The ORPHANS

Fiona McIntosh is an internationally bestselling author of novels for adults and children. She co-founded an award-winning travel magazine with her husband, which they ran for fifteen years while raising their twin sons before she became a full-time author. Fiona roams the world researching and drawing inspiration for her novels, and runs a series of highly respected fiction masterclasses. She calls South Australia home.

BOOKS BY FIONA McINTOSH
AVAILABLE FROM PENGUIN RANDOM HOUSE

Fields of Gold
The Lavender Keeper
The French Promise
Nightingale
The Tailor's Girl
The Last Dance
The Perfumer's Secret
The Chocolate Tin
The Tea Gardens
The Pearl Thief
The Diamond Hunter
The Champagne War
The Spy's Wife

In the DCI Jack Hawksworth series:
Bye Bye Baby
Beautiful Death
Mirror Man

FIONA McINTOSH

The ORPHANS

MICHAEL JOSEPH
an imprint of
PENGUIN BOOKS

MICHAEL JOSEPH

UK I USA I Canada I Ireland I Australia
India I New Zealand I South Africa I China

Michael Joseph is part of the Penguin Random House group of companies
whose addresses can be found at global.penguinrandomhouse.com.

Penguin
Random House
Australia

First published by Michael Joseph, 2022

Cover photography by Collaboration JS/Arcangel
Inside front cover by kwest/Shutterstock
Cover design by Louisa Maggio Design
Typeset in 11/16 pt Sabon by Midland Typesetters, Australia

Printed and bound in Australia by Griffin Press, an accredited
ISO AS/NZS 14001 Environmental Management Systems printer

A catalogue record for this
book is available from the
National Library of Australia

NATIONAL
LIBRARY
OF AUSTRALIA

ISBN 978 1 76104 156 3

penguin.com.au

MIX
Paper from
responsible sources
FSC® C009448

*We at Penguin Random House Australia acknowledge that Aboriginal and Torres Strait Islander
peoples are the Traditional Custodians and the first storytellers of the lands on which we live
and work. We honour Aboriginal and Torres Strait Islander peoples' continuous connection
to Country, waters, skies and communities. We celebrate Aboriginal and Torres Strait Islander
stories, traditions and living cultures; and we pay our respects to Elders past and present.*

Frederick Richards
1926–2019
Your brilliant smile, wit and love are deeply missed.

1

FARINA, SOUTH AUSTRALIA

April 1914

Something about this moment felt unnerving to Tom Catchlove. It was as though the world around him was physically quietening down in readiness. Tom couldn't pinpoint why. He glanced again through the binoculars around his neck but saw nothing out of the ordinary. He could sense a strange, almost sinister frisson across the desert landscape this morning, and it was making his skin crawl.

Six feet up on one of the twisted limbs of an ancient coolabah tree on the edge of the waterhole, ten-year-old Tom sat, legs swinging as he chewed on some ruby-coloured saltbush berries. They were like gleaming jewels in the parched wilderness and the citrussy explosion on his tongue as each tiny berry popped made his mouth water and eyes squint. He was being careful not to spill the scarlet juice on his shirt; he didn't want to create more work for his mother.

He batted away the annoying, sticky-footed flies that always tried to get into his eyes and looked up through the tree into the depthless vault of the sky – his upside-down sea. The colour lightened towards the horizon but directly above it was such a brilliant Egyptian blue that he could pick out each gumleaf with precision against it. His mother, Moira, had taught him that while Nature had created the many hues of the sky, the ancient Egyptians had reproduced this particular one for their art by mixing limestone with azurite.

'Azurite contains copper. They'd heat it, Tom, and turn it into glass that would then be crushed and combined with egg whites to create a glaze the colour of this perfect Australian autumn sky, untouched by clouds.'

Learning this sort of random fact was all part of his education, she'd assure him, and although Tom wasn't convinced it would be handy for his inevitable future on a sheep station, his enquiring mind enjoyed expanding itself. Moira had plenty to share from her private school education in Adelaide and her travels in Europe.

He heard the screech of a kite in the distance. It was hovering, on the hunt. The waterhole had been filled with some welcome and abundant spring rains, so the small creatures were plentiful, the creeks were running, and wildflowers had pushed through formerly parched wilderness. The sound of the lapping Paradise Creek wouldn't last, though. It was a transient awakening, a tease that reminded the families of pioneers why their forebears had thought this land would reward them. But that had been a false hope; it could not reward them in agriculture. It was a tough enough land-scape that only the hardiest creatures like sheep could survive, and even they needed so much help.

The rains had barely finished and already the waterhole was no longer deep enough to swim in, but Tom had enjoyed a week of joy playing in it. Water was so elusive in their lives out here that they usually had to fetch and carry it from the railhead in shippers and then be strict about its use. It would be gone – drained, evaporated, drunk away – in a week or so, he guessed, but for now the waterhole was populated with all the birds he liked to spot and identify. This morning alone he'd seen cheeky willy wagtails, honeyeaters, variegated wrens, even doves. And then the raptors had arrived, hunting for the rabbits that he tried to trap for his mother to vary their daily diet of mutton. There were always crows around, of course, making their raspy caws. Ever observant, cunning crows.

They were not so talkative today. Odd.

He didn't want to miss the approach of the train into Farina this morning. Its erratic arrival fuelled his dreams that there was more to life than this lonely existence; the train often felt like a shiny treat in his isolated life. He'd look for its billowing steam in the distance from his vantage and leap down to hurtle across the desert towards the rail tracks. Racing to be near the lines before it passed was part of the fun and the challenge. It was over a mile from the waterhole, and he had to skip over cottonbush and watch out for slithering creatures but never drop his speed so he could arrive out of breath but in time to wave to the driver. The blast of air that would hit him as the train thundered past knocked all the last breath out of him. It always felt exciting. He would listen to the piercing sound of metal on metal as the train wound its way to the siding, where a different sort of train, a line of camels, would be waiting. There, the shippers would load up the camels with water and then their Afghan handlers would take their camel train on to far-flung parts of this enormous sheep station.

One million square miles, Vern Catchlove, Tom's father, had told him with an awed sigh. Tom had been impressed – he knew how to write that number and it had an awful lot of noughts in it. He understood that the station was enormous. Tom remembered how he had looked at his mother and seen only misery at his father's words. Why was she here? Why was she married to his father, a cattle drover, gone for months at a time?

He'd asked her once, a couple of years ago. She'd simply shrugged.

'Your father made me feel special, Tom, at a time when I needed to feel . . . something,' she said, unable to find the right word, it seemed. 'He wasn't who my family chose. He is who I chose.'

It had sounded too complex and vague a notion to press for further understanding. He'd not asked again.

He'd been born in January on a day the mercury had reached one hundred and seventeen degrees Fahrenheit in the shade, his mother told him.

'You came quickly, Tom. The town's midwife, Mrs Moffatt, said I needed to be grateful for that and not groan about the heat.' She had tousled his hair with affection. 'You've always been an easy, cooperative boy and I'm still grateful to you for it.'

He smiled at that fond memory, that and her horror that he'd eaten goanna with a couple of the local Aboriginal families. Their children were his friends but living out here on the station, he saw them rarely. Some of the Afghan children were his friends too and he loved to see the handsome Gool Mahomet, who had moved to their region from Afghanistan. Moira had shown him on a world map where that was, and Tom had stared at all the countries around the world as she pointed, the great continents picked out in pastel colours against the pale seas. He'd squinted at Afghanistan, shaped like a sausage and nestling among romantic-sounding places like Tehran in Persia, Tashkent, Samarkand, Peshawar and the Khyber Pass.

Gool had been born in a city called Kabul before he travelled to central Australia and into South Australia to bring all his experience as a cameleer to their region. Tom always thought Gool was magnificent, sitting astride his tall charger. He wore a turban and had a strong profile with his long, straight nose, blue eyes and fair complexion. His beard was black and woolly. This man, of high caste in his country, had married a woman from Paris of all places, making him quite the celebrity. Tom had heard a number of rumours about this woman: everything from her being a governess in the Goldfields, to a prostitute in Kalgoorlie.

They were a colourful couple, but Gool was also the leader of the Afghans who lived on what was known as Afghan Hill in a camp not far east of the main town. It wasn't often that Tom spoke to the wise man of the Afghans, but on the rare occasion he did, he had smelled chlorodyne on Gool's breath; all the Afghan men seemed to sip it from blue bottles. His mother had said it was medicine but Tom suspected it had something else in it.

He realised he'd become lost in his thoughts and time had slipped by. The train was late today. It often was. He'd enquired with the guards about the curious timetable and the response was, 'We get here when we get here,' which seemed to amuse the adults around him. For Tom Catchlove, though, the response made no sense. He liked precision. Finding order helped him to make sense of his world that felt increasingly disordered as he grew and his father stayed away for longer periods.

The need for accuracy certainly wasn't a trait of his father, who was unreliable at best; instead, Tom's mother said he got it from her family, the Darnells, although he'd not met any of them to verify her claim. Now her mind was blurry, always distracted. This lack of sharpness from the woman who had given each day of the week a specific title, from wash day to bake day, had him troubled. Now she had become as unreliable as his father – just in a different way.

Tom returned from his musings, flicking at the flies and becoming aware of the new and sudden silence.

Something was not right. All the birds who should have been singing and flitting about had become still. The kite had disappeared too. Did they all know something he didn't? Was he imagining their silence or was this sense of being unnerved to do with his mother's 'turns'? They were happening more regularly now – she was ill. The adults who came through their lives referred to it as 'her nerves' and at ten he had no idea what that actually meant, but he knew it was more about his father's absence than his own presence.

He didn't know how to help her and all he could do when she was lost in that silent, staring broodiness she slipped into was to take her hand and hold it in his lap. They might sit like that for hours, occasionally through a night, and then at daybreak she'd surface from the mire of whatever it was that sucked her down into its depths. She'd look at him as if recognising him again and ask him how he was and shouldn't they be getting some food organised, or was it time to feed the horse?

Tom shouldered a lot of chores and did his best to be the man around the house, as Vern had instructed him to be when he had left. He tried to remember all the smaller tasks too that his mother was becoming forgetful over, like moistening the clay pot, in which they kept their butter. In summer, the pot was stored in the fireplace where it was cool. He kept the lanterns filled with kerosene and he kept a watchful eye on the slightly temperamental Coolgardie drip safe to make sure it was working, so his mother could rely on her precious food remaining cool. He helped her to grow onions and potatoes, which were their mainstay of vegetables unless they could be treated to some carrots and the like when the train came in. When it did, the kids, like Tom, knew to grab a spoon, plate and a copper penny because they could buy a big scoop of delicious vanilla ice cream, the treat of the gods as far as Tom was concerned.

His father had now been away for eight weeks. Tom knew it was that long because he had diligently counted off the days, as they turned to weeks, on a sheet of butcher's paper. As the sun slipped away each evening, his job was to light the lamps that he and his mother would eat by. He'd gaze at the homemade calendar that appeared gloomier for its seemingly endless rows of crosses in the low, flickering light.

Moira didn't always eat but Tom would encourage her, keeping up a one-sided conversation, making sure she could hear the gentle clatter of his fork against his plate. She insisted they eat from china crockery and observe good manners, and Tom rather liked the unexpected pleasure of elegance it leant to their meagre, lamplit suppers and humble surrounds. His once statuesque mother had become five and a half feet of bones encased in fragile flesh, in stark contrast to how she looked in the two photographs they had of her life before Vern Catchlove. Her shoulders poked out squarely and her elbows formed triangles when in motion. While he enjoyed a rare hug from her, they were fleeting, angular; he could feel the ridges of her ribs like the washboard in the laundry when he pressed his face against her.

But recently he'd noticed her body was changing – becoming plumper. He couldn't understand it because she ate so little . . . and she seemed constantly fatigued. He often heard her throwing up outside. He hadn't wanted to ask in case it meant she was ill; what if she was getting ready to blow up and explode as he'd seen with some dead, bloated animals? But her new shape had got the better of him the night before last.

'Mum, you feel softer,' was the only way he could say it.

She'd given him a wan smile that tried to glow out of her pale, once-pretty face that was now hollowed into a ghostly version of itself. 'I'll explain soon, son,' she'd said, ruffling his hair, which had turned its traditional darker shade now that summer had passed.

It sounded ominous. *Explain what? That you're dying? That I'm going to be left alone? That my father is lost? That your heartbreak or your nerves at such a thought is killing you? Is that what you meant?*

'What about Dad?' he'd asked, knowing instinctively that she wanted to talk about him.

'I'm hoping they'll have heard some news. It's been long enough.' She began to frown, as though counting in her mind. 'He needs to be home soon,' she said, her voice rising. 'Before . . .'

'Before what, Mum?'

'Oh, nothing. Just home – where we want him.'

Tom had nodded. He wanted his father home too. They were opposites; where Tom was quiet, thoughtful, precise, his father was a loud, often raggedly drunk but ever-cheerful person of height and stringy muscle that roped around his limbs. His face had been etched by the sun's artistry over years of exposure, its pencil drawing deep lines as if it were a blade into the leathery skin. Vern, when home, was usually smiling or whistling some tuneless melody. And often he'd burst into song and grab Moira to twirl her around the hut. The sand of the red earth they lived upon, no matter how hard they swept, was always present and sounded gritty beneath their dance steps. Tom would clap a rhythm to his father's cheerful singing, longing for the moment when his mother would reach out and draw him into their private moment to pirouette as a trio. His father never reached for him, but that's how men were, his mother would assure Tom. He'd hug his parents around their hips, revelling in the notion of love that existed in their simple lives.

His mother was no doubt longing for the bluster and laughter of Vern to echo out across the lonely landscape once again. But there was still no sign of the men on horseback and the beasts they were driving down from Queensland.

He'd offered to help with extra chores but this morning she had told him to go and play, looking paler than ever . . . and sweaty.

Horses sweat, he remembered his mother correcting him. *People perspire*. She liked to educate him, insisting on teaching him over and above his school hours.

So here he sat, in the venerable coolabah, squinting through his father's binoculars so he could focus on the township of Farina and look for the telltale plume of steam and the screech in the far distance.

But that's when it struck him how still everything had suddenly become. Up on the hill there was usually some sort of breeze, just enough to lift a few of the hairs that flopped across his hairline over his forehead. But the air wasn't stirring.

The sudden cacophony that pierced the silence of the prairie was not from the train that had hauled itself north out of Adelaide twenty-four hours earlier, but from the birds nesting in the gums by the creek. Cockatoos rose alongside galahs, who moved quicker than the heavier crows, who were also lifting off in instant and collective alarm. There was a great excited discordance as the birds cried their agitation.

'What the . . .' Tom murmured, watching the birds explode into the air like a dark cloud.

And then he heard it. A groan, like an ancient giant awakening. It continued, growing angrier. The rumbling came from deep in the earth and shook him. He felt the power of that shaking through every muscle and cavity of his body until he could swear his teeth chattered. It was an earth shock, he realised, something he'd only heard about, and he crouched for fear of toppling, marvelling at the powerful vibration as though the cave-dwelling giant deep in the earth's core was shaking the foundations of the land on which they walked . . . angry at being disturbed.

And then, as abruptly as it began, it stopped. The birds silenced once again and an eerie hush laid itself back down like a picnic blanket after being flipped.

He would later learn it had lasted thirty-five seconds, which was exactly how long it had taken his mother to realise that what she'd feared most was happening. While the land had shuddered,

Moira Catchlove's baby had chosen to start her journey into the world. But Baby Amy had made her decision far too early.

Tom could hear his mother's screaming from the homestead, all the way to the waterhole. The steam train was forgotten. So was the earth shock. Clutching his father's precious binoculars, Tom began to run, praying to whichever angels might hear him that they were not sending darkness his way.

He harnessed up Bonny and somehow half carried, half walked his mother outside and into the wagon, where he urged Moira to lie down, wrapping her in a blanket.

'Mum, you have to tell me. What's happening?'

She shook her head as if denying it, but the words finally spilled out. 'You're going to have a brother or sister before the day's end, Tom.'

He opened his mouth with a thrill of delight. At last. Someone to talk to, to play with, to teach about the desert life. 'It looks painful.'

'It is,' she gasped, and to him it looked agonising. 'I'm going to need help.'

'Why are we frightened?' he asked, thinking aloud, wishing he hadn't. He wanted to be very strong for her.

'Because your brother or sister is arriving too early,' she ground out. 'And that puts them in danger . . . especially out here. Now, stop talking and get me to town.'

With a grim expression, he began the bumpy journey of eighteen miles to the town of Farina, propping blocks of wood behind him so he could reach the reins and control the pony properly. His mother would yell out from time to time in what seemed to be torture and then it would subside. At first he'd thought it was the rutted dirt path they were following that was upsetting her, but why was she quiet at other times on the same uneven surface? No, this was the baby. Why was his tiny brother or sister – such a helpless thing – so dangerous? There was no point in asking; a glance backwards showed only a tense grimace in her expression, while her hands clasped her belly.

Tom gritted his teeth and encouraged Bonny to move faster if she could without wearing herself out. Fortunately, it was a mild day. April was the month that he and his mother always craved because it began the slide into autumn; the summer's heat could reach one hundred and twenty degrees. He was reminded that newborns were often laid under the shadowy cool of their mother's bed. Where had he heard that? His thoughts were like skittles, ranging off in different directions with no attachment. He was trying not to let his gaze land on the desolation of the wilderness. This was not sand like the Sahara Desert, which his mother had described to him, where the golden dunes were soft and hot, 'looking silken from a distance,' she had explained. No, their desert was a relentlessly nuggety and unforgiving gibber plain.

He felt a fresh wave of panic warble through him: what if he couldn't get her there in time? *What if she dies?*

This was too daunting to contemplate. Tom forced his thoughts away from what scared him most towards ordered, rational memory that could deliver up a fact and distract him from the threat at hand. The earth folded in and faulted on itself more than five hundred and forty million years ago, Tom had read in an encyclopaedia up at the main house, called Witchelina, which ran the station and he let that fact resonate now and take over. He deliberately occupied his mind with this sort of mundane detail for a few more miles, even managing to eclipse his mother's intermittent yells by thinking about the morning's earth shock, which was related to the plate tectonics he'd learned about. He reminded himself to try and record five hundred and forty million as a number.

'Come on, Bonny, not much further now,' he lied, because he had no idea how close – or far – they were. He'd lost track and so it was with surprise and trembling relief that he spotted the outskirts of the town and its activity. He could see people, like ants moving around, and across the distance left to cover he could make out the iron sounds of a forge, while the odd voice pierced the distance in a shout or burst of laughter.

He glanced over his shoulder where his mother lay, death still. 'Mum . . . Mum!'

She groaned in answer.

'We're here. We'll be in Farina in minutes. At the hospital.'

All she did was nod. Her eyes remained closed.

'Hospital' was a loose term even in the mind of a ten-year-old. The rather grandly titled Transcontinental Hotel had been converted into a hospice of sorts and depended on bush nursing and a series of travelling doctors who arrived by train from Quorn. Tom knew from the adult conversations he'd overheard that finding a permanent doctor had proved impossible and it was hard enough to get nurses to stay. He'd heard one of the townsfolk admit that any serious injury likely meant death. Out of need, most of the locals knew how to set and mend bones themselves, his mother included.

He began yelling from the fringe of the town, drowning his mother's cries and attracting a host of people who soon pushed him out of the way. Within minutes he was watching the person he loved more than any other be carried away from him towards the long stone building with its cheerful, striped tin verandah. Two women in starched nurse's outfits were taking control of proceedings.

In the activity, Tom was barely noticed, but he was used to that and he remembered his father's rules. Horse first. His mother was now in the best hands – the only hands – that could help her. He led Bonny slowly back down to the stables behind the Exchange Hotel before unharnessing her from the wagon, tying her up and seeing to her care.

The voices of men drifted through to the stable from the busy hotel; someone was playing a mouth organ on its verandah, which lent a melancholy note to an otherwise raucous-sounding gathering of workers after a long day. The evening was closing in and the smell of old beer wafted through to where Tom was stroking Bonny's neck.

'There's fresh water and food. I don't know how long we'll be here, but I'll be back soon. All right?'

Bonny snorted and bent her head to her pail of hay that he'd already paid the stablemaster for; luckily he'd had the foresight to bring his mother's purse. He tucked the tiny leather sack back beneath his shirt on the thong she wore around her neck for safekeeping.

He tapped Bonny's rump affectionately. Moving into the darkness away from the lights, laughter and even the mournful music, he rounded the back of the hotel to go in search of his mother. The strains of the sad melody were cut short by a loud voice.

'Hey, Knackers! Play something decent, will you, mate? Making us all cry in here.'

As Tom picked up the pace heading back into town, he could hear the tune of the jolly lumberjack that his father sometimes played and it made him smile.

But Tom's smile was short-lived.

2

PORT ADELAIDE

April 1914

Fleur knew the rain of the last two days had slowed the decomposition of the corpse. She had listened and memorised what she'd heard – the deceased was a woman named Mary Oaten and she was a shopkeeper – but she had learned in her eight short years as an undertaker's daughter that, for the dead, what one had done in life no longer mattered.

'Dying makes everyone the same, doesn't it, Dad?' she'd offered not so long ago, lifting her father's eyebrows in surprise at the sophisticated notion from such a young person.

'That's true. The dead begin a new passage, my love,' her father had replied.

'How can you be sure they're going anywhere if they can't tell us?'

He filled his cheeks with air and blew it out gently at yet another complex thought from Fleur. 'I can't be sure, but we're all taught there is a different sort of life after death. Not one that the living are privy to, obviously.'

Henry Appleby had learned long ago to answer his intelligent daughter honestly and as if he were conversing with an adult.

To placate, or worse, talk down to her, rarely worked. At least this way she would know he'd respected her question and done his utmost to respond fully.

'But it's up to us, the living,' he continued, 'to make sure we guide them gently on their way and make it as easy as possible for the family. As funeral directors, we *undertake* the care of their loved ones.'

Fleur had appreciated him pausing to discuss her thoughts. She peeped around the doorway to watch her father speaking gently to Mary's kin in the hallway; she heard him explaining that they might like to pick out a gown for their mother to be buried in.

One of them glanced her way. 'Mr Appleby, should your daughter . . .?'

'Don't mind her,' her father reassured them. 'She's been around those at peace since she was old enough to walk.'

Fleur smiled at his careful wording. At eight, she already knew her father was avoiding using the word 'dead', which might feel blunt on this day. 'At peace' was a kinder expression, he'd explained to her, when the grief was fresh. Even so, she could see the alarm passing across the faces of the adults that a stranger's child was near the corpse, but Fleur also knew that heartache would press in and her presence would be ignored, if not forgotten.

Her father had not lied; since being adopted as a newborn by Henry and Mae Appleby, she'd known nothing but the world of funerals, and her father was one of the best – no, he was *the* best.

She glanced around the door again as she heard him clear his throat and admired how splendid he looked, dressed in his under-taker's garb of striped charcoal trousers with a black frock coat that cinched at the waist and flared into silken lapels. Beneath that he wore his close-fitting waistcoat of the same gaberdine and his shirt and stiffened collar that her mother worked hard to keep so white and starched. The suit was a perfect fit because Henry was tall and trim, so his waistcoat sat flat against his belly and showed off the glint of his fob watch to perfection. Before he left the house of the grieving, he would reach for his shiny top hat and give a short bow of respect. His longish face, which looked especially sombre in repose, added a final flourish of reverence in the moment.

Yes, indeed, Henry Appleby was the funeral director of choice for the people around the Port of Adelaide, although listening to him of an evening she knew the business, which he had grown out of his father's milk delivery rounds, was changing.

'We have to adapt and change too, Mae,' she'd overheard him saying to her mother only the previous evening. 'There are lots of opportunists moving into our area of work. It's not as though one has to prove their qualification. Any old Jack the Lad can hang up an undertaker's sign and accept business.'

'What will you do?' her mother had asked, deftly allowing Henry to continue airing his thoughts. Fleur knew her mother had little interest in the funeral business and that her role was to support her father, which was no challenge for Mae. It was obvious in all she did that she adored Henry and knew exactly how to handle him.

'Well, we have to modernise. We're the ones with the reputation to protect, so we must get better at every aspect of our business. Do you know what I heard the other day?'

'What did you hear, my love?'

'That upstart Johnny Dale – a butcher and small-time criminal – has set up a funeral parlour next to his shop! Suddenly now he's Mr John Dale, Undertaker.'

Fleur could almost see his disgust like a shadow near him, and heard a few sonorous ticks of the grandfather clock in the hallway before Mae replied.

'Why does that trouble you, Henry?' she finally asked in a reasonable tone. 'Don't compare yourself to him.'

'I'm not, Mae.' Fleur heard exasperation creeping into her father's tone. 'Sorry, my love,' he said, always quick to apologise, 'but he undertook to prepare the body of that sailor who fell off the ship at the port.'

'Another drunk one?'

'Yes. The man's wife could barely scratch a shilling together, what with looking after three youngsters. The ship's captain paid but chose the cheapest option. Johnny Dale was laughing in the pub that he hosed down the sailor's body in the backyard behind the butchery. Poor man's not even on a slab of ice and I thank heavens it's not summer. They need to get that fellow into the ground urgently.'

There was another careful pause. 'Henry, I can remember a time when you did something similar when you were first starting out.'

Fleur heard a snort of derision. 'Mae Appleby, how could you compare the situation? I washed those bodies with great care—'

'In the backyard, with a bucket, as I recall. Nothing terribly dignified about that situation.'

Fleur smiled on the stairs. Her mother knew just how to challenge her father without provoking him too much.

'Ah, Mae, we didn't have the set-up that we do now, but I still showed them the respect they deserved . . . and I didn't laugh about it in the pub later.'

'Indeed. No one would ever question your care, Henry. It's undoubtedly why you're in such demand. But everyone starts somewhere, and while I'm not suggesting John Dale is in your league, I would urge you to let your reservations go. You told me that sailor was a good-for-nothing drunk at the best of times and the captain did the right thing by his poor wife. I say we give her some money for those little ones and then you know you've done more for that family than any fine burial of their useless father might.'

Fleur heard her father give a grumbling sound in response.

'You have more than enough work and reputation for ten new undertakers,' her mother continued. 'Everyone would choose Appleby's for their funeral, if they could. Hold that close and don't allow the newcomers, still needing to find their way and build their business, to trouble you. This Dale fellow won't last if he's no good, but he'll learn and improve if he means to survive in your arena.'

'Always the voice of reason, my love. You're right, of course.'

It was Fleur's habit to sit on the stairs and listen to their unguarded conversations at night. With no brother or sister, she considered them her friends as much as her parents. Besides, Fleur didn't particularly care for the company of her peers. Children seemed so distractible, often mean to one another; she preferred adults, none of whom were perfect, of course, but she could enjoy a mature conversation with an adult. She had tried but failed to achieve the same with people her own age.

Her mother regularly clicked her tongue at Fleur. 'You'll end up being a loner, my darling, if you can't make friends.'

'I *can* make friends, Mum. I choose not to because I think I'd let them down by getting bored. Perhaps it's because I'm an orphan.'

The remark had made her mother sigh. 'Fleur, you're not an orphan. You are an Appleby with two parents who love you. I never wished to know where you'd come from – that made you new and pure for me – but you're an old soul, that's for sure.'

Her radiant mother, with her pretty hair that shone red beneath the sun and lightened into a rosy gold come summer, had planted a kiss on Fleur's head that day. 'You're a gift from the gods, child. And we're blessed to have you.'

Fleur had looked at her mother's pale complexion and light freckling and wished she had the same colouring, desperate to belong wholly to this wonderful woman from whom she'd never felt a cross word and had experienced only affection. She was the blessed one, to belong to the Applebys; they could not have children of their own and she'd overheard them finally agreeing not to bring another adopted child into their lives, and to concentrate on Fleur.

She remembered another evening she had sat on the stairs, listening to her parents talk softly, this time about the future of their business.

'Henry, you know I'm not ambitious. I derive all the reward I need from being a good wife to you and a good mother to our little girl. Now, I'd love for you to have had a son to inherit this company, but it's surely becoming obvious that Fleur is more than capable.'

Peeking out from the shadows of the stairwell, Fleur heard her father's leather chair creak as he sat back, the low lamplight casting a golden spot to illuminate his helplessly serious countenance. She watched him nod. 'I won't deny that. With Fleur I often feel like I'm talking to another adult.' He sipped from the glass of whiskey he had been cradling in his lap.

She heard her mother's knitting needles clink. 'That's my point, dear. Can you imagine Fleur and a babbling toddler, or a noisy infant who grows into a highly active, perhaps cheeky boy?' They both chuckled at the thought. 'She's got an old head on her shoulders, my love, and we should be grateful for that. She will do you proud and become a great boon for your business. I don't want her being pushed aside simply because she's a woman. Fleur has so much to give. Let's be thankful she's ours and so clever and grown up at eight. Imagine what she's going to be like when she comes of age.'

'Intimidating,' her father quipped but Fleur heard only tender affection in his voice, so she imagined it had to be a compliment.

'What a modern thinker you are, dearest. There are many who would not consider the needs of a daughter.'

'Yes, well, I'm not like all those others who only seem to see a future in their sons. She's *our* only child and I'll consider her every need, especially her future. And that should not rest on whom she marries. I want our girl to marry for love, Henry . . . not security or status. I want her to experience what I have in my marriage. Promise me, won't you?'

'What's that, my love?'

'That you'll never corner Fleur into marrying someone for anything other than love.'

Fleur heard her father's chair creak again and saw him lean forward to plant a soft kiss on her mother's forehead. 'I promise you.' As he sat back, he cast another affectionate smile towards her mother. 'You know she talks to the dead?'

Her mother must have put down her knitting, because the regular click of needles stopped abruptly. 'I do. Some may find it strange, but given it's what she's been raised around, I'm not surprised she finds solace with people who don't answer back. I think she's marvellous with them. I admit, I can't be as comfy around the corpses as Fleur is. I don't even like walking near your mortuary.'

Fleur was pulled out of her recollection as she heard the Oaten family members begin to disperse and her father's footfall coming in her direction. She tiptoed up to the still, silent woman with a soft, encouraging smile and said, 'We're going to take good care of you, Mary.'

Back at the funeral parlour, Mary Oaten was laid out on Henry's table. While he knew most would baulk at the sight of an eight-year-old participating in the process that was about to unfold,

Henry also knew that his young assistant could maintain clear focus for hours, and was certainly as able as anyone more than twice her age.

He glanced up as his child entered what they privately called the sanctuary. It was quiet, as clean as they could achieve, with plenty of ventilation. Toxic fumes from the chemicals they sometimes used during the embalming process could overwhelm at any time and had the potential to kill, so unlike other undertakers, Henry had avoided locating his mortuary in the cellar. The glazed windows overlooked a walled garden, which ensured the room remained private and gave Henry something pleasant to glance towards during the work that went on in this room.

'Mum says there's an urgent telephone call,' Fleur told him. 'I told her you wouldn't want to be disturbed right now.'

He was once again impressed that his daughter was ahead of him in her thoughts; she knew how inconvenient the request was. 'And?'

'She's insisting you telephone the family immediately.' Fleur paused. 'It's not like her to insist on anything,' she added, echoing his private thought. 'You go, Dad. I'll stay with Mrs Oaten.'

He gave a sound of soft frustration. 'All right. You can take off her boots and stockings, start unbuttoning her overall. You can also unpin her hair and comb it out but—'

'I know. Gently, to protect the scalp's skin.'

She was such a smart little button. He cut her a soft smile, meeting her eyes. They seemed capable of changing colour based on mood, the light, and even what she was wearing. Henry had read a bit about eye colour through his embalming studies and according to some experts, the hazel eye colour that Fleur possessed was potentially the most alluring and mysterious because of that capricious nature it seemed to possess. Fleur had on her funeral smock that was a deep olive green, and her eyes, which had seemed brown in Mrs Oaten's bedroom earlier, now appeared the colour of a faded gumleaf sprinkled with gold. Whatever their colour, these were eyes that read the world deeply.

'I'll be back shortly.' As he left the room, he glanced back and saw that Fleur, without being asked, was testing the rigor remaining in Mary Oaten, gently easing a limb to loosen it. She'd listened carefully to the family, who believed that Mary had died just after four this morning. It had been approximately seven hours since she'd passed, so the stiffness of death would be making itself evident, and Fleur was taking care to ease the onset of rigor mortis so they could clean and prepare Mary's body swiftly. In another day, the corpse would have relaxed again, and Mary would be ready to dress in her burial outfit and for the family to farewell her at a proper wake. He nodded to himself. His young child had learned all of this with intense concentration. Mae was right, he thought. *Who needs a son and heir, when I have Fleur?*

Arriving into the family parlour, Mae didn't waste time explaining who had called. 'It's the Darnells.'

Henry frowned. 'The wool people?'

She nodded. 'One and the same.'

'Has someone died?' *Silly question*, he berated himself. A posh family like the Darnells would hardly be calling for any other reason . . . but why him, when they had undertakers much closer to their city address?

'It's a woman,' Mae confirmed.

His frown turned to dismay. 'Is Elizabeth Darnell—'

'No, Henry. There's another. An estranged sister, apparently.'

He blinked in consternation.

'I don't know the details, and nor would I be so bold as to ask. What I do know is that Elizabeth Darnell is just short of demanding your presence at their home.'

'But I—'

'She was rather forceful, my love. I think she knows her family name is too important and influential for you to ignore her request . . . more of an order, actually.' Mae pulled a face of concern.

'They're in the city,' he thought aloud.

'Then you'd better get going. Hugh will be in shortly. He can attend to Mrs Oaten and since it's a weekend, Fleur can—'

'No, Mae. I need Fleur with me. She's my eyes and ears sometimes. They mostly overlook her but she misses nothing, and this seems a strange request when surely one of the prominent city funeral houses can undertake the care of their deceased.'

Mae shrugged. 'Take Fleur, then, and stop wondering. You know, Henry, I think you sell yourself short sometimes. Let it occur to you that maybe word of your reputable services has travelled from the port to the city of Adelaide.'

'What would I do without you thinking so highly of me all the time, my dearest?' They shared a smile of affection. 'I'll scribble out some notes for Hugh. Fleur and I will take a train—'

'Not a train, my love. By the sounds of that call, you will be bringing a body back for burial preparation. You'll need the hearse. I'll get Fleur dressed properly.'

3

Inside the two-storey villa on Carrington Street, Fleur followed her father towards one of the back rooms, aware of the pinched look of disapproval from the woman who wore a long apron over her dark, ankle-length dress. Fleur surmised this was not the lady of the house but her housekeeper.

'Are you sure you wish to take the child in?' the woman said in a superior tone that was barely a question, turning at the entrance to the room.

'There's a child already inside – two, in fact, if you count the dead,' Henry replied, nodding towards someone Fleur couldn't see. She recognised her father's gentle but firm business tone.

'He is the dead's family.'

'And Fleur is my family and very helpful in these situations. She might even be able to comfort the child, who perhaps shouldn't be alone.'

The woman sniffed. 'That boy refuses to move. Wait here, please. I'll fetch the mistress.'

Fleur stepped into what appeared to be a less formal sitting room behind her father. All the furniture had been shifted against the walls to make way for a coffin, which sat in the centre of the room on a high trestle table that looked as though it had been carried in from a shed. Emerging from behind her father, she saw the wide-eyed lad staring at them, wringing his cloth hat in his hands.

'Good morning, son,' Henry said. 'I'm Mr Appleby and this is my daughter.'

Fleur eyed the boy, noticing his slightly scruffy clothes; they were not dirty, but well worn. His boots were scuffed, desperately in need of a good polish and the jacket he wore was slightly too small for him, although he looked lanky, like it didn't matter what he wore because by next week he'd have outgrown it. The thought made her smile, as did his thick and unruly fair hair that she found herself rather taken by.

'I'm Fleur. My mother's mother was called Flora and so I was named after her, but using the French version because my mother's father had French ancestors. What's your name?'

He didn't speak immediately, blinking at her in slight puzzlement and taking a moment to digest the information as much as to assess their presence. 'I'm Tom,' he finally said. 'It doesn't mean anything, I don't think. My father is Vern Catchlove and he doesn't know yet, about . . .' He looked towards the coffin.

Fleur moved towards him and noted that he took a small step back into the corner. 'My father will make sure the family reaches him. And I think the name Tom means "strong". It certainly sounds strong. We're here to help,' she offered.

'No one can help me. My mother's dead. My sister died too.'

Fleur looked at the simple pine coffin, schooling herself not to wince or reel back at the telltale odour of a body beginning to ripen. 'Is your sister in here too?'

He tipped a nod at the box. 'She only had a few breaths, I overheard the nurses say, but my mother refused to let her go. Said she'd take her to Adelaide and farewell her here.'

'So your mother didn't know she was dying?'

He gave a light shrug. 'I didn't see her before she died. She probably did. All I know is that she called my sister Amy.'

They heard women's voices. Fleur was aware of her father stepping out of the room, but she continued with Tom without turning. 'Where's your father?'

She didn't think Tom minded her question; he seemed ready enough to answer. 'I don't know. He's droving . . . bringing animals down from Queensland into South Australia. Do you know where Queensland is?'

She couldn't fully disguise a scathing look. 'Of course I do.'

'Sorry. You look young.'

'And you look rough, but we're probably both wrong.'

Fleur saw the surprise in his expression.

'How old are you?' he asked.

'Eight. You?'

'Ten. You sound older.'

'You just said I seemed young.'

'I know. You confuse me.'

'Why aren't you crying?'

'Will that prove I'm sad?'

'It might get you some sympathy. Why isn't there family around you?'

'I don't have any.' He tipped another nod, this time towards the door. 'None of those people out there have ever seen me. They just wanted my mother's body back, or so they say. I think I'm a nuisance for them.'

As he said this, they were interrupted by the bustling arrival of the lady of the house, smelling richly of floral perfume.

'And who is this?' she queried.

Her father stood a step behind her. 'Er, this is my daughter, Fleur.'

Fleur curtsied as she'd been taught. 'Good morning, Mrs Darnell. I'm sorry for your bereavement.'

'Good gracious,' the woman breathed. 'How precocious.'

Henry Appleby gave an awkward twitch of his mouth, hidden by his moustache and beard, that approximated a brief grin. 'Would you believe that Fleur knows almost as much as most apprentices in the funeral business? Right now, I suspect she might be a good distraction for your sister's boy, while we . . . er . . .' Henry gestured towards Tom.

'Yes, indeed. You children might like a glass of milk in the parlour while Mr Appleby and I talk. Miss Jackson will help. I would introduce my own daughter but she's rather sickly today. Off you go, you two. Make no noise, please.'

'Come on, Tom,' Fleur urged after glancing at her father and observing his nod. She offered a hand and was surprised when he took it. They left the room where his dead mother lay. 'Which way?' she whispered.

Tom pointed. 'Through here, but the housekeeper is mean,' he whispered.

Fleur grinned. 'Leave her to me.'

Inside the parlour, the woman who had greeted them, still with a disapproving expression on her face, did indeed await them, and Fleur positioned herself slightly ahead of Tom to face the housekeeper

'Hello, Miss Jackson? Mrs Darnell wondered if you'd be kind enough to pour Tom here some milk . . . and perhaps offer some biscuits? Nothing for me, though, thank you.' She gave a sweet smile. 'I've had a big breakfast,' she lied.

Tom was right. Miss Jackson's mouth had a mean-spirited cast to it – thin and straight, as though it had been drawn permanently in ink and was forbidden to move from its original horizontal line.

'Go into the garden,' she said, motioning with a dismissive wave. 'I don't want you spilling crumbs on my freshly swept floor. And don't make a noise.'

'No, we've already been told that,' Fleur said, managing to sound sweet and yet somehow defiant.

The woman stared at her, obviously trying to make up her mind as to which.

Nevertheless, Fleur and Tom obediently followed her instructions, making their way to a bench as far from the back door as possible so they wouldn't be overhead.

'What a witch,' Fleur said and liked the sound of Tom's laugh when it came. It was gone in a heartbeat. 'I feel like walking in some mud and deliberately striding back inside.'

'You're brave for someone so small,' Tom said, sounding impressed.

Fleur shook her head. 'She couldn't do much with my father in the house, but then she may take it out on you.'

'I won't be here long enough.'

'Why not?'

Before they could say more, Miss Jackson appeared at the back door. Fleur stood up as though ready to take her on. 'Wait here, Tom, I'll get it.' She ran towards the housekeeper. 'Thank you so much,' she said, feigning polite sincerity as she took a small tray from the housekeeper.

'He'd better not make himself sick on these biscuits,' the pursed lips managed to grind out. 'They're rich butter shortbreads.'

'Oh, I'll make sure he doesn't, Miss Jackson,' Fleur said, as if those same butter shortbreads couldn't so much as melt on her sweet-sounding tongue.

'Mind you do, girl.'

'My name is Fleur, Miss Jackson. I don't think you'd like it if I simply called you "woman", would you?'

'I beg your pardon!'

'Yes, that was too forward. My parents tell me I should not always speak my mind.'

'Indeed, you should learn to hold your tongue,' the woman snapped, her mouth pressing together until even the original line disappeared.

Fleur wanted to laugh; she knew that in this moment alone, she was untouchable. But Tom wasn't. And she didn't want him to bear the brunt of her cheekiness. She formed a contrite expression. 'I am very sorry. I did not mean to be rude. In fact, I try very hard to be polite at all times to everyone because my mother says that everyone – even children – deserve respect.'

'Your mother's right. You mind what she tells you.'

'Oh, I will, Miss Jackson. I'm glad you agree.' Fleur wondered if the housekeeper would catch on to what she was actually saying. 'Thank you again.' She turned away and walked carefully back towards Tom, determined not to spill a drop of the milk they'd been given, along with the shortbread.

'You took a chance.' He looked impressed.

She shook her head. 'Not really. My mother scolds me. She says that speaking the truth isn't always considered polite and gets me into trouble.'

He grinned. 'Sometimes you have to fib to protect someone's feelings.'

She smiled. 'Do you do that?'

'Yes. I think we all have to.'

'I suppose, but I have to learn how to. So you have a cousin? Your aunt said she was ill.'

'I haven't seen her. It's as though Mrs Darnell is keeping her hidden in case she catches a disease from us.'

Fleur laughed but then stopped as Tom continued.

'Mrs Darnell told me we're not family.'

'She didn't!' Fleur said, sounding appalled.

He simply nodded.

'Why do they want your mother's body, then?'

He shrugged. 'Because she's a Wintrow.' He adopted a mocking tone. 'And no Wintrow is buried in forsaken land.'

'They said that?'

'Mrs Darnell said it to the doctor at the bush hospital when he contacted her.'

Fleur sensed she was pressing a bruise and needed to change the subject for Tom's sake. 'What are your interests, Tom?' she asked, remembering that it was important to put a grieving family at ease. She didn't remember her father ever asking such a question of the bereaved, but he normally didn't speak to children.

'I'm from the wilderness beyond the Flinders Ranges, so I am interested in its landscape and the work we do out there.'

'Tell me more. I have never seen where you come from.'

'I'll show you one day.'

She smiled. 'All right.' It sounded as though they'd made a deal so she turned it into one, pretending to spit on her palm before she held out her hand to shake. 'Is that a promise?'

'It is,' he said, mimicking her and holding out his own.

She grinned as they shook on their agreement. 'You have to take me now. But until that day, you'll have to describe it to me. Can you do that?'

'Yes, I can.' He got a faraway look in his eye as though he was conjuring a picture in his mind. 'Where I live, I think the sun is always trying to kill us, while the howling wind sounds like a soul in constant despair . . . that's what my mother used to say, anyway.'

Fleur caught a slight hint of a smile on his face at her memory and then it left as he continued.

'We get huge dust storms and many times I've had to crawl

out of the single window in our cottage to clear the sand that blows against the door and locks us in.'

'That sounds scary.'

'It can be. My father once said that if you survived sun and dust, drought was never that far behind, determined to kill everything.'

'Why live there?' she asked, appalled.

He shrugged. 'I don't know. It's where we live. The mountains are ancient. I've learned about them. They're called the Flinders Ranges and they were formed by the earth's surface folding.'

She grinned. 'Are you fibbing? How can it fold?'

'It can, I swear. It's called plate tectonics.' He rubbed his forefingers together, hands held flat, to demonstrate. 'One great mass of land collides against another, and it's felt tens of thousands of miles away. That land, all that distance away, is bent, pushed up to form wrinkles in the earth and that process can form mountains.'

She gave a low whistling sound of awe. 'So your Flinders Ranges were pushed up against each other,' she said, moving her hands together to form a gesture of prayer.

'Exactly!' Tom said, sounding delighted that she'd caught on so fast. 'And I learned from one of my father's friends who knew about stuff like this that these mountains were once covered by an ancient sea so many millions of years ago that I'm not sure I know how to write that number down.'

She giggled and he smiled back at the sound of her amusement. 'I like you, Tom. You're interesting.'

'I can tell you more. Flies are the greatest pests in our life but there are snakes, spiders, scorpions, lizards, mosqui—'

She shuddered. 'Ugh.'

He gave a shrug. 'They're fine if you leave them alone. Thanks for the biscuits. I would never have asked.'

'You look like you need a good feed.'

He grinned. 'No, I always look like this.'

'Serious, you mean?'

'I don't have a lot to laugh about right now.'

'No,' she agreed. 'What will you do?'

'I suppose I'll go back on the train and wait for my father. The news may have reached him by now.' Tom nibbled on another biscuit.

'And when he comes home, then what will you do?'

'Grow up. Become a wool classer, I suppose.'

'What's that?'

'You've heard of a shearer?'

'Of course.' She began to sing. '"Click go the shears, boys, click, click, click."'

Tom grinned. 'Well, the classers – they sometimes call them "guessers" – are the men who look at the wool and they make decisions about it.'

'What sort of decisions?' Fleur frowned, thrilled to be learning more new knowledge from Tom.

'The man studies the shorn wool and has to decide on how clean that wool is, does it have a fine crimp, or—'

'Crimp?' Fleur interrupted. 'My mother has crimping shears that have wiggly blades.'

She saw dimples deepen at Tom's cheeks and his eyes seemed to glisten brighter than the navy she'd initially noted them as being. The smile seemed to cast an inner light.

'Exactly,' he said, his tone enthusiastic. 'The wool fibres have crimps . . . wiggly bits. Some are fine, with many wiggles, and others are broader.'

'And? What does it mean?'

He looked galvanised by her interest. 'The finer crimped wool is used for garments while those of a rougher nature . . . we call it coarse . . . might be used for . . .?' He looked up as though the sky might deliver the answer. 'Well, for carpets and the like. You know, rougher use.'

'And that's it? I could do that.'

They both began to laugh at her cocksure remark.

'No, there's more. I've made it sound too simple. In moments these men can fling out a fleece – that's the shorn wool in one piece – and decide on the crimp, the feel – it's called texture – the colour, cleanliness, strength. And all the while, the classer is keeping an eye on all the shearers and what's going on in the shearing shed. He's keeping the work flowing at a steady rate and even teaching the rouseabouts at the same time. He has to run across and get the wool pressed into bales, too – that's why they used to be called pressers. But he's got so many skills and he has to – as my father told me – think on his feet all day long. He can speed up and slow down, depending on the Gun's pace.'

He must have seen her moment of puzzlement because he continued. 'That's the top shearer – he's called the Gun because he's the best in the shed and the fastest. Everyone shears, as best they can, to his speed but most can't keep up. But the wool classer makes sure he keeps up, while also doing everything else. I think wool classers are brilliant.'

'Well, I think you're brilliant that you have this dream. I'd like to watch you working as a wool classer, Tom Catchlove.'

'Maybe you can visit. How about you? What do you want to be when you grow up?'

'Oh, I'm going to be the best mortician in this state – no, the best in the country.'

'Mortician? I don't know that word.'

'I help prepare the dead for their burial.'

At first Tom appeared shocked, and then he frowned. 'I thought your father is an undertaker.'

'He is. He takes the dead into his care and prepares them for their final journey. But there's a lot of work to be done on a body to make that person ready for burial. He's very good at it. I shall be even better.'

'Are you going to look after my mother?'

'I'll help to take care of her . . . and Amy. You can trust us. My father is the kindest man there ever was. He is very gentle and respectful.'

'Good. I'm glad you'll be there to watch over them, because they're sending me home tomorrow.'

'You won't be here for the funeral?' Fleur was surprised.

He shook his head. 'I think Mrs Darnell wants to be rid of me.'

'Why?'

He shrugged. 'I really don't know.'

'Yes, you do.'

He cut her a glance. 'I don't think I'm good enough for them.'

'They don't know you, you just said, so how can you not be good enough?'

'Oh, probably because we're poorer than them and live so far away.'

She nodded. 'What horrible people. Oh, look up there!'

Fleur had happened to glance to the top storey of the house and saw a pale face pressed against the window. It was the face of a child – a girl – who looked utterly miserable while she stared at them. Her hair was long, with a fat satin ribbon tied high at the back, just peeping over the top of her head.

Fleur was aware of Tom lifting his hand in salutation, but the girl stepped back into the shadows and disappeared. 'Who's she?'

'No idea,' he replied.

'Shall we ask?'

'Best not to be nosey with them,' he cautioned her.

'As I say, horrible people,' she repeated.

'Well, my mother came from them, but she wasn't horrible . . . she was wonderful. It's all right. I'd rather remember my mother dancing and laughing than lying in a closed box and being lowered into the ground.'

'Children!' Miss Jackson was back at the door. Fleur and Tom both threw a glance upwards, but the girl with the ribbon had not reappeared. Fleur instantly forgot about her as she turned her attention to the housekeeper.

'Bring that plate and glass back now, child,' Miss Jackson said, her glare landing firmly on Tom. 'And you,' she said, pointing at Fleur, 'hurry along. Your father's ready to leave.' She didn't wait for their reply, slamming the door shut behind her.

'I better go,' Tom said.

'I hope we'll meet again, Tom Catchlove,' Fleur said, and she surprised herself by stepping forward and, on tiptoe, planting a kiss on his mouth. It was over in a blink and he stared open mouthed at her. She giggled. 'I thought you needed one.'

He wiped the back of his sleeve over his mouth. 'Thanks.'

They emerged from the parlour into the hallway, where Fleur could see her father still speaking quietly with Tom's aunt. As Mrs Darnell looked towards her housekeeper, Miss Jackson pushed past them both to fetch her father's hat. Fleur skipped into the room that held the coffin, where Tom had darted. He looked suddenly bereft.

'They're gone,' he said unnecessarily.

'My father brought the hearse . . . that's the big car to carry coffins. He'll have taken her there.'

'I wanted to say goodbye.'

Fleur stepped forward and took his hand. 'Tom, it's important to bury your mother and Amy very soon.'

'I know, I could smell it,' he admitted, and she was pleased she hadn't had to explain that the dish of purplish, almost black water beneath the table was a special substance to mask the odour of death.

'I'll just take this and empty it. Anyway, they've already gone.' She walked back towards the parlour and the sink.

He followed. 'What do you mean?'

'Their bodies came here with you on the train, but their spirits were set free back in your Flinders Ranges. Now they're following you, looking out for you. They'll go back with you.' She tipped the purple contents into the sink and had to stand on tiptoe to reach the tap.

Tom helped her. 'Do you think so?' He turned that soulful gaze on her. Fleur nodded. 'Will I see you again?'

She rinsed and flicked the water away until the dish was dry enough. Tom obliged, turning off the tap. 'I hope so,' she answered. 'We're friends now and I don't have any my own age.' She grabbed his hand gently to prove it was true.

He held their linked hands up and surprised her again, this time by kissing the back of her slender hand. 'I won't forget you, Fleur Appleby.'

'Promise?'

'I have to show you the Flinders,' he said, grinning. 'We made a deal.'

She laughed. 'Then I'll wait for you.' She wished she could protect him. Take him home with them and ask her parents to adopt Tom Catchlove as they'd adopted her and given her so much love and security.

'Fleur?' Her father was at the door, his voice gentle as always.

Tom dropped her hand.

Henry turned to him and lifted his tall hat. 'I'm sorry for your loss, Tom. We'll take good care of your mother and sister.'

'Bye, Tom,' Fleur said. 'Keep your promise.'

On the journey home, Fleur pestered her father. 'What will happen to Tom?'

'I don't know. He has family. They'll step up.'

'His aunt doesn't want him.'

'No,' her father agreed, sounding contrite, as if caught in a lie. 'But Tom's father will be returning soon and will take charge of his son.'

'What if he doesn't?'

'Then others will.'

'Other strangers? Tom said he had no friends.'

'Fleur, this boy is not our concern.'

'Why did they bring him here?'

'They are quite well-to-do, as you can see. Tom's mother is one of two sisters and the family wanted her returned to Adelaide to be buried.'

'They live up here in the city. If they've called you, it means they want her buried around the port. Why is that, Dad?'

First he cut her a smile. 'You're very perceptive, Fleur, and yes, it's true. They want Tom's mother buried far away it seems.' He sighed. 'I don't know why people think as they do, Fleur. Decisions are made for all number of reasons and it's not our business to enquire. I still don't know why they chose us to manage the burial other than we're based at the port.'

'They're rich enough to have a family plot,' she remarked in a huffy tone.

'They are indeed. But clearly they don't want Tom's mother buried there.'

'That's cruel.'

'Not really. It's honest, perhaps. I sense that Tom's mother has not been within the family bosom for years. She's a wayward, and perhaps they're simply doing what she might want. Maybe it's a kindness. We can't know.'

'Well, if they're that kind, why isn't the family taking care of Tom?'

'It's complicated, Fleur. Families often are. You'll discover this in time. We're very lucky that we have such a happy little trio in ours. But let's not forget our task is as funeral directors. We've been asked to do a job and we've accepted. Our task is to prepare Tom's mother and sister for burial. They insist on a private funeral, so it's going to be swift. I know you want to learn more because you've struck up a friendship with that lad, but we must be careful that we don't appear too curious around the affairs of others. We must be relied upon to be trustworthy, especially as we're entering their homes.'

'Did she say what's going to happen to Tom?'

'Tom will go home. I can't imagine he wants to be anywhere else.'

'But there isn't anyone there.'

'They'll sort it out, Fleur.' He gave her a soft smile. 'You mustn't worry. Even if his father is not yet home, there will be neighbours and townfolk who will know him and do the right thing. Now, let me concentrate, my darling. The traffic is busy and I don't want any problems. The bodies we're carrying are ripening too fast.'

Fleur wanted to interject and let her father know that Tom lived in a situation of no neighbours and no townsfolk close by, but she could hear it in his voice that he was keen to get Moira Catchlove and her daughter properly prepared and buried. He wasn't lying. The odour was leaking out of the pine coffin like an invisible wraith, surrounding them in the familiar aroma of human decomposition. It was unpleasant, but a smell that Fleur had become used to, just like the harsh-smelling formaldehyde that her father used with so much care.

Henry had counselled her on this since she was young enough to make sense of language. She could clearly recall the first time she'd been shown the formaldehyde.

'This is toxic,' he said, pointing to the large bottles. It had a skull and crossbones on the label to make the point, which he tapped, making sure she understood. 'Never be curious about it. It can kill you. Never smell it directly. You see how I make sure all the windows are open and we are well ventilated? I don't care if it's the middle of winter and your fingers are frozen. Promise me, dear one, you'll never open the bottle alone.'

She was excellent at taking instruction and knew she would never disobey his teachings.

'I don't think those Condy's Crystals they had below Tom's mother are going to be much help by the time we get back to the mortuary,' she said, sounding as cynical as someone quadruple her age.

Henry laughed. 'No, I think you're right. We're past potassium permanganate being able to absorb the smell. This body needs to go into the ground by tomorrow. We'll be working fast on Moira Catchlove all day today. Mrs Oaten will have to wait – she's on some ice anyway.'

Fleur knew all the stages of death already. The rigor mortis, then the flaccidity, the grey pallor that took over, while the pooling of blood in the lowest cavities created the purplish mottling. The eyes and cheeks sinking as the skin lost its elasticity and the inevitable putrefaction that was so evident now. She turned away to look out of the window and forget the smell of Tom's mother decaying behind her, but she couldn't help wondering about that wide-eyed boy, so contained, so intense. She wished she could write to him and keep him company through the lonely days ahead.

Her father's voice startled her. 'Still thinking about that boy Tom?'

She nodded as they passed the expanse of the parklands. 'I am.'

'Let your thoughts about him go, Fleur. You're likely never going to see him again.'

4

FARINA

January 1935

Over the last couple of decades, Tom had come to believe the woolshed was like the wild, wild West of American fame. Fierce, single men, sometimes lawless, usually with daily hangovers, and as tough as the quartz of the mountain range that hugged this sheep station, came together under one roof. This motley mob, as varied in character as a bunch of blokes could be and of all ages, were required to live, sleep, eat and play together, not to mention work at speed and in hellishly hot conditions most of the time. With the collective attitude of being 'guns for hire', they roamed the stations from state to state, shearing most of the year. It wasn't just a way to earn money; for most of these hard blokes, it was a way of life. Given the choice, Tom was convinced none would give it up.

Now in the summer months, the gang were at Witchelina Station. Thirty-five thousand sheep would be shorn during January alone. Tom had the numbers in his head for this push: ten thousand ewes, plus their eight thousand lambs. Seven thousand hoggets who were last year's lambs, and then nine thousand or so wethers this summer, and then the big boys . . . at least three hundred rams.

The woolshed's cauldron of unpredictable components was no doubt why Tom had followed through on his promise to become a wool classer rather than a shearer. It allowed him to take a more omnipotent view of life in the shed and take a step apart from the unruly mob mentality . . . but it required him to take responsibility for all of them. And he was still considered young in the role.

The shearers were paid by the fleece, so that added an additional element of tension. The competition within the shed was palpable. Skilful shearers soon became rivals and vied for that top spot called the ringer, or the Gun. No one liked being number two, although someone had to be. The Gun was king, and he set the speed for the day, everyone else aiming to keep up with him.

Most here at Witchelina were part of the 'northern run', which, Tom had learned over the years, allowed individual shearers to join a team and travel through South Australia, into New South Wales and even up to Queensland.

The Gun this season, Big Jim Farrow, or Granite to most, had also done several stints in Western Australia, way up north, where some of the biggest sheds in the world resided and maybe one hundred thousand sheep awaited shearing. They didn't come any tougher or more experienced than Granite.

Tom found himself feeling dwarfed by Granite during the nine-thirty smoko after he had sighed, straightened from his final sheep of the first session and yelled that it was 'Time to boil the billy and get ourselves a rollie'.

This group called their king 'Granny'; they'd clearly been together a long time for that to occur. Peter, a new rouseabout on the gang, had been nicknamed Sparrow, or 'Sparra' as they said it, because he was so small. Tom was looking out for Peter, because he was still very green in his role with lots to learn; Tom hadn't forgotten what that felt like.

'Hey, Sparra,' Granny called out from his seat on a hay bale. 'I want to check my shearing comb. Get me the left-handed one, eh?'

'Righto,' Sparra said good naturedly. He leapt to his feet to go see Bill, the man known as 'the expert', who was in charge of keeping the shearing handpieces constantly oiled and in good order through the working day.

Loud laughter accompanied Sparra as he rushed off and Tom grinned. It was always going to be a trial by fire with a mob of men like this. Peter would learn, and in the meantime he'd take the merciless ribbing until someone new and naïve joined the gang. It was an old joke that Tom himself had fallen for years ago: when someone in the gang told him to fetch the left-handed screwdriver, he'd spent ages looking at the range of screwdrivers, trying to work out which that was.

Sparra returned, grinning sheepishly. 'The expert sent me with this one. Is this right?'

'Bloody hell, mate. What, no left-handed shearing combs?' Granny replied, sounding offended.

Sparra shrugged, handing him the universal tool. 'It's all he had.'

'Well, then, Sparra, fetch me some right-handed pliers from that box and pay attention. I'm going to teach you something now.'

The lad was yet to catch on but Tom knew he needed to work his way through the hoops that had to be jumped. He watched the youngster dip into the mobile toolbox nearby and pull out the only pliers, dutifully handing them to Granite. Peter looked like he was holding his breath, fearful of being wrong.

Granite took them and put them against his right palm, the shearing comb still in his left. 'Now, in New Zealand, those sheep-shagging Kiwis, like Donkey here, are allowed to use a much wider comb than us. Isn't that right, Donkey?'

The men sniggered at the insult, affectionate in its biting fun.

Donkey didn't seem offended; Tom was sure he'd heard the insult many times. 'Yep, sure is,' he said. 'Means we're faster. What takes me five minutes takes you blokes ten.' Except with his intriguing accent, it sounded as though he'd said 'teen'.

'Well, I can't have you Kiwis bragging. So, watch this, Sparra.' Granite used the pliers to bend the furthest tines on each side of the shearing comb so that they stuck out at an angle. 'Now I have a wide comb like the cheatin' Kiwis.'

Time to step in. 'You know that's illegal, Granite.' Tom kept his voice even. 'In Australia, anyway,' he qualified. 'It's written into the Federal Pastoral Award that we use combs of two and a half inches only.'

'Yeah, but who's going to say anything?'

It was a challenge. Either he stood up to Granny or for the rest of the month he would burn with the knowledge that he had been weak in front of the other blokes. 'I'd prefer you didn't, Granite. If an inspector—'

'But will he?'

'He might. And it's my duty to keep the shed in line with all the rules – particularly the union regulations, which includes making sure you're well fed and watered, mate.'

'*Oooh.*' The others were enjoying the cheerful threats being exchanged.

Granite paused dramatically and then shifted his weight onto one buttock and let rip with the loudest of farts. 'Ah, you see, Sparra, all that gas was obviously making me grumpy. Now that's out of my guts, I see the world in a better light and young Tommo is right. We can't break the rules. Give that comb back to Bill. He'll straighten it again.'

Sparra obeyed and Granite tipped Tom a wink. It wasn't an apology and it wasn't backing down. Tom suspected Granite was simply testing before the main push of the shearing day began.

'Just educating the lad.' Granite smirked. 'Anyway, what's for our midday meal?'

'Mutton!' everyone chorused.

That was the diet. Mutton chops for breakfast, roast mutton for midday, and cold mutton for tea . . . seven days a week. They'd bled a sheep only a couple of days ago and wrapped it up so the flies couldn't make a complete mess of it.

Tom grinned to show there were no hard feelings. As the chorus died down, he saw a cart arriving. 'Watch your manners, boys. Ducks on the pond.'

A murmuring went up at the signal that women were in their midst. Right enough, sitting alongside the driver was the lady of the homestead and one of her daughters.

'Morning, Tom,' the lady called from her seat, holding onto her hat. She looked beautiful all dressed in white. 'Morning, lads.'

Tom glanced at the men and they stood as one, pulling off their sweaty hats. 'Good morning, Miss.'

'We're going into town. We're helping to plan the summer fete.'

'Are you planning to win the ladies' running race again, Miss?'

She laughed and it sounded like the tinkling of a piano. 'No, that was an aberration, Tom.' He understood the word but many of the others might not. 'There's some fresh fruit and green vegetables for you men. I'm having them sent down to the cook.'

It normally wasn't her role but Tom had always thought the family from Witchelina were particularly good to all their workers. They murmured their thanks.

'You're most welcome,' she said. 'We have to keep your strength up. I hope the meat is staying fresh?'

'It is,' Tom said.

'And the beer's cold,' the Gun piped up.

'Well, now, I'm sure that's very important,' she replied in a wry tone. 'We won't keep you, Tom.'

Tom lifted a hand in farewell. Despite the mild morning, Granny's bare chest was slick with the sweat of his labour, which had begun promptly at seven thirty. While it wasn't Tom's fault the man had no shirt on, he was glad the visitors did not linger.

'Very good of her,' Granny acknowledged, taking a drag of his rollie.

Tom nodded, noticing Granite's fingers were stained with nicotine. This morning's cigarette looked fragile, glowing brightly as Granny took another suck, holding it delicately between thumb and forefinger. Most held their cigarette using the first two fingers, but Tom had worked out that Granny like to smoke his down to the last moment it could be alight without burning him.

On their own again, the huge shearer began a tall tale and all the blokes visibly relaxed as he started in.

'You know, I once sheared with a bloke called Maggot. He got that name because he smelled so bad, though he didn't seem to mind. I reckon for the whole month we worked at one shed he didn't change his clothes. Didn't even take his trousers off to sleep. One day we all got together, and dumped him in a cold bath – held him down while the cook soaped him up good and proper. We found a pair of underpants actually stuck to him. Maggot didn't even know they weren't his skin.'

All the men reeled back, making sounds of disgust.

'It's true, I tell yer! I was there. We burned those underpants, probably with a layer of old Maggot's arse still clinging to them. Anyway, one day he found an old kite, probably blown away from one of the children who'd gone off to boarding school. So Maggot took to learning how to fly this kite. Every afternoon he'd wander off into the bush and catch a breeze. And one evening before dinner, this overseer is riding through and sees Maggot.

'"Hey, you a shearer?" "Yep," says old Maggot. The bloke nods. "I've got a pen spare from tomorrow. Want some work?"

So old Maggot gets behind on the horse and goes with this bloke. His name was Runt, so you can imagine what everyone called him.'

All the blokes sitting around smoking exploded into laughter.

'He even began introducing himself that way. "Hello, I'm Runt the C—" he would say.'

Again, the gang chortled as one.

'He was small, you see. Youngest of six sons and I think stunted. But he was bloody tough and had the smarts to match,' Granny said, tapping his temple. 'He could outwit anyone. So the bloke takes Maggot and sets him up at this other shed on the neighbouring property and off he goes.

'Maggot's wife, meanwhile, goes to collect his wages. He came from Queensland, so his wages were paid up there and he got beer money down here when he worked. The paymaster tells his wife that there's no money because Maggot hasn't worked this last week. All us blokes in the original shed – the ones who bathed Maggot – begin to worry, you see, as the wife is now howling for wages and her husband, who she's convinced is hurt or dead. I have to be honest now, I too reckoned he's disappeared and been got by a snake while flying his blasted kite. So they send out a search party. The homestead rings through to the next property that a man's gone missing, so now that team calls for volunteers and Maggot puts his hand up.

'Off they go. Maggot's now in a truck searching for the lost shearer, and they meet up with the other search party. Maggot gets out and goes over to those blokes and says, "Who is it that you're looking for?" And they say, "You, you stupid bastard!"'

Even Tom had to chuckle.

'He left soon after, headed back to Queensland and the shed never smelled better, fair dinkum.'

The men sitting around Granite laughed, as he stood to get rid of his stub.

'We're throwing butts in the tin, everyone,' Tom warned. 'Place is like a tinderbox, so we have to be careful. Bingo, you make sure these are dampened before they're tipped out.'

Bingo nodded. He was one of the younger rouseabouts and had earned that nickname for having an uncanny knack of losing every bet he made, every card game, and even the simplest of contests. He didn't seem to mind, glad to be around the older blokes.

Smoko was almost over and they would begin again, working on the lambs first. Their mothers would follow. Tom had been part of the muster to move the sheep from their traditional watering spots into fenced-off areas that would be the only place they could find water now until they were shorn. Once the whole mob had come to water, Tom lent another pair of hands to clap and a mouth to yell at the easily startled animals, who were being expertly herded by a fast-moving and alert trio of dogs along with their masters to the transition yards. Here they waited to be gradually coerced into the shearing-shed pens.

Tom looked over at the lambs, all pressing into one corner, understandably anxious for their mothers, who were waiting to be shorn too before being reunited. It amazed him how those hundreds of lambs could each find their own mother when they were released, far in the distance of the shed and even over hills.

He turned back to Granite at the sound of his deep voice. 'Am I going too fast for you, lad?' he rasped, before sipping from a mug of strong tea that looked like stirred mud.

Tom had met Granite's kind so many times before. They fed off bravado, especially in front of the others, needing the laughter and banter to fuel them for the next two-hour session of brutal work.

'I've never done anything else but wool classing since I was fifteen,' he said in reply. It was his calculated way of impressing upon the Gun that he could cope with whatever the mountain of a man might like to throw at him but without letting him feel undermined or even challenged.

Granite nodded. 'I began shearing at fourteen. Couldn't wait to leave school and join the gang. I did the long run a coupla times . . . that's ten months away on the hardest of roads.'

Tom gave him a nod to show he understood the harsh nature of those long stints. 'This is home. My father became the station supervisor here for a few years after my mother died, before he passed.'

'The orphan wool classer?'

'That's me,' Tom admitted. No one had ever referred to him as an orphan before – or at least not to his face. The word put a strange new slant onto his life, and he wasn't sure if he was grateful or irritated by the title.

Granite nodded at him. 'Probably did you a favour, mate. Made you grow up quick. I hear you're unbreakable.'

Tom grinned despite not feeling in any way amused. 'Is that right?'

Don, the number two, joined the conversation, tipping out the dregs of tea from the mug in his hand. 'Granny hasn't hit his top speed yet, Tommo,' he quipped.

Tom couldn't remember suggesting anyone call him that, but Granny had once and it seemed to have stuck. Even so, his mother would turn in her grave, hating his name being shortened. Vern had laughed at her reluctance. 'Listen, love. The boy's a country lad and will never be called anything else. Let him get used to it.'

Tom recalled his father reaching down from his lanky six-feet plus to offer one of those rare moments of affection, ruffling his hair. It had felt good. He must have been five then, unable to contemplate not having his parents in his life.

'I said he hasn't even moved into top gear.' Don repeated, dragging Tom from his memories.

'Neither have I, Don,' Tom replied.

Granite caught his eye and winked. 'Let's see just how good you are then, Tommo. Come on, lads, smoko's over. Let's get back to it. I've got an itch to hit a personal milestone today.'

The men stood with sighs and made their way back into the earthy-smelling shed, where the pens of sheep were ready to be hauled in by their front legs one at a time to be fleeced. In here, the long timber slats they stood upon with gaps wide enough to let through the sheep dung, created a warmth of their own. The timber, coupled with the golden tones within the cocoon of the shed, felt familiar and safe.

Tom knew every inch of this shed, having grown up around it. His father had returned a fortnight after Moira died and was obliged to stay, given there was no one else to care for Tom. They'd stayed on in the cottage, Vern now supervisor and Tom finding new responsibilities of his own, from making the morning porridge for the station hands to feeding, watering and rubbing down all the horses.

He'd learned a wide array of jobs but had developed a hobby for carpentry, which spoke to his need for precision. The shearing shed had become a home, and he liked that every tool had its spot, and nothing was ever cast aside; you never knew when that bit of rope or old piece of leather might be handy. He'd learned his craft as a rouseabout; he was young and strong, quickly moving through the junior roles to become a wool classer in his own right.

Tom had learned that his wrists ached and sometimes flared up with terrible pain as a 'roller'; that was the fellow who rolled the soiled edges of the fleece away so the senior classer could focus on assessing the quality. So he'd taught himself some exercises to strengthen his hands so he wouldn't fall prey to the injuries that could finish a man chasing the demanding wool-classing role in the shed.

Tom waited while the shearing team readied themselves – nine stands were occupied – most keeping one eye on Granny as he went through his ritual of tying himself into a thick belt of his own design; it strapped his back for the relentless bending that was required. One day, Tom thought, they'd design equipment to help a man to bend so he wasn't relying entirely on his hard-working spine to do all the work – something that allowed him to bend, stretch, reach, twist but take the greater burden of all that strain. That felt a way off, but the shears were now mechanised, with power transmitted to the blades that formerly relied on the strength and adroitness of a shearer's hand. It still took one man, one pair of arms, one sheep at a time, but the mechanical piece meant a shearer could cut a lot closer to the sheep's skin, and that translated to millions of pounds more wool to the world.

When everyone was busy, Tom likened the flecks of wool, invisible until the glints of sunlight slanting through the narrow wooden slats of the shed caught their dance, to a snowstorm in the shed. Dust hung in the air as well, lurking on every surface, under-foot at every tread. To Tom, the familiar sound of his life, no matter the situation, was the sound of grit beneath his boots.

He capitulated to the need to swat at some flies and then knew he wouldn't bother again once the work began.

The lambs were small and easy; once on their backs, they mostly stayed still with fright. The older sheep could kick and struggle, making it a much tougher job. Tom knew that hauling just one sheep, particularly a ram that weighed up to three hundred and thirty pounds, was enough to create an injury, but repeating the action daily while the spine was bent was asking for problems. He'd seen many a shearer crippled by back injuries and pain, having to leave the shed for good; some only lasted a few years. Others tried to keep going because these were not times to be looking for new work; Tom was only too aware of the crowd of impoverished blokes living out of swags by the creek hoping for someone to quit or get injured. For every man in this shed, there were at least another two eager blokes outside who would stick their hand up for the same back-breaking work.

But there were few wool classers, so Tom felt secure. He would always be in demand as long as there were sheep to be shorn and he stayed fit.

'Tom, I've done the count.' Ronnie, the eldest rouseabout, the one he trusted to be accurate, appeared at his side.

Tom had worked with Ronnie over a couple of seasons now and liked the young man, who had an eye on Tom's job. Like Peter, Ronnie was a beanstalk of a lad but, nearing twenty-one, was stronger than his build suggested. He was also a quick learner and possessed a passion for the wool classer's role. Tom pushed him hard only because he could see a bright future for Ronnie and wanted him to be the best he could be when he went out alone.

'And?'

'Five hundred in the pen.'

'You're sure?' As boss of the sheep pen, Tom needed to know what he was up against with each shearing session.

Sparra arrived as Ronnie nodded firmly. 'I counted twice.' By count, he meant estimated, but there was a skill in that too and Ronnie had proved himself reliable.

'That will see us through to dinnertime. We've got to keep a pace of twelve hundred fleeces a day, lads, so each of these blokes is going to be doing around one hundred and forty, perhaps one-fifty each a day.'

'Granny reckons he'll do half that twelve hundred himself,' Sparra said.

Tom gave a soft snort. 'He can try, and we'll be ready, right, lads?' He looked hard at each of the youths in his care who were now going to assist with the task of classing the wool and baling it. 'Nobby, you need to roll faster. Until you get all those flyblown and scraggy edges away from the fleece, I can't class and you're in my way. Jacko is nipping at your heels.'

Jacko gave a snapping sound with his teeth. 'I'm twice as fast as you, Nobs.'

'But not as thorough,' Nobby replied, with just enough disdain to wipe the grin from Jacko's grimy face.

Tom smacked Jacko's arm with the back of his hand. 'Righto, now listen up. That ringer is going to try and humiliate us, and we're not going to let that happen. We have to work fast but, as Nobby says, thorough. I am only as fast and as accurate as you lot are neat and swift. You each need to be doing your job as efficiently as possible and that means getting out of my way. Dooley, you hear me?' He glanced at a tall, physically strong-looking lad called Doolan. 'I'll do the throwing this session.'

The boy looked wounded by the statement. 'But—'

'No buts, Dools. You're learning and learning fast, but this joker at number one is testing us. You can go back to throwing this afternoon, but right now I want us waiting for him because we're that good. He's not waiting for anyone. So, Dooley, you focus on skirting the moment I throw. All right, lads?' They all nodded and murmured assent. 'Keep sweeping, Bingo, and Sparra, keep everything clear. I don't want to trip, and I want to shave off some extra seconds between this table and the wool press. You do anything that the others ask of you without hesitation. Right?'

Sparra nodded.

Tom glanced over at Granite, who was testing the sharpness of his blade. No matter what he said, Tom knew Granny pulled the fearsome teeth wider on either end of the handpiece to grab a little more fleece off and add to the speed of each shearing. Tom looked away from the unlawful practice; he'd already said his piece and all the men were witness to it. 'Looks like he's ready. Are you ready, lads?'

'Ready,' they chorused.

'Here we go. Keep up.'

5

Despite his earlier promise, Tom flicked again at the tiny, annoying flies that plagued their days in the shed. He suspected his back was already covered with the creatures and knew the sensation of legs as thin as hair landing or padding across his skin would have to be ignored. He'd never got used to them targeting the corner of his eyes, after his tears, but bush people learned not to keep brushing at them because it was an action in vain. There were too many to fight and those flies were going to share their lives for as long as the sheep were here, and the men were sweating over them.

Granny strode into the pen and grabbed a lamb by its forelegs and the session began. He had the wool off his first animal within four minutes, and he was only going to get faster. Jacko leapt to the cast-aside fleece and Bingo began sweeping, while the Gun pushed his sheep through the hatch, sending it skittering outside, and was already reaching for the next terrified lamb.

Tom grabbed the small fleece and tossed it easily. It landed perfectly on the long, narrow timber slats of the table as he knew it would; he had known how it would land from the second his fingers let go.

'It's an art, Tom,' his father had said when Tom had first said he was interested in classing.

As young as he had been during this conversation, Tom had been able to make his point eloquently. 'Wool classing takes concentration. I've watched Lou for years, Dad . . . a wool classer only has moments to make his decisions and has to be confident in making them, plus they have to make that throw land every time, hundreds of times a day. I'm not saying shearing isn't skilled but it's about brawn . . . doesn't need any calculation.'

His father had shrugged. 'It's your funeral, Tom. Shearing pays well.'

'Wool classing won't ruin my back.'

'If Lou will take you on and teach you, I don't care what you do, so long as you earn your keep.'

It was a harsh response but since his mother's passing, Vern had lost his happy-go-lucky approach to life, becoming brooding, aggressive at times. When Tom turned eleven, six months after they'd lost his mother, his father disappeared for ten weeks. Left Tom to fend for himself, or rather to get on with life among the station hands. He kept cooking their breakfasts, stirring an enormous bowl of porridge or cooking eggs as best he could, or grilling chops and looking after the animals. Soon enough he found himself hanging around the sheds and watching its high activity over summer. He'd taken on a rouseabout role as soon as he was old enough and began to earn for himself, living at and working for Witchelina Station as opposed to joining one of the shearing gangs.

The family at the homestead had known and liked his mother and saw to it that the boy who had been born there now had a permanent role, doing all sorts of jobs around the place when the shearing or crutching seasons had passed.

Most of the rouseabouts took on shearing roles when they were of an age, but Lou had given Tom the chance he craved to learn how to class wool. Once he'd spent a few years as the rouse-about, Tom had become Lou's roller.

'Never worked with anyone this young on the table before, boy. Don't let me down,' Lou had warned.

He hadn't. Tom's ability to concentrate, take instruction and learn fast meant he was rolling and skirting the fleeces efficiently far earlier than most apprentices had in Lou's estimation. When Lou had finally retired, Tom had stepped up and taken on the role gladly, but he still resisted joining the roving shearing gangs.

His father, due for retirement himself, had asked why only once. 'What's wrong with you, lad? Guaranteed work most of the year and top dollar, no less. You shouldn't be sneezing at that, not in these tough times. Chance to move with the rest of the blokes.'

Tom had shaken his head. 'I'm happy here. I don't care much for change.'

Vern had grumbled at him and Tom could believe his father had lost faith with him. No more singing and dancing. Barely any amusement. He couldn't remember the last time he'd made the man smile, probably when his mother had still been alive. It seemed to Tom that his father had begun treating him as a stranger from the moment he was no longer a dependent child, which, in Tom's estimation was age ten, the day Moira had passed.

Perhaps that was harsh, Tom mused. Maybe more like an un-welcome relative. He was perceptive enough to sense his father felt obligated to acknowledge him, but there was no affection left for his son, or so it seemed to Tom. Tom couldn't work it out then and was none the wiser now, nearly two decades on, as to what he had done wrong.

In recent years, when Vern was in his cups he'd cry and talk about Moira . . . and the baby. And so it was that Tom had begun to blame himself for his mother's and sister's deaths. He hadn't done enough, hadn't driven Bonny fast enough, hadn't sought help urgently enough; they'd died because of his inaction or carelessness.

The notion was terrible but as seductive as it was infectious, colouring his thoughts with deep regret whenever he had time to himself to think. The silence he'd once considered a companion was now his enemy, because it reminded him of loss – all of it, his fault.

Vern had died, not saying it, but conveying blame on his son to his last breath, so Tom believed. How could he not? He'd held his father's hand as his breathing had become laboured and told him that he loved him, but in a final and shocking gesture, his father had found the strength to pull his hand away with a grimace. There had been such naked aggression to the gesture and to this day Tom wondered what his father's hostility meant.

'Ready, Tom? He's nearly finished,' Ronnie warned. 'And the others aren't far behind.'

Tom snapped out of his memories and gave an almost imperceptible nod; in the same heartbeat the rouseabouts moved in to do their skirting. Suddenly there was no time for anything other than getting that fleece sorted and fluidly over to the wool press, which was already groaning its metallic sounds in readiness. Sheep bleated, not in unison, but layered so the sound was discordant and pitiful. There was fear from the animals and tension around the troupe of shearers as sweat already gleamed on straining muscles. The mechanical shears hummed beneath the higher pitched shriek of the blades being sharpened by the expert. Granite liked to swap his blades every couple of fleeces. It added time but Tom admired his confidence that those extra moments spent changing over made him faster overall.

Tom could remember early autumns when the wool was so flyblown and dirty that he spent far too much time separating out the maggots while the fleeces piled up. But not today. This wool already looked top quality to him.

The two lads rolling either side stepped back and Tom was touching the wool in the next instant. His expert gaze had already told him most of what he needed but now his fingers would confirm what he had sensed. The quality was excellent; he knew from a quick click of his thumb and second finger that the tensile strength was superb, while the value of the wool grease was high. That meant the fleece was in top condition. The colour was bright, with no daggy yellowing, and the neat, bold crimps that were neither too curly nor hairy meant the 'style' was tip-top, as Lou used to say.

'Three AM,' he murmured, more for Ronnie's benefit as the apprentice began his new layer of learning. 'Get on with the other bits.'

The 'other bits', which were the bellies, locks and top knots, were now Ronnie's responsibility. He would rapidly check for stains, vegetation and any other matter that might contaminate the main fleece, which Tom had classed as the best merino available. Meanwhile, the other hands got busy sweeping as Tom insisted on a clean working space.

Ronnie began his task as Tom was striding to the bin, folding the fleece as he moved, then tossing it neatly into the press. By the time he turned, Ronnie was moving to put the other bits in their respective bins and he was back at the table ready to roll the second fleece within seconds.

Tom was not looking at anyone now. It would be fleece after fleece until the session was done. His focus was complete. After half-a-dozen fleeces, he knew he was hitting his best speed and was pleased to note that Ronnie was keeping up and not getting in his way. Once Tom hit his stride, he would give himself only ten seconds to look and feel each fleece, plus another twenty seconds to walk it to the bin and be back in position.

He caught a wink from the number two. 'Granite reckons he's going slow, mate.'

'He can go as fast as he likes,' Ronnie said, taking up the challenge on Tom's behalf. 'We're yawning back here.'

Tom heard the laughter, the exchange of friendly insults, the growling of Granite as he complained that the ewes coming in had full bellies and were cranky.

'They need more rest after a full feed!' he yelled at the station manager who had made the error of coming into his eyeline. 'That mob can cause accidents when they're angry.'

The man must have nodded, or moved on, or offered placation; Tom couldn't hear. He heard only the scream of his mother in the sound of the bleating sheep and the soft smile of a generous stranger, younger than him, who promised to take care of the dead women in his family. Why that little girl haunted him still, he couldn't say. It had been such a brief moment in his life and yet she had a big effect, giving more comfort in the few minutes they spent together than any adult could, especially his father.

The midday meal bell heralded the arrival of cold mutton and freshly baked bread, which Bingo had been sent to collect. It was still warm from the oven of the underground forge at Farina.

Relieved to take a break after the morning's work, Tom was helping himself to the food set up on the tables when the expert sidled up.

'I think we need some maintenance on the shaft, Tom.'

'Going slow?'

The man nodded. 'The Gun will complain otherwise – just gives him something else to blame if he doesn't hit his goal. I can hear it beginning to struggle.'

Tom gave a nod. 'Sparra?' The lad looked up, his mouth stuffed with bread. Tom smiled; he could remember a time when his belly felt like it could never be filled fast or often enough. 'Can you get up and oil the shaft before we start again? Say, in the next few minutes.'

'Yes, boss.'

'Like I've taught you. Careful at every stage, right?'

Sparra grinned around his mouthful. 'I know.'

Granite looked up from his midday meal. 'Yeah, watch ya head, boy. I was workin' a shed not so long ago up in New South Wales, and a bloke got his whole scalp fair torn off. We had to take his skin with him so they could sew it back on.'

The lads thought he was joking and laughed, but Tom knew Granite was not entertaining them.

'Sparra, all I need is for you to top up the oil and keep the bearings cool. I'll switch off the engine now. You finish what you're eating quickly and then get the ladder.'

Sparra took another huge mouthful of the sandwich he'd created, juice from the mutton rolling down to his wrists and beyond.

Tom blinked; he'd surely never be able to chew it, let alone swallow it. He left the lad to his dilemma and walked away to the engine room, flicking off the switch that turned everything quiet around the shearing shed as the drive wheels spun to a halt. He headed back out and away from the men to eat alone somewhere. It wasn't friendly, he knew, but he preferred his own company away from the pointless ribbing and banter that would inevitably ensue once the chewing was done.

He pretended he was checking on the bales from the two morning sessions and looking over the new mob of sheep they would tackle in the afternoon sessions, getting a measure of the quality coming through. From the corner of his eye, he saw Sparra setting up the ladder before he went in search of the oil can to fill the individual bottles that fed the bearings. Everything had its place in Tom's neat shed; Sparra wouldn't have to hunt for it.

Tom leaned back against a fence post, chewing thoughtfully as he recalled a pair of intriguing hazel-coloured eyes that had once regarded him over a generous smile. He wasn't surprised by the thought. The young friend from Adelaide had invaded his thoughts regularly over the years. She had been eight then. He began to wonder what she might look like now.

Distantly he heard Granny beginning another story about a shearer with an 'arse that was feeling rough', as he'd put it, who decided he'd cool it down by sitting in the flour sack that the cook used to make their bread. 'I tell ya, we were all very suspicious of our damper each evening.'

Tom tuned out the laughter and let his thoughts roam back to Fleur Appleby, who had been arresting even at eight. He'd never forgotten her name or those large enquiring eyes. They seemed to know him even though they'd just met, and were not ones to easily tear one's gaze from. They held you while they studied you. The hair around her heart-shaped face was darkish but could hardly be called just brown. It was rich like polished Australian black-wood, striped with warm tones of treacle and even burnt umber. Fleur Appleby had her own special drawer in his mind, which he slid out from time to time to ponder what Fleur was doing now. She would be in her late twenties . . . Was she engaged? Married? Probably. She might even have a clutch of children already. Her husband would be someone of standing in the community and no doubt smart; he'd have to be to contend with Fleur's quick-witted ways.

Distantly he heard the engine grind into motion again in the shearing shed. Sparra had likely finished the oiling and was running the machinery through its checks. He smiled absently, remembering the little girl who had taken on that horrible housekeeper in Adelaide. She'd been quite a cheeky thing, so confident and disarming in her directness. It would be intriguing to see whether she'd become—

Tom's notion never reached any further.

The gut-twisting shriek chilled his thoughts, froze him momentarily as he blinked through the sharp sunlight to the shed and realised it was the young apprentice screaming for help. Tom flung away his bread and mutton and launched himself from the fence, yelling at the others, who were already in motion.

The sound of Sparra's shock and pain stopped him once again as he skidded onto the gritty boards in the shearing shed, startling the mob of sheep waiting. They too kicked up a pile of dust as they tried to push away from the disturbance and Tom had to blink it away, looking up to where the trainee rouseabout was trapped, being hurled about in the overhead shaft, the bearings complaining loudly.

Others arrived a heartbeat behind him, full of exclamation and looking up to where Sparra writhed, begging for it to stop.

'What the bloody hell?' It was Bill the expert.

'Ah, you poor bastard,' Granite murmured.

Tom raced to switch off the engine that would end the mechanical motion overhead, but he already knew it wouldn't end the cries of agony. Granite stepped forward but wasn't quick enough to catch Sparra, who fell heavily the six feet or so, crunching to the boards in a thumping sound Tom knew would haunt his dreams. He looked to be unconscious as the men hurried to his side. But no, Sparra's eyelids flickered open.

He groaned softly as Tom touched his shoulder. 'Sorry, Tom.'

'Don't move, mate,' he urged. It was too late now to ask the youngster why he had risked being on the ladder while testing the machinery. It was the first rule: only test the machinery from the ground and away from harm. How many times had he drummed that into the lad?

Tom grabbed one of the others, open-mouthed and wide-eyed in fright. 'Bingo, go fetch the truck.' He flung the lad the keys he hauled from his pocket. 'Move!' Tom yelled as the youngster's gaze seemed to swim. He turned to Nobby. 'Go fetch some grog. Not beer, proper liquor – you'll find some in the cupboard in the hut. Be quick, Nob. Fast as you can.'

Jacko and Doug already knew to give their boss their full attention and stepped up with fright in their expressions, awaiting an order. 'Jacko, fetch a pillow and a blanket. Hurry.' Now Tom turned to the men. 'Granite, you're the strongest. I'll need your help, mate, if we have to get him into town.'

Granite nodded and relief flooded Tom that the Gun wasn't going to start complaining about his numbers or loss of time.

Tom eyed Granite's number two. 'Don, fetch some water.'

'Yeah, for sure.' No wisecracks for once. Don straightened and headed out of the shed.

Finally, Tom turned to the expert. 'Call the hospital, Bill, can you? See if there's a doctor anywhere close. Ronnie, you, Granite and me – we'll lift him on to the truck when it gets here.'

All shearing forgotten, the men worked together to make Sparra as comfortable as they could without moving him too much. His body looked strangely twisted as they lifted his head to first get some water into him.

'Tom, I can't feel my legs.'

'You're in shock, that's all. It's to be expected,' Tom lied. He had no doubt that Sparra's spine was injured and his rouseabout days had finished before they'd got going.

'No, I can't feel my fingers either. I don't think I can move my hands.'

'You lie still, Peter. Give your body a chance. It's been hurt, and you've gone into shock,' Tom tried again. He glanced at Granite, who met his gaze with a small shake of his head. Tom had to look away from the truth in that gesture.

More brandy helped to quieten the growing panic that Sparra was displaying; they began pouring copious slugs of the liquor into his mouth. Anything to dull his anxiety, because he wasn't complaining of pain, which felt ominous. The sounds of the bleating sheep, even the touch of the annoying flies, were forgotten.

'Do we get him up?' Doug asked, looking like a frightened child.

'We don't move him an inch until we get some advice,' Tom said.

Granite pointed to Sparra's shredded shirt. 'This is what got caught. Seen it happen before but the bloke didn't get twisted up like this, poor bastard.'

Bill returned with features grimly set. 'No doctors in town. Maybe day after tomorrow.' The men cursed as one beneath their breath. 'The nurse said they'll do what they can for him if you get him to the hospital.'

Tom, reminded of his previous experience, wanted to ask 'What hospital?' but held his tongue and nodded instead. 'Let's get the truck backed up to the door and then we'll carry him slung on a sheet so we're not hurting him any more than we need to. Give him more brandy. Best he's out of it for the trip to town.'

It was Bill who spoke up. 'Tom, let the station hands take him into town.'

'You're joking, mate. Sparra's my respon—'

Bill didn't flinch. 'So are all these men and their livelihoods . . . and all these sheep to be finished today. Your responsibility is first to the station owners. You can't do any more for the boy today, but others can while you keep the work going – keep us all distracted if nothing else.'

It was the voice of reason. Neat, ordered, clear thinking. Tom couldn't argue with it. 'Right,' he murmured. 'Bill, will you—'

'Already done, Tom.' They heard the truck arrive. 'Let's get him loaded on the flatbed and you boys can get back to work.'

With Tom barking instructions, the drunken Sparra was slung

gently in a sheet and carried to the truck. He moaned as he was laid onto the bed of the truck.

'I thought he'd carry on more,' Doug commented, tapping into Tom's great fear, because he had expected more protest too. The thought leapt around his mind that Sparra's back had been broken, which might account for him not feeling much any more, but he refused to say it. He'd let the others think it was the grog . . . and hope they were right.

The first station hand was a young fellow called Stu. Tom eyed him hard, like a hawk watching prey. 'Now, Stu. This young bloke is very badly injured. You have to drive slow, mate, all right? Real slow.'

Stu nodded, looking terrified. 'I'm bringing Wilko with me so we can carry him into the hospital.'

'Good idea,' Tom said, finding a grim smile that he was struggling to feel. 'Right, you two, thanks. Just be gentle with him.'

Bill added his two cents' worth. 'Something might be broke on that boy, lads. You don't want to make it worse.' He cut Tom a look and Tom knew that Bill was thinking along the same lines as him.

The rest of the afternoon passed in a blur of horror. For the most part the men were uncharacteristically quiet, working hard, fast and no one complaining for any reason. For once Tom's ability to withdraw into himself was a genuine advantage as they worked on. And Ronnie stepped up, taking on more responsibility. Being one labourer down did slow the work, but Granite seemed to understand and compassionately slowed his shearing too, and because all the shearers took their lead from the Gun, the work kept flowing at its new, less frenetic pace. They might not make twelve hundred today, but they would try.

The wait for news was like a wraith darting around them, poking and prodding every now and then but invisible nonetheless.

It felt like a chill each time it stole up and reminded Tom what was happening beyond the shed in Farina town.

The news finally came long after the day's work was done. Four sessions completed and all the blokes were sitting around the verandah once again, contemplating a roast mutton dinner and drinking long-necked beers. The sun had set. No one seemed in any hurry to stop drinking or start eating. Granite had showed the youngsters how to cool their beers with a wet linen wrapped around them that would evaporate its moisture in the breeze.

'Takes the boil off, you see,' Granite explained, trying to brighten the leaden mood and Tom liked him more for it.

Still, the heavy atmosphere clung on as the day's light disappeared. Tom heard the truck's arrival. He was planning to use the same vehicle to go to the hospital and stood up impatiently. He half hoped, knowing it was a vain notion, that Sparra might be seated in front, giving a thumbs up with his lopsided grin.

There was no sign of him, though.

A pit opened in Tom's belly and the smell of the roast coming from the oven, which would normally cheer everyone, seemed to do the opposite. The truck drew to a slow stop and even the two lads' reluctance to get out of the vehicle told Tom that the news was not going to be good.

Broken back? Crippled? He'd look after Sparra. They'd work it out. The shearing team stood as one, bottles of beer in hand and moved to cluster around Tom as though to offer comfort.

Stu killed the engine and finally opened the door. Even in the dimming light his eyes looked red.

Tom could barely find the right words. They came nevertheless, arriving into the awkward pause and not bridging the gap smoothly. 'They've kept him, then?'

'Yep,' Stu said, averting his gaze, and tears arriving. 'In the morgue, boss.'

Tom blinked. He couldn't have heard right.

The blokes around him gave soft gasps. One whistled a sound of disgust.

Tom stared so hard at Stu it was as if his gaze had the power to lift the lad's chin and demand he look at him. 'Sparra's dead?'

Stu swallowed and knuckled away his tears. He nodded. 'The nurses said it was the kindest thing anyway. Nothing they could do. His spine was broken, they reckoned, and even if they had been able to get him to Adelaide, there was little to be done to fix it. He'd have had no life, the senior lady said.'

That was more words in one breath than he'd heard Stu say in any given week. He looked traumatised and his mate, Wilko, shifted uncomfortably from foot to foot.

Tom walked up and squeezed Stu's shoulder. He cleared his throat. He wished now he had taken the lad himself and not let these youngsters bear the brunt of the rouseabout's death. 'You did your best and I'm grateful – we all are – that you got him to hospital. Join the boys . . . have a drink and have a meal. You'll feel better, Stu.' What else could he say? He looked at the other station hand he didn't know well. 'Thanks, Wilko, for being there.'

The lad tried to say something but clearly couldn't find any words and Tom understood.

'I'm taking the truck. I'll go pay my respects to Peter.'

He couldn't wait to leave the line-up of shocked, unhappy expressions but he drove towards Farina as slowly as he dared. He was in no hurry to look upon Sparra's broken corpse.

Mother, sister, father . . . Peter. Death seemed to be Tom's regular companion.

6

PORT ADELAIDE

April 1935

Henry Appleby shook his head and flapped the page with disgust, reaching for his glass of ale nearby. It would become a glass of brandy later, Fleur thought with sadness as she sat quietly between her parents at the dinner table. Except they weren't really her parents. Only one parent sat at the head, vexed at some item of news in his evening newspaper. The other – an impostor, as far as Fleur was concerned – sat with pinched lips where her real mother once sat.

Irma was Fleur's stepmother, but even that term was loose, in Fleur's opinion. She thought of her more as a conniving limpet of a woman, who had clung fiercely to Henry from the moment he had looked at her and used his grief at being widowed to steal Mae Appleby's role for herself. To Fleur it had been a sly and orchestrated campaign to win her father's affections; the horrible woman who now sat in Mae's chair had shown such patience that Fleur almost believed that beneath Irma's skin lived a reptilian creature of ancient cunning. She had tried over and again to find qualities to admire, just one thing to like about Irma – perhaps the affection between her and Fleur's father – but she had come up wanting.

She had never seen a fondness coming from her father, nothing even resembling love.

Now, as an adult, Fleur believed the marriage had been one of convenience on both sides. It suited Irma's social climbing aspirations as much as her need for security. And what her father got out of this arrangement, Fleur had often worried over, and she had finally settled on him simply wanting a wife to run a household and the child within. It appalled her that he'd relegated her mother's role to something so practical, given how loving they had been towards each other.

These days her father made no pretence of his indifference towards Irma and had taken to reading the evening newspaper at the dining table, something Fleur knew her darling mother would never have tolerated. What's more, her father would never have put up such a barrier between himself and his women had Mae still been living. Her early death from influenza had changed all their lives in so many ways, reading at the dinner table one of the least intrusive. The worst was making Henry so vulnerable to a predator such as Irma.

'You can clear the dishes, Nan,' Irma said with her fake smile, dabbing at those mean lips that seemed to be permanently chapped. 'Coffee for Mr Appleby.'

'I don't think—' Henry began.

'Nonsense, dear.'

Fleur would have gladly helped but she knew it would raise her stepmother's ire. She continued to find new pretensions to focus her attention on. The last few years had been about jewellery and acquiring more of it to show her husband's wealth. Right now, though, Irma was fixated on the notion of domestic help, and how that spoke of wealth and position.

The household currently had a staff of two. Nan was a sailor's wife with a clutch of children and a need for income, and had entered their lives just a few weeks prior as a cook and server. Fleur didn't believe she was particularly competent at either but she was cheap and looked the part in her new uniform. A cleaner, Jean, had been keeping the house dusted and tidied for half a year now.

Fleur thought about her lovely mother, who had happily run the household alone, raising a child among those duties, but was now eighteen years in her grave. Her father had held out for a couple of years; it was hardly a happy life without Mae, but they'd managed well enough as father and daughter, despite the hole she left because of the deep affection between them. And yet somehow Irma had got beneath his skin and, likely during a drunken moment, coerced him to get married.

So here they sat. The world's unhappiest trio around a table where the happiest of families had once eaten. Fleur shook her mind free of the past. It did her no good.

'What is happening in the world to make you cross, Dad?' She knew he still enjoyed a conversation about news and events with her. Irma would only join in if it was salacious, involved some sort of purchase or, best of all, offered an opportunity to make money. He didn't look well; he was pale but it would only vex him to mention it.

'Not cross. Concerned. This beef riot they're talking about is going from bad to worse. We'll be busy if they keep this up, because people from the port are going to get hurt or even die with all this hostile feeling flying about.'

Fleur sensed Irma's interest was piqued at the mention of bodies and burials.

'Nothing is bad that's good for business, Henry,' Irma predictably said, as though making some grand philosophical point. 'Er, Nan, we'll take coffee in the drawing room now,' she said in the lofty voice she reserved for servants or her father's funeral workers.

Drawing room. It made it sound as though they lived in a vast manor. Fleur's mother had called it the sitting room, which sounded far cosier and was more accurate, given its small size.

Fleur returned her focus to the news item, eager to hear more and keep her father engaged. The riot her father mentioned had broken out somewhere near the city when the unemployed discovered that mutton would be substituted for beef on the ration list.

'Henry, shall we go through, dear?' Irma put down her napkin and made to stand, leaving a ghastly imprint of her lips on the starched fabric from the plum lipstick she favoured. 'Henry?'

There were times when Fleur believed this careless attitude was deliberate, to show disdain for the woman who had come before her. Irma knew how much Mae's belongings still meant to the people she had left behind and now, watching that oily stain landing in full view, Fleur was convinced that Irma meant Fleur to see it. She looked away as her father growled.

'What?' he said rudely, frowning as he again folded back the newspaper, disgruntled to be disturbed.

'I said, Henry, we're taking coffee in the drawing room.'

'You go through.' He flapped the paper again.

Irma glanced at Fleur, who maintained a neutral expression. She hoped it conveyed a sense of 'don't blame me', but what she really felt was helpless delight. When had she become so petty that she would inwardly smile if her father favoured her over his wife? It seemed that she and Irma had taken positions on opposite sides of her father. Anytime he moved against Irma – even in a tiny way, like choosing to stay seated a little longer where Fleur happened to be – was apparently a choice in his daughter's favour.

'Tell me more about what the article says,' she said, turning back to him, far more interested in her father's doings than Irma's.

'Henry?' Fleur could sense her father's blood pressure rising as Irma nagged again in her sniffy nasal voice. 'Don't let it go cold, please.'

Henry gave another grumbling sound and Irma left, her wide hips grazing the tablecloth and rumpling the corner. Fleur straightened it – it was her mother's lace and she hated that Irma made use of her possessions. This was one of her mother's favourites and yet Irma used it for midweek suppers; she could see where Nan had dripped stew from the pot to her father's plate, but she couldn't blame Nan, who was a former flower seller, not a waitress. It seemed Henry was oblivious too; either he chose not to see the stains on his first wife's precious lace, or he no longer cared.

'Here, listen to this,' Henry said. 'Apparently the unemployed in our neighbourhood are demonstrating in the streets tomorrow against the abolition of beef in their meat ration. They're mustering at the Waterside Worker's Hall.' He folded up his newspaper and sighed. 'There's two thousand going from Port Adelaide, but they're meeting up with plenty of others once they hit town. They're threatening to carry signs with the hammer and sickle!'

Fleur gave a soft shrug. 'They have legitimate grievances. I was talking to Mrs Brown the other day – you know her husband hasn't had work for a couple of years, and they have five mouths to feed?' She didn't wait for him to answer. 'She told me their rations had gone down from four loaves to three in the last year, and even the value of their groceries were reduced by threepence. She said they had more at the height of the Great Depression a few years back than they do now.'

Henry clicked his tongue with disgust, reassuring his daughter in doing so that he still did feel something for others. She watched him reach for his glass again to drain the ale and winced internally. He was drinking heavily. It had been escalating since her mother died – year after year it became more noticeable but now she was convinced that her father was an alcoholic. It didn't matter that he was sober for the day's work; come the evening – and Irma – he let go into his cups. She reckoned he'd suffer coffee in Irma's drawing room briefly but would be out to the pub as fast as he could.

'Dad?' She might as well strike while he was lucid, and especially because life in this household was worsening by the week.

'Hmm,' he said, absently, folding his glasses into their case.

'I've got some ideas I'd like to discuss.'

He closed his newspaper, obviously aware that he was being impatiently awaited in the other room. 'What ideas?'

Fleur smiled. 'Mainly for our business, but one personal one I would like to talk over with you. Can we arrange to sit down together tomorrow, perhaps?'

'Your mother's insisting—'

'She's not my mother,' Fleur said, helplessly fast, like a whiplash. She wished she hadn't, because his eyes narrowed.

'She's the only mother you have and—'

'I didn't ask for one. I was happy with just us.'

Henry sighed. And she understood – it was an old bleat and she should have resisted making it once more. 'Don't start again, Fleur, I'm tired of it.' His expression looked suddenly wearied, as if he alone carried all the weight of the world's troubles.

But Fleur knew exactly what his private troubles were, and they all focused around one topic. 'Why did you marry her, Dad?' she murmured. 'You look unhappier now than you did years ago when Mum became sick.'

'Too late for regrets. We have to make the best of it.'

'I don't have to. I want to leave.'

He looked stricken. 'The business?'

Fleur shook her head. 'Just the house, Dad. I don't think I can live here much longer.' It was all tumbling out the wrong way.

'She's so grasping, I can't bear it. You give her everything and it's not enough. She'll ruin you, Dad.'

'She's just uncertain of her place,' he said, falling back on his usual generous way. 'You're so assured and reminders of your mother are all around us. It's probably hard for her.'

'Oh, Dad,' Fleur said, sounding frustrated. 'There's nothing hard for Irma in the life you've given her. She's fortunate you're so big-hearted.'

'You miss your mother, I underst—'

'Don't *you*?' She regretted the accusatory tone immediately as pain fleeted across his features, taking them from that resting expression she knew and loved to one of grief again.

'Every day, child. But you needed a mother back then, can't you see that?'

She nodded but it was a lie. She had never needed anyone but the person who had died, and once Mae was gone, Fleur would have got along as best she could with one parent. But she knew he would tell her that Irma came into their lives for the right reasons. And she would take that moment, if it presented itself, to express as sharply as she dared that Irma was an actress and only pretended to love them, that she hadn't had much to say to Fleur since she'd first bled and been considered a young woman, no longer a child.

'Irma sees you as family, Fleur.'

She fixed her gaze to his. 'Irma sees me as a rival, Dad. For your love, for your business, for your property – and especially your bank account.'

He gave a groan of despair as the very woman they were discussing called out again.

'Henry!' Her shrill voice came from the room where the coffee was clearly cooling to where they were now all but whispering.

'Come on,' he said. 'We'll talk at length about what you have in mind tomorrow, when we're in the mortuary. Right now, let's just keep the peace, can we?'

She gave her father a small smile with a nod and stood. The meeting tomorrow was a positive step. 'All right. Tomorrow.'

They moved to the sitting room where Irma waited. 'What were you both whispering about in there?' she asked in the caustic tone that was natural to her.

'Nothing of importance, dear.'

Fleur refused to let her father be interrogated in front of her or to make excuses for having a private chat with him. She was more than comfortable telling untruths to Irma if it protected him. 'We weren't whispering, just speaking quietly about work. I was reminding my father of the embalming we are doing for not one but two people in readiness for a family viewing.'

'Ugh, don't talk to me about corpses, child,' Irma said, with a glare at Nan. 'Pour the coffee and that will be all,' she said to Nan in a dismissive tone. 'Mr Appleby's here now.'

Fleur cut Nan a look of apology. 'Actually, Nan, I can do this. You finish up in the kitchen and get back to your family.'

Nan curtsied and couldn't get out of the room fast enough.

'Fleur, I'll thank you not to interfere with the home help. I am training that woman.'

'You're frightening her, Irma. She'll respond easier to a less cutting tone.'

'Don't tell me how to run my household staff.'

Fleur wanted to laugh at her stepmother's pretensions, and remind her that they were living near the port, surrounded by the families of sailors and dock workers, but she saw her father's forehead wrinkle into a deep frown.

'Now, now, please,' Henry spoke up. 'Let's drink our coffee in calm. I think Nan's coming along well. You're doing a good job, my dear,' he placated Irma.

Irma, trembling slightly in her pleasure at being exonerated, slung a look of triumph in Fleur's direction. 'Let me pour.' She did so, handing her husband his cup and saucer and leaving Fleur to fetch her own.

Henry swallowed his coffee in two gulps, giving a sigh. 'Our coffee tastes strange these days.'

'I'll make the next pot, my dear. I don't think that woman knows how to make it.'

'No, no, it's fine. Well, ladies, I shall be on my way.'

'Oh, Henry, please. Not the Prince of Wales tonight.'

'My dear, the pub is where us undertakers do our business in Alberton and discuss matters relating to our industry. And I must keep an eye on my competition.'

Irma put down her cup and saucer, her rings constricting the fattened flesh around several fingers. 'Well, don't forget what we discussed.'

There was a pointed tone to Irma's words that Fleur picked up on instantly. She looked between them over the rim of her cup and saw her father's expression of consternation as he rummaged back through what must have been various forgettable conversations with his second wife.

'Sorry, my dear . . .?'

'What we discussed,' she said again, slightly sharper, as though he were dim and she had to find a way to cut through the fog of his mind. 'Mr Coglin?' she urged, sounding outwardly vexed now.

'Coglin, as in the coffin-maker, Coglin?' Fleur piped up, annoyed that her stepmother was having any conversation about anything to do with the family business.

'Oh,' Henry said, in dawning. 'Yes.' He looked sheepish, glancing Fleur's way.

'Bert Coglin is unreliable and that's a nice way of putting it,'

Fleur said, wondering what they were up to. 'I'm glad we don't use him as our permanent coffin maker. Why are we having anything to do with him?' She directed this towards her father, determined not to engage in business talk with Irma.

'Fleur, please don't fret,' her stepmother said in a soothing tone. Irma knew just how to poke hard enough to bait and win the reaction.

'I'm not fretting,' Fleur replied. 'But if it's to do with the business, then it is something that I have some say in.'

Henry sighed. 'It is not business, my darling. And it is not Bert Coglin.'

'Shall I tell her, dear?' Irma asked.

'Tell me what?' Fleur was aware she sounded demanding, petulant even, but she couldn't take it back now and her attention was riveted on her father. Something ominous was approaching; she could feel its stalking presence making her skin prickle.

'Irma!' Henry snapped.

Her stepmother ignored Henry. 'It's high time you were stepping out with a young gentleman, Fleur. It really isn't very natural to be your age and so ignorant of men. Actually, let's not beat around the bush. You're in your late twenties and in old-maid territory, my girl. Your father and I think it is—'

Fleur's mouth was open in shock listening to Irma. 'You know nothing about my private life and social engagements.' She turned to her father. 'You're talking about Jimmy? Jimmy Coglin?'

Irma put her cup and saucer down noisily. 'So what if we are? James is quite taken by you.'

Fleur looked back with incredulity. 'Irma, have you taken leave of your senses?'

'How dare you!'

'No. How dare *you*? What makes you think I need your assistance in my life, romantic or otherwise?'

Henry made soothing noises but both women ignored him. 'I'm going,' he said, sounding as wearied as a man could.

'Mind what I said, Henry,' Irma pressed.

Fleur looked to her father with an aggrieved expression, and he turned away from her. 'Don't wait up,' he said, not even looking back.

It seemed she would have to fight this battle alone. She returned her gaze of scorching disdain towards her stepmother. 'I am not interested in Jimmy Coglin.'

'And I am no longer interested in having a 29-year-old spinster living off us for much longer.'

Fleur could barely believe what she was hearing. 'Irma, I think you've got that twisted around. My father and I were doing just fine until you came into our lives. You were his secretary, let's not forget. Now, suddenly, you're a lady of means and it's my father and I who work very hard to provide those means for you.'

Irma stood. She wasn't tall, but Fleur watched the hateful woman swell to her full height and inhale so that her large breasts loomed like a shelf before her. 'You're not happy here, Fleur,' she mused, adopting a conciliatory tone. 'And I no longer feel it's necessary for us to be pandering to your needs. Time for you to make your own way and stop leaning on this family.'

Fleur couldn't imagine feeling angrier than she did in this moment. *This family?* She opened her mouth to respond but Irma continued in her mock sympathetic manner.

'I know you've stepped out with some young men, but dear, it's time you stopped searching for that grand love like all those books you read and films you watch. It isn't like that in real life. It's like your father and me. No fireworks, but loyal and solid.'

Fleur blinked. She was sure her father would not describe his present marriage in this way. No spark at all. Stolid, more like, she thought, and that was being generous. 'I can assure you my father does not feel about you how he felt about my mother.' It was an uncharacteristically cruel barb, but Fleur felt herself losing control. *Rein it back*, she pleaded inwardly.

'Maybe not,' Irma replied, annoyingly calm, deflecting the arrow that was meant to wound. 'But he's married to me, isn't he? I am legitimately Mrs Henry Appleby. Meanwhile, Fleur, you are the orphan that was taken in. You're not blood.' She gestured towards a photo of Mae in a silver frame over the fireplace. 'Mae couldn't have a child, as I understand it. If we're going to sling the idea of belonging at each other, then you are as much an interloper into this family as I am. You may bear his name, but it was never yours to begin with. I gather your surname was Mason.'

Irma chuckled and it had a horribly tinny quality to it. 'Oops. You didn't know that, I see,' she said, looking like she wanted to hug herself. 'Yes – Mason. As in the jar. As in the stone worker. Nothing too high and mighty, then. Given up by your own mother . . . Who knows if she was even married. Probably not. She could have a been a street walker, for all we know. Whatever she was, you were not in her plan. Unnecessary. *Unwanted*. Tossed away like rubbish. And yet here you are, clinging to Henry Appleby as if you are of his flesh. You're not, dear. I've as much right to his name as you do. We're equals, you and me. You're just another name on his will, and you'll get less than you imagine if I have any say. Your father's drinking himself to an early death each night at the Prince of Wales, or hadn't you noticed?'

Irma gave a theatrical shrug. 'I can't save him from himself. Pity, but there we are. I'll just have to soldier on, do my best with the Appleby name and its fine business.' She strolled over to the mantelpiece and made a show of staring at the photo of Mae Appleby. 'Pretty young thing, I'll grant you. I must get Jean to dust here properly.' To Fleur's complete horror, Irma hawked up and spat a gob of saliva at her mother's picture. 'Needs a good clean,' she said, turning to give Fleur, rigid in her shock, a disarming smile. 'I'll invite young Jimmy over for dinner. I think he has something important to ask you.'

And Irma left her turning slowly back to the only woman she had ever loved, to watch the saliva smearing her features as it dripped down the frame.

7

FARINA

They'd left him to sweat it out. Tom was distantly aware that outside it was an unusually warm autumn's day, but here on his cot he was shivering as if he was living through midwinter. The fever had come on fast. He was an easy victim, no doubt; low in mood as much as physically run-down. Peter's death had hit him hard.

After the accident, Tom had moved around in a daze as he carried out his duties; he'd felt like his mother, going about his tasks from memory. Now he knew what it felt like to have someone watching you with a frown; the same expression he'd worn while he waited for his mother to come back from wherever she went in her thoughts. Had she suffered some sort of trauma to make her like that? There was so little focus. He'd tried hard to shake himself from the malaise, but he'd begun to feel convinced that something sinister had caught up with him and taken advantage of his weak state.

Right now Tom was flat on his back and hoping to ride out the storm of his illness. The doctor, who had come up from Adelaide, suggested it be treated as a bacterial infection like flu. He'd muttered it briefly, shaking his head, and Tom had just surfaced in that moment to hear it before drifting away again, voices blending until they sounded like murmurings on the edge of his world.

Tom's teeth chattered, and his body shook. The fever finally broke on the fifth day after his arrival at the bush hospital. He could hear a woman's voice, felt a cool hand on his shoulder. His vision swam, finally focused and he opened crusty eyelids to slits. He thought he'd answered as she called his name but the sound he made was little more than a grunt.

Soon enough he felt warm water on a soft rag held against his eyelids as she gently soaked away the five days of feverish sleep.

'Try again,' she encouraged him.

This time his eyes opened fully but still he struggled to focus again.

'Hello, Tom. I'm one of the nurses at the Farina hospital. My name's Dorothy.'

'Dorothy,' he croaked, never more glad to see a friendly face. 'I thought I was dying.'

'We thought you might be too at first, but you're strong, Tom, and very determined to live, I'm pleased to say.'

'Ah, welcome back, young man.' Another voice, another face hovering above him. It was the doctor. 'Glad you've pulled through, because we don't have much to work with in terms of what I think you're suffering from.'

'Which is?' He didn't mean to sound rude but it was hard to talk.

'I think you've had a dose of Q fever. Only recently discovered in Queensland – fortunately by a colleague of mine, who happened to share his findings with me.'

'What is it?'

The doctor shrugged. 'A bacterial infection, a lot like a flu. It's believed to be passed on to humans through animals. First thought of as a disease from the abattoirs, but people like you, who are around animals a lot, perhaps a bit low in health or . . . Anyway, look, Catchlove, you're young and robust. You'll be up and around in no time.' He looked towards the nurse. 'Lots of water, rest and thin broth, please, nurse. Get him moving as soon as possible.' He tapped Tom's shoulder, said, 'Good luck, lad,' and departed from Tom's bedside.

Dorothy turned back to Tom and gave him a beaming smile. 'You're going to feel weak, so don't try and do too much immediately.'

He nodded. 'How long has it been?' he rasped.

'You were two days at the homestead, I gather, and then you were brought here. A week, I reckon.'

'Bloody hell,' he murmured.

She grinned. 'Don't let Sister hear you curse!'

'Can I sit up?'

'You can try. Here, let me help you.'

With some effort from the two of them, they managed to get Tom propped up against the pillow in the iron bed. He felt dizzy but stayed patient and the world stopped spinning after a moment.

'Right, you need to start drinking plenty of water, as the doctor says,' Dorothy instructed, pointing to a pitcher and mug next to his bed on a small table. 'Start now,' she added, handing him the mug, 'while I go and see about some broth for you. We've got to get your strength back up.'

Tom began drinking, as she watched her patient carefully. It felt good to feel the water slipping down his throat. He noticed an older fellow sitting in a chair next to a nearby cot and tipped his head in his direction. 'Who's that?'

'That's Jonesy. I haven't heard him called by any other name, although Sister calls him Lord Jones and it seems to amuse him. He's gravely ill. We're just keeping him as comfortable as we can.

He loves to talk, if you're in the mood.' She smiled kindly, squeezed his arm and left.

Tom looked at the bloke, who was staring straight ahead. 'I'm Tom,' he said. Jonesy didn't seem to register his presence. 'Hey, I'm Tom,' he said louder.

'Heard you the first time,' the man growled. 'Dying, not deaf.'

'Sorry.'

'It's okay, mate,' Jonesy replied, finally turning to look at him. 'I just don't feel ready to go, but it seems upstairs has other plans,' he quipped and smiled without mirth. 'Glad you pulled through.'

'Thanks. I have no idea where I've been for a week.'

'They were pretty worried about you. Some bloke called Bill visited and told Sister that he thought you'd lost the will to live.'

Tom shook his head. 'No, I lost a good man – a young one – to an accident in the shearing shed.'

'So I heard. Took you bad.'

Tom nodded. 'I don't know how to do anything else but wool classing, and yet I don't feel like going back. I had to ring his brother and then write to his mother.'

Jonesy sighed. 'Yeah. You don't realise life is precious until it's gone . . . or going. Did he have a large family?'

Tom nodded. 'Three brothers and a sister, as I understand.'

'Ah well, that mother of his, she's got family to love and be loved by. Tougher when it's an only child.'

Tom grinned bleakly. 'Like me.'

'I knew your father, you know.'

That caught Tom's attention. Until now he'd been making conversation because he thought the nursing team would appreciate him chatting to the older man, but Jonesy's comment made him sit straighter. 'You did?'

'Used to drove with him, until my lungs stopped working. He's gone now though, right?'

Tom nodded. 'Died twelve years back.'

'He was a good man, your dad was.'

'Not much of a father, as it turns out,' Tom remarked, more to himself.

Again his companion proved he was not deaf. 'I suppose if you walked in his shoes, you couldn't blame him.'

Tom wished he could shake how gloomy he felt. 'I do blame him, though. We only had each other but we became like strangers after my mother died.'

'No, I mean you can't blame him because he wasn't your father, was he?' But it wasn't posed as a question. As far as Jonesy was concerned, he was stating a known fact.

Tom blinked at his companion. 'What are you talking about?'

Jonesy shrugged. 'Sorry, mate, didn't mean to shock you. I thought you'd know.'

'Wait! No, that's not right. I don't think we're talking about the same man. My father was—'

'Vern Catchlove, yep, I know. I met you when you were a young tacker. Met your mother too. Now, she really was a sight for sore eyes. Vern certainly got lucky there.'

Tom felt momentarily lost. Either an insistent whistle was being blown somewhere or it was an alarm deep inside . . . he could hear it, shrill and distressing. He didn't know how to respond.

'I thought he would have told you. He should have, if he didn't.'

Tom slowly put his feet on the floor and moved until he was sitting on the edge of the bed. He shook his head slowly. 'Why would he have told you?'

'I dunno, mate. Men talk. Especially when you're far from home and in the middle of nowhere. And Vern liked a drink. He only mentioned it once, as I recall.'

'Jonesy, tell me what you know.' Tom stood with difficulty and padded over to his companion's cot. The dizziness loosened his resolve momentarily, but he held on, grabbing the side of Jonesy's iron bedstead before he reached for another chair and sat next to the older man. He wanted to look him square in the eye.

'I don't want to upset you, lad,' the older man grumbled. 'They'll blame me if you sink into your thoughts again.'

'I won't. I want to know.'

'It isn't much. Your father was pretty full when he shared it.'

'Tell me.'

'He loved your mother to distraction.'

'I know. I thought he cared about me too, his only son.'

'I can't speak to that. He told me your mother came from a well-to-do family.'

Tom nodded. He'd known that.

'And she fell in love with some bloke,' Jonesey continued. 'I can't remember what he did for a living; some sort of traveller. Not a salesman, but he might have been a musician or something like that. Either way, it didn't suit her family, according to Vern. She was forbidden from marrying him, and your father said they near locked her up to prevent her trying to run away with him. They started making arrangements for her to become engaged to the right sort, but from what Vern said, your mother was not one to be pushed around.' Jonesy began to cough. 'Bastard thing,' he cursed. 'My lungs are shot, son.'

All of what Jonesy had said was news to Tom but somehow it was like finding missing jigsaw pieces, watching and feeling them slip into their correct spots to make sense of a bigger picture. He helped his companion to sip some water. Jonesy sighed his thanks.

'Where did she meet my father, do you know?'

'That I do. Apparently, they met at the Royal Adelaide Show. He was there performing.'

'What?'

'You didn't know he was a wizard with a whip?'

'Ah, yes, I did know that. He used to make me hold his burning cigarette and he'd crack it out of my fingers. I wet myself once, I was so frightened.'

Jonesy chuckled and it sounded like a drain emptying.

'But I didn't know he performed for others,' Tom remarked.

'Maybe before your time, son. He did a circuit of the shows. Adelaide was his final one and that's where he met your mother. She was in the audience with some friends who were clapping and cheering, he said, and she was like a radiant cheerleader, applauding just for him. All very romantic, I gather, because it was muddy – isn't it always at that Adelaide show? – and without permission he picked up your mother and carried her over the puddles. He admitted to me that he fell in love with her the moment she started laughing in his arms, and before the next day was out, he had proposed.

'He was a good-looking man, Vern, and I can imagine your mother was taken by the cowboy showman that he was. We certainly were. He used to entertain us blokes all the time with his singing, harmonica playing and whip-cracking. I once bet him my week's wages he couldn't knock the ash off a cigarette in my mouth with his whip.'

'You didn't.'

'He suggested it! And I wanted his money.' Jonesy laughed and got lost in another wet coughing fit. When he'd recovered he continued. 'I didn't get my hands on his money, of course, and he knew I wouldn't before he took the bet. Your father snapped off that ash from fifteen yards away as neatly as if he'd stepped up and cut it off with a knife.'

Even Tom had to smile. 'And you didn't wet yourself?'

'I might have done worse, actually. Lucky my trousers were brown, eh?' He had another coughing session before they shared a grin in memory of the man.

'How do I fit into this story, Jonesy?'

'Ah, well. As his story went, your mother was in the family way when he married her.' As Tom opened his mouth, Jonesy cut him off. 'Pregnant with the other bloke's baby,' he qualified. 'But it made no difference to Vern, apparently. He was obsessed with your mother. Wanted her so bad he agreed to raise another man's son as his own. When Vern told me the story, he started laughing at the storm in your mother's snooty family when she said she was going to marry this rough fellow from Crystal Brook in the southern Flinders Ranges. He reckoned none of her family had been further north than Prospect, which was just a few miles from the city. Anything further out to them was desert . . . unchartered land.'

He grinned at the thought. 'Vern said they were preparing to stop the wedding at all costs until she dropped the bomb that she was with child. He said that was it – they gave up on her after that, believing it was good riddance to all of them and the problem she was posing for the family's reputation. Her parents, especially her mother, wanted nothing to do with her any more or the potential shame she would bring. Vern married her within the week and brought her to this very town. No one else ever knew you were the other bloke's boy.'

Tom wanted to deny it all. Wanted to rage at Jonesy, and yet everything the older man had said fit. It explained so much of what he'd not understood while growing up. He took a breath, then spoke.

'I sensed that my mother found little to enjoy about her life out here, except me and my father, but she never complained. Not about the hardships or the fact she had to work so hard. But from the moment my mother died, Dad changed towards me. I thought it was because he couldn't get past his grief. I was still so young, but he left me alone in the care of the station. It seemed so ruthless. He accepted jobs that took him as far from home as you can imagine and for such long periods. I was passed from person to person; all the folk around the station looked out for me. I slept in with the station hands, ran odd jobs, learned to cook for them. The family at the homestead took pity on me, made sure I had clothes, shoes, that I was taken to school until I was about fourteen. By fifteen I was a rouseabout. By seventeen I was throwing wool and by eighteen, skirting it alongside the guesser.' Tom shook his head. 'And all the while my father was absent. He came home from time to time, but by then we really were strangers. When he took his last long trip I was all grown up and he was an old man – and a sick one at that.'

Jonesy gave a shrug. 'We all make our choices, lad.'

'So he never talked about me?'

His companion shook his head. 'Apart from that one time when he was drunk.'

'But you worked with him after my mother died?'

'I did. And I agree, he was different after she passed away. He didn't sing. Didn't entertain us with his whip or showmanship. And if he played his harmonica, they were sad songs around the fire. The cancer took him fast. I think your father welcomed death, to be honest.'

'I think he did too. I hate him now for keeping the truth a secret.'

Jonesy gave a sound of disgust. 'Don't waste the energy, lad. Your mother loved you and Vern provided. He did the best he could. He loved her with all his heart and most of him died when she did.'

'The best he could?' Tom repeated, sounding incredulous.

'Yes,' Jonesy replied, 'under the circumstances. Another man might have been stronger, less jealous, more capable of showing love to someone else's child. But Vern's shortcomings haven't hurt you. I'm guessing you're strong of mind and character; you're independent, capable of earning well for yourself.'

'You're not suggesting I should thank him.'

'No, I'm not doing that. But we all make choices in life. Just accept he made his, as your mother made hers . . . and you'll make yours. You wouldn't have been any better off for knowing the truth, I'll wager.' Jonesy took another long drink, and then took a while clearing his throat, a wheeze now arriving. 'But I doubt you'd have had a better life if your mother had stayed with her posh family. They'd have punished her daily and treated you with their sneers of disappointment. At least with Vern, your mother found some measure of happiness, and you probably grew up happier and more in control of your life than if you'd been raised alone by her within their house. They say ignorance is bliss, don't they?'

Tom nodded.

'Well, then. Move on. He's been gone twelve years and if you feel he wasn't a good father, then you lose nothing in the knowledge that he wasn't your father anyway.'

'That's a strange logic, Jonesey.'

'Yeah, well, a dying man can think this way, lad. Get on with your life, making it the best it can be. Find a good woman and love her. Start your own family and be the best father you can be and make up for the shortcomings of the man who helped raise you.'

The neatness of Jonesy's advice appealed to Tom. But could he let it go that his mother and father had upheld a lie to their deaths?

Jonesy leaned back in his chair, closing his eyes and Tom realised he'd slipped into sleep. He returned to his cot and stared at the ceiling. The more he prodded at what he'd learned, the more it felt like the truth and the further he felt himself drifting from the compass of his life, which had always pointed to Paradise on Witchelina Station and life as a wool classer.

He thought about school and how proud his mother was that he was doing well in his spelling, dictation, essays and grammar. His teacher at the time, Mrs Napier, had sent home a report that

Tom was excelling in geography and arithmetic. For no reason that he could fathom, carpentry was his favourite subject. He decided his pleasure in it was the challenge of and the precision required to make perfect joints for the timber shapes he crafted. He'd made his mother three fine vessels: one for her sewing, another for her outdoor tools and had been working on a new box for the kindling when she'd died. He liked building her practical gifts. He recalled how, even at his young age, he'd designed the box – more of a cradle, really – to stand above ground so the sand could blow through it rather than pile up on one side during dust storms.

He looked at the shadows on the hospital ceiling through the mosquito net that was not yet in use and remembered how he'd completely lost interest in his schoolwork after her death; there was no one left to impress with his high marks and academic tasks. Within a year, he'd found himself cutting up newspaper into rough six-inch squares to be used in the school's pit toilets; that had been his punishment for not doing his homework.

And then Witchelina rescued him. He'd waved farewell to school and joined the station full time. He'd known no other life, but suddenly that life felt false. He knew he was probably being irrational – perhaps the fever was making him think unreasonably – but Jonesy's revelation was still hurting. It hadn't been just an emotional jolt . . . it felt now like a stabbing pain in his throat, as though he wanted to howl his despair to the skies.

But that wasn't his way. He kept his hurts tight within.

'Here's your broth, Tom. Do you feel like trying some?' The cheerful nurse was back. 'Did you speak with Jonesy?'

Tom nodded. 'Yes, but not for long,' he lied. 'Didn't say much.'

'Ah, well, it would have brightened his day to have a conversation with someone who wasn't a nurse.' She smiled.

It hadn't brightened *his* day, though. In fact, it had cast a shadow over his already darkening thoughts. A notion that had been niggling before his illness had been let out to roam his mind again. Jonesy's truths had unleashed it fully.

Leave, it said. *You've always wanted to see what was beyond the desert. Go find out.*

8

Port Adelaide

Fleur was finishing some final touches on one of the coffins. Now that her father had some casual workers, she no longer had the unpleasant task of painting the bottom of the vessels with tar. It was necessary to seal the wood and keep the contents within the confines of the chest as it decomposed deep in the ground, but she hated it.

She had learned from an early age that this sort of fact, such as tarring the bottom of coffins, or setting out a bowl of Condy's Crystals (or a plate of coffee grinds if the crystals were not available) to help with the odour of decomposition, was not to be raised in polite conversation, despite how interesting she found it. Fleur had absorbed, rather than needing to be told, that almost everything her father did in his work – and she now did too – was not for general discussion.

'Death needs its mystique, Fleur,' Henry had counselled his child when she had not even reached double figures. At her frown, he'd explained. 'No one really wants to know what we actually do. It's a kindness to them – the mystery of our undertaking needs to remain that way. We handle the care of the dead privately. Then the death of a loved one is easier to cope with. Does that make sense?'

'But I would want to know,' she said, sounding puzzled.

Her father had smiled. 'I don't doubt it, with that inquisitive and intelligent mind of yours, but trust me, my girl. Most people are frightened of death, quietly terrified of the process of embalmment, and certainly cautious, even at the lightest conversation about it, because death can be confusing as well as being final.'

'I'm not scared,' she'd countered.

And he had given her an indulgent sigh. 'No. You're not frightened, mostly because you're very young but you've also been around death all of your life. I might add, Fleur, that even those who are not afraid often prefer to stay in the dark about what is happening when we step in and take over the care of their beloved.'

'So not everyone is like us, you mean?'

'No one is like you, Fleur. You're unique.'

Though she hadn't really known what unique meant, she'd understood her father was giving her a special compliment. She knew now, though, and had to wonder whether her father had forgotten all that love and affection. He had changed so much since her mother died. It was as though he no longer cared. Irma was right; he was willingly drinking himself to an early grave. But worse, he no longer seemed to care about the daughter he had once shown so much affection towards. Was he really comfortable pushing her into a partnership with the coffin-maker's son? Why did he look so grey? He wasn't that old. And how about the way his mind wandered now and then? He seemed blurry, as if too often distracted.

'Jimmy Coglin!' she muttered, still shocked, as she sewed the final run of stitches on the calico she was using to trim the inside of the coffin.

She was being especially careful, as this coffin was being prepared for a mother and her child who had died at birth; the woman had bled profusely and died soon after. Fleur had insisted that she take care of both bodies alone, even though her father had frowned, and she'd had to help him grasp why this felt so important.

'But I have time, Fleur,' he argued. 'We can do it faster if we each take one of the Savilles.'

She had shaken her head. 'It's a mother and child. Hard to explain, but do you recall being called away by the hospital mortuary staff when we picked up the bodies?' He frowned and then nodded, remembering. 'One of the nurses spoke to me privately. She said she was sure the mother had died of instant heartbreak at the news of her child being stillborn.'

'You know that's unlikely—'

'Dad, I can't speak for affairs of the heart or what it is to be a mother who is heartbroken. But Mrs Saville had experienced eight miscarriages. Eight! I don't think you can imagine what that can do to a woman. I don't think I can either – but I believe I can get closer to understanding than you. Men seem to deliberately keep their distance from children until they're sure they're robust enough . . . healthy and strong and destined to survive the lives they're born into. But women, Dad, we're different. Each pregnancy is something special, especially if it's a wanted child. And to be denied that child for whatever reason is painful, and I don't mean physically. I mean it is mentally harmful.' She tapped her temple. 'Mrs Saville went through that agony eight times before she carried a baby all the way through to her delivery date, and then that precious child died before she could take a breath.'

Her father had stared at her; his expression was neutral but she could see he was still at a loss.

'Dad, I don't want them separated. I want to keep that baby in her arms while I work on them.'

'Don't be rid—'

'I'm not ridiculous. This is not just any corpse. This is about a mother and her child for me. I can't help approaching it

95

emotionally – I feel it at a different level. It's hard for me to explain, but when I'm preparing her, I know I shall feel as though I'm communicating with her on the other side. Reassuring her. Letting her know her baby is coming with her and will never leave her arms. That I'm there to protect her and her child to their final rest.' Fleur had paused and looked him in the eye. 'Let me do this my way.'

Her father had shaken his head. 'This is why others in the business don't let women do these things. Too emotional,' he admonished.

Yes, he'd certainly changed if he believed that. In years gone, his frown would have relaxed and his smile softened; he would have patted her shoulder and said something like, 'Thank goodness for your sensitivity, Fleur.' Now her father was suddenly impatient with her ways.

But their new life had become shaped so that he was happier at the pub than at home and, in a way – as much as she hated to admit it – that increasingly suited her. She was shouldering most of the work behind the scenes now, although her father continued to meet with the bereaved and transport their dead. Fleur was perceptive enough to understand that, although the day was coming when women undertakers would be accepted, most people did prefer to greet a sombre male funeral director in his mourning suit when organising the event or attending a burial.

Even so, there was an important conversation Fleur wished to have with her father about taking the business in a new direction. He wouldn't like it, but she had convinced herself that he would understand because he was the one man in South Australia – possibly the whole country – who was essentially pioneering the introduction of women into his industry. He hadn't meant to, she knew that; it had occurred naturally because he had adopted a precocious little girl in need when his wife was unable to give him a child – particularly the son he'd hoped for. He could not have known that Fleur would become intrinsic to his business, but she was the best possible advertisement for female undertakers, no matter how much the male fraternity resented her.

Last night Henry had agreed to having a serious talk this morning, but he had not woken in a good mood and she'd sensibly left him to his headache, porridge and Irma's fussing. Irma had now taken control of everything Henry ate and drank, often preparing some of his food, certainly his beverages, for him. It was curious, but Irma was so horrible that Fleur didn't want to think about her any more than she had to.

Fleur calmed her tumbling thoughts, reassuring herself that her father would be more receptive tonight after the pub; she would wait up for him, catch him before he flopped into bed next to the tutting Irma.

The shock of Irma spitting on Mae's photo had not abated; the memory of saliva, launched with such ferocity and slipping down her mother's face, was about as vicious a gesture as Fleur had witnessed. Irma had intended it to offend at the deepest level, but perhaps what she hadn't grasped was just how revealing her action was. Now Fleur was convinced she had her stepmother's full measure. There was no doubt at all in her mind about Irma's intention, which was to remove Mae completely from her father's life and potentially make a solid case for shifting Fleur as well. The push towards marriage was the first move on Irma's chess-board towards check-mating Fleur; Jimmy Coglin was her pawn and she was using the King – Henry – to lure Jimmy into her trap.

Well, Fleur would not stand for it. She shook her head with disgust and blew out a long breath to clear her mind. She bent down to bite through the thread and stood back to admire her work, pushing the needle safely through her blouse like a brooch, so she knew where it was until she could put it away.

Inhaling again to settle herself, she could just smell the still-rich aroma of the freshly ground coffee that now sat between the tarred bottom of the coffin and the calico lining that awaited Mrs Saville. She had been dead for two days and Fleur had worked hard on the lividity of the body once the rigor had passed. Removing the copper pennies that the woman's family had placed on her eyes to keep them closed, Fleur pondered the nagging thought that there needed to be a better way; the heaviness of the coins only made the eyes sink further. It had taken all her skill with soft cotton wool behind the eyelids to plump them realistically.

Her father had taught her how to make stitches behind the lips that tracked invisibly into the septum of the nose and back again. When pulled gently, they closed the person's mouth permanently, but Fleur had recently designed her own method. She hadn't shown her father yet, but it took fewer stitches via a gentle looping action that remained hidden but was more effective in ensuring a firm close. It also did not require anything such as a milk bottle or a rolled-up towel to hold the chin in place until these adjustments were made. She was proud of her invention and felt it was kinder somehow, since it required fewer needle punctures. She shuddered at the notion that some morticians used wire and a nasty-looking implement to push it through the gums of the corpse.

She had dressed her client in a charcoal-coloured worsted dress, which made even the slight colouring that Fleur had achieved by softly applying rouge at her cheekbones seem almost too warm and lifelike. It was as though Mrs Saville might wake from a swoon, but the tiny infant cradled in her arms looked to be in her final sleep. Fleur had added nothing to the child's pale skin but simply dressed her in the robe intended for her christening day.

Fleur had managed to wash and dress both bodies without the precious child ever leaving Mrs Saville's embrace entirely.

It had been an exceptional challenge and one she was glad no one had witnessed because others would think her mad. She didn't pretend for a moment that Mrs Saville would know it, but perhaps spiritually – wherever her soul was travelling – she might sense that her baby was still in her arms, her spirit travelling alongside. For Fleur it was an important kindness she was performing for a woman who deserved this regard, after her years of despair and loss.

Thinking this made Fleur maudlin and her eyes watered. In times gone, the mother and child might have been photographed together in their death embrace for posterity, but that habit had lost favour, probably because people were living longer, living healthier and especially because children were surviving more readily. The mortality rate today compared to when her father had begun his role as an undertaker was far more optimistic – but none of that mattered to Mrs Saville, lying here with her newborn.

Fleur clasped the mother's cold hands that were clutching the child. It had taken quite an effort to position the baby safely and reliably so she wouldn't fall at the slightest shift of her mother's body. Invisible stitching that bound mother's and daughter's outfits at the right point had made this possible. She'd used the cunning inspiration making her father blink with consternation when he checked in on her progress.

'Stitched them together?'

'Their clothes, Dad, not them.'

'How odd.' He had shrugged. 'Once the coffin is hammered shut . . .' He didn't finish the sentence.

'No, it matters that they are never parted.'

Her father had departed, shaking his head.

Looking back at mother and child, Fleur was suddenly reminded of a little boy with a serious countenance at odds with his head of summery golden hair. Tom Catchlove had been grieving the death of his mother and new sister and the memory of him came back to her in full detail, trapping her breath and forcing her to pause. How amazing that she was recalling from so many years ago that newly bereaved little boy with his wide eyes of navy and his knowledge of geology.

She felt taken with him all over again. He had remarked that she was brave, but she was nothing of the kind. Fleur had always had the privilege of status, along with the inherent confidence that came from being loved – no, adored – by the Applebys. It was from that status and adoration that she possessed so much self-belief, which only served to fuel a naturally precocious manner. But scrawny Tom, helplessly handsome behind that reticent manner . . . *he* was the brave one, facing the death of his mother and his sister, as well as a long journey home on his own, and his father far away.

She wished she'd been old enough to care for his mother and sister with the same tenderness as she had as the Savilles. 'Where are you now, Tom Catchlove?' Fleur asked the universe quietly as she let go of the dead woman's hand. She looked again at the sweet face of the newborn, relaxed in her death pose despite how pale and tiny she was. And Fleur thought of Amy, Tom's little sister, who never took more than a breath or two, it seemed, and had never known she had a brother who loved her. 'Did you become that wool guesser, Tom?' she asked the silence with a small smile as she pretended to talk to him.

'I wish I could see him again, Mrs Saville,' Fleur remarked to the woman over whom she was now making a final sweep with a careful eye. She reached for a comb to smooth a wayward hair that had escaped. 'There was something about Tom that appealed to me. I was only eight, but he was ten, so he'd be in his early thirties now. He's probably married with a brood of his own. I hope he's happy. When we met he was desperately sad and alone, so I hope he's got a house full of children and lots of laughter in his life.'

Mrs Saville couldn't answer but Fleur heard the woman's voice in her mind all the same. *That's something you need to strive for, my dear. Laughter, company, marriage, children.*

'I don't want to marry Jimmy Coglin, if that's what you mean, Mrs Saville?'

No, but you need to change your lonely existence.

'I was going to speak to my father about moving out, having my own place . . . we'd all be much happier.'

Your father is never going to be happy again, you know that. And you will still be alone.

'But not lonely. I think too many people presume they mean the same thing. I don't mind being alone.'

Your mother wanted marriage and children for you.

'And if the right person comes along, so would I want both of those.'

The right person can't find you if you don't make yourself available to be found, Fleur.

It was the baby talking to her now. Alice was her name.

'And what do you suggest, Alice?'

Well, perhaps if you step out with this Coglin fellow, you may meet other people. How can you know who you wish to spend time with if you keep yourself tucked away in a mortuary?

'I suppose not,' Fleur agreed. 'I don't want to lead him along, though.'

You're known for your honesty. Why would he feel led? Mrs Saville offered.

Fleur smiled. Now even the dead wanted to marry her off.

Not marry you off, Mrs Saville corrected. *Help you look for happiness.*

'All right. I'll be more open to gentlemen callers and I'll agree to the dance with Jimmy . . . but only so I'm being social and meeting others.'

The mother and daughter fell silent in her thoughts as Fleur made a final adjustment to the buttons on Mrs Saville's gown. Fleur wanted them to sit perfectly straight. She busied herself with a soft piece of lace she'd saved from an old nightdress for just this sort of occasion. It was a small milk-coloured panel of delicate fabric she'd laid behind Alice's head. Against her mother's dark gown, the webbed design created a beautiful resting spot.

Satisfied that she could do no more, Fleur rang a bell that she kept nearby. Soon enough a couple of the lads who worked for her father arrived at the mortuary door, rubbing their hands on their trousers.

'Thanks for coming so fast, boys. Can you help me get Mrs Saville and her daughter into their coffin, please? Mr Saville is coming to farewell them in about one hour.'

'When's the burial, Miss?'

'Tomorrow morning.'

Both pulled off their caps and she noted they wiped their boots on the mat at the door. They were both good lads.

'Wash your hands, remember.' She smiled, gesturing towards a trough at the entrance. 'I always do,' she assured them, so they didn't feel she was being bossy.

She took a last look at her sleeping friends and bid them a silent farewell. They couldn't have looked more beautiful, she thought. 'Very gently lads, please. I don't want either of the bodies to be disrupted.'

They did an excellent job of transferring mother and daughter into the coffin. After thanking them, Fleur folded soft muslin to cover Mrs Saville up to the crook of her elbows. Mr Saville could look upon his wife and child now with pride at their beauty, even in death, never knowing how hard Fleur had worked on his beloved girls.

She went in search of her father.

In the house there seemed to be a flurry of activity with Irma supervising the laying out of the best dining crockery, admonishing one of the new staff who was cleaning Mae Appleby's silver.

'Have you seen my father, Irma?'

'Not since he left after breakfast,' she replied, sounding distracted. 'No side plates this side of the dinner plate,' she snapped, pointing, and then making a tutting sound at poor Nan.

'Why is my mother's best china coming out, Irma?'

'Well, it's doing no good sitting in a cabinet as dead as she is.'

Fleur gave a low gasp. Both women working paused to glance at her, looking shocked.

'Get on with your work!' Irma snapped. She looked back at Fleur. 'I'm only speaking the truth. Tell me what good crockery is if it's not used or admired.'

Fleur blinked. The hateful woman's question was not without logic. 'I asked why it's being used. I didn't say it shouldn't be,' she replied, surprised by how rational and, indeed, neutral she sounded. It felt like a triumph to hold her anger in check, entirely under her control.

Fleur's reply must have taken Irma by surprise because her small eyes flared, unsure, searching for guile. She had been expecting an argument. Fleur kept her own expression even but enquiring, and watched her stepmother's chins settle back towards her broad neck, where they found wide support against the crepe-like skin.

She imagined how tricky it would be to work on Irma's corpse because of all that soft, flabby skin, which would fall to the sides and flatten out. There would be little that someone, even as talented as she was, could do to combat gravity's pull. It emboldened her to think such dry, bruising thoughts about Irma, who seemed to lack any compassion for anyone.

'We have people coming for dinner on Saturday,' Irma confirmed.

'I see. Well, enjoy the—'

'And your father and I expect you to attend.'

Attend? What an odd word to use for a member of the household. Irma never let any opportunity pass to alienate Fleur, having not yet worked out that Fleur did a reasonably good job of that all on her own.

'Leave us,' Irma said to Nan and her companion, still holding the side plates. 'Go put some coffee on. Mr Appleby will be wanting his noon meal.'

The women couldn't get away fast enough.

Fleur could tell this discussion was going to be akin to gunfighters squaring off in the cowboy movies she'd seen at the local picture theatre. 'They have names, you know, Irma. One is Nan and the other is Jean. Why don't you use them instead of simply barking orders?'

'I pay them. I'll call them what I like.'

'My father pays them, and it could be said that I earn most of the money that allows my father to pay for your indulgences. But if you insist on having waiting staff, please address them with some basic courtesy. They are not slaves. A please and thank you now and then wouldn't go astray.'

'Don't lecture me, Fleur. It's just noise and wasted breath. I can't wait for you to be married and living elsewhere.'

'Who are your guests?' Fleur asked, knowing it was exactly what Irma wished her to ask so they could get their duel going.

'The Coglins,' Irma replied.

Fleur felt the rise of frustration and it momentarily silenced her. This father and son, who, as it was, ran a suspect coffin-making business that she was hoping to detach Appleby's from as soon as possible, were now being given Irma's full welcome treatment. And as Irma did nothing without an agenda, Fleur imagined she had already hinted at a possible engagement. It made her inwardly gag. 'Of course. Well, unfortunately I shall be—'

'Right here,' Irma interjected, pointing to a place at the table. 'At your father's behest. Our guests are arriving at six. Don't be late, Fleur, and do not disappoint your father.'

She couldn't think of anything to say that would express how angry she felt without letting herself down. Instead, she sniffed. 'Good luck having my father stay long enough. I'm afraid you simply don't have the attraction any more for him to linger.'

'Oh, you poor, clueless child. Do you think I really care? I've got what I need.'

That stung. Irma had been well armed and more than ready for her. 'Just need me out of the way, do you?' Fleur's voice sounded brittle in its icy tone.

Irma shrugged but Fleur was clearly correct. 'I'm just doing what's expected of any mother.'

'You're no mother of mine. You're an impostor . . . a conniving thief who stole my father's heart under—'

'Do be quiet, Fleur. I don't think the servants need to hear your pathetic accusations. Henry Appleby made his choice – now he must live with it. And shortly I shall make a choice of my own – for you not to be in my house any longer.'

'*Your* house?'

It was the smuggest of gestures when Irma shrugged at her. 'I hope you don't think it's yours, little miss orphan?' She didn't wait for Fleur's shocked expression to dissolve, nor for her step-daughter to find an appropriate response. 'So let's just both make ourselves a lot happier by getting you out of it for good, shall we? I think Mrs James Coglin has a very nice ring to it and I, for one, will be very glad to remove you from the Appleby name.'

Fleur couldn't feel more stunned and was sure her face reflected how Irma's cruel words had injured her. 'Well, at least now we're being honest. I wonder what my father will make of this?'

'I don't know why you'd think your father wouldn't agree

with me,' Irma baited her. 'I think he'd settle for any answer that rids him of the fractiousness in this house.'

'You are the reason for it, Irma. We were happy enough before you pushed your way into his life.'

'Fleur, I am not going anywhere. I am Mrs Henry Appleby and you are an ageing spinster and adopted child from a previous marriage who really does need to take stock. I'd call you an old maid.'

'And I'd call you a grasping, ageing, desperate woman with secrets!'

Irma laughed but Fleur could see one of her insults had landed a surprise blow. Which one? They were all offensive, but Irma had seemed to flinch at the notion of secrets.

Fleur decided to test it. 'What secret are you hiding from my father that you think he's too lost to alcohol and grief to discover? Perhaps I might find out what you're hiding because I don't like you and have never believed you had a place here.'

'You've been a snoopy, self-assured and annoying child since I first arrived—'

'As a secretary,' Fleur qualified. 'Don't suggest my father went looking for another wife. You used your wiles to convince him he needed a mother for his child, and what a dreadful mother you have been.' She watched Irma wince again. Fleur couldn't imagine Irma cared a hoot for how she was regarded by her step-child, so why that remark might cause even a single feather to ruffle was intriguing.

The woman's lips flattened, lifting into a sneer at their edges. 'I want you out of this house, Fleur. I don't even know that we'll need you in the business for much longer. I shall be talking to your father, when he's sober, about bringing in new people.'

'What?' It came out as just short of a shriek. 'Now I think you are going around the bend, Irma.'

'Perfectly sane, actually. I see things clearer than your romantic lens.'

'My father needs me.'

'Your father will be dead sooner rather than later. His liver is shot.' She smirked at Fleur. 'Hasn't told you, I see. Oh dear. Well, he hasn't got long and now that he's listened to my reasoning that he shouldn't be holding back his daughter from marriage and starting her own family, it suddenly all makes sense to him to encourage you to become engaged.'

Her father was dying? *No!* It couldn't be true. Why wouldn't he have told her? Fleur took a deep breath. She felt like packing a bag and running away, but of course that too would play straight into her stepmother's game. Instead, Fleur knew she needed to stay in her home and resist the woman's manipulations as best she could until, on her terms, Fleur could leave. 'Irma, stop talking. I will not go along with your plans.'

'We shall see, dear.' Irma pushed past her, turning briefly in the hall. 'Remember, Saturday at six o'clock, looking your prettiest so James can take you to the Palais. Oh, and I gave Mae's photo another spit and polish today. Don't want her memory being lost, do we?' She chortled as she walked away.

9

Tom found it hard to believe he was finally here, even after all the hours on the train, watching desert give way to greener pastures and ultimately into civilisation. He'd never seen so many people at once, he thought, as he alighted at the main terminus in Adelaide.

On the concourse he passed various refreshment rooms, including a grand dining room, and even a hairdresser was doing a good trade with the travellers from far and wide. The hall was lined with a marble so highly polished that he could see his own reflection staring back. And he soon learned not to stop suddenly and gawp, because it frustrated others in a hurry to get to wherever they were going. Stepping to the side for a moment to look up to the ceiling, Tom noted that a vast dome helped to create a lofty, dignified space in which travellers could sit on the concourse and wait for their connections to be announced. He was thrilled to be experiencing the new art deco building, which was fashioned in the neoclassical style and now served as the central city railway station, its administration layered in the levels above.

When he finally reached the street, he couldn't help but turn back to regard the sandstone edifice that cast a pinkish glow in the afternoon sun, looming over several storeys. The station clock on this main facade told him it was nearing three. His intention was to travel down to the port to see about some casual work, but, excited by being in the state's capital, he made the decision to walk around the city and acquaint himself with its layout.

That exploration took him down to the River Torrens for a while, before he strolled through the Botanic Gardens and came back onto North Terrace, one of the four main arteries encircling what was known as the 'square mile'. He'd read that this was the grandest, and ran east to west along the northern edge of the city where many of the capital's cultural institutions were based. It was elegant and leafy and he was contentedly taking in the scenery as he walked along the pleasantly wide streets, not focused on anything specific, until his attention was caught by a modest sign painted on the glass above a front door of a terraced house: Tillet & Associates.

Tom blinked. It felt to him as though all motion stopped in that moment, when it was him who had halted. A man who nearly bumped into him gave a sound of disgust and looked back over his shoulder with a vexed expression, but Tom didn't respond because all of his focus was riveted on the door and the memories that it prompted. How many times had his mother made him repeat the name of Tillet & Associates? How could he have forgotten? He could only blame the grief and the strange time of isolation and confusion that had followed.

Should anything ever happen to me, Tom, you have to go and see a firm of solicitors called Tillet & Associates.

Tom, if I die suddenly, you get yourself to Adelaide somehow and visit Tillet & Associates.

What's the name of that firm I want you never to forget?

He'd duly repeat the name, sounding almost bored, never believing anything would happen to his mother that would force him to go in search of these people in Adelaide. It was only now that he recalled his mother murmuring to him about Tillet & Associates while he raced against time over the desert to get her and his soon-to-be-born sister to Farina. She'd said it so many times as he had driven Bonny faster than she cared to go while he grimly set his sights on the bush hospital. 'Tillet & Associates, Tom. Don't forget,' she'd panted.

His eyes watered at the memory as he realised that perhaps his mother had begun to believe that she might not see another day. And she hadn't. He swallowed, returned to the present and became aware of more people flowing around him as he stood, staring, in the middle of the pavement. He straightened himself, breathed in and knew that he would need to confront the firm of Tillet & Associates, to see what secrets lay behind that black door.

But not today.

It was getting on towards late afternoon so he turned away and wended a path through to the famous Hindley Street on his way back towards the station. He'd actually heard of it for its debauchery of pre-war times, but he wasn't observing much of anything too racy. Instead, he gathered that the street likely lit up the city of an evening with colourful, blinking lights and sounds of excited audiences attending the theatre.

As he reached the station where he'd begun the afternoon, it was approaching sunset and the people moving around now were the theatre-goers and early diners. Given the pleasant evening, there were also plenty of strollers taking a walk near the river.

He stood in the wide boulevard of elegant North Terrace and knew a decision had to be made quickly. Either he found accommodation in the city, which would be expensive, or he should make his way down to the port before dark and find a guesthouse or hotel room over a pub. Once night closed in, everything would seem more strange, more difficult.

However, the smell of cooked pastry wafted over, making his belly rumble. He'd not eaten anything at midday, saving his money and relying on breakfast to carry him through to an evening meal, and right now, the irresistible fragrance of meat pie was calling to him. He followed the scent to where people were queuing at a kiosk with a canvas awning. Two men in white baker's hats were serving a dish he overheard people ordering called a pie floater. It seemed to have appeal to all, from workers ending a busy day to the theatre-goers in their finery, as he watched them experiencing what looked to be a guilty treat, laughing and dabbing at their mouths with paper serviettes. Craning to see the dish, he spotted a thick slurry of mashed peas, halfway to a soup as far as he was concerned, and then a square pie placed lid-down to float in the pond of vivid green. Odd but irresistible.

Well, there was nothing for it, he decided, but to join the herd. He gathered from the talk around him that the van would be twice as busy once the drinkers poured out of the pubs. So within a few minutes he was one of the smiling people standing around and eating, chatting with his fellow diners.

'Your first? Really?' one man said, sounding astonished.

Tom grinned. 'I come from the outback, up north. No pie floaters there, although I think my father once mentioned that his folk used to have a pea-and-pie supper in England where they came from. Maybe it was this.'

The man nodded. 'Could be right. Although visitors from the other states turn their noses up. They just don't get it.' He grinned, dragging a spoon around the last of the thick gruel of peas. 'It's twice as good after a skinful,' he continued.

'Is that right?'

'Oh, my word. It's as though you're enjoying the final meal of your life. You'll see. So, what's a fellow from the far north doing here? Looking for work, are you?'

'Yes. I thought I'd head to the port and ask around.'

'Not an easy time for anyone to find work,' the fellow said, apologising with a shrug for stating the obvious.

Tom nodded his understanding.

'But you're on the money – the port is probably the best place. Have you heard about the Black Diamond?'

Tom shook his head.

His companion smiled. 'It's at the intersection of Commercial Road and St Vincent Street. Busy spot, overlooked by a silent cop.'

Tom didn't know what that meant but he nodded all the same, encouraging the man to continue.

'Black Diamond refers to coal, of course, but it's that corner where men gather and find out what work is going at the port. In days gone, the lucky ones would be given a piece of coal as their pass to get work – hence the nickname. Anyway, head there. You're young, strong, fit . . . you should be able to find some manual work.' He pointed down North Terrace. 'Follow the road but it's a long way. I'd recommend you take the train. Have you sorted your accommodation?'

'Not yet. What about a tram?' Tom asked, preferring to watch the street life go by rather than rattling on a track that would likely snake around Adelaide's hustle and bustle.

'No trams here – take a motor bus from over there by the Gresham Hotel.' The man pointed to the opposite side of the great terrace, back up towards the intersection of King William Street. 'I think you'll have to change, but ask the conductor. Go down to Alberton, find rooms, and it's a short walk to Black Diamond Corner.'

'That's perfect.'

'There!' The man pointed. 'A motor bus like that one. You'd better ask which number, or you'll be off to Largs Bay,' he warned with a grin.

Tom scooped up his final mouthful and then bent down to pick up the small bag that he slung over a shoulder. 'Cheers, mate.'

'Good luck,' the man said, giving a casual salute of farewell, and they parted ways.

Tom returned his plate to the servery and gave them a thumbs up in thanks. Wiping his mouth with the handkerchief his mother had drummed into him to always carry, he skipped across the wide road, dodging trams, buses, cars and the horse and carts that made up the cacophony of traffic. Since his arrival, Tom had successfully blocked out the noise, mostly due to his wonder, but now, with a full belly and fatigue beginning to niggle, he suddenly felt the full weight of Adelaide's city life start to overwhelm him. What had been a novelty earlier in the day – even exciting – suddenly made him feel lonelier than he'd ever felt in the great outback when little more than an owl's mournful screech pierced the night.

The constant motion and claustrophobic presence of so many people and vehicles, as well as air that felt thick and clogged with fumes, was oppressive as he made his way towards the tram stop across the road. He could almost chew on the dust and grit of the city, which was so different to the earthy taste of the sands in the wilderness. He had been warned by several people to expect a reaction to the commotion; while he could hardly have prepared himself, he also knew not to feel besieged, and began to school his thoughts into a soothing focus.

One foot in front of the other. Find the bus. Pay for your ticket and find a quiet seat at the back. Calm.

Tom leaned towards a couple of young men joshing each other near the queue. 'Hey, mate? Er, which bus goes down Port Road?'

'Simple. Just look for the bus that has Port Adelaide on its front.'

Tom felt stupid for asking but nodded his thanks and started scrutinising the buses turning the corner. Finally one had a sign for Port Adelaide. Others looking out for that same bus picked up bags or straightened their coats, shuffling forward a few steps in anticipation as more people than Tom expected alighted the vehicle.

'It's the double-deck Garford,' one woman said, rather obviously but sounding relieved.

Another gave her a gentle shove. 'Let's hurry for a seat downstairs. Then you won't get your vertigo.'

Despite the cold, Tom decided he would climb the curling steps to the upper deck to enjoy the city mostly to himself. Only a couple of hardy smokers sat up here, faces burying into scarves, and he found a seat tucked into the corner. He pushed his bag between his feet, checked his money was still in his breast pocket and let out a quiet sigh, relieved to be heading at last towards accommodation and a bed. The bus lurched, stopped, lurched forward again and finally got going. Tom picked up a strange new waft of metal mixing with perfume and the aroma of burning tobacco, along with the scent of baked pastry and stewed meat that hadn't left him yet. He imagined he must look like a wide-eyed child at a funfair, bamboozled and awed by all the new sounds and colours and smells.

The conductor ambled up. His uniform was filthy with caked dust. He saw Tom staring. 'You wouldn't think I brushed it before each shift, would you?'

Tom shook his head, offering a sixpence. 'I need to get to Alberton.'

'So, mate, to get there, I'm going to give you two tickets. One for this part of the journey, which will take you to Albert Park. You'll get out there and transfer to a tram, probably a bouncing Billy if you're lucky,' he said with a wink, as though it may not be quite so lucky to do so. 'And then you can show your conductor the second one. All right? It's not far – a few minutes. You shouldn't be waiting long.'

Tom nodded, inwardly sighing that his journey to a pillow still had two stages.

The conductor continued. 'On a wintry night in a high wind, I end up looking like this at the end of each shift,' he said, handing Tom an oblong ticket the colour of furiously blushing skin. 'That's tuppence ha'penny and your change.' He dropped two pennies and a halfpenny into Tom's palm. 'Out of towner?'

'That obvious?'

'It is. Where are you actually headed?'

Tom gave a soft sigh. 'Tomorrow I'm planning to get to Black Diamond Corner for work at the port, but I need to find accommodation for tonight.'

The conductor nodded. 'There're some guest houses around Albert Park but I agree Alberton's probably a good bet. Remember, the conductor needs to sight this one, all right?' He pointed at the second ticket. 'The Alberton Hotel is probably your best chance.'

'Righto. Thanks.'

'Friday nights are always busy like this,' the man quipped. 'You're doing the right thing by escaping. And there's a big match tomorrow down there. I presume you're a Magpies' fan?'

'Of course,' Tom replied, knowing it was the right response.

The fellow winked again.

As it turned out, the journey was enjoyable once they'd cleared the stop-start nature of the city and hit open fields. The bus veered to the right and Tom gathered they were finally heading in the direction of the port. He alighted at the nod of the conductor, who also helpfully announced the Albert Park terminus, and was gratified as the man pointed towards a tram about to arrive.

'That's your ride to Alberton, mate.'

'Thanks,' Tom said and grinned to himself, noting how the tram, as it stopped, did seem to rock at each end. Bouncing Billy – now he understood. Tom showed the tram conductor his second ticket and found a seat at the back, suddenly wishing he hadn't devoured his pie floater quite so greedily as the tram began its near-drunken-style bounce down towards his destination.

―――――――

As a wool classer from Farina finished his first taste of a pie floater in North Terrace, Fleur and Henry were standing outside their funeral home, facing Commercial Street, which led down towards the port. Henry was forbidden from going to the pub this evening but his sour mood seemed to be easing as he smoked and relaxed, watching dusk settle across the port region of Adelaide as workers headed home, most via one of the pubs. Trams rumbled by and the distant sound of the dock workers began to fade as they finished up for the day.

A man hurried by, heading towards the bus that was lingering at the bus stop nearby. 'Mr Appleby, Miss Appleby,' he said, touching his flat cap.

'G'day, Thomas,' Henry said and the man flicked a glance back with a grin.

'Thomas Williams was always nice to me at school,' Fleur commented. 'Others not so, from memory.'

'That's because you took a lofty approach to school, Fleur.'

'I'm different now, though, Dad, aren't I?' She hoped he'd confirm that she was.

'My word, yes. As much as we admired your self-assurance, your mother and I used to worry whether your confidence would isolate you, that and your somewhat dismissive attitude at times.'

Fleur laughed. 'It did, Dad. I didn't know how to control it then but I'm better at it now. And I don't believe I'm dismissive.'

'No, my dear, that was probably the wrong word. You don't suffer fools easily, but you see, fools often present as ordinary people with the kind of questions or outlooks that most share.

And people like you, who already know the answer or don't necessarily share their view of the world, need to find tolerance.'

'I hope I have.'

'Well, you're certainly much better at disguising your disdain when it erupts.' He gave her an affectionate smile, rare these days. 'It's not a criticism, just an observation. We all have our prickly bits. I wish you could be more patient with Irma, for instance.'

'I wish I could too,' Fleur answered, remaining neutral.

'I would have an easier, less irritated life and wife if you were.'

'Do you love her, Dad? I'm sorry to repeat the query.'

He looked at her in soft pain. 'I've never thought about it,' he said, looking embarrassed, and she knew that was an admission of truth.

'But you loved my mother. I know it.'

'That I did. But there was only one Mae Appleby, and I accepted that a long time ago.' He shook off his recollections. 'Do you know why this road is so wide, Fleur?' He took out his gold Hunter watch – a wedding gift from Mae – and flicked open the lid to reveal the large white porcelain face behind its glass. 'Getting late,' he murmured.

She did know why the road was so wide; he'd told her this a couple of times previously. Was her father getting old, or suffering dementia? 'Tell me,' she said, not wishing to tarnish the pleasant moment or bring the conversation to an end yet.

'The plan was to make this a canal. Can you believe that?' He glanced her way and she could see his face was filled with animated pleasure. He was surely losing his memory. 'So they dug out this wide channel, the idea being that all the goods going to and from the port could be barged into and out of the city. A masterstroke.'

'But it didn't happen,' Fleur said gently.

He shook his head. 'Big plans. Too big, probably.'

'But it's still brilliant, Dad. All these shops do well, and the new trolley buses are coming.'

'Yes. Still, I just love the idea it might have been a waterway – such a grand vision.'

'I have a grand vision,' she said, surprised at herself for leaping in so blatantly.

'Do you, my girl?'

'You know I've been wanting to have this conversation, so let's have it now while we're alone.'

He nodded, looking trapped. 'All right. Tell me what you're thinking.'

'I think women are kept out of this industry . . . deliberately.'

'Not by me!' he said, sounding injured.

'No, you're nothing short of a trailblazer,' Fleur complimented him. 'My mother wanted this for us too, didn't she? She always encouraged me to keep my interest in your work and, even though I was adopted, she used to say I was my father's daughter through and through, showing knowledge far beyond that of other under-takers' sons.'

'She was on the money, Fleur. You've been nothing but exemplary in this field, and I truly applaud your committed studies into the human body and its physiology.'

'Even so, it doesn't matter how qualified or exemplary I am – your colleagues don't want women in the funeral business, Dad. I don't know what you all discuss at the Freemasons Hall or in the pub, but they seem to be so suspicious of the notion of women working in undertaking.'

'Women are too emotional, Fleur.'

'Really? Have I ever been so emotional as to compromise your position, or even a single client? I have never lost my calm or wept in the presence of your clients or their loved ones.'

'No, I can't say you have. But you are rather overly connected to children. You get yourself in a private state over how you want them prepared, and you spend so much extra time on their coffins.'

'Is that a bad thing?'

He shrugged. 'You let emotion creep in. But it's not just you we're talking about is it, my dear? You mean other women. Not everyone has your constitution, and very few would have been raised in the environment that you have or had the exposure . . . and education. And if we start letting inexperienced women in, there's going to be a lot of . . . well, histrionics.'

She resented his choice of words but she knew why he might fear such a situation. 'But that's my point, Dad. More *should* be exposed, to get used to the funeral business. I think women can bring something very special to the industry.'

Henry made a scoffing sound. 'They only got the vote in England after the Great War!'

She didn't know if he was aiming for levity or really believed it was relevant, but either way his remark felt patronising. Irritated, she continued. 'Yes, and they had to be thirty years old and meet property qualifications. Very short-sighted, I'd say. But it's different here. This is not England. We not only gave all women the right to vote a quarter of a century ago, but South Australia was the first place to allow women to be elected to Parliament – you surely can't overlook that?'

Her question was rhetorical and she didn't wait for her flustered father to answer, pressing on. 'We were the first city to admit women to university on equal terms as men, more than half a century ago. Adelaide elected the first woman to an Australian university council. I won't labour the point, Dad, but if our city, and our state, can be that forward thinking, don't you think it can embrace the idea of women entering the funeral business? Or are all your cronies too scared of us?'

In that moment, she regretted her final words and looked down. 'I didn't mean that. My blood's up, that's all.'

'Is that how you see me? A crony?'

'No, I certainly don't. But maybe the other men in this business. Your colleagues seem to think they own the world of grief and dying, of burials. Stodgy, suited-up and looking sombre isn't the only way, Dad. It likely was at the turn of the century, but we've fought a war since, we've had Spanish flu rage across nations and a worldwide Depression on top of that, which we're only just emerging from. And in all that upheaval, women shouldered a lot of the burden for keeping their nations looking forward. They raised children, found ways to feed them, worked untold hours and when the men were at war or incapable, they did their men's jobs as well and kept countries safe, fed, productive. Seriously, now – don't you think we can arrange funerals and acquit ourselves appropriately during them? I would go one step further and say there are instances where I believe women can handle aspects of undertaking better than men.'

He narrowed his eyes over the vapour he puffed out from his pipe. She noted once again how grey his pallor was. Irma was right: her father was either desperately ill or dying, and his mind leaking its memories was part of it, she was sure. 'Would you indeed? It seems we've come full circle, Fleur.'

She knew exactly what his pointed remark was aimed at. 'But that's my point. No one in our line of work is offering any special handling for women and children who die, or even for those women who are grieving over dead children. Ask any woman, Dad, and learn the truth – most women would far rather have someone like me preparing her for a final farewell or that of her mother, sister, aunt or any child. And I suspect when a child is involved there's a sense of tenderness that a woman can bring. Men just don't understand.'

'What don't we understand?' He sounded wounded.

'That there's pain, Dad. Probably everlasting. It doesn't matter that a woman can have another child, or ten. That's how most men would comfort her. *Bear up now, you can always have another,*' she mimicked. 'The fact that she's lost a single child comes with heartfelt and lifelong regret. You know there are plenty of men out there who just ten years ago didn't allow themselves to get caught up in the excitement of a newborn because they weren't sure it would survive its early days, or even its early months.'

'Yes, well, they didn't,' he replied, sounding frustrated, tapping out the contents of his pipe against the wall. 'So what?'

She smiled sympathetically, as if the gesture would help him to grasp her point better. 'But women do, Dad. If they want a child, the pregnancy is welcomed with joy. Losing that child through the pregnancy, or worse, at birth or soon after, is a torture beyond your reckoning. But it's not beyond mine. Even though I've never had a child, I can empathise with a woman's trauma of loss. And it's those women who might welcome more female involvement in preparing their precious loved ones. Can't you see that allowing me into your business is one of your genuine strengths? It's a masterstroke, to be honest.'

He looked slightly baffled. 'Most of my peers think I'm mad letting you work with me.'

'Most of your peers don't have your foresight, or so much success attached to their funeral home. Appleby's is the gold standard in so many ways. I salute you, Dad, as a forward thinker and modern man, but your colleagues are frightened of women being in their clubs, their hotels, their workplaces, their industries.' She gave a wry smile. 'And if I'm being honest, they should be . . . because we're coming.'

He didn't share her smile. If anything, he looked unbalanced. 'What do you want from me?'

It was now or never, Fleur decided. She held up a finger. 'First, I'd like to set up a new business, separate from our existing one, that only cares for children and mothers who pass away during childbirth or soon after.'

'And you'd call it AppleBaby, I suppose?'

Her father's mirthless jest fell flat and it was her turn to frown. 'Don't make light of it, Dad.'

He cleared his throat. 'Why does it need to be separate?'

'Because it does. I plan to give it a new look – no black; white and pale greys. I want to align it with the young and rid us of our Victorian approach to all things funereal. And I'd also like to handle the work slightly differently. I will use women only to tend to women and children under twelve.'

'And this is to be yours alone?'

'I'd prefer it that way, although I would agree to Appleby and Daughter. I'm not trying to cut you out.'

'Appleby & Co, it would have to be,' he said.

It was a start. She should take the higher road. 'All right, but it must be a new business that is not financially attached to the old.'

'What is your problem with the business that has fed you and raised you and given you such a good life, Fleur?'

'It's not the business.'

'You said you're not trying to cut me out, but why are you trying to carve yourself away from all that we've built?' He stared at her and she knew he was demanding a truthful answer. They both already knew it but he needed her to say it.

'I don't want Irma involved. I don't want her to be in a position to interfere at all in this new venture.'

And in that admission she saw his expression close off. 'You really do hate her, don't you?' he said sadly.

She really didn't want to answer that question so she dodged it with a shake of her head. 'I cannot think of her as a mother, Dad, no matter how much you wish it to be so. And I know you'll argue that she's been in my life since I was small, but if you're really truthful with yourself, you might admit that Irma would have preferred there to be no child existing in the marriage.' She was being careful. She didn't tell him about all the times that Irma was hurtful or cruel to her behind his back; to his face she'd always played stepmother as a fine actress.

'Irma came into my life at a time when I needed her, Fleur.'

'I know,' she said, dropping her gaze. She wanted to add some accusations but she wisely held her tongue. 'And perhaps she was good for you at that time.'

'You seemed happy enough at first, weren't you?'

Nothing was further from the truth. She had simply tried to appear happy for his sake, and she continued to lie for his feelings now. 'I was so young. I was in grief. I clung to you, and Irma seemed kind and affectionate at that stage.' She paused; time to lean into some honesty. 'But then I grew up, Dad. And I realised that while Irma might feel affection for you, there was and still is no fondness for me. I've become a burden for her, which is why there's one more part to my vision.'

'Which is?'

'I want to leave home. Find my own place.'

'Live alone? Don't be ridiculous. What would people say?'

'Why should we care?'

'Because I have a reputation to protect, Fleur, that's why?'

She wanted to ask him how much he valued his reputation as he lurched a slightly weaving path out of the pub most evenings. But all the men who went drinking were the same. Those who called in for a beer after work were just one of the boys, but the hardened drinkers like her father were drowning invisible sorrows, in no hurry to return home. They were alcoholics; they just wouldn't admit it. But she didn't want to argue, so she tried to inch him forward with her plans.

'There's a lovely flat available. I could live above the florist, just a short walk away.'

'No, Fleur, absolutely not. You might be unhappy at home but it's not Irma's fault,' he said. 'You're a very headstrong young woman and you want it all your way.'

'So let me live alone and have it my way,' she said, feeling suddenly as though her father believed all the fractiousness in the house was her fault. Perhaps it was . . . That felt like a revelation. Immediately, she wanted to tell him about Irma spitting at the photo, to accuse him of being absent or witless when it came to the conniving Irma; she wanted to rage that his wife was trying to heave her out of the business and was probably looking forward to the day Henry died and she could get her hands on the proceeds of his will, but she realised she had no proof. It would sound like a petulant grievance against a woman who managed to give a solid impression – even Fleur had to admit that – of trying her utmost to be accommodating . . . supportive, even.

Her father's lips had thinned and she knew she had lost him before he'd even opened his mouth to speak again. 'She wants to see you married with your own family, Fleur. What's so wrong in that?'

'Nothing, Dad,' she said, in a neutral voice, 'but she doesn't get to choose who I marry, and right now you're allowing her to choose Jimmy Coglin. *Jimmy*, Dad! Even you've started complaining about the quality of their carpentry. Can't you see why Irma thinks now is the time?'

'No,' Henry said, sounding both perplexed and frustrated at once. 'Irma thinks the match with James is perfect because he's part of our industry.'

'Dad, you've got blinkers on, or the drink is dulling you. I don't know how Irma does this to you, but somehow she gets you to see only what she does. The Coglins want your business. You know they want to move into undertaking, but no one is taking them seriously because of their shadowy past. Blimey, Dad. I think

Irma wants to sell off your business so she can live off its fat – and probably without you.' There. She'd said it.

'What do you mean *without me*?'

'She's gloating that you don't have long to live.' That was not something Fleur had wanted to slip out but she couldn't take it back, so she pressed on. 'Did you plan on mentioning this to me . . . your only child . . . that you are dying?' Tears were glistening in her eyes now, threatening to run.

'I don't know what you're talking about, Fleur. Who says I haven't got long to live?' he blustered.

'Irma!'

'And Irma's a doctor, is she?'

Fleur felt stumped. Perhaps Irma had lied. Why, Fleur couldn't imagine, but she shouldn't be so surprised; it could be anything from wanting to unnerve her stepchild to simply being cruel. Irma was capable of anything, Fleur was sure. And there was no point, she now realised, in pursuing this conversation, because Irma would simply deny it, making Fleur look stupid and forcing her into finger-pointing and accusations. Well, she wouldn't fall into Irma's trap; she needed to be smarter.

'No, I must have misunderstood,' she answered, realising her father was waiting for a response.

'You must have. I am not at full health, I'll grant you. I've been feeling fatigued and not very hungry. But that's just a phase. I'll be fine once summer arrives and I get some warmth on my back. Let me say firmly to you, child, that Irma has no interest in the business . . . only in a happy life.'

Oh, Dad, she thought. *You are delusional. That woman wants you gone and that's how she'll achieve her happy life, the chance to start again as a wealthy widow without an annoying stepchild.* But she sighed the thought away and managed to keep her tone neutral.

'Well, let me be clear. I will not marry Jimmy Coglin,' she said, drawing a firm boundary line.

'All right, Fleur. But the least you can do is attend Irma's dinner. Be polite, be convivial, and step out with Coglin for an evening. Just go along with it and make her happy.'

'And then I don't have to see him again socially?'

It was her father's turn to sigh. 'Fine. I really don't want to be involved.'

'Nor do I want you to be, Dad. I don't need anyone involved in my romantic interests.'

He frowned. 'You don't have any, do you?'

'Not yet.' She shrugged. 'He needs to be special.'

'Oh, Fleur,' her father began in a tone that sounded condescending.

She knew he didn't mean it and responded before he could continue. 'No, Dad, what I mean is that he must be special to me. I must be left alone to recognise what it is about a man that makes me notice him. And it won't necessarily be that his business interests match ours, or that he's a good catch from a social-standing point of view. My mother would not have stood for anything but me choosing to marry someone I love.'

'Love is all well and good, Fleur, but—'

'You can't sweep that away as though actually loving, even *liking* one's spouse is a bonus. It's the beginning of everything that contributes to a successful marriage. That's how you and Mum had it so good and could cope with every obstacle . . . even not being able to have children of your own. You loved each other.'

'That's how a young woman thinks, Fleur. That's perfectly natural, I'd say, but—'

'You don't love Irma,' she said, cutting again into his patronising tone. She lowered her voice. 'If you did, you'd be with her right now, chuckling about something or chatting together as you used to with Mum.' She lifted a shoulder in a soft shrug. 'You made a pragmatic decision with Irma, Dad, and that was yours to make, but don't insist my life has to go that way too. I'd rather run away and join the circus.'

'I'm not. But you are old enough to be married. Old enough to be starting your own family.'

'Yes, but I'm also old enough to live alone and run my life.'

He shook his head emphatically. 'No, Fleur. You will be married out of this house. I want no tongues wagging and compromising Appleby's.'

She blinked with exasperation and disappointment that he was so closed in his mind, but he continued.

'I expect you to attend Irma's dinner and speak in a civil manner to James and his parents.'

'What about my business idea?'

'I'll think on it.'

'When do you—?'

'I said I'll consider it. We'll talk about this again another time.'

She heard the adamant note in his warning and knew to let it be; she had pushed her father as far as she dared. 'One more thing, Dad.' She didn't wait for his permission to continue. 'Whatever else happens, will you promise me that I will still inherit the pocket watch that my mother gave you?'

He took it out again, and she saw his gaze soften as he looked at it. She reached out to touch the gloriously intricate pattern on its shiny surface; she could feel the warmth from his body on the gold.

Henry nodded. 'Yes, it should be yours, for my first grandson.'

He smiled and she returned it, squeezing his hand, wishing she didn't feel like sobbing right now in this moment of tenderness.

Fleur noticed a man walking towards them, shrugged deep into his coat, its lapels pulled up almost to his mouth against the wind that was whipping up off the sea. She saw a thatch of blond hair but no other features as she deliberately turned away, not wanting him to see the moisture in her eyes that the prickly conversation with her father had provoked.

The man stopped in front of them. 'Excuse me, sir.'

'Yes, son? How can I help?'

'I'm looking for the Alberton Hotel. I might have walked too far.'

'You have,' Henry said, stepping out onto the street and pointing. 'Follow your footsteps back, but I'd suggest you cross the street because it's going to come up on that side in about ten minutes.'

'Many thanks.'

'Stay warm,' Henry said as the stranger departed, angling across to the far side.

Fleur turned back, watching the man as he navigated first a bus, and then horses and carts on the wide Port Road, waiting as a tram rumbled by. And then he was lost to the shadows of the lowering light.

She wished again she had the freedom to come and go as she pleased. 'I'll see you inside, Dad,' she said, stepping close and squeezing her father's arm. As she did so, she smelled a faint, stale odour coming off him. It was hard to pinpoint but the most accurate way she could describe it was mousey. She made a mental note to check if he was using new chemicals in the mortuary.

She also made the hard decision that she could no longer count on her father's support – it was time for her to make a break from Appleby's and forge her own path. It felt like something broke inside herself to realise that this was the only way she might achieve her vision to bring women into the funeral business, but she couldn't let her father see the welling tears.

She had lost him anyway. Irma was winning. It was time to harden her resolve and face her foe.

10

As he stepped off the bus at the terminus, Tom thought about finding a connection but decided it was better to walk until he found a local hotel. The conductor had suggested the Alberton Hotel, mentioning it would probably take Tom about fifteen minutes to get there on his long legs.

Tom began the walk, looking around to spot the pub that he hoped would offer him a room for a couple of nights, but he became lost in his thoughts, striding through the dark, and realised too late that he'd been walking longer than fifteen minutes. He saw a couple standing in a shadowed doorway; the older man looked disgruntled, and the woman, who pulled a shawl protectively, almost fiercely, across her chest, looked equally unhappy. She turned away before Tom could get a good look at her face and the action looked deliberate. He didn't want to interrupt what appeared to be an awkward conversation, but he was lost and cold.

The interaction was short but there was something about the pair that struck him as familiar. He wanted to look back but made a dash across the wide road as a bus began moving towards him. By the time he'd dodged a horse and cart and a tram had gone by, he saw the woman had left. The older man remained in the doorway, but there was no streetlight to make out his features or even the shopfront from the opposite side of the street.

Tom let the thought go and hunched deeper into his coat, glad of its heaviness, protecting him from the shear of the wind now at his back. He followed the man's instructions, retracing his steps, until he spotted the glimmer of the hotel's lights, surprised he had missed it.

A room was available and he didn't even bother to pause for a beer, heading straight upstairs where he flopped onto his bed, fully clothed, asleep within moments.

When he woke he felt it had been a restorative and mercifully dreamless sleep. It was still dark, but his father's fob watch told him it wasn't long until sunrise. He yawned but got out of bed immediately so he didn't drift back to sleep and he stretched to wake fully, realising he would be first into the bathroom with luck. He wasted no further time.

Tom took care to look neat even in his working clothes, combing damp hair into a slick parting. He quickly ate a bowl of porridge before pulling on a cap and heading out, once again retracing his footsteps to the terminus, where he knew he could catch an electric tram down to Black Diamond Corner. The conductor said he'd recognise it by the major intersection and the 'silent cop' at its centre. Tom finally worked out that this referred to the concrete pillar in the middle of the intersection, the second iteration of the traffic signal because the first, which had been introduced to keep traffic flowing to the left, had been knocked over. The famous corner was hard to miss; he'd never seen so much traffic in such a small space honking and easing its way around itself. Bicycle riders jostled against horse and carts, while cars seemed to feel they had superiority until a bus thundered close. It was a stream of metal and grinding gears.

Tom positioned himself at the crossroads, on one of the corners outside a sweep of shops with everything from a newsagency, a books and stationery outlet through to a general store. Further around the corner was a big shop called Ezywalkin, clearly a boots and shoes shop, and he imagined how his mother might wince at the cannibalisation of the spelling.

Men in work clothes began arriving and by a few minutes past seven, there was a small crowd of shuffling blokes in shabby attire, each with a hungry look. Tom no longer wanted to be viewed as one of these impoverished men. He made a snap decision, not at all sure it was the right one, but determined to follow his instincts, he wended his way to the port, scanning its skyline for the woolstores he'd heard so much about.

Tom reminded himself that South Australia's entire clip passed through the Port Adelaide woolstores, its warehousing responsible for storing, loading and routing the state's wool trade through to the busy looms of Britain and Europe. He knew to look for the towering structures erected by those enormous graziers, the powerful Elder, Stirling & Co. There was surely a job for him in that warehouse, where wool needed to be unpacked for the buyers to value, and where it was sorted and baled for transport overseas. Few men as young as he would have his knowledge to class the wool before export.

Although the size of the woolstores made him blink upon arrival – it was a giant, no other word for it – Tom's instincts were rewarded quickly. His credentials as a wool classer got him tested and he impressed the bloke, who offered him a job immediately, saying he'd be back in a flash.

As he waited at the door for the man to return, he craned his neck to take in the towering three storeys of bluestone.

A man nearby, smoking a newly lit cigarette, winked. 'Fresh in?'

Tom nodded. 'Farina. Tom Catchlove.' He extended a hand.

'From Witchelina?' the man asked, looking impressed. 'Yes, I know it. You're certainly far from home. I'm one of the stock agents from Wesfarmers – Charlie Hunter.'

They shook hands.

'Well, I'm actually from Paradise Station on the Witchelina property,' Tom explained. 'I'm a wool classer.'

'You're so young.'

'Never done anything else.'

'Why did you leave? Good money for a young bloke like you.'

Time to lie. He gave a shrug. 'Just want to see more of the world, experience the Big Smoke for a bit.'

Hunter was looking at him slightly perplexed, so Tom added some drama to his story. 'My father passed away. I just needed a change of scenery.'

The man nodded. 'Fair enough.'

Tom gazed around the enormous warehouse. 'I don't think I've ever seen any space this big under one roof.'

Hunter chuckled. 'Wait until they get going for the day and constant activity fills this quiet space,' he warned. 'But it is impressive. See that sawtooth roofline?'

Tom looked to where he pointed, nodding.

'Lets in loads of natural light, which I'm pretty sure you wool guessers appreciate. Bit different to the shearing shed, eh?'

'Sure is,' Tom said, just going with the stranger's conversation.

'Full of the same boozers and bullshit artists, but you'll find some former cockies and ex-shearers. And, of course, the ladies.'

Tom frowned. 'Ladies?'

Hunter grinned. 'A grand old gang who do the catering for the buyers and staff. Top tucker,' he said with a wink. 'D' you smoke?' When Tom shook his head, the man's jaw dropped open. 'Bugger me, what's wrong with you?'

'Bad lungs,' Tom lied. He'd just never taken to it, having grown up watching too many men with hacking coughs end up spitting blood into their ragged handkerchiefs.

'Ah, well, you're lucky then, because there's a smoking ban in the woolstores. Bit of a bastard, but that's how it is. Good luck, Catchlove. See you round.'

The man in charge of the wool balers for the day returned. He signed a chit and handed it to him. 'Show that to the bloke in charge.' And before Tom could ask more, the man had turned away and was dealing with selecting another worker from the anxious group of men waiting to be picked.

Tom made his way inside. Years of wool passing through the vast space meant the timber floors had absorbed lanolin and the familiar, earthy smell comforted him immediately. Towering timber supports held up the enormous floors where the wool would travel up the various levels and ultimately to be loaded onto ships.

Tom understood he was to work on the ground floor, where the bales came in for weighing, cataloguing and, of course, testing – his role – ensuring the wool inside each bale matched the description branded on its outside and that it had been properly skirted and classed at its origination. The man who'd hired him impressed upon him that the top-line reputation of Australian wool internationally had to be preserved through this final rigorous testing; Tom's new role carried that weight of responsibility.

The workday began with a loud whistle and turned the stores into a beehive of relentless activity. Everyone had a job and they got busy, each focusing on their individual role. It was a flurry of motion and noise, from the sack trucks being used to unload the wool bales from the lorries, men weighing them, and others hauling them off to line them up. Buyers streamed in to value the thousands of bales. All the rookies and casual fellows lucky to get a day's work were given the unenviable task of what was called the 'oddments' section. Tom could see that this included sorting the crutchings, which were stained, maggoty or flyblown, all the bits they collectively knew as 'dags'.

Meanwhile, the wool that really mattered was lined up in bales and opened for checking. Tom's job, alongside a small mob of classers, was to help the stock agents as they made their appraisals. He was one of the fellows who would pull out roughly ten pounds of the wool and drop it on the floor to be inspected. Depending on Tom's decision the bales would then be moved up the floors to the top where agents awaited to do their buying. But first Tom had the tricky task of cramming that ten pounds of wool back into the bale by hand. It was as arduous as any day's work in the shearing shed, but he enjoyed the familiar ache in his muscles as he began to expend his energy.

The hard work was the perfect distraction too, and the hours passed quickly in this experience that was new and yet somehow so familiar; the smell of the wool, the feel of the lanolin on his fingers again, the muted sound of the floorboards and the tufts of fibres floating in the air was all reminiscent of home and his beloved shearing shed. Now and then it also reminded him of a twisted and broken young man bleating like a frightened sheep, and that led him to think about the death of his parents and his helpless sister, and just how alone he felt. On they went – the thoughts couldn't be stopped, but they could be diverted, redirected.

Tom knew he needed to let the past go. He needed to make sense of this new life he'd thrown himself into and find where he might fit.

If Fleur were being honest, she would have to admit that Jimmy Coglin – or James, as Irma had begun referring to him – had turned himself out better than she'd imagined he might for the snobbish dinner that her stepmother had organised. It was laughable how her manner of speaking had changed to reflect her hostess role in front of the Coglins. Suddenly she was using tongs, linen napkins, smiling a strange new smug smile, and communicating with poor Nan as though she were a royal servant and a subtle wave of Irma's bejewelled hand needed to be interpreted precisely. It could mean one thing or something else entirely; that was Nan's problem to navigate.

Irma was powdered and rouged from forehead to the lace collar of a navy wool dress Fleur had not seen before. That would explain her almost secretive trip into the city earlier that week; Fleur had seen the box from the Myer Emporium in Rundle Street. It must have cost her father a princely sum, going by the quality of the dress. Clearly Irma was out to impress from every angle, although the new sleek lines of the current fashion did not suit Irma's rotund, shorter stature.

Fleur knew the fashionable tailored looks suited her taller, slimmer shape well, but she had not dressed to please Jimmy Coglin – or his father, who kept staring at her from the other side of the table. She had dressed with some care only because she'd wearily agreed to go to the Semaphore Palais with Jimmy after an early dinner with their parents and Irma. It was her way of escaping the orchestrated event, which was trying so hard to be something it could never be and seemed to have a more sinister aspect: Fleur was concerned that by sitting down with the Coglins, she was giving her tacit agreement to an engagement with Jimmy and that felt repugnant. She would have to explain to him after the dinner that she was simply being sociable.

Irma, meanwhile, looked delighted. Fleur believed her stepmother was imagining herself seated at a long, polished table over which hung chandeliers, set with crystal, solid silver and the finest European china. Somewhere like East Terrace, where the grand bluestone homes were stacked over several stories with lacework and balconies. Irma had forgotten, or chose to ignore, that they were near the port, so far from East Terrace that most of those city dwellers had likely not seen the port since the day they'd arrived. While the Applebys were perhaps considered a family of means, their home was modest, with none of the grandeur that Irma was projecting with her lace and linens, her strange new accent and pinched lips, her expensive garments and the sugary glances she kept casting towards Jimmy as though the deal was done.

The excursion to the Palais was Fleur's only ticket out and, given it was a dance gathering for autumn, she was outfitted in a favourite evening dress she'd owned for a couple of years but not got much use from. It was fashioned from a new fabric called rayon chiffon that was crease resistant, and it was cut on the bias to follow the lean lines of her body masterfully, with the flourish of short butterfly-style sleeves and a ruffle from her knees. The dress was essentially white but featured an artfully washed-out geometric pattern of red and charcoal. A patent black belt cinched her waist, matching black pumps that had low-enough heels for dancing.

Her plan was to accompany Jimmy to the dance hall and then gently explain that Irma's plans were premature, unfounded in any reality, and that she was sorry he had been misled. She was sure she could walk the tightrope between honesty and giving offence, putting it to Jimmy in such a way that he would not feel jilted. However, going by the nervous glances full of expectation that he kept sliding her way, she would need to work fast. This evening she would nip any anticipation of marriage firmly in the bud.

'Are you looking forward to the Palais tonight, Fleur?' Jimmy asked now, as if he'd dropped in on her thoughts.

Stars! Now he was putting on some sort of performance too.

'Er, well, it's quite a long time since I've attended a dance there, Jimmy. I'm certainly intrigued to see it again.'

'I wish the Palais de Danse was still operating on the Torrens,' Irma joined in enthusiastically, dabbing at the last remnants of steamed treacle pudding and custard on her mouth. Fleur watched the laced-edged napkin come away not only with custard but a waxy carmine imprint of those lips, and her insides clenched again with anger that Irma was so careless with Mae Appleby's treasures.

She desperately wanted to correct Irma's pronunciation of the floating dance boat that had been all the rage during the 1920s on Adelaide's main waterway. Irma had slaughtered the words but it seemed no one but Fleur minded. Instead, Irma's comment set off the older people at the table on a trip down memory lane, including her father. She didn't mind his indulgent smile and remarks about its Arabic decoration because she knew he was probably remembering happier days with her mother.

'James, can I offer you a glass of port?' Irma asked, cutting across Henry's reminiscences about dancing with his first wife on the floating palais.

'Er, no, thank you, Mrs Appleby.'

'Oh, do call me Irma,' she said. 'We're going to be family soon.'

'Right, well.' Fleur stood up to stop her stepmother from continuing. 'Jimmy, if we're going to avoid the queues, I suggest we get going.'

'Off you go, you lovebirds,' Irma said and won a scowl from Fleur.

'Please don't embarrass Jimmy, Irma.'

'Oh, come on. You young things shouldn't be so shy.'

'We're not, but we're also not lovebirds.'

Irma tapped her nose and gave a knowing smile, as if communicating some great secret, and clutched at Henry's hand, repulsing Fleur even more. This wasn't some big emotional moment.

'Shall we go, Jimmy?' Fleur said pointedly. She moved around the table to kiss her father, who had been noticeably quiet this evening. She wondered if he was feeling as dismayed as she was to be seated around the table with its sinister intention . . . or was he as fatigued as he suddenly looked? She frowned at his pale complexion, which was bordering on grey. 'Dad? Is anything wrong?'

He stood unsteadily and patted her hand. 'All is fine. You look lovely tonight, Fleur.' Then he leaned in so that only she could hear. 'Your mother would be proud.'

Fleur wished he hadn't said that in this moment, because it only made her more aware of the hole in their lives and the imposter who had claimed Mae's place.

'Goodnight, everyone,' she said, letting go of her father's hand, which felt papery dry. She let Jimmy say more formal farewells to the other two people around the table.

Outside the house she gave a sound of despair.

'You all right?' Jimmy asked, falling back into his normal way of speaking.

'No, Jimmy, I'm not. I hate this charade.'

'Shar . . . what?'

'Forget it.'

Jimmy gripped her elbow a little too hard. 'Don't speak me to me like that.'

Fleur was determined not to wince and let him win the satisfaction of her pain. 'Like what, Jimmy?'

'Like I'm less than you.'

'Is that what I did? Or did I just use a word you don't know how to say, spell or understand?' What was wrong with her, being this cruel? She'd promised her father she would try harder.

'You won't be talking down to me when we're married.'

'No, I won't. Because we aren't getting married, Jimmy.'

'We are! I've been told.'

'By Irma?' Fleur shook her head with what he couldn't know was despair for them both. 'She's lying. There's nothing assured about this mad idea, Jimmy. I'm really sorry, but she's got you hoodwinked because it's not happening!'

'But why?' He frowned. He looked Neanderthal as his forehead creased, making his brow appear even more hooded and protruding.

She shook the churlish thought away, flicking her hair. Kindness – wasn't that her mantra in the mortuary? *And so it should be outside of it*, she heard in Mae Appleby's voice. There had been nothing kind or gentle about her words, so she tried again. 'Let's just say we aren't suited and leave it at that.'

'I think we are. And my father and your mother think so too.'

She wished he wouldn't badger her. 'She's so far from my mother it's not worth discussing, and it's certainly not up to your parents who I marry.'

'You'll need a man when your father's dead.'

She knew Jimmy didn't mean it as an insult. He was too much of a blunt instrument to fashion anything so subtle; he was simply stating the facts as he understood them. But his words still managed to land a bruising blow, and she felt as though all the wind had left her lungs.

'My father is not dying,' she ground out.

Easily distracted, Jimmy saw the bus hove into view and pointed, grinning, his mood changing in a heartbeat. 'Come on, the bus is coming.'

Fleur sighed, grateful for the breeze that blew their sour words gently away. The early evening was not as cold as she'd thought and the milder weather, as well as being away from Irma and her pretensions, improved her mood. As much as she didn't like the Coglins, with their less-than-professional ways and rather grasping idea to enter undertaking, the engagement was certainly not Jimmy's idea. This plan had Irma stamped all over it, and the more Fleur turned it over in her mind, the more she became convinced that there was something greater at stake here. Irma had been looking very pleased with herself recently, while Henry was barely a shade of the tall, strong man she knew. He was only just sixty.

Fleur frowned into her thoughts, resigning herself to the fact that her father looked to be sickening. Irma was right. Perhaps his drinking was taking its final toll, although she knew plenty of other alcoholics far older than her father, who were still getting on with work and life. She recalled how her father had apparently dismissed the doctor's warning. *Had* he seen a doctor, or was Irma lying?

11

Fleur and Jimmy made their way down to the promenade at Semaphore and before long had joined the happy throng filing into the grand ballroom of the former bathing pavilion known as the Maris Palais. She could remember being brought here as a youngster to the ground level, where there were lockers and showers – one could even hire bathing costumes, although she and her mother had owned theirs. And she could recall the special treat of being taken upstairs to the café/kiosk for an ice-cream sundae. Her father had spared no expense for his favourite girls.

Now she was back at this space of former dreams and delights with someone she didn't want to be with, being forced to dance in his arms towards an engagement she had no intention of making.

'I'm happy to buy your ticket,' Jimmy said, sounding pleased with his offer, their terse exchange apparently forgotten.

'That's kind, Jimmy, thank you, but I'm happy to purchase my own.'

'My father and Irma said I should.'

'And did they give you the money for it – all one and sixpence for the entrance?'

He grinned. 'It's three shillings all up. Yeah, Irma gave it to me . . . bit rich for me.'

She nodded. It wasn't Jimmy's fault that he was being manipulated by a woman way ahead of him in her cunning. Even so, she wondered how Jimmy felt ready for what Irma was planning. 'How are you going to afford to get married, Jimmy, if you can't afford three shillings for a dance?'

'You might need me as a husband more than you realise.'

Now she cut him an enquiring glance. 'Why would that be?'

He lifted his shoulders in a defiant shrug. 'Face it, your father looks unwell,' he said, and she hated that he had seen it too. 'You're lucky to have such a good offer, because once he goes, you've got no one, Fleur.'

'Once he goes?'

'You know what I mean.'

'No, Jimmy, I don't. He's just a bit tired at the moment,' she deflected.

'He's hitting the bottle too hard, if you don't mind me saying,' he countered.

'I do mind. My father's drinking less these days than he ever has in the past.' She wasn't lying. The past week Irma hadn't let him get down to the pub as he preferred, instead insisting that he join her in the sitting room for coffee.

'Well, if we're going to be family, we have to talk about these things.'

'What things?' she asked, astonished.

'The future of his business when he dies.' Her companion was looking over his shoulder, maybe deliberately giving an air of nonchalance to his words.

'Jimmy?'

'Yeah?' He was giving the thumbs up to some mates he could see queueing behind them.

'Jimmy.'

'What?'

'We definitely need to talk.'

'What about?'

'About us . . .' She took a deep breath; it was kinder to do this now, and as directly as she could so he understood. 'I don't see any engagement working between us, and my father's business is not part of the deal.'

Jimmy surprised her by grinning, but it was not warm. 'You'd better talk to your mother about that.'

'My mother is dead.'

'You know what I mean,' he snapped and she lifted an eyebrow. 'Talk to Irma. She's the one with all the plans.'

'I will, Jimmy. Whatever Irma is planning should not involve me – I'm not one of her chess pieces. And it shouldn't involve my father's business, which she has no place in.'

He frowned. 'She sees it differently.'

'This is a conversation for another time with a different person.'

The line moved up suddenly and they arrived at the ticket booth, still scowling at each other.

'Two tickets,' Jimmy said to the small, bespectacled woman behind the glass and grille.

'Please,' the woman uttered in an admonishing tone. 'You shouldn't forget your manners, young man.'

Fleur had already palmed the coins and now placed them into the little metal cup. 'I'll pay for myself, but thanks, Jimmy.'

The woman glanced at Jimmy and back at Fleur.

'I told you—'

'No, Jimmy, you don't tell me anything. You've become Irma's mouthpiece,' she snapped. 'I don't need Irma's money . . . which is in fact my father's money, anyway!'

'You two need to cheer up,' the woman said, taking the coins and putting the tickets into the cup in exchange. 'This is meant to be a happy evening.' She gestured towards a poster promising that the orchestra of five would be led by Ken Wylie and there would be balloons, streamers, prizes and dancing until ten.

'Excuse us,' Fleur said, stepping away from the window as Jimmy scowled at the woman before turning away.

'Here's your ticket,' he said, pushing it into Fleur's hand.

'Thank you,' she ground out and barely waited for Jimmy to catch up as she stalked into the ballroom.

———

On Friday, Tom had moved through a long day at the woolstores but he had never been shy of hard work or days that felt like they had more hours than others. He could feel the familiar ache of honest toil in his body.

'Hey, Tom?' He looked up to see Charlie Hunter, the stock agent he'd met earlier and had spent some hours with that day. 'A few of the lads are going down to the Palais tomorrow evening.'

'The Palais? What's that – a pub?'

Charlie gave a burst of a laugh. 'No, mate. It's the ballroom down on the Semaphore beach.'

Tom frowned.

'A dance,' Charlie continued. 'You know, pretty girls. Tell me you can dance.'

Tom gave a shy smile. 'Yes, I learned.'

He received a slap on the back from the grinning Charlie. 'Then you'll have a girl in your arms tomorrow, big fella. I'll come by and pick you up at seven forty-five.'

'I'm not sure . . .' Tom began.

'Don't be daft. I need you there to attract the girls for me, mate, even if you don't want to dance with them. You'll be like a beacon.'

'Shut up, Charlie.'

'Seriously! Who's going to notice me in the crowd? I'm five foot six, and you've got seven or eight inches on me. You'll glow like the Christmas angel on top of the tree when they turn on the lights.'

Tom had to laugh. 'All right, all right.'

'It's one and six to get in, but well worth it. Bring a few bob so we can have some beers. I'll see you tomorrow.'

So now here he was, hanging back in the shadows as the band hit its first number. He watched couples skip onto the polished boards that had been chalked and made ready for a full evening of happy people twirling around the ballroom.

'What do you think, mate?' Charlie asked, dark eyes shining in the glittering ballroom lights.

'I'll admit, it's fun. Thanks for bringing me.'

'Right, now stand proud, Tom. I want the girls watching you and that means they're watching me.'

Tom laughed and straightened his back amenably as he took in the room. He was impressed that the ballroom overlooked the sea. The sun had lowered beneath the horizon, scattering rose gold and soft orange hues and bleeding away into the darkening twilight claiming the sky. He was mesmerised until his attention was caught by a flick of darkly golden hair at the corner of his eye. It belonged to a woman he recognised as the one he'd seen standing in the doorway a couple of nights ago. Had to be her. The hair was identical in colour, and he now saw it framed her face in soft waves. She was with a man who looked to be around her age, hovering on the other side of the large ballroom, and they seemed to be having words. The last time he'd noted her slim height she'd looked equally unhappy. Tom couldn't help but wonder what was making such an attractive woman so miserable. She still felt strangely familiar to him, though he couldn't pinpoint why.

'What, or should I ask who, has caught your attention?' Charlie gave him a nudge.

Tom didn't drop his gaze fast enough and Charlie was able to follow it directly to the woman.

'Mmm. You don't waste time, do you? She's got to be the prettiest girl here. Out of my league, but not yours.'

Tom didn't reply.

'Well, don't stand here like a shag on a rock, mate. Go over.'

Tom cut him a withering look. 'Beer?'

'Buying already? Sure. I'll just wait here and work out who will have the benefit of my twinkle-toed brilliance tonight.'

'Goose,' Tom replied, shaking his head and departing towards the bar. When he returned, carefully balancing a couple of schooners, the band had taken the energy up a notch. The dance floor was full of eager dancers and he could no longer see the girl with the tumble of loose waves. Charlie had disappeared too; no doubt the opportunity for a twirl with a pretty woman in his arms was far more alluring than a schooner of West End.

Tom drifted to the back of the room, where he found a small table to put down Charlie's beer. His height gave him a good head above most in the room and as he sipped his deliciously cold beer, he scanned helplessly for the lovely but sad woman.

A flash of pale fabric caught his attention and there she was, moving around the edge of the dancefloor, looking – in his opinion – awkward in the arms of the bloke she'd obviously arrived with. They weren't talking and were instead looking in different directions, although he, from what Tom could tell, was joshing with friends nearby with their dance partners. The group of four men all looked to be ignoring the women they were with. And then they were gone again, lost to the crowd.

Tom caught sight of Charlie, chatting enthusiastically to a woman in a pink dress; her chin was tipped back as she laughed at whatever Charlie was saying. There was no doubt he was fun company and Tom knew he wouldn't have come to an event such as this without Charlie's encouragement. He was going to have to shake off his reticent, country boy attitude and learn how to be a city dweller, integrating more with others. People couldn't be avoided. Life was never going to be quiet again unless he moved back to a station – and right now nothing struck him as less palatable. He imagined there may well come a time when he could face a shearing shed again, but not yet . . . not nearly.

Charlie twirled into view again. 'Hurry up, mate. The dance will be over before you get going.'

Slightly stung by Charlie's friendly sarcasm, but also able to see across the dancefloor to where something was unfolding that he didn't like the look of, Tom moved into the crowd.

———————

Fleur was trying to make this evening work, but Jimmy was frustrating. They were so mismatched in every way that it was hard enough just finding something to talk about. She thought dancing might help, but they'd been even more awkwardly silent as they moved around the ballroom.

She'd hoped they would be able to take the woman at the ticket counter's advice and put their hostile words aside, but her patience was wearing thin. Jimmy was a clumsy conversationalist anyway, but his suggestion that Appleby's should really be using the Coglins exclusively for their coffin-making was ill-timed. She refused to get into a heated exchange over why that was a supremely poor idea. While she acknowledged that he was making an effort to find a shared topic to discuss, she resented that he seemed to feel he could discuss her father's business with such familiarity and, worse, propriety. What's more, his tone held a sense of entitlement that Fleur couldn't go along with; she hoped no one had overheard her withering response, which was probably the reason Jimmy was now disinterested in talking to her.

The truth was, there was so little to say to each other unless they were talking about funerals, but she had no desire to discuss business with him. He and his father made coffins, but not so well any more. Fleur began to imagine the horror of allowing Jimmy free rein in a mortuary; he would surely take their business back decades. There was simply nowhere that they comfortably connected to help this night along. He was a mad-keen footy fan – a diehard Port Adelaide supporter – still mooning about losing to South Adelaide by just over a goal at last year's Grand Final. As he carried on next to her with his mates about the next weekend's match and whether Jack Dermody would kick a swag and take his boys a step closer to another battle for the premiership, she realised that she not only barely understood him, but she wasn't interested in learning anything more about him – or the football, or the new pub that was opening at Alberton, or that one of the freemasons was going to sell him an Ariel Square Four motorcycle . . . On it went.

'I can attach a dusting sidecar,' he said, casually flicking a thumb her way.

The gesture only made her irritation feel more heated. It was rude of Jimmy to ignore her, rude of all his friends to forget they each had a girl in their arms, but if she was going to shine an honest light, then she needed to accept that she was at fault too. She had nothing to offer him. She played no sport and had no interesting pastimes, nor did she really have a close set of friends. And if she was completely truthful, her attitude towards him was wrong. She didn't particularly like Jimmy or his lack of imagination; she felt sorry that he was being used by Irma, but he was obviously happy to go along with her plans with no aspirations of his own. No, they had nothing in common.

She had the dead. She was their friend, and they were hers.

Fleur looked to the young women she was supposedly with and yet here she was, standing slightly aside from the three excited girls who'd come on the arms of Jimmy's friends. They didn't seem to share her indignation at being ignored; perhaps this was how these things usually went. Instead, they were sparkly eyed and seemingly enjoying the evening, as she knew she should be, but didn't really know how to join in. The current conversation between the girls was about how to change the contours of their faces using clever make-up techniques.

'No, Joanie, you *can* have high cheekbones,' Shirl was saying. 'You can make your whole face look longer by shifting your hair back like this, for a start,' her friend said, lifting Joanie's curls away from her forehead. 'And then you need to apply rouge at this angle . . .'

Fleur looked away, sipped her lemonade and watched Jimmy laugh about something; it was to do with the footy again, she realised, and was about to turn away when he seemed to sense her attention. He moved closer.

'Why aren't you talking to the other girls?'

'They're not talking to me.'

'That's because you're so snooty,' he accused her.

She wished she could tell him the truth – she'd happily take the blame that she simply wasn't very good at being sociable – but Fleur didn't think Jimmy would understand. 'No, it's not that. I just don't feel—'

'Why are you always so moody?' Jimmy snapped, making her flinch with surprise. Now all his friends had turned at his tone, and the women had shifted their attention to them as well.

'Just leave it, Jimmy.' She realised he was drunk; he'd downed at least three beers already and who knew if he had been swigging something else from a flask.

'No!' he said, full of fresh hostility, suddenly gripping her arm for the second time that evening. Not tightly enough to bruise, but sufficient to make Fleur wince and believe that he might lose control; if he exerted just a fraction more pressure, she might be marked. 'You're a stuck-up bitch, you know that?' he growled. 'Irma's right. You need taking down a peg or two and I'll make sure that begins on our wedding night.' He pressed harder.

Fleur refused to give him the satisfaction of seeing that it hurt, but she also didn't want to cause any more embarrassment than they already had, snarling at each other. But Jimmy wanted to hurt her, it seemed, and he clenched his strong fingers, apparently determined to leave the impression of his grip in purple bruises.

It was too much for Fleur to tolerate any longer. 'Let me go!' She wrenched her arm away. 'Don't you ev—'

'Care to dance?' A new voice broke the moment.

Neither Fleur nor Jimmy had seen the man arrive but now all heads turned to the stranger, a tall man about their age with thick blond hair, neatly parted on one side.

Jimmy looked over his shoulder with a slight snarl still on his face. 'Bugger off.'

'I wasn't asking you,' the man said for all in their group to hear. 'I was asking *you*,' he said, turning a clear, grey-eyed enquiry at Fleur. 'Would you like to dance?'

She wanted to accept for his welcome interruption alone, though she sensed a collective envy emanating from the girls nearby. He was handsome with that smile in his eyes and his clearly broad frame beneath the suit she sensed he was not comfortable in. Even so, he emanated self-possession; she sensed this was a man who wouldn't be pushed around by anyone.

'If she won't, I will!' Shirl said, stepping forward.

He didn't even look at Shirl, much to Shirl's apparent chagrin. His gaze was firmly on Fleur.

'Yes, I would,' she answered. With a smile, she eased past Jimmy and his flaring nostrils. 'Excuse me.'

'Hey, she's my date!'

Fleur looked at the man whose hand she hadn't realised until this heartbeat she had taken. It felt calloused, presumably from hard work, and despite its strength, it held her smaller hand so gently and without any sense of ownership. His attention remained riveted on her, and she could tell he was waiting for her to respond to Jimmy's claim.

'I'm not anyone's date,' she told him, loud enough for Jimmy to hear. 'I accompanied Jimmy, but only out of politeness to our parents.'

'You bitch!' His voice was louder than it needed to be and his face was flushed with anger combining with humiliation; she watched the colour climbing from his scrawny neck. His Adam's apple bobbed in anger as he was forced to swallow his pride.

The girls gasped. Two couldn't help nervous giggles.

'Steady on, mate,' one of the blokes said, reaching for Jimmy, but he shook off his hand.

'We're getting engaged,' Jimmy announced, bringing fresh gasps from the girls. 'The silly cow needs to understand that.'

'Well,' the stranger said into the frigid atmosphere surrounding this group, 'I think the lady disagrees.' He finally looked at Jimmy. 'And you need to watch your mouth around women or someone might shut it for you.'

Fleur turned her gaze back to Jimmy as well. 'For the last time, Jimmy, we are not getting engaged – not now, not ever. There! Is that clear and public enough?' She didn't wait for his answer, although she heard the other couples laughing at Jimmy's discomfort, and turned back to the man who still had her hand. 'Shall we?'

They moved into a convenient gap that opened on the dance-floor and joined a slow foxtrot. Fleur felt instant gratitude to be moving away from her party. 'Thank you,' she murmured. 'I'm so embarrassed.'

'Don't be. He's an oaf and a fool. He's the one who is suffering the embarrassment. You handled yourself well.'

'Is everyone still staring?'

'No, but we can stay on the other side of the ballroom for a while,' he said.

'You're that good a dancer, are you?' She grinned at him, surprised to be looking up at a man, given her reasonable height. He had to be six and a half feet tall.

'I am,' he replied with a soft chuckle. 'My mother insisted I learn from a young age.'

'She's a good woman – taught you well.'

'*Was* a good woman, yes.'

'My mothers are dead too.'

'Mothers?'

She smiled, finding it easy to do as she looked into his interested expression. 'Long story. For now, I appreciate you rescuing me.'

'Did I?'

She nodded. 'You can't know just how much I needed it.'

'I think I can. I noticed from this side of the ballroom that you really didn't want to be where you were.'

Fleur shook her head. 'It's not the dance itself, it's him.'

'And I can understand why,' he remarked.

She liked that he wasn't asking any hard questions, wasn't acting curious; he was simply following the conversation where she allowed it to roam. 'I'm Fleur.'

'Fleur,' he repeated. 'I love that name.'

'Oh, come on. Don't disappoint me.'

He caught on. 'I'm not flirting. It's an unusual name.'

'True. I've never met anyone who shared it.'

He smiled. 'I have. I met a girl once, when I was just a boy. Her name was Fleur and . . .'

She watched his gaze turn wistful as he trailed off, trying to find the right words.

'I felt like she saved me in a moment of tremendous grief. I was lost and I know this sounds fanciful but, just as you felt a moment ago, I think she rescued me. She showed me a kindness and interest that made me feel like I could face . . .' He trailed off again. 'Sorry, we hardly know each other, you don't want—'

'No, I do.' She gave him a gentle smile of encouragement. 'What did she help you to face?'

He shrugged. 'A terrible time. I'm a country boy. I was ten. My mother and newborn sister had just died, I was suddenly alone in the city to accompany their bodies to where her family wanted and I was . . . well, I was lost,' he said again, finding a smile despite the memory. 'And this young girl called Fleur arrived at the house where they had my mother and sister in a coffin. This little girl, full of confidence, took charge, not letting anyone bully me. Her whole name was pretty – I've never forgotten it. I think I fell in love with her then and there, but she was only eight. Fleur Appleby is one of my fondest memories. You're every bit as pretty as she was.' He shook his head. 'You know, as odd as this sounds, you even look like her.'

He grinned at this fanciful notion, while she blinked with private astonishment as the music ended and all the dancers stopped to clap and smile at each other.

He looked a little bashful. 'I'm sorry, I didn't mean to say so much. I *never* say that much. I didn't mean to embarrass you either, but after how that bloke was treating you, I reckon you could do with a compliment.' He shrugged again. 'Can't escape the fact that you are pretty, and brave to stand up to those jokers.' Now he looked awkward, as if he was blushing, but she couldn't tell under the lights. The music struck up a fast dance and people streamed onto the floor.

As they both turned to watch, Fleur replied. 'You were the brave one. I just stood there.'

'No, you defied him. I think you surprised everyone.'

'Including myself,' she said, watching the women on the ballroom boards looking adoringly at their partners. She could never, not in a lifetime, look at Jimmy Coglin like that . . . even if he did claim to have twinkle toes and all the right dance moves.

'I doubt it, Fleur. I think you'd have found a way to leave him even if I hadn't happened along.' Her new companion cut her a glance. 'Would you like a drink?'

'Not really. I'd prefer to go. Sorry . . . what I mean is, I'd rather just leave the dance.'

He watched her carefully. 'All right. Have you got everything? I'd be happy to take you home if you wish.'

She nodded. 'Thank you. How about we walk? It will take an hour but it's a lovely evening out there.'

'I'm in no hurry. By the way, I'm Tom.' He offered a handshake.

'I know,' Fleur said, a warm smile breaking across her face to reach her eyes. She clasped his hand. 'Hello again, Tom Catchlove.'

12

Tom was still looking at her in wonder when they stepped outside. The sea breeze stirred their hair as Fleur pointed.

'Let's walk the Esplanade.'

'You knew?' he said, framing a question while feeling awestruck.

She chuckled. 'Not until you mentioned the circumstances. But I remember that brief time we spent together as vividly as you do.'

'I can't believe it's you!'

'It is . . . the girl of your dreams,' she jested, not realising how her joke hit its mark.

He couldn't talk about his feelings yet so he steered the conversation to Miss Jackson. 'That awful housekeeper,' he said. 'She terrified me . . . but not you.'

'I hate injustice at any time. She was being deliberately cruel to you, when you deserved a big hug and lots of empathy. I worried about you after we left with your mother.'

'Thank you for whatever you did. As young as I was, I felt as though you and your father would take good care of her and my sister.'

'We did, I promise you that. Have you visited the grave yet?'

'No, planning to next week. I arrived a few nights ago and have been finding lodgings and some work, getting myself acquainted with the neighbourhood.'

'Attending dances,' she said, matching his slightly weary tone.

He grinned. 'That was a mate's idea but I don't regret it,' he said, casting her a shy glance.

They passed the rotunda. Lights were strung between lamp-posts, achieving a sparkly pathway along the shore.

'The bands will be playing most weekends come summer,' she remarked. 'It's lovely down here and everyone is usually in such happy spirits. Shall we walk the jetty?'

'I'd like that,' he said, wanting to pinch himself that this was the same Fleur Appleby he'd carried a torch for most of his days. How strange and wonderful life could be.

'Are you always this economical with your words, Tom?'

He smiled at her teasing. 'Probably.'

'Never turned into a chatterbox, then?'

He shook his head.

'I remember liking that about you all those years ago,' she said, smiling back.

The breeze stiffened slightly but it was pleasantly mild and he loved the way it teased a few strands of her hair free from their neat styling. She didn't disappoint from his vision of how she might have turned out. Her hair was slightly darker than it had been as a child but remained a mystery colour between blonde and brown. There had been moments earlier in the evening when it glowed like a summer sunset, though right now, beneath the moonlight, it appeared fair.

He glanced back at the Palais and she followed his line of sight.

'This is a bathing pavilion, which apparently can cater to five hundred bathers,' she explained.

'Why the tower?'

'Oh, just an attractive addition, I think. It serves as an observation tower. People sneak up there.' She pointed. 'I think I can see two pairs of lovers right now,' she said, grinning, and then quickly moved on. 'There's a rooftop garden as well.'

'I think the lovers are staring at us, wishing they were out on the jetty instead.'

Fleur smiled at him. 'So, are you visiting for long, or . . .?'

'I'm not sure. I'm working at the woolstores.'

'Oh, right. Did you become the brilliant wool classer you told me you wanted to be?'

He laughed. 'I became a wool classer, that's for sure. I'm still one.'

She frowned. 'Just taking a pause?'

'Not quite.' As they walked the length of the jetty, he told her what had occurred.

She sighed in sympathy. 'That's a lot of pain.'

He nodded. 'How you felt just now in the ballroom is how I felt about my life. I needed to walk away from it.'

'So, what's next for Tom Catchlove?'

They reached the end of the jetty and stared out at the sea. 'I don't know,' he said, revealing his deepest anxiety. 'I need to find something. As much as the work in the woolstores is welcome, I've got to make some decisions.'

'Do you want to keep wool classing?'

'The only way to do that is to return to a shearing shed and, as cowardly as it sounds, I don't want to be in one again. I love the shed, but it holds bad memories for me now. My mother died during shearing time, my father did too, and then the business with Peter . . . I learned something about someone I loved during shearing time that has shocked me so deeply, I can't think straight. So, everything about the shearing shed feels bad to me at the moment.

Even the smell of the wool bales in the stores sends me right back there, so I think I need to find something new.'

'I don't think it's cowardly, Tom. I think it's more cowardly not to face one's demons. You couldn't be more honest than you're being with yourself right now. Most people would probably prefer to put their head in the sand and ignore that inner voice. But yours has spoken, and you're paying attention and allowing it now to guide you. I think that's brave.'

He gave her a nod. 'You certainly know how to throw a good light on my situation. That's what you did the last time we met.'

They shared a sad chuckle.

'You know, I think I saw you the other day,' he said.

'Really? When? Why didn't you say hello?'

'You were standing in a doorway down the road from the pub at Alberton, where I've got digs. You were with an older man.'

She frowned as she thought back. 'Yes, that probably was me. I was with my father, trying to have a private conversation – the walls have ears in our house.' She turned away and he followed her path as, side by side, they strolled back down the jetty.

'I've not seen the sea before, so thank you for—'

'What?' She stopped walking, looking back at him with an expression of shock.

Tom shrugged. 'I grew up a million miles away, Fleur. We didn't take holidays or go to the seaside like you lot.'

'Shouldn't you be whooping with joy to gaze on it for the first time?'

'I am, in here,' he said with a grin, touching his chest.

Fleur shook her head. 'Oh, Tom. Come on, you have to dip your toes in and have a yell or two.'

'What, now?'

'Yes, now!'

'Be cold, won't it?'

'I've just finished telling you you're not a coward. You aren't scared of a bit of cold water, are you?'

'Cold might be understating it.'

She tugged at his sleeve. 'I insist. I want to be at your side when you first feel the foam of the sea touch your toes. No further, I promise.'

'Only if you will as well,' he challenged her.

'Right, I will!' She began to run and he followed, breaking into a jog.

'Get your shoes and socks off, and roll up your trousers,' she urged.

He laughed. 'Still bossy. People are going to stare.'

'Does it matter? It's harmless. You've never seen the sea, Tom!' she exclaimed again as if still unable to believe it. Fleur pulled off her own shoes quicker than Tom and dropped them onto the beach. 'We'll leave them here. Don't worry, no one will touch them.'

She offered her hand and he took it, allowing her to lead him down across the sand. The reflected light from the Palais and the jetty allowed them to see where they were walking.

'I love the sound of Nature's power,' Tom said, exhaling softly as they stopped just out of reach of the water's edge. 'Even when she's gentle like now, you know she can take it up a few notches. It's very soothing tonight.'

'It is seductive,' Fleur agreed. 'Do you have anything similar in the landscape you grew up in?'

He nodded. 'The wind can tousle your hair when it's hot and make you sigh with pleasure, but when it roars across the plain, that same wind is Nature showing off her power. It can create a storm like you can't imagine – there's nothing to shield you from the sand it whips up, or the rain it drives . . . or the heat it carries, which can kill.' He watched her shake her head gently in wonder. 'And on the day my mother and sister passed away, there was an earthquake in our region. I'll never forget it. That was Nature at perhaps her most dramatic . . . it made me realise we're like grains of sand by comparison to her power. She shook me until my teeth rattled, like she was able to wake up some prehistoric beast deep in the earth and make it shift.'

Fleur smiled. 'I like that you make me see it and feel it with your description, Tom. So, now, step into the water and enjoy a whole new experience.'

Still holding hands, they stepped forward and allowed the sea's tumbling edge to race up and greet them. The foam curled around their toes and Tom chuckled.

'That's amazing. No longer a sea virgin.'

She laughed. 'I'm glad I was here for your first time,' she said, smiling back at him. 'I find your joy irresistible.' And as he turned towards her, it seemed she chose not to resist the impulse as she reached up and kissed him swiftly but gently. 'Are you going to wipe your mouth now with the back of your sleeve?' she murmured.

He blinked. 'I didn't, did I?'

'You most certainly did.' She laughed again at the memory.

'Not this time.' He leaned in and kissed her again. 'Thank you.'

'For what?' she asked, looking puzzled.

He looked around. 'For this. For dancing with me, for remembering me. For a kiss from the most beautiful woman at the dance.'

The sea surged again gently around their feet. Fleur tugged on his hand. 'Let's walk a little. Not too far, because it's a bit dark.'

'Fleur, when we spoke the other evening, I didn't know it was you, but you looked unhappy.'

'I was. I am.'

'What's going on?'

Now it was Fleur's turn to spill the past, and Tom learned how her mother had died, how the arrival of Irma into her life had turned it upside down, about the change in her father, and now the campaign to get her married to Coglin and out of the house . . . out of the way.

'Out of the business, do you mean?' Tom asked.

Fleur nodded. 'Probably. I think she wants it for herself. Although she's covering all the possible angles.'

'What do you mean?'

'Well, by trying to marry me off to Jimmy.'

'Why him specifically? Is he rich?'

She smirked. 'Now you've got her measure, but no, Jimmy is not rich. His father owns a coffin-making business and both father and son want to move into undertaking.'

'Oh, I see. That's neat.'

'It is, certainly in Irma's conniving mind. Ooh, my mother is likely turning in her grave.'

'You said before you have two mothers?'

'Three, in fact, but one doesn't count.' She laughed without mirth before explaining about her adoption, Mae's death and Irma's insinuation into their lives. 'So, yes, while I was a pitiful orphan, as Irma likes to remind me, Mae Appleby is the only mother I've loved. A woman – a stranger – gave birth to me, but it was Mae and Henry who became my parents. I freely admit that I resent Irma being in our lives, claiming to be a mother to me. But my negativity is not all about emotion. You see, Irma knows nothing about undertaking, funerals and the work of a mortuary, or all the companies that work with us, from coffin to calico makers. I think she's using me as her way of being able to continue the business should anything happen to my father.'

'And is anything happening to him?' Tom asked.

Fleur nodded, and he saw how the directness of his question made her tear up.

'Fleur, I'm sorry, I—'

'Don't be.' She chose that moment to bring their paddling to an end, moving out of the sea's reach. He followed her up the sand as she continued. 'I must face it – my father is likely dying. I don't understand, though. He was hale three months ago and now suddenly he's ashen, weak, and even his personality is shifting.'

'Pain can do that.'

'But he's not in pain. He assures me he's just getting older, a bit more fatigued, and that Irma's claim about the doctor only giving him weeks to live is a lie.'

'Why would she say such a thing?'

'Because she's cruel and wicked and scheming. Pretending to know something I don't, simply to be beastly. And especially because she knows I'm trapped in a way and can't respond. I don't want to hurt Dad any more than he already has been. Having two women at war in his household makes him feel wretched.'

Hearing the note of despair in her voice, Tom pointed to a nearby bench. They sat together to dry their toes, dust off the sand and put on their shoes. 'She certainly sounds like a pot stirrer.'

'She's so much more devious than that. Irma makes trouble. She also makes me see red,' Fleur admitted. 'Sorry, Tom, you don't need to hear all of this.'

'I want to. I want to know everything about you.'

She sighed. 'Losing my mother was catastrophic for both of us – few would understand that better than you – but Dad and I worked out a way to manage our lives. We're close – and we're a good team in the business. We look after one another. Above all, we love each other. We made it work. And then Irma arrived and everything began to go wrong.'

'How did they meet?'

'Irma was brought in part-time to help run the house while Dad worked, but then she rather loftily took on the job of sorting out the mountain of paperwork after my mother passed away. Irma wasn't especially good at it, as I understand, but Dad had no time, and I was still at school. She began calling herself his secretary, and attached herself firmly to my father as his very private assistant. Suddenly she was opening all the mail, handling all calls, organising the bookkeeping and making appointments. She began to embed herself in every facet of our life, finally going out on Dad's arm to events that she organised.'

At Tom's nod, she continued. 'All the while, she did very little in the house – the tasks she was employed to see to, I mean. I was still quite young, a new teenager. Irma acted caring towards me, but only in front of my father. When he wasn't around, she was mean about everything. I disliked her from our first meeting, and she felt the same way about me, I'm sure. All these years it's as though I've had her hands on my back, waiting for the right moment to give me a shove.'

'Could you be mistaken?' Tom asked. At her frown, he gave a shrug of surrender. 'I mean, could you be reading more into her actions because you simply don't like her?'

'Tom, she spat on my mother's photo right in front of me, ensuring I was paying attention, taking delight in it – she left her spittle to run down my mother's face. This happened just a week or so ago.'

He couldn't hide his shock then. 'Bloody hell.'

'Exactly! And she's made it very clear to me she wants me gone from the house. Not in any subtle way, Tom, but in clear, compelling English. My home . . . the only one I've ever known. The one she plans to take from me.'

'And your father's all right with this?'

'That's the thing. It's as though Dad's in another world. He's becoming forgetful, he's caring less, he's allowing me to take on more and more of the business, while allowing Irma to negotiate its future without any say so from either of us. She's got him under some sort of spell. I work most days of the week in my father's funeral parlour, while Irma does nothing. She gave up her clerical duties years ago . . . It was always a sham. She set her sights on my dad and she got him to marry her. Now I could believe she wants us both out of the way.'

'How so?'

Fleur gave a moue of bafflement. 'I don't know. If neither of us were around, she could probably sell the business to the Coglins and live very comfortably on the proceeds. If I was still a thorn in her side, but married to Jimmy, they could gang up on me. Either way, she needs my father out of the way but I think she'd love it if we were both gone.'

'You say your father hasn't seen the doctor?'

'Well, that's according to him. Irma intimates otherwise. I'd believe Dad any day over her, even with his being so vague lately.'

Tom nodded thoughtfully. 'If Irma is really trying to unsettle you and put doubt in you, then perhaps this is her way of playing with your mind.'

'What do you mean?'

Tom began to tell her about life in the shearing shed and how the gun shearer would create banter at smoko to deliberately make the wool classer feel he would never keep up.

'Why does he do that?'

He laughed. 'It's hard to explain. It's men, living and working together. Ego, power, status – men in competition with one another. You know, the ape beating his chest.'

Fleur nodded, smiling. 'Good image. So you think Irma's beating her chest?'

'She could be. She wants to be number-one gun in the house and needs you to know that. You are two women under one roof, and it sounds like you're competing for one man's attention.'

'One's a wife, one's a daughter; we could have been friends. Instead, we're enemies.'

'My mother always said it takes two hands to clap. Sounds like you dislike Irma as much as she does you.'

She nodded readily and that gesture brought relief to Tom that she seemed unoffended by his remark. 'I do. But she had the chance when I was young to play it all so differently – she was the adult. She could have helped me grieve, and come to terms with the new situation. Instead she chose to belittle me, to ridicule me and pitch me against her for my father's affections. She did all of this behind his back. Until I became an adult, I felt defenceless. Now I'm pushing back.'

He nodded. 'If you can keep a clear mind like that, you'll find it easier to be around Irma. Let her behave however childishly she chooses. You take the high road and keep your conscience clear.'

Fleur blinked away from him to look across the beach to where the moon's light picked out the horizon. She looked back at him, the same light casting her serious expression into one that was ghostly grave. He loved how she leaned into him at that moment. 'I've never had a real friend. As of this evening you are the closest I have to one . . . so you're now officially my best friend.'

This time Tom initiated the kiss. He put his arm around her, careful not to presume too much and leaned in. As he hesitated for a second, she reached up to touch his face, and it was the permission he sought. He let his lips find hers – soft, not insistent. They parted but neither leaned back. He could smell her perfume, not at all floral as her name might suggest. Instead it enveloped him in a citrus and spice vapour that was intoxicating. Tom was sure he would hold that fragrance in his mind from now on, yearning for it to lift from her skin in warmth and affection.

He dared another kiss and she returned it; it was longer this time, deeper. They stared at each other in the lamplight coming from above.

'Best night ever,' he said, grinning.

Fleur nodded. 'Started badly, ended brilliantly.'

'Come on, I promised to walk you home.' Reluctantly they stood, but they now held hands, confident in each other's affection. 'Perhaps you should ask your father to be honest about his health. Maybe he's deliberately not telling you everything to protect your feelings.'

'That certainly sounds reasonable, Tom, and perhaps in an ideal world it's wise, but I don't really know my father any more. His moods are unreliable, and he doesn't like me asking too many personal questions. He quickly gets cross with me if I criticise Irma.'

'So he can't see the same failings that you do?'

'I've always thought I saw her more clearly, but you've made me think tonight. I do look for her flaws, so it is easy to find fault. However, I have a strong impression that Dad has regrets regarding Irma, but he's too proud – perhaps too far down the road of this marriage – to admit as much to me. I think he feels he's failed me, failed my mother. But he hasn't. He married Irma for the right and caring reasons, but she was the wrong choice.'

'I know it's unlikely, but perhaps he could divorce her,' Tom offered, his tone reasonable, deliberately not leaning one way or the other.

'He would never want to humiliate her in such a way.'

'What are you going to do?'

'I'm going to make my own way. I have to.' She nodded once firmly.

He grinned. 'Did you become that amazing mortician you promised you would?'

She laughed. 'You remember.'

'I remember everything about that meeting. I can even tell you how you were dressed.'

'Well, I have become a professional mortician . . . the only woman in the state.'

'That's brilliant, Fleur. I'm proud of you.'

She smiled with pleasure. 'You may be surprised to know how much your pride means to me. Most men consider it an imposition. Here, we can walk on a bit further here, and then cut up left in line with St Vincent Street.' She pointed.

'Not me.' He returned to what she'd said. 'I was raised by a brilliant woman. She was educated, wealthy, full of spirit.'

'As young as I was when we met, I remember wondering how a woman from that wealthy family ended up on a sheep station.'

He nodded, embarrassed. 'You've told me your secrets, Fleur, so I'm going to tell you mine.' He was glad that she didn't pounce on the idea of hearing a secret, waiting through his lengthy pause while he arranged how to say it aloud. 'I was in hospital recently – nothing serious,' he said before she could enquire, 'and in the bed next to me was an old fella who knew my father . . . probably knew him before I was born. And um . . .' Tom trailed off, giving a sigh.

'Go on, Tom. You're safe with me.'

'I know. It's just hard.' She waited again for him to continue. 'He told me that my mother was already pregnant when my father married her.'

'Is that it? Tom, you don't have to—'

'No, you don't understand. She loved someone else. But her family refused to let her be with him, as I understand it. She defied them and kept seeing him and then realised she was going to have a baby. I don't know what happened in between that time, but she met my dad at the Royal Show. He fell in love. Not hard to do with my mum.'

'And the family didn't mind her falling for a drover?' Fleur sounded incredulous.

'I'm sure they did, but by then they were probably tired of her rebelliousness. And while I think she did enjoy him – perhaps even learned how to be in love with him – I can now see there was a defiance in her marriage to him, not to mention a practical side, with me coming along.'

'If we walk up here we'll come onto the main street,' she said softly, clearly not wanting to interrupt him.

He nodded as they passed a couple of pubs, one on either side of the street. Ahead they could see the lights of what he presumed to be a theatre. It was still relatively early, so the patrons would still be inside enjoying the film, but the traffic was thickening now that they'd come off the Esplanade and were heading back towards Black Diamond Corner.

'Go on,' she urged gently. 'We seem to have similar situations.'

He shrugged. 'I won't say she regretted it entirely, because she was very fond of my father – that's how it felt anyway, when they were together. But now I feel sad, responsible even, that she couldn't have all that she wanted in life. There was so much more to her than being known as Vern Catchlove's wife, or Tom Catchlove's mum. Neither of us were particularly special, but *she* was. She could have been with the man she really loved . . . and not us.'

'Don't put yourself down. I think you're one out of the box, Tom, and she chose to remain in that life because she loved you.'

'I think she could have been anything she wanted to be, but the only avenue to escape her awful family was marriage and motherhood.'

'No, listen to me. The fact that they wanted her body back here means they felt she was always theirs. Your mother made her choices – we all do. My father has too. Your mother's desire to thumb her nose at her domineering family led to Vern. She chose to marry him and chose to raise you as his son. Don't ever forget that you are the product of her true love, so you were her most precious person.'

Tom gave a sad smile. 'They both chose to keep it a secret, though. Finding out the way I did was like the final blow and another reason I'm here and no longer in Farina. After she died, my father changed towards me.'

'What do you mean?'

'We became like strangers living together.'

'Oh, Tom—'

'It's all right,' he assured her, shaking his head. 'I've been making my peace with it. Being away from all things familiar helps. But it's the truth that after her death he no longer treated me the same way. I couldn't work it out, you know. He'd leave me – young as I was – for long periods of time and I'd knock about with the shearing shed gang . . . the rouseabouts especially. I was raised by others from age ten until my fifteenth birthday, when they all considered me old enough to fend for myself.'

'I'm so sorry, Tom.' She let go of his hand and put hers on his arm instead, pausing for a moment in sympathy.

'Don't be,' he said. 'It wasn't bad. It just wasn't family.' He placed his hand on hers. 'Don't you make that same mistake as my mother, Fleur. You were smarter at eight than any adult I'd met. I hope you fulfil all your ambition.'

Fleur gave him a sidelong glance that was filled with pleasure. 'Remind me to tell you about my ambition?'

'All right, but only if you promise to let me take you out properly, perhaps for the day.'

'That's easy. I promise. When?'

'Tomorrow?' He looked hopeful.

'Sunday . . .' she said, thinking, and nodded. 'Providing we have no call-outs in the morning.'

'You can choose where we go. I have no idea where to take you.'

'Oh, Tom, let's go to the zoo. I haven't been for years and there's a new hippopotamus. He's called Newsboy and came from Auckland Zoo.'

'The zoo.' He knew he sounded excited. 'I often think I like animals better than people, Fleur . . . present company not included.' He grinned. 'I've never been to a zoo. I couldn't think of anything more thrilling for a day out.'

'Gosh, you're fun, Tom. Everything's a new experience. That's a date, then.' She gestured at a doorway he recalled. 'We're here.'

'I'm staying not too far up the road at the Alberton Hotel.'

'Oh, yes, I know it. Is it all right?'

He shrugged. 'It'll do for now until I find more permanent lodgings.'

'You know your mother is buried about five minutes from the pub?'

'Really? That close?'

She nodded and smiled. 'Don't hesitate. I'm sure just being near her will help to settle some things in your mind.'

'I will go on Monday.' He grinned. 'Can't wait for tomorrow.'

'Counting the hours?' she shot back cheekily.

'I don't think I'll be able to sleep,' he replied just as fast, causing her to throw back her head with delight.

'Feels good to feel good,' she said. 'You do that to me. Kiss me goodnight, Tom.'

It felt both impossible and beyond his childhood dreams to be kissing the girl he'd loved for twenty years. The childish crush had turned to a deep fondness almost instantly, and to imagine that the Fleur of his dreams had this very evening been in his arms, beneath his lips, made him believe it was this doorway and her embrace that he had been travelling towards all of his life. His mother's death, his father's rejection, the years of raising himself and carving out his path in the shearing shed, the trauma of Sparra's death, the fever that took him to hospital and the revelation that Vern was not his real father . . . every one of those turning points had contributed to sending him to Adelaide. And not just Adelaide, but down to the port's woolstores and to agreeing to the dance that would have him cross the path of Fleur Appleby again.

It was meant to be. Did he believe in destiny or was it fate? He wasn't sure. He just knew as he deepened the kiss that this was where he wanted to be forever, and nothing else mattered any more except loving Fleur.

13

It had been more than a kiss. Fleur had sensed that immediately. It had felt like home . . . or at least how home used to feel when Mae had been alive and Henry had been a happier man. Back then, the house had been a vessel for love, laughter and hugs. Now it felt like a repository for dislike, silences and awkward meals of polite conversation at best. Even the two women who worked for Irma rarely cracked smiles; they barely spoke unless answering a question fired at them by the lady of the house.

But kissing Tom changed everything.

It prompted all her pleasurable memories at once, wrapping them into a neat, tender feeling of joy, allowing her to glimpse all that she missed about her childhood. He suddenly felt like her safe harbour away from the rocks of misery, or the currents of despair, with his strong arms encircling her and the way he looked at her with what seemed like awe or disbelief. She loved knowing that he couldn't hide his own pleasure at being with the grown-up Fleur. He had certainly grown into a fine-looking man but, more importantly, Fleur could tell he was the best sort of man – someone to rely on, who would be the closest of friends, the gentlest of lovers.

She had decided all of this as they kissed. It felt like their lips had wanted to touch again for all these years and now that they had, she wanted them to touch forever. She hadn't wanted to let him go after their final kiss and when she finally did, it had led to a lovely moment of embarrassed laughter between them.

'I don't want to leave you again . . . not ever, Fleur,' he'd told her, and she loved how vulnerable he could be in his honesty. He was stroking back a wisp of her hair that had come free.

She'd cupped his jawline in her hands . . . strong, with just the first rasp of evening stubble against her skin. 'Then don't, Tom Catchlove,' she'd whispered back, kissing him again and smiling at the sound of a distant wolf whistle coming from across the wide road. Someone had noticed them, maybe envied them.

They pulled away.

'I have to, though,' he said. 'Tomorrow feels like a lifetime to wait.'

She grinned in the dark. 'I might be able to get one of the boys to drive us up to the city. I'll meet you outside the pub at ten.'

'It would take several strong blokes to stop me,' he assured. Tom kissed her hand softly. 'Tomorrow, then.'

'No church this morning, Dad?' Fleur enquired brightly at breakfast.

Henry frowned. 'No, I didn't wake you because I have a call-out. Old Mr Jones.'

'Oh,' she said sadly. All of her father's peers were dying. 'He was ailing, though.'

He nodded. 'I'll go shortly.'

Fleur watched again as Irma joined Nan at the sideboard, where she now preferred breakfast to be laid out so that the family could help themselves. It was beyond pretentious and, given that all they were eating this morning was porridge, it seemed a waste of time, effort and washing up.

Her stepmother's latest decision, though, was to insist on pouring Henry's coffee herself and she seemed to take an age over it.

'It's my pleasure to look after my husband in this way,' she insisted to Nan, who offered to pour. Irma's voice grated; to Fleur it sounded insincere with its high-pitched, nasal tone that she managed to achieve without really trying. 'You can clear the table instead.' Irma kept her back to Henry and Fleur, finally returning to the table with two steaming cups.

'You can fetch your own, can't you, dear?' Irma said lightly to Fleur. The arrangement of the words probably sounded caring to her father but all Fleur heard was Irma's careless attitude towards her.

'Of course.' Fleur frowned. 'I thought you prefer tea in the morning, Dad.'

He flicked the newspaper. 'I do. But Irma believes the tea is giving me indigestion.'

'Nonsense. You've drunk it all your life,' Fleur said, giving Irma a perplexed stare. Her father was not giving any eye contact, apparently more interested in his morning news.

Irma returned Fleur's stare with a mind-your-own-business glare. 'Well, I spoke to my doctor, and he said we should eliminate certain things one by one. We've begun with tea.'

'But your doctor doesn't have my father's history, does he?' Fleur countered.

'You came home late.' Irma changed the subject, as dismissive as ever, faking a smile. 'I presume your evening went well?'

'It did.' Fleur allowed her question to be set aside, giving an overly sugary smile to her stepmother.

Irma looked vaguely surprised and even smacked at her husband's newspaper. 'Henry, dear, please pay attention. This is about Fleur and her engagement.'

Fleur tried not to bristle at Irma's rudeness, and instead decided to use it to her advantage as her father reluctantly folded up his newspaper and sipped his coffee. She watched him make a face as he tasted it.

'So . . . last night? Is that what I've been interrupted for?'

Irma gave him a warning glare. 'Tell us about it, Fleur, dear.'

Ooh, she could be so phoney. It made Fleur want to shake her father. Instead she smiled. 'I did have one lovely dance in the arms of a man I haven't seen since he was a boy.'

Irma's expression dissolved into confusion. 'What do you mean?'

'Dad,' Fleur said, ignoring Irma's question and touching his arm. 'Do you remember that funeral we prepared for the Darnell family in the city many years ago?'

Henry frowned and then the skin on his creased forehead slackened. 'I do. Mother and newborn had died. The other child, a son, accompanied them.'

Fleur grinned. 'Nothing wrong with your long-term memory. That's spot on. The little boy's name, you may recall, was Tom Catchlove. I met him last night by chance at the Palais.'

Her father gave a sound of surprise. 'Ah, yes, I do recall. And this is the fellow you danced with?'

'It is.'

'What about James?' Irma demanded.

Fleur turned to her. 'Jimmy couldn't care any less, actually. He was quite unpleasant to be around.'

'Who wouldn't be if his date was whisked away by another man?'

'He was rude, Irma, and he had nothing to say to me or I to him.'

'And I suppose this Tom chap had plenty to say for himself?'

'We seemed to have a lot to say to each other, if I'm truthful.'

'I'm glad, Fleur,' her father said, wincing as he finished his coffee. 'It's nice to see you so bright.'

'Henry!' Irma was unable to conceal her frustration. 'Your daughter was meant to be stepping out with James Coglin. He's going to be her fiancé.'

'He most certainly is not,' Fleur replied firmly. 'I agreed to go to the Palais with Jimmy to keep the peace in this house, but what I've proved to him and to myself is that we have nothing in common and nothing that we admire about each other.'

'That's because you're too high and mighty, Fleur Appleby.'

'Now, now, Irma,' her father tried to soothe her.

'Stay out of this, Henry. You've done enough damage.'

Fleur could feel herself turning snake-eyed. 'You're the one doing damage, Irma.' She just stopped herself from adding *And I just have to work out how*. Instead, she cleared her throat. 'I'm going out with Tom today, as a matter of fact, and I am going to ask him to join us for our evening meal on Tuesday. Please, can we have anything but roast mutton – I'm sure he's had enough of that in his life.'

'You're what?'

'You heard me, Irma. I have as much right to invite guests as you do. If you don't wish to join us, feel free to remain absent from dinner. I don't want anything special laid on for Tom. I'd simply like him to meet Dad again.'

'And how long is this new friend here for?' Irma said, sounding scornful.

Fleur shrugged. 'I'm not his keeper. He's working at the wool-stores and staying at the Alberton Hotel until he can find some proper lodgings.'

Her father placed his hands either side of his empty porridge bowl as though he was ready to flee the conversation. 'He's most welcome around our table, Fleur. Tuesday, you say?'

She nodded, ignoring the look of hatred Irma gave her.

'Good, that's settled. Irma, we shall do a roasted chicken.

Tell the lad five o'clock, Fleur.' Henry pulled out his fob watch and flipped it open. 'Right, I can't be late for the Jones family.'

'I'll take care of Mrs Chambers before I go. Er, Dad, would it be all right if Robbie drives us into the city, please? It will take hours on a Sunday to get there by bus.'

'And where, pray tell, is he taking you?' Irma demanded.

'To the zoo, Irma. And before you sneer, it was my choice.'

Her stepmother made a face anyway. 'Not very romantic.'

'It's not meant to be. It's a day out and what a beautiful day it is,' Fleur said, unable to hide her pleasure at knowing she would be with Tom in a few hours. She stood. 'Thank you for breakfast, Irma.'

Henry stood too, giving Irma a perfunctory peck on the cheek. 'Yes, thank you. Fleur, my love, I hope your day is splendid with your new young man. I'm looking forward to meeting him again.'

Fleur revelled in the twisted expression on her stepmother's face and knew she would probably have to pay dearly for her revelation of this morning.

At the Royal Zoological Gardens in Adelaide's Frome Street, Fleur queued with Tom alongside a horde of other sightseers and pleasure-seekers, dressed up in their best for a day out.

'It's busy,' Tom remarked, looking around wide-eyed.

'It's Sunday and it's sunny,' Fleur said. 'I'm actually surprised there aren't more people.' She stood on tiptoe to sneak a view of the turnstile. 'Ah, we're finally moving,' she confirmed.

'You look beautiful,' he said.

She smiled. 'So you've told me.'

'Well, all that colour really suits you.'

Fleur smoothed the floral frock made of what the lady at Foy & Gibson had described as novelty crinkled crepe with a riot of tiny flowers in myriad colours against a cream backdrop.

'All these new fabrics, dear,' she'd said. 'Hard to keep up with them, but you do look most delightful in it. Fits as though it was tailored for you.'

Fleur had demurred, needing to be convinced. 'I must admit that I prefer the dropped waist or looser fittings of a few years ago.'

'My dear, the waist is back! And your neat figure and slender looks couldn't suit it more if you tried.'

Fleur had glanced again in the mirror, not wanting to like it but aware of how attractive the dress looked on her. It cinched at the waist but had a loosely frilled neckline that was echoed by a slightly fluted hemline not too far from her ankles. The sleeves were three-quarter length and while it was a modest dress, it was helplessly pretty.

'I'm not used to being this colourful – I'm always in my dark formal outfits for work,' Fleur told Tom, coming out of her recollection of buying the dress several months ago when summer was still in full roar. 'But I'm glad I wore flat shoes. I want to walk until my feet ache and I see every creature in the zoo.'

He grinned. 'Come on.' He clasped her hand in his rough one and it felt warm and safe as they shuffled towards the turnstile.

Finally it was their turn and Tom quietly paid a shilling for both of them. He was so different to Jimmy, not needing to be showy. The metal bars twisted with a creak to let them through, and the man at the gate offered some tips as he handed back the entrance tickets.

'I'm sure you'll find your way around, but most people want to see Newsboy, so if you follow the path to the left, you'll pass the wallabies first, before you round a bend and Newsboy is on your left. Opposite him are the alligators and then you can walk on that same path towards Lillian, although she's giving rides today.' He smiled at them.

'And the monkeys?' Fleur asked, helplessly excited. As if they'd heard her, a sudden caterwaul began and everyone queueing behind them laughed.

'Follow the noise,' the ticket-seller suggested, joining the laughter. 'They're just warming up. The monkey enclosure is right in the middle – all paths lead into the centre, so you can do a big circle and then take any one of the paths to the monkey house and the kiosk, if you feel like some refreshment.'

Fleur and Tom thanked the man and moved together into the zoo, where it felt suddenly cooler for all the greenery that lined the pathway.

'So why is everyone so excited about Newsboy?' Tom asked, a light-hearted tone of bewilderment in his voice.

'Tom! You don't know about Newsboy?' she asked, incredulous, watching him shake his head without shame. 'Well, there is a story to it. Our hippo called Daniel sadly died after someone threw a ball into his enclosure and he swallowed it. It created a big stir and South Australians were collectively devastated. Anyway, a couple of years ago our afternoon paper – *The News*?' She paused and he nodded to show he knew what she was referring to, so Fleur continued. 'It made a public appeal, asking for donations for our zoo to have a new hippo. The newspaper kept the promotion going so long as we agreed to name the hippo what it wanted.' She gave an enquiring smile.

'Newsboy,' Tom said on cue.

'Exactly. So Newsboy eventually arrived from Auckland Zoo in 1934, courtesy of a big effort from so many people in this state, including schools and firms – it was brilliant, really. Appleby's donated twice. There was a huge celebration when he got here, and the enclosure was covered in a special wire mesh to prevent anything being thrown in there.'

'I'm impressed you know so much.'

'I'm a member of the South Australian Zoological and Acclimatisation Society.'

He smiled. 'That's a mouthful.'

She gave a shrug. 'I do love animals.'

'And the dead.'

Fleur smiled in agreement. 'Neither bring anything but privilege into my life.'

'How do you feel, though, about these amazing creatures from all over the world being caged like they are? You don't think they should be left to roam free?'

'Not in Adelaide, no,' she said dryly but quickly addressed the gravity of his question. 'Tom, I agree, this isn't ideal to have a city growing up around a compound of caged creatures, but it's their very exoticness that makes them special for city folk to see.'

He shrugged, clearly opposed to it. 'It's a tricky one. I'm as thrilled as the next person to see a lion or a polar bear, but it's not natural, is it?'

'Neither are sheep in Australia, but the First Fleet didn't seem to care about them not belonging.'

'Fair enough, but the sheep clothe us, feed us, make money for us. These animals are for our entertainment and that feels cruel.'

Fleur nodded. 'They are, but a lot of good research is done at this zoo, which they exchange with others around the world. Imagine, for instance, a world without lions, or giraffes, or monkeys.'

'I've never seen any.'

'But you want to.'

'I do. So, I'm a hypocrite, I suppose?'

'Not at all. You work with animals, you take care of them. That's what every zookeeper will say to you here – that they put the animals first. I'd rather be one of the people that campaigns for better facilities, more research, more suitable conditions. The zoo is an educational establishment as much as a pleasure park. All these people today will hopefully leave with a fresh appreciation for the creatures of the world, so when donations are needed or campaigns for new enclosures and so on are launched, they'll support them.' She raised a hand. 'Anyway, enough philosophy. Let's enjoy looking at these beautiful creatures.'

She knew Tom was about to agree when he halted, staring in wonder as an enormous grey-brown animal emerged from a hut inside the enclosure to their left. Children began to wave and call out his name as the crowd, including Tom and Fleur, hurried forward. A keeper dressed in sandy-coloured shorts and a matching shirt lifted a pail of water from the pool that Newsboy was wading through and poured it over the head of the giant, almost prehistoric-looking animal.

To shrieks of delight from the onlookers, Newsboy opened his jaws wide and the water tumbled into his gaping, cavernous mouth. Tusk-like teeth stood like sentinels at either side of his large pink tongue.

Tom laughed. 'He's brilliant. Do you know what the word hippopotamus means?'

'Oh, Tom, are you going to impress me?'

He laughed again. 'Perhaps.'

'Well, I don't know. It's such a strange word.'

'It's ancient Greek – I'm sure you can guess that much.'

She stared back at him, loving him even more for being interesting, for knowing something she didn't and for not being boorish or boastful about it. 'All right, but what does it mean?'

'It means river horse.'

'Ah.' She sighed, full of wonder. 'I like that. What else do you know about hippos?'

'You should never get between a mother hippo and her calf. Mothers have been known to kill lions, crush crocodiles and bite them in half, if her baby is threatened.'

'I knew I liked them for a reason.' She chuckled. 'Most mothers feel the same way about their young.'

Tom grinned. 'You're going to make a great mother.' He kissed the top of her head fondly and Fleur, who'd never allowed herself to dream about motherhood because she'd not met the right person, felt the rush of a strange new pleasure at the mention of it. The joy of that thought . . . to be a mother. How extraordinary and wonderful at once.

The sound of complaining metal announced the arrival of the miniature train, whose diesel engine had been designed and built by zoo staff. It eased around the corner, passing them to deposit another pile of families excited to see Newsboy.

'We'd better let others get to the front,' Fleur suggested, breaking out of her happy thoughts, and they moved on. 'We've got two ageing lions remaining and some tigers here too – two parents and three cubs . . . all grown up, though.'

'Is that the giraffe house?' Tom pointed, laughing at the height of the enclosure they were approaching.

'No giraffes at the moment, sadly. Our last one died a few years ago and, before you ask, we don't have any rhinos – but we want one. I imagine it's a case of remaining patient. We do have two female polar bears and some sun bears, though.'

They walked around the full circumference of the zoo, holding hands, smiling affectionately at excited children and being amazed by everything from the incredible pink of the flamingos to the shagginess of a new llama baby. The day was neither warm nor cold, but it wasn't windy either, so Fleur was glad she hadn't saddled herself with a coat to lug around. Besides, she was sure if she felt suddenly chilled, Tom wouldn't think twice about taking off his jacket and placing it around her shoulders.

The more time she spent with Tom, the more Fleur began to enjoy the comfortable silences between them and how unaware he was of all the women's glances that sliced his way and lingered. She allowed herself to privately enjoy their envy.

'Last night you promised to tell me about your ambitions, Fleur . . . I'm keen to hear them.'

'I've not spoken this aloud, other than alluding to it with Dad, but it seems easy to say it to you.' She smiled. 'I want to open the first all-female undertaking business in Australia.' As they continued walking, enjoying the sunshine and pleasant noise of the crowds, she explained her rationale in a similar way to how she had presented it to her father, but giving Tom plenty more detail because he seemed keen to hear it all.

Tom finally gave a small whoop of pleasure when she shrugged as they walked, suggesting that was it, he'd heard all her plans. 'That's really clever, Fleur.'

'I'm glad you think so. I'm intrigued to hear why, though.'

He seemed to sense this was a test, as though she wanted to be sure he was not just paying her lip service. 'I suppose when the time comes, I'd rather have someone like you preparing me and my loved ones than someone like Jimmy Coglin. You care. It sounds as though he cares more about income and profit. But perhaps, just more objectively, your idea is unique. Anything with a fresh approach to how we have always done things is going to win attention. I could apply that thinking to sheep shearing and wool classing and even . . .' He paused for a moment, thinking of an example. 'Well, those new electric buses. Who would have thought twenty years ago we'd have those carrying people to and fro? I imagine you have new techniques, new ways of doing things in your business from time to time.'

'We do – regularly.'

He grinned. 'But this is a big leap, I imagine. Right now, it's likely few may think what you're suggesting is a great idea, because it's so radical and it probably feels threatening too. You're going to really shake up the industry.'

'A lot of the undertakers in this state and everywhere else belong to the Freemasons. The funeral business, like the Lodge, is a male-only domain – an industry that is increasingly worth a fortune, I might add. I pay attention to news both here and internationally. I watch what's going on in our industry and, Tom, the Americans are eyeing off Australia. Their industry is massive; you'd think there would be more than enough business to go around. But I can feel their collective eyes on our nation, and I sense they think we're ripe for the picking. My father doesn't share my sentiments but he's older, set in his ways. He believes in doing things the old-fashioned way. But the very history he's come from proves that generations don't sit still. They change with the times. He changed his father's business and somewhere along the line he's forgotten that.

'I'm the next generation, and I can bring the change, but those men who dominate the funeral business sit around in their meetings and plot ways to keep it wholly male-owned. I know they've criticised my father down the years for involving his daughter, but there wasn't much they could do because Dad was one of the first in the state and certainly the first in this region to offer a proper undertaking service. They'll be overrun by the big American companies who will gobble them up.'

'Not you, though, Fleur. I can see the local blokes won't enjoy you striking out in this way.'

'I'll probably receive threats,' she jested.

'I'll protect you.'

Fleur squeezed his arm. 'You were sweet at ten, Tom, and you haven't changed despite all that's happened.' She paused walking and he followed suit, their gazes locking, and she felt as though a current had been encircling them. It had begun with slow revolutions drawing them towards one another, first relying on that childhood familiarity but increasingly over the journey of the past hour it begun to travel faster, bringing them so much closer as they shared their innermost thoughts and feelings.

Now it felt like an invisible rope bound them . . . it had connected them two decades ago but was now finally secured around them with a firm knot of secrets and emotion.

By the time they made it back to the gates, she was ready for a break. 'Shall we have a pot of tea?' she asked, checking her wristwatch. 'It's past eleven.'

'Great idea,' he said, and led them down the nearest pathway that would take them into the deepest part of the zoo. 'I know you want to see the monkeys, so let's save them to last. If we wait until noon, all the children will need feeding and I imagine picnics will be laid out, so it will be quieter at the enclosure.'

She tapped her nose. 'Smart move, Mr Catchlove. Tea and cake, then.'

14

They wound their way towards the kiosk, which was easy enough to spot with its roof brightly painted with stripes. It was already teeming with people queuing for takeaway items and outdoor tables.

'If we go inside, we might stand a better chance,' Tom suggested.

Fleur nodded. 'More expensive, though.'

'My treat.' He grinned and took her arm, guiding her into the restaurant part of the kiosk, which had bright chequered table-cloths and jugs of flowers on the tables. Sharp-eyed Tom spotted a couple preparing to leave. 'There,' he said, pointing. A waitress met them. 'May we?' Tom asked, gesturing to the table that was suddenly absent of guests.

'Of course. I'll just lay it fresh again if you don't mind waiting.'

Within minutes they had each ordered a pot of tea and a slice of cake. Fleur had gone for a wedge of jam and cream sponge cake, while Tom couldn't resist the ginger fluff sponge.

They both groaned with pleasure at their own cakes but before long they began to share.

'Can't take the country out of the boy, eh?' Fleur jested. 'I don't think I've ever tasted that before, but I think Dad has mentioned eating it as a boy.'

'Mum used to bake them for my father. Her cake would stand this tall,' he said, gesturing with hand away from the table.

She laughed. 'That's very fluffy.'

'No, that's very delicious!'

Fleur refreshed their cups of tea and sighed. 'This is lovely. Thank you for treating me like this.'

'What else can I spend my wages on other than a wonderful day out alongside a beautiful girl?'

'Any old beautiful girl?' she enquired.

He became serious, his features straightening from his previous look of amusement as he shook his head. 'There's only ever been one for me.'

Fleur covered his hand with hers and tried to convey silently through touch that she felt the same way. As she did so, she became aware of a baby's insistent cries. When Fleur stole a look, the child's mother, sitting nearby with a family, appeared calm but Fleur's impression was that she was deliberately ignoring those who had begun to stare; a quick glance around the restaurant showed several looks of pointed objection and pursed lips of disapproval at the noise interrupting their morning teas.

Fleur looked back at the scene, where a man with only one arm, it seemed, was gathering up three children, while steering the crying baby's pram, obviously making to leave. The children were clearly unhappy at being hurried away from their treats, the remainders of the famous green, pink and chocolate frog cakes, unique to Balfours Bakery of South Australia, still on their plates. The older child, a boy, turned first and ran back to the table to grab his green frog. Then the other, presumably his younger sister, howling at the notion of leaving behind her own pink frog, twisted out from her father's gentle hold. Her much younger brother also joined the charge back to the table, rushing forward and getting tangled in his sister's legs and knocking over a chair.

Fleur heard gasps from nearby tables and saw the mother's cheeks flush with embarrassment at her children's behaviour, while the baby had by now reached a new level of despair and was turning purple with the effort. A senior waitress came over and said something to the children that brought a stammering apology from the family before she turned on her heel and stalked away.

'Tom, I have to do something,' Fleur said, letting go of his hand and walking over to the table, while casting admonishing glances to all the nearby pinched expressions. He rose too, and as she admonished the diners within earshot, Tom calmly bent and picked up the chair, setting it straight. 'They're just children,' she said, exasperated, 'excited to be at the zoo and enjoying their cake. I'm sure they didn't mean to misbehave – that was a simple accident.' Not waiting for a reply, she turned to the mother. 'Excuse me for interrupting, but can I help?'

Close up, Fleur realised the mother was older than she'd appeared, perhaps in her early forties, but her figure was so trim and her complexion so lovely that they seemed to defy her age.

The woman gave Fleur a soft look of thanks. 'Our baby's not well, as you can hear, and my husband is struggling a bit with the other three.'

Fleur nodded. 'Take no notice. Perhaps these people have forgotten what it is to nurse an upset baby. What are your children's names?'

The woman told her.

Fleur smiled. 'If you'll permit me, perhaps I could take them to the monkey house? We were headed there anyway, and then you and your husband can settle down the baby. I'll keep your other children distracted but within your eyesight. I'm Fleur Appleby, by the way, and this is Tom Catchlove.' He and the woman exchanged a smile. 'Tom, would you buy some sweets please, and also some peanuts for the elephant if you can?'

'Of course. I'll settle our bill and I won't be far behind.' He nodded at Fleur and the woman, and departed.

The woman seemed to sink a little in relief. 'I'm Claire Wren. My husband is James . . . er, Jamie. And thank you, that sounds perfect.'

Fleur grinned. 'See you at the monkeys,' she said and didn't linger, making a beeline for the children who were following their father out of the restaurant.

She skipped to their side. 'Hello, I believe you are William.' The boy nodded. 'And this must be Susan.' The girl smiled shyly. 'And you must be little Matthew.'

'Matti,' he corrected.

'Right,' Fleur said, giving him a salute. She felt a moment's awkwardness reaching for their father's hand, helplessly glancing at the empty sleeve of his jacket, which he'd tucked into his pocket. 'I'm Fleur, a friend of your mother's,' she said to the children before smiling at their father. 'And you're Jamie, I gather.'

'I am, and you're . . .?'

'I'm Fleur Appleby. I offered to help out momentarily. Now, my friend Tom,' she said, pointing him out from where he stood, holding the door open for their mother, 'has bought us a bag of peanuts and I wondered if you'd like to have an elephant ride and see the monkeys?'

Their faces lit up, looking at their parents.

'Go on,' Claire said to her children, and she nodded at her husband to say all was fine.

'Mum and Dad are right behind us,' Fleur said, taking the little girl's hand. She presumed William, who looked to be about ten, wouldn't want anyone holding his hand but she saw Tom give him a wink when he looked up. She reached for Matti's tiny hand and he didn't mind a bit. 'Is that a baby sister or brother?' Fleur nodded at the pram.

'His name is Alfred, but we all call him Alfie,' Susan said.

'But he's not very well,' William chimed in.

'Yes, your mum mentioned.'

'She says we have to be prepared to let Alfie go.'

The bluntness of the statement caught Fleur by surprise and she glanced at Tom for support. He looked as disheartened as she did. 'Oh,' was all she could say as Matti decided to no longer walk, but jump each step as they started off towards their destination. She smiled sadly at his golden head.

Susan continued. 'Alfie's been sick since he was born. But Mummy says we've had Alfie in our lives for four months, and we need to be very grateful for that blessing.'

Fleur had to swallow the rise of emotion at this statement.

'Dad was in the war,' William said, oblivious to the pain their honesty was causing. 'He was badly injured and lost an arm.'

'He's a brave man, your dad,' Tom said, ruffling the lad's hair. 'Now, Fleur tells me we're off to meet an elephant.' The children laughed. 'And we have peanuts and we know her name is Lillian. Are we ready?'

'Yes!' they chorused and Fleur cut him a look of thanks for changing the atmosphere. She looked over her shoulder to where Claire and Jamie were following with baby Alfie, who was presumably settling as all the wailing had dissipated. Claire wore a look of total gratitude.

Fleur felt something pass between them. She had such a strong connection to the intense sorrow that these parents were feeling over their sick infant, while no doubt trying to keep life normal and happy for the other children. Her heart felt heavy for the family. She wanted to help them.

Tom led them down the path towards the rotunda, where the three children stopped with wide eyes to see Lillian, the young elephant, hauling around a wagonload of people. Tom cut Fleur a look of soft despair and she gave him a sympathetic smile in return. It seemed rather unfair that Lillian spent her time doing this, but Fleur would also argue that the elephant was given lots of love, plenty of food, safety and daily care by her keepers.

'So, Tom is going to help you to put peanuts on those posts all around where Lillian walks.' She pointed. 'And this clever little elephant is going to use her trunk to snaffle up your peanuts with thanks.'

Susan clapped with pleasure and William already had his hand open to be loaded up with peanuts. Tom led the children forward, while Fleur dropped back a couple of steps to their parents.

'Is this all right?'

Jamie looked relieved and Claire, expertly balancing the sleeping Alfie in one arm, squeezed Fleur's elbow with her free hand. 'You're an angel.'

Fleur shrugged. 'Not really. Your children are charming.'

'Not back in the restaurant, I don't think.' Jamie grinned. 'I might join Tom.' The women nodded as he moved off.

'I'm betting they were perfectly behaved until Alfie got upset,' Fleur reassured Claire, who nodded and looked momentarily sad. 'Susan said he's not well.'

Claire looked down for a moment. 'I can't bear to talk about it, to be honest, but the reality is that our darling Alfie won't be with us for much longer.'

Again Fleur felt like she'd been punched in the stomach by the rawness of the admission. 'Words fail me—'

'Nothing to say, truly. We've known for a while. I'm a nurse, and I've learned over the course of my career to make peace quickly with the inevitable. We've explored all avenues . . . Alfie probably shouldn't have lived at all, but he's a little fighter, like his father. This is a battle he can't win, though.'

They stood in silence for a moment, looking at the sleeping baby.

'Claire, I'm so sorry.'

The woman found a brave smile. 'I have three other beautiful children, Fleur. I must remind myself constantly to stay grateful for being as blessed as I have been. Plus, I have Jamie. For a while during the war, I didn't think I'd ever see him again.'

'He's had his own battles, I can see.'

Claire nodded. 'He says he stayed alive for me. We were both at the front in France, neither knowing the other was there. We met at Gallipoli.'

'What a story you both have.'

Now Claire smiled easily. 'It is romantic. I'll tell you about it someday.'

'I like that we might see each other again,' Fleur said, meaning it, feeling a curious and instant kinship with the older woman.

'Are you and Tom . . .?'

Fleur nodded. 'I hope so. We first met when we were young children and then didn't see each other again until yesterday.'

'Good grief! And I thought my romance was fashioned by the gods.'

Fleur laughed with genuine pleasure. 'I barely know him and yet . . . I know him. Does that make sense?'

'More than you can imagine. I think it's wonderful.'

They watched the children clambering up onto the wagon that Lillian was going to pull around the rotunda.

'The last elephant, Mary Ann, carried her passengers on one of those Indian howdahs,' Fleur explained. 'Poor little Lillian, but she is growing. They ride her to the East End Markets to an enormous weighing station.'

'You mean where they sell all the fresh goods?'

Fleur laughed. 'Yes, and the flowers and herbs. Darling thing stomps up North Terrace with a rider on her back so she can be weighed, and the zoo can make sure she's doing well.' She chuckled. 'I think I might have made a good zookeeper.'

'And what do you do, Fleur?'

Fleur cut her a cautionary glance. 'Don't be shocked but I'm a mortician.' She paused fractionally but when Claire didn't react, as many people did, she continued. 'Our family have been undertakers for several generations. I . . . er, I specialise in women and . . .' She didn't – couldn't – finish her sentence.

Claire blinked and seemed to understand. 'Well, what a special role you have.'

Fleur nodded. 'It's hard to say this to most, but I love my work. People think it's bleak or frightening, but really it's the opposite. It's uplifting . . . an honour to take care of the beloved for *their* beloved.'

'I understand. As a nurse, I always felt it was a privilege to hold a soldier's hand and hear his last words, or to sit with the dying, see them through to the end with tenderness, but also a smile. It's not a miserable thing, is it? An honour, as you say.' Claire glanced to where the two men were lifting the children down from the wagon. 'And Tom?'

'Tom is a wool classer, but he's left the sheep station to come to the city and start afresh . . . to sort of find himself.'

'Instead he found you, Fleur.'

Fleur blushed. 'I think he needs to work out his next step.'

Claire's kind eyes sparkled a little. 'It's pretty obvious to me that you are his next step.'

Fleur smiled. 'He's a country boy – I don't want to force him to stay in the big smoke.'

Claire nodded. 'So's Jamie. I'm from England and we've quite recently moved to Australia to be near Jamie's family. I have no family left, but he's from a place called Quorn, way out in this state's mid north. He tells me it's about four hundred miles north of here.' She smiled. 'You could travel from John o' Groats in Scotland to Land's End in Cornwall, and it would probably only be that far as the crow flies. Australia has such great distances – I can barely think in the vast numbers it is from place to place, and let's not forget we're still talking about the same state!'

Fleur was stunned. 'That's quite a coincidence, actually. Tom's from the north too – much further on, as I understand it, at a place called Farina, but in the same direction. They'll have plenty to share. So, are you moving to Quorn?'

'No,' Claire gusted, as though scared of the notion. 'But we'll visit soon while it stays cool, Jamie says. We thought about moving there – the bush needs more doctors and nurses – but there's nothing for Jamie out there any more . . . not in his, er, situation. So I've agreed to take on a role here in the city, in which I shall be training hundreds of new nurses, and I promise to encourage them to look to the rural regions. We've bought a big old place in an area called North Adelaide. It's a lovely, draughty old home, two storeys, big garden, and the children can walk to school. I know you feel a bit sad for us,' Claire said, glancing at Fleur, 'but don't. We have a lot to be grateful for, especially that my love came home from the war.'

Fleur withdrew a calling card from her handbag. 'Here. If you ever find yourself in need of a familiar face or a babysitter, or just a companion for the day, please don't hesitate. I'd love to talk with you again.'

'Then we shall be friends from today, Fleur. I can tell my children are already as much in love with your Tom as you seem to be. They'll never let anyone go who does that for them,' she said, pointing.

Fleur laughed as she looked over to see Tom with Matti on his shoulders and Susan balancing on his feet as he walked, arms encircling his waist. William stood next to them, laughing loudly, amused by how awkwardly Tom was being forced to move. Even Jamie was grinning.

'That one, Fleur, is a keeper,' Claire said, touching Fleur's cheek gently. 'Do you love him?'

Fleur found herself nodding but shyly. She'd never thought of herself as self-conscious, but to admit to this about a man she barely knew was a novel feeling.

'Then don't you ever let him go, no matter what. Jamie and I were suddenly separated in the early part of the war and we had no idea where the other was. But I never gave up on him. I kept faith he'd survive. And he kept faith that I would keep my promise to meet him when the war was over at a London hotel.'

Fleur smiled. 'Oh, how romantic.'

'Outrageously so and, yet, we were so in love it felt such a normal promise to make to one another, just in case we were forced apart. And then we were.'

'But you found each other,' Fleur said, sounding awed.

'Not without our private struggles, but we trusted our love was strong enough to bring us both through . . . and it did.'

'I won't doubt what I'm feeling, or him, I promise.'

Claire squeezed her wrist. 'Thank you for being so kind, and changing my day.'

Fleur felt entirely encircled by Claire's warmth and easy manner. It was as though they'd known each other for years, and she was convinced that she'd just made the first real female friend she'd ever had.

———————

Fleur and Tom farewelled the Wren family with promises to meet again soon, and then, holding hands, they returned to the monkey cages. It had been fun to share the monkeys with the children, but she'd been so focused on making sure they had a good time. Now she wanted the chance to watch the primates more closely, try and engage with them.

'It's really Mary I want to see. She's the sweetest little thing and quite the performer. There she is!' Fleur said as she spotted her leaping about with her companions.

'How do you know it's her?' Tom asked.

'She's the smallest. Arrived for Christmas a year or so ago.'

'From Africa?'

She grinned. 'Africa via the zoo in Scotland. We exchanged her for some Australian native animals and seventy pounds.'

He touched Fleur's temple. 'You carry all that information around,' he said with awe.

She grinned. 'Not much good to me. But it goes in and sticks.'

'Imagine what you'll do when you are let loose into your own company. I think we'll be able to hear that big brain of yours whirring into action.'

She smiled. 'I hope so. I've had the best day, Tom. Thank you.'

He shrugged. 'It was your idea. I should be thanking you.'

'No, you see, someone like Jimmy Coglin would never have found today as interesting as you have. You raised questions that forced me to consider how I feel about cages and zoos in general. Jimmy would have thrown peanuts at the monkeys or got up on that wagon and expected Lillian to drag him around. He's the kind of fellow who'd throw a ball into the hippo compound . . . Jimmy is a lightweight, immature, not nearly enough man for me.'

'I hope I am?'

'Well, there's plenty of you for a start,' she said, letting her gaze roam over his height and width.

Outside her home, because it was daylight Tom seemed to take the precaution of kissing her gently on the cheek before kissing her hand. 'I'll see you day after tomorrow for dinner. Thank you again for the invitation.'

'I can't wait for Dad to meet you again. He's going to get such a surprise.'

'Why?'

'You were a weedy sort of kid, I recall. Nothing weedy about you now.'

He winked. 'Nothing,' he said, raising an eyebrow and she burst into laughter at his cheekiness as he hurried away, laughing too.

15

Today was going to be as busy as it would be physically demanding. Fleur had two corpses to care for; one for local burial, which would be the simpler of the two, and one who would be sent to Port Augusta on the train. She anticipated embalming the latter – usually an all-day task – so she would have to work intently and swiftly today. Replacing someone's entire network of veins and arteries with chemicals after draining the blood required as much mental focus as physical exertion; making sure a pinkish complexion could be maintained through the journey this person was yet to make was the challenge. Fleur wanted his relatives to be able to grieve over someone they recognised, who didn't frighten them with a grey pallor.

The knowledge that she was seeing Tom again tomorrow evening made it easier on her mind and it was the evening meal that occupied her in this moment.

'Nan, is there anything I can do to help? Any shopping you need?'

Nan did most of the cooking now that Irma no longer even pretended to attend to duties in the kitchen. Fleur had to wonder exactly what Irma did with all her spare hours.

'No, your father ordered a roasted chicken. I have all we need for this evening, Miss Appleby, but we've run out of some staples that Mrs Appleby wants and I'm nervous that I won't have time. Jean isn't here today to help.'

'Then let me fetch them. I've got to go out briefly, so give me a list. I'll do them now before I begin my day's work.'

'Are you sure, Miss Appleby? I don't want to get you into trouble.'

Fleur laughed. 'You won't. And Nan, I've told you before, please call me Fleur.' She worried that Nan was so spooked by Irma's rules that she might just curtsey, but fortunately, she gave Fleur a shy smile.

'I'm sorry, I will. I forget.'

Fleur smiled back. 'I'll make the list, hang on.' She fetched a used envelope and licked the pencil she kept tucked into her hair during her working day. 'Right, fire away.'

'We'll need some more butter, Miss, and some, um, white pepper. Mrs Appleby likes to have marmalade and we're running low on Yo Yo biscuits. Oh, and a fresh tin of chocolate powder, please, if you can. Mrs Appleby likes to make your father a milky drink at night . . . er, if he's home.'

Nan met Fleur's gaze and she flushed slightly; she hadn't meant it pointedly but they both knew he was so rarely home of an evening.

'My father never used to drink anything before bed; he always said it gave him indigestion.'

Nan shrugged. 'Mrs Appleby insists. She likes to make it and carry it up to him just before bed, so she tells me.'

Fleur shook her head, baffled. 'Anything else? Meat, cream, salt, sugar, flour, tomato sauce?'

Nan shook her head at all those suggestions. 'No, we're good. Oh, yes!' she said, looking relieved to have remembered. 'We need more rat poison.' She blew out a breath. 'Mrs Appleby would have skinned me if I'd forgotten that.'

'Rat poison?' Fleur repeated. 'Whatever for? I haven't seen any rats.' As she said it, she privately corrected herself, imagining Irma as a huge rat using all the same conniving intelligence.

Nan shrugged. 'I might have seen one when I first arrived, but not in the house – it was out in the street, actually. I haven't spotted any since.'

'Nan, you said more rat poison.'

'Yes.' The woman sighed.

Fleur shook her head in query.

'We had a box, because I picked it up for Mrs Appleby when I started. But she reminded me yesterday that we need a new one.' Nan shrugged again in a don't-shoot-the-messenger kind of way.

Fleur's forehead creased deeply. 'But Irma doesn't lift a finger around the house. Why on earth would she be attending to rats?' She bristled. 'Non-existent ones.'

'Maybe it's the mortuary,' Nan offered hesitantly.

'Nan, Dad and I are clinically clean in there. Never any food or drinks taken in, not even drinking water. Every receptacle, every piece of equipment, is scrupulously cleaned daily, plus once bodies are dealt with they're sent on or certainly closed up and gone within a day. And I doubt Irma has ever set foot in there to know. She wouldn't have a clue about it.' Fleur frowned. 'No, we've not seen a rat in as long as I can recall.'

'Please don't get me into trouble,' Nan said, looking suddenly mortified.

'May I see the old box?'

'I might have thrown it away. Wait a tick.' Nan returned soon enough with it. She rattled it for effect and they both heard the remnants of crumbly dust.

'May I? Thanks.' Fleur took it from Nan. 'I'll make sure to get another one now I know the brand she prefers.'

Tuesday morning arrived, bringing the news that her father wasn't feeling well.

'What do you mean?' she asked Irma, who was tucking greedily into eggs and bacon at the breakfast table.

'I mean he's not well,' Irma repeated, sounding exasperated by the enquiry.

'What sort of unwell?'

'Fleur, I'm many things but I'm not a doctor,' she replied, effectively closing her part of this conversation.

Fleur decided she no longer cared about the pretence of courtesy, especially as they were alone. 'You are indeed many things, Irma, and among them is that you lack a shred of empathy for anyone.'

Irma slammed her cutlery down onto her plate. They locked gazes of hate.

Fleur hadn't finished. 'Why are you not up there with him, instead of feeding your face down here?'

'I'm also not a nurse.'

Fleur could see she was deliberately trying to enrage her step-daughter in saying so and she had to admit it was working.

'I'm no use to him,' Irma continued, feigning helplessness.

'I agree. You are absolutely no use to him at all!' Fleur flung down her napkin next to her cooling porridge and walked upstairs to her father's room. She knocked gently, and then stepped into his bedroom. The curtains were still closed. 'Dad?' She moved across to the window and opened them slightly, watching him wince as the sunlight hit his gaze. 'Sorry, Dad. Let me open these and get some air in,' she said, taking the liberty of opening the window a crack.

She was at his bedside in moments and took his hand, noting the roughness of his skin, as though small warts were appearing. She made an effort not to show how worried she was by the change to his skin colour. She could see patches that had darkened, while other areas looked livid. He also looked confused.

He blinked at her, his expression groggy. 'What time is it?'

'Past eight, Dad.'

'I won't make church.'

Fleur gave a small gasp. 'It's Tuesday, Dad.'

Henry frowned. 'That can't be right.'

'It is. We have to pick up from the Bedfords, and Mrs Smith from hospital.'

'Already?'

She nodded. 'What's going on, Dad?'

He shook his head. 'I don't know, Fleur. I feel so drowsy and blurry in my mind.'

'I think I'm going to call for the doctor.'

'You'll do no such thing, my girl. I just need some help.'

Fleur crooked her elbow around his and watched as he swung his tall, suddenly painfully thin legs around and placed his feet on the ground.

'Give me a few moments.'

She waited. 'Have you let it slip your mind that Tom Catchlove is coming this evening?' Fleur asked, simply for something to say into an otherwise tense silence.

'Tom? Ah, yes. I'm looking forward to seeing him. Right, help me to stand, please, my love.' She did. 'There. I'll go bathe.'

'Dad, you won't make the Bedfords.'

'Then you'll have to go.'

Fleur paused, shocked at his remark.

'What?' he asked, as though what he'd suggested was the most obvious idea to ever pass his lips. 'You've bleated about wanting to give women an opening into undertaking. Here's your chance. Prove it . . . prove to me that a woman can.'

She didn't know whether to laugh or weep. Instead, she kissed her father. 'I'll take care of it. You get ready for the day and for picking up Mrs Smith.'

'No, you can do her as well. I think I'll work on accounts today. I want to be as fresh and alert as I can to meet your young man.'

'He's not my—'

'Fleur, my darling,' he interjected. 'You forget I've known you since before you knew yourself properly. I know all your moods, all the subtle shifts within your temperament, and when you so much as say the name Tom Catchlove, your eyes light up.'

Fleur was relieved to hear him sounding more himself.

'They certainly don't light up for Jimmy Coglin, Dad,' she said, taking her chances.

'No. I don't know what was in my mind agreeing to that.'

'Irma is in your mind and your ear about all that she wants. Jimmy is her plan, not yours or mine. My plan is to protect your legacy and our business.'

He hugged her and in that embrace it felt as though she had her father back, the one she remembered alongside her mother.

'I hope Tom is the right person for you, Fleur. It would please your darling mother, may her soul rest, for you to be happy in marriage and family.'

Fleur nodded, her eyes watering with emotion. 'I hope he is too. I like him and I want you to like him.'

'I'm sure I shall. So, off you go. Prove to me you can take over this business and set it on its new path, Fleur.'

Fleur stared at her father. 'You mean that, don't you?'

He sighed with a soft shrug. 'Look at me. I'm getting old, getting weary. I must hand over to the next generation at some point, and it's no good me hoping things will remain the same when

I do. I changed things from when my father had the business. Why shouldn't you have the same freedom?'

'Dad,' she murmured. 'I . . . I'm stunned. I don't know what to say.'

'Say you'll make me proud, as you always have.' He found a tender smile and she kissed his cheeks. 'Go on, you don't want to be late. Make my apologies and let's see how they cope with you fetching Mrs Smith. Robbie will drive. He's become very reliable behind the wheel.'

———

Fleur had secretly designed and ordered a charcoal outfit in the hope that this day might eventually arrive. It was a dress made from mourning crepe, a special fabric that had allowed the Courtaulds brand from Essex, England, to build a new and extremely profitable empire. While she had chosen it so that the widows she met might feel comforted, she privately acknowledged that the need for special fabrics for the grieving was on the wane. It was her intention to help speed that process; not only was it expensive, but it was cumbersome. She far preferred the idea that widows – and all grieving women – could feel confident to wear the colours of half mourning as soon as they felt capable of facing everyday life again. Those colours ranged from subdued greys to quiet violets, purples and heliotrope.

However, for now, on her first official visit as the undertaker of Appleby's, she wanted to observe every respectful part of the 'code' that she could, so while black felt too much, the new charcoal dress felt deferential. It included a soft lace in white at the collar and sleeves, which she hoped would subtly encourage women in sorrow to not feel ashamed of adornment. She also wore her mother's modest and very simply designed Whitby Jet ring that her father had given Mae following their marriage. Fleur had effectively stolen it from her mother's jewellery case soon after her passing and was glad that at eleven she'd had the courage to do so, because Irma had pillaged everything her mother had owned. This was all Fleur had of Mae's jewellery and, although it was a rather Victorian notion to wear a mourning ring, it felt precious to Fleur because it spoke to the work that had given their family its livelihood.

The man who answered the door at the Bedfords' blanched. 'Sorry, no callers, please. We were expecting the undertaker.'

'Good morning, sir. I'm Henry Appleby's daughter, and I have been undertaking with him since I was old enough to work,' Fleur said, glad her voice did not shake.

He frowned. 'But you're a woman.'

'Thank you for noticing, and I gather I'm here to meet another one – Mr Bedford's wife?'

In his confusion he nodded. 'Helen, yes. My sister.'

'Ah, thank you,' Fleur said, stepping forwards gently but firmly, not waiting for permission.

He had no choice but to step aside but Fleur paused and held out a hand. 'Fleur Appleby,' she said.

'Allen Dawkins,' he replied, looking perplexed as he met her clear gaze.

'Is Mrs Bedford through here?' Fleur pointed down the corridor of the small house, and now she did await his permission.

He nodded. 'In the back. He's laid out there.'

She returned the nod with the barest of smiles. 'My colleagues, Robbie and Albert,' she gestured, 'will wait outside until Mrs Bedford feels ready.' She didn't wait for him to say any more but stepped down the hallway, trying not to let her heels make any noise on the boards.

She found herself in the parlour, where a corpse was laid out in his pyjamas and dressing-gown on the table. Before she even looked around the room, Fleur automatically began making plans for his preparation. She judged that he was likely five hours dead at worst;

rigor was in the face for sure, so it was travelling now through the body, blood pooling at his back. She needed to get Arthur Bedford to the mortuary and change the angle of his body to help prevent signs of lividity.

Satisfied with the beginnings of a plan, she looked up. A woman with swollen, red-rimmed eyes regarded her.

Fleur introduced herself quickly. 'My father isn't very well today, Mrs Bedford. I work with him daily and so I hope you don't mind that I have come to attend to your husband.'

The woman blinked. 'We . . . we brought him down here.'

Fleur nodded. 'Do you have children?'

'Two. They're at school. The doctor came yesterday, and warned me my Arthur wouldn't make it through the night. Well, he did. He called to me as the birds began singing. Had time to kiss his son and daughter farewell.'

Although she felt her emotions being stirred by Helen's words, Fleur let a small smile break across her face, sensing this is what was needed in the moment.

'Arthur said he couldn't see anything but he could hear the dawn chorus and it was calling him to rest. "I won't be going to the docks today, love," he said,' Helen recalled aloud, tears welling and spilling down her cheeks.

Fleur wanted to get the lads in immediately to cart Arthur Bedford away but that wouldn't do. A family needed time to let go. 'Would you like a cup of tea, Mrs Bedford?'

The widow looked up in surprise. 'Thank you. I haven't eaten or drunk anything. It was all I could do to give our children some porridge and get them away this morning. They were so good . . . I was in too much of a state. They helped draw the curtains and stop the two clocks in the house.'

'What time was the sad hour, may I ask?'

'It was three minutes to six when my Arthur passed.'

Fleur glanced at her watch and calculated that Arthur had passed about three hours and twenty minutes earlier. 'Thank you, I'll remember that for our arrangements,' she said, thinking about the small cast-iron piece her father had commissioned. It showed a clock face, beautifully rendered in iron, with curiously delicate hands that could be set to the time of death. He placed it on the coffin to inform mourners and prevent the upsetting question that always seemed to be on people's lips. It was a small but special kindness to protect the grieving family, but Fleur understood it to be yet another reason that Appleby's had flourished. 'It's the small things that add up, Fleur, remember that,' he'd counselled. 'No matter how inconsequential to you, it's resonating somewhere with someone. If it has a positive effect, it will be remembered.'

Making her client a pot of tea was another small kindness. 'No, don't get up. Let me,' Fleur said, filling a kettle.

'My brother needs to get to work.'

'Let me tell him to carry on. I'm here now. I won't be leaving you and I won't be hurrying you. Is anyone else coming over?'

Helen nodded. 'My mother and Arthur's sister are coming over this morning.'

'Good. Then I'll wait with you until they do.' Fleur lit the stove and put the kettle on; the sound of the gas flame gurgling was comforting in the most domestic of ways. 'You can tell me about Arthur. I'll just speak with your brother.'

She found him lurking uncomfortably in the short hallway and Fleur suggested he go to his work.

He looked confused. 'But who will . . .?'

'I will, Mr Dawkins. I shall sit with your sister and your brother-in-law until the relatives arrive. Then, when I know Mrs Bedford feels ready, I will have Mr Bedford transferred to our funeral home and we will take care of him until all the arrangements are made for his interment.'

'You'll do this? I mean, you personally?'

Fleur nodded. 'Of course. I'm an Appleby. It's what we do.' Her father might have slid her a glance of caution for showing too much pride, but she had a different style and he'd urged her to prove she could do this alone.

Mr Dawkins found a smile at her remark.

'Please don't worry,' she reassured him. 'I'll keep your sister comforted until she has family around her. We're about to have a pot of tea together . . . You get off, don't be late.'

He shook his head, and the gesture spoke of gratitude mingling with wonder, she decided. Fleur could tell he was impressed.

'I'll just say my goodbyes, then.'

Fleur gave him a smile. 'And I'll let the boys know outside to cool their heels a while.' She stepped out, informed her two companions that they were waiting for family members to arrive and took from them the items she had deliberately brought with her.

'Thank you again,' the brother said as he pulled on his cap and left the house, and she could tell he meant it.

Fleur returned to make the tea, taking the time to warm the pot. Helen was resting her head in her hands, and Fleur understood the woman was coming to terms with the fact that the man laid out on the table was no longer her husband, but the vessel that held him. That's what Fleur needed to see happening; then she knew she would feel comfortable to make a bolder move when the right moment came along. Arthur's soul had already been set free, and Fleur saw the kitchen window was open to permit that; the window in the bedroom where he'd died was probably open to the chill morning air for the same purpose. She reheated the kettle, bringing it back to boiling, and while she waited for the telltale whistle, she reached for a tin, guessing that it might be the tea caddy as she didn't wish to disturb the widow's thoughts.

'Er, no, the other one,' the woman said hastily as Fleur paused, her hand on the tin. 'I use that one to store rat poison.'

A chill went through Fleur as the pieces clicked into place. Fleur stared at her half-amused, mouth open. 'Good grief!'

'We have a bit of a problem in this street and I can handle the odd mouse, but the rats look large enough to carry my children away.' Helen made an attempt at a smile.

Fleur gave the chuckle that was needed. 'Do you know, I've learned we may have a similar problem in our street.' She still didn't believe it, but Helen's admission gave more credence to Irma's actions.

'Arthur put the rat killer in there. I told him at the time it wasn't a bright idea to put it in the old tea tin, especially not having it in the kitchen.' Tears welled again. 'That was only two days ago when the new box he bought got damp.'

Fleur spoke quickly to distract her. 'Shall I put the tin up on this shelf instead, nice and high?' She opened it first. 'I've never actually seen rat poison. Can it kill us as well, I wonder?' Her question was rhetorical; she knew it was toxic.

'Awful stuff. Liver goes first. You've heard of arsenic being the best way to get rid of your husband?' she quipped and then realised what she'd said. Her expression crumpled. 'Oh, no!' She began to weep.

Fleur quickly put her arm around the woman's shaking shoulders. 'Come on, now. I know you didn't mean that. Tell me more about Arthur while we wait.'

After sharing the pot of tea she'd made for them, and listening to Helen Bedford's tears come, dry and then return at happier recollections of her life with her husband, Fleur removed a small box from the bag she'd brought.

'Helen,' she said, glad to be on first-name terms now. 'I've brought two items for you. Firstly, I want you to have this gift.' She handed the box to her companion, who frowned as it was placed in her hands.

'What's this?'

Fleur smiled. 'A small token from Appleby's. Thank you for choosing us to look after your husband until he reaches his final resting place. We hope you can enjoy using this to keep remembering all the good times,' she said, nodding so Helen might feel encouraged to lift the lid.

She did, and gasped. 'A locket. For me?'

Fleur couldn't help the jolt of delight she felt inside at Helen's pleasure. This was something she'd wanted to do for a few years, but she had only recently had the courage to have the lockets made. She'd ordered only a dozen, using her savings, but she knew they would be a powerful way of spreading the good word. Helen's response only reinforced what she'd anticipated, and Fleur knew she would now produce many more with company money – if her father was prepared to provide it – to give lockets to widows and grieving mothers as part of her service.

'It's engraved,' Helen said, in awe.

Fleur didn't wish to correct her that it was enamelled, and simply smiled. 'It says "Not lost, but gone before", which I think is a rather lovely sentiment to keep in your mind about Arthur.'

'Oh, Fleur, it's beautiful.' Helen wept.

'Open it,' Fleur encouraged her. 'And perhaps you can put a small photo of Mr Bedford in there so he's always close to your heart.' She quickly handed Helen a handkerchief. 'Don't apologise,' she said before Helen could remonstrate. 'It would be unusual if you didn't cry. These are good tears on behalf of a good man who will be missed.'

Helen nodded. 'But never forgotten,' she whispered, dabbing at her eyes. 'Oh, I know just the picture to use. Thank you. I don't know what to say. This is most touching.'

'I'm glad you like it,' Fleur said. 'And in the hallway, Helen, I've put a laurel wreath. With your permission, I might hang it on your door, so your neighbours understand there has been a death and you won't be disturbed by casual callers. But maybe the close neighbours will want to visit and commiserate.'

Helen shook her head in disbelief. 'I can't believe how kind you are, Fleur. I'm going to have to tell everyone at work about you – I'm a nurse at the hospital. I hope you don't mind?'

'I don't mind a bit! I'd love you to let all those you know that Appleby's is developing its service. I want to offer grieving women especially a small sense of lightness in their hearts in whatever manner I can, whether it's by being supportive of their needs, or through these tiny gifts to show we care about those left behind as much as we care for those who have passed.'

Helen nodded. 'I called Appleby's because your father collected and organised the burial of my father. Are you in charge of the funeral parlour now?'

'One day. I think my father would like to retire and hand over the reins.'

'I didn't think a woman could . . .'

'What?'

'Oh, you know.' She shrugged.

Fleur thought she might as well start presenting her argument now. 'I think a woman can do anything she sets her mind to, and I personally think the time is here for us to become more visible in funerals.'

'How brave you are.'

'Not really,' Fleur said. 'I don't have a family to care for – not yet, anyway. I love my work and I want to do it to the very best of my ability . . . and I think I'm every bit as good as any other funeral director in Adelaide, to be honest.'

Helen leaned forward. 'No, Fleur, you're better,' she said, looking surprised by her own admission. 'You're not stuffy or frightening. When my uncle died, I was young. He lived with us, and I think I was more upset by the careless attitude shown to his body when they were collecting him than his actual death. And their sombre faces only made the atmosphere worse.' She held up a hand before Fleur could respond. 'Not Appleby's, of course. When my father passed, yours was kind but he was nonetheless grave. You've helped me this morning to breathe again.'

Fleur nodded. 'I do think a woman's touch can make a difference . . . especially to widows and grieving mothers.'

'I believe you. I like the idea that my Arthur will be taken care of by you.'

There was a soft knock in the distance.

'Ah, that might be your family coming to offer comfort,' Fleur said. 'May I let them in?'

Helen sighed and nodded. 'May we have a little more time with Arthur?'

'As long as you need.' Fleur smiled gently. 'And Helen, when you're ready to face work, don't go to the hospital. Please come and see me. I think I could use someone with nursing experience.'

She rose to let the murmuring family members in, smiling softly in welcome and pointing them towards the back of the house, and departed as quietly as she'd entered.

16

Once she had returned to the mortuary, Fleur immediately got to work preparing Arthur Bedford. The family wanted him buried as soon as possible, and Helen's mother had just rung to say they had spoken to the church and organised a service for the day after tomorrow.

Fleur checked his pyjama pocket to make sure nothing valuable was left behind and found a fresh flower tucked inside. She felt the precious love of that moment, wondering if Helen had done this . . . or perhaps it was her daughter who'd placed that flower before she left for school, trying to comprehend that her father was dead in his bed.

Shaking off the thought, Fleur immediately set to the business of getting Arthur readied. That was how she thought of him now; he was no longer Mr Bedford, but her new friend and companion for the next couple of hours. She busied herself elevating his head and hands to minimise the lividity that was already beginning to show itself. She did not want to be fighting against the eruption of dark red and purple on his face or hands that the accumulation of blood after death brought. She cast a glance at the clock;

it was now seven hours since his death. Fleur took the precaution of lowering his legs, using the clever table her father had designed and had made just for this reason. Its levers meant she could effortlessly ensure that gravity would drain away the various fluids from the man's visible features without requiring any strength.

Fleur turned slightly to where a pen and her mortuary book sat. She had already recorded the name and details of her 'guest', and now she would make quick notes about his preparation in case they were ever needed. She could not recall a time when they had been called upon, but her father was meticulous and had insisted that when the day occurred that someone did need a question answered, Appleby's would be ready to supply that answer to the best of its ability.

'Take notes about everything that you do or you observe. It's professional . . . good practice,' he'd told her many times from when she was old enough to be in the mortuary, when she had asked him about his big book – which would soon become *her* big book, she supposed.

There were many similar volumes filed on their shelves, all identical in appearance. She smiled, never failing to be impressed by her father's diligence. She felt determined to follow his footsteps, but perhaps taking a parallel path that looked to new ways without losing those old, important practices that had built their reputation.

Helen had placed a heavy penny over each of Arthur's eyes; it was a death ritual that went back centuries to when pebbles were placed over the eyes, back even to the ancient Egyptians – masters of the death ritual – who would paint eyes on the stones. Fleur had noted that Helen, from an Irish family, followed the old ways, including opening the window to let her husband's spirit out to roam free, shutting curtains, stopping clocks, covering mirrors and insisting he be carried out feet first from the house. None of these practices were new to Fleur and she had observed Helen's wishes good naturedly, smiling at the memory of Helen claiming to have heard a dog barking just moments before her husband passed.

'It was the omen,' she'd told Fleur, who chose not to mention that there were plenty of dogs in this neighbourhood and it was highly likely that barking occurred most nights. 'That dog foretold my Arthur's passing,' Helen had assured her family as Fleur waited in the shadowy hallway.

Fleur now removed the coppers gently, surprisingly still warmed from Arthur's eyelids. She clutched them in her palm and spoke a short blessing over his life, asking that his spirit would find its way home safely. It was curious that they were both 1933 pennies, but Fleur had become accustomed to the detail that people observed for even the simplest of acts while in shock at the death of someone close. Perhaps 1933 had been a special year for their family or a milestone for the couple, like a wedding anniversary. She rather enjoyed wondering about these aspects of the person she was preparing; the diversion of thought somehow helped her to focus on the mostly mechanical tasks even more intently. It also prevented her from regarding the person as a corpse, when every inch of them was still someone's child, someone's parent, someone's lover.

The weight of the coppers felt reassuring, their engraving still unworn. One side clearly depicted the King, the other the Commonwealth of Australia. Fleur neatly placed the pennies, one on top of the other, on the page of her book next to the wilted flower; she would return them to Helen Bedford with a kind note, along with Arthur's pyjamas and dressing-gown, knowing it would reinforce the thoughtful service of Appleby's. However, there was a likelihood that Helen would not want her pennies returned. They were, after all, a tithe, attached to the notion of paying 'a penny for the ferryman' so Arthur's soul could move safely over the infernal rivers in Hades.

One of the lads arrived to help undress Arthur. 'Gently, Robbie,' Fleur said, as she always did.

He grinned and nodded. Out of respect, she averted her gaze as Robbie removed the robe and pyjamas and, when she turned back from her book after recording the presence of the two pennies and the flower – a daisy, she had noted – Arthur was naked but his modesty had been protected by a wide piece of linen across his hips. She and her father had set up this practice from many years ago, not because a woman was present in the mortuary, but to show respect for the person lying on their table.

'Thank you, Robbie. Can you and Albert be back in about'— Fleur frowned as she checked her wristwatch—'an hour and a half?'

'Easy,' he said.

'The coffin's ready?'

He nodded. 'I've put on the handles. You just have to do your bits inside, Miss.'

'That's good. Do you want to do the packing?'

He looked hesitant. 'I've only done it twice with your father.'

'That's all right. I'm here, I know exactly what to do.' She nodded her encouragement. 'Let me clean him first. Ten minutes?'

He departed, leaving Fleur to the first of the jobs to prepare Arthur for his coffin.

'I'm going to give you a nice soothing wash,' she said to her silent companion. Fleur began sponging every inch of Arthur's exposed body, then took care as she washed his hair. Robbie arrived in time to take care of the regions that he'd covered earlier with the linen, which included packing the orifices to minimise odours or leakage. She was sure that the time was fast approaching where even this nod of courtesy would likely fall away, and the team of women that she planned to assemble would take care of preparing the bodies fully, whether they were male or female. Her argument would be that in days gone it was always the women of the household who prepared a corpse for its final journey, irrespective of its sex. It was done with love, mostly, and a lot of respect, and gave the woman of that house a special time during her early grieving to show her care for whomever had passed within the walls of her home.

Fleur loved this traditional role and was keen to be part of returning that responsibility to women again. *We just do it better*, she thought, reaching for the shaving kit. Then she spoke aloud, making Robbie smile as he finished up his task. 'Let's get that chin of yours beautifully smooth, Arthur, so the family can kiss you goodbye without getting poked by your whiskers.'

Fleur spent another ten minutes carefully shaving Arthur's stiffened face and was grateful that he had no moustache to contend with. She dabbed his face dry of all soap and water, satisfied the early preparation was now complete. She checked quickly over his exposed body for any wounds or sores and found none.

It was time to close Arthur's mouth. No one at the Bedford home had thought to put a towel beneath his chin, so Arthur's jaw gaped helplessly and was now set in that expression by rigor. She would need to suture. She moved to her side table to thread her needle with the fine black thread. There were simple sutures or more elaborate, invisible stitches that her father had taught her from a young age. Appleby's always used the invisible technique, while others chose to go the easier, faster route, but Fleur's slim fingers made swift work of the looping stitch, which began on the inside of Arthur's mouth at the base of his teeth in the lower jaw. She ran the stitch expertly up through the gums of his upper teeth, just above the front pair, and her needle moved deftly and unseen through one of the nostrils, piercing the septum to arrive into the other nostril, before travelling invisibly back into the mouth cavity, where the thread could be gently pulled to close the jaw.

She watched Arthur's chin move precisely to her instructions and, satisfied that his mouth would sit neatly in rest, she tied off the thread. The skin of Arthur's face was still malleable and she knew she had time to set his lips so he would look relaxed and untroubled, should Helen wish to see him once more. Fleur checked Arthur's newly washed hands and decided to clip his fingernails, which she did quickly and then filed down any sharp edges. 'Now we can fold your hands and they'll look neat and groomed,' she assured him.

'Time to close your eyes now, Arthur,' she said, always comfortable talking to the people in her mortuary who never replied. 'You've seen your children grow, you've lived a good life with a good woman, and now it's time to sleep.'

As she spoke, she lifted the lid of Arthur's right eye, which hadn't closed and was wanting to pull open even further – and would, without her ministrations. The iris gave the appearance of having been drained of colour and was now greyish. She hadn't known the true colour of his eyes, but the opacity that occurred in the cornea after death meant that everyone's eyes tended to appear a flattish blue-grey. His pupils were predictably enlarged, another sign of death.

'Being able to narrow the pupils requires muscles in motion, doesn't it, Arthur? Your muscles are now quiet,' she continued amiably, as though keeping him company through her process. 'I want you to look your best for Helen and the children, so I don't want to risk your eyes flattening behind your lids . . . I'm just going to do this gently,' she said, beginning to pack a pledget of lint behind each lid. Fleur had done this so many times now that her fingers worked with expertise to fashion a smooth layering, indistinguishable behind the eyelid. Again her invisible stitching prowess came to the fore.

His eyelids now firmly closed, Fleur stood back. 'Let's get you dressed into your smart Sunday suit.' She cast a soft smile of thanks to Robbie, who had been hovering to help.

'You're amazing, Miss. He looks so good.'

Together they dressed Arthur, and Fleur was pleased to note that Robbie moved in perfect concert with her, rolling the body and lifting the head as needed. While he did up Arthur's trousers, she focused on achieving a neat knot at his tie.

They both took a step back to check their work. 'You look very handsome, Arthur,' she remarked and gave Robbie a nod. 'I'm just going to work on Arthur's face for a few moments, so you can bring in the coffin.'

'Will do,' he said and disappeared.

Fleur spent a final couple of minutes smoothing Arthur's skin with a make-up she had carefully colour-matched. It was the lightest of applications, simply to give a covering against the inevitable mottling that would occur between now and tomorrow. Next she dusted on a thin layer of powder to set the stickier make-up and finally she tidied his eyebrows, manipulated his lips, though they didn't need much manoeuvring, and reached for her comb.

The lads arrived with the coffin. Fleur looked at the portrait of Arthur in life. In it his hair was cut neatly around his ears, and she decided she might just give him a trim now. With the pair of sharp scissors she kept for this task, Fleur did her best to approximate the neatness of Arthur's hair in the image. She knew a lot of the funeral homes didn't pay sufficient attention to these actions and so often family members wept, claiming they didn't recognise their loved ones lying there in their final sleep. Fleur wanted her dead to prompt a soft smile of affection from their families. They would look like the person they remembered, as though they were simply sleeping; that was always her aim. It wasn't always possible, of course, depending on the state of the body. Sometimes the person had been dead for too long or had been involved in an accident. That was usually when Henry suggested to the family that they didn't have an open coffin for viewing.

'But you look at peace, Arthur, and now I'll just comb your hair how you like it,' she said, wetting the comb and dragging it expertly through his already moistened hair. She achieved his straight parting on the correct side. 'There!' Fleur finished with soft triumph.

Both lads nodded their approval. Fleur supervised as they carefully lifted Arthur into his coffin, and she smoothed a hand beneath him to keep his jacket straight as they laid him down.

'Right, I'll just get the inside sewn up and his hands in place.' She sniffed. 'What's that awful smell, boys?'

Robbie nodded. 'I got that earlier. I thought it was him,' he said, tipping his head at Arthur.

'It's not,' she assured him. 'But whatever is causing it is turning rank.' She pulled a face. 'It smells like fish.'

They both agreed.

'Best close the door. I don't want it corrupting the mortuary.'

She frowned as they left the room. Fish certainly wasn't being cooked today for the dinner with Tom. But she didn't have time to think further. She had other corpses to attend to.

17

The table was simple; Fleur had taken care of setting it herself. The menu of stuffed roast chicken, accompanied by peas and mashed potato made creamy with hot milk and butter and a good pinch of salt, would be enjoyed by all. She enjoyed the domesticity of shelling the peas while Nan stepped out to their tiny herb patch to pick some parsley for the stuffing and some mint to boil up with the peas.

'Phew! Smells out there,' Nan said, bustling back in with a small bowl of herbs. The grassy fragrance of the curly parsley was pleasantly overwhelmed by the fresh scent of mint, cool and woody, and filling the kitchen with its potency.

'All I can smell is beautiful mint,' Fleur said, rubbing one of the leaves and inhaling. 'Is it the traffic fumes?'

Nan frowned. 'No, it's a bad smell. Something's off.'

'Ah, that again,' Fleur said. 'We'll hunt that down. Now, how's the pudding coming along? Anything I can do?'

Nan smiled. 'I've made a lot of jam roly-polys in my life. This is a good one.'

'Lovely. Thanks, Nan. Dad said in his day they called it "dead man's arm".'

Nan chuckled. 'In our house it was "dead man's leg".'

'Seems appropriate for Appleby's,' Fleur remarked, as they shared a grin. 'Well, if you want me to make the custard or—'

'All under control, Miss. Why don't you go and get ready for your young man?'

Fleur did, and just before five she found Henry and Irma already awaiting their guest. Henry was in the armchair sipping an ale. He looked ashen but seemed to be in bright spirits.

'I heard about the good work you did today, Fleur.'

'Did you check in on Mr Bedford?'

'I certainly did. He looked exceptional, my dear. Perfect skin colouring.'

'His eyes?'

'I couldn't have done better and before you ask, yes, I looked in his mouth. You really did an amazing job on him. Very neat. You've done our family and his family proud.'

Fleur sat up straighter. It had been a long time since she'd received this sort of praise from her father, and a glance at Irma told her that her stepmother was not enjoying it.

Irma's pinched lips moved. 'Dinner is rather early, isn't it?'

'Only by half an hour. Besides, Dad likes to eat early.' Fleur shrugged, knowing it was so he could make it to the pub for a quick one. 'He might take Tom to the pub for a drink after dinner.'

Henry nodded as though he didn't disapprove of the idea.

'Tell me again why we're meeting this fellow? I really don't like strangers—'

'He's not a stranger, Irma. We've known him since I was a child; I just haven't seen him since those days. But he's lovely and I like him even more now.'

'How much more?' Irma demanded. 'It seems you're going to a lot of trouble.'

'Not really. A mere fraction of the effort and money you put into the Coglins.' Fleur kept her tone sounding reasonable but hoped it felt like the barb she intended.

'I was going to get Henry some lovely Coffin Bay oysters for tonight, but he stopped me.'

Henry gave Fleur a look of soft despair. 'No one is to fuss. I seem to remember suggesting a roast chicken anyway.'

Fleur frowned. 'Oysters, though . . . tonight? Normally we have them Friday night.'

'What's wrong with that? You father enjoys them and they're good for him. They'll restore his strength.'

'How do you know this, Irma?'

'My father always spoke about the power-packed oyster, if you don't mind.'

'Speaking of seafood, there's a strange smell around,' Fleur commented.

Irma gave a grimacing smile. 'Well, I wonder what that could be?' Her sarcasm was on display, but it didn't have its usual cut. 'I'll just check on Nan.' She excused herself and left the table.

'Dad, it's not the mortuary but it's lingering around there. Smells fishy.'

Irma bustled back in. 'I'll get some fresh oysters for you tomorrow, Henry, how's that?'

'I will, Irma,' Fleur replied. 'That's always been my job. I've been collecting the oysters from our local pub since I was a child.'

'And I can't?' Irma asked airily but before Fleur could respond, she shrugged. 'Fine. Is a dozen enough, my dear?'

Henry smiled wanly. 'Perfect. Thank you, both. Always nice with a dark ale,' he said, as though trying to appease each of the women in his life. He changed the subject. 'Where's your young man then, Fleur? Didn't you say five?'

'I did,' she agreed, glancing at the clock as her father checked his gold fob watch. She knew it would tell him that Tom was running late.

'Not a very good start, is it?' Irma said, leaping onto any opportunity to wound. 'I mean, here we all are, ready to receive. To keep one's hosts waiting is just rude.'

Receive? Fleur wanted to laugh. Instead she stood. 'I'll go and look out for him, in case he's lost,' she said, glad to avoid the snide attacks and Irma's pretentiousness.

Outside she scanned the street leading up towards Alberton and then the other way down to the port. There were plenty of people around, moving into and out of the pubs or cutting down streets on their way home, and traffic had thinned as it always did at this time. There was no familiar tall man striding towards her. She waited, all but counting the minutes until it was twenty past five. She knew something was wrong, but she had no choice but to return inside and do her best to rescue the situation.

'No sign?' Irma asked none too sweetly. 'Fancy standing you up, Fleur. James Coglin didn't.'

'He also didn't entertain me, include me, or even care about me. What he did do is bore me . . . when he wasn't annoying me. Let me add, Irma, in case you think I'm being churlish'—she deliberately used a word she hoped Irma did not know—'I bored and annoyed him just as much. We are not a good fit.' She looked away from Irma to her father. 'There is surely something amiss for Tom to do this.'

'You barely know him, you admit yourself, so how can you possibly know what he may or may not do?' Irma continued.

Fleur looked on with horror as her stepmother reached for a small bell and gave it a solid jangle. 'I think we should get started. Your father needs his food.'

Nan hurried to the doorway, glancing at Fleur and then at the bell, which was now back on the small side table, but still beneath Irma's bejewelled sausage fingers.

'We're ready for our meal to be served, Nan.'

'But what about—'

'Please get on, Nan!' Irma snapped.

Their cook fled with another anxious look, blended with sympathy, towards Fleur.

'Don't yell at her,' Fleur appealed to her stepmother. 'She does her best. Irma, you are not going to do that with the bell each evening, surely?'

'Why not? Saves me having to get up and fetch her.'

Fleur closed her eyes momentarily to find her calm. She would be playing right into Irma's trap if she began to argue in front of her father. 'Whatever suits you, Irma.'

'Thank you, I shall suit myself,' she said, and paused as Mae's china sauceboat from the good set was plonked down on the table by Nan. 'Oh good, I must admit I am a bit partial to gravy.'

They stood and made their way to the table, Henry gently shaking off Fleur's help to find his seat.

The meal would have been delicious in its simple, clean flavours – and cosy in its familiarity – but Fleur might as well have been eating the wood shavings from the coffins. She tasted nothing but an increasing sourness that had begun to leak into her mouth. Something was wrong. There was no chance, she was sure, that Tom would have carelessly stood her up . . . not after the two of them had found each other again. It was as though Irma's and Jimmy's underhanded plotting was all part of fate's plan to bring her and Tom together, from their first sweet kiss when she was eight to their deeper, more affectionate kiss of a couple of nights ago.

'Coffee, Henry?'

Fleur came out of her thoughts and realised the meal was finished. She'd pushed her food around her plate, eating no more than a couple of mouthfuls.

'Oh, I don't know,' Henry replied. 'It gives me stomach acid.'

'I'll make it milky, dear, just as I take mine,' Irma said with her back to them both.

Fleur stood and cleared the plates to the end of the table. 'I'm very sorry that Tom is not with us. I feel something is wrong, so I'm going to look for him.'

Her father smiled with sympathy at her.

'A woman should never chase a man, Fleur,' Irma said, over her shoulder.

Fleur had hoped Tom would be around this evening to support her in her suspicions, but she would have to handle this alone. Despite her misgivings, she intended to test Irma – to test her own theory, in fact, which was feeling like a demon in her mind, laughing and pointing at her.

'Here, let me help,' Fleur said, arriving at Irma's side.

'Oh . . . er, no need, dear.'

'I want to, especially since tonight has been a flop. You sit down, Irma. Let me carry these over.'

Their gaze met and held for a heartbeat, and Fleur could sense Irma's indecision.

'Right, well, this one's your father's,' Irma said, pointing to the cup on the left.

'All right,' Fleur said and made a show of picking up the cups and saucers, her father's coffee in her left hand. She waited for Irma to leave her side, then, making sure Irma saw, turned around carefully, balancing the drinks, arriving between her father and Irma. She watched Irma's eyes widen as she realised Fleur's left hand was now closest to her and the coffee she had intended for herself was now closest to Henry. Fleur watched with interest as something – what was it? Fear? – flashed in Irma's eyes.

Yes, dear stepmother, I think you're worried, Fleur thought.

She deliberately placed the coffee in her left hand in front of Irma, and gave the other to her father.

He took a sip and sighed before anything could be said. 'Oh, that's better, dear,' he said, sounding vaguely delighted. 'Excellent flavour. New beans?'

'Er . . .' Irma hesitated. 'I think you may have my coffee, Henry, dear. I told Fleur yours was on the left.'

'Oops.' Fleur smiled, feigning innocence. 'Doesn't matter, does it?' she queried. 'You said you'd make Dad's just like yours. It's milky as you wanted. Drink up, Irma.'

'It's very nice, thank you,' Henry remarked, taking another sip. He sighed again with pleasure.

Fleur stared at Irma and the hideous suspicion that had begun to claw at her seemed to take shape, telling her that a monster was seated before her. Should she believe it?

'Drink up, Irma, before it goes cold,' Fleur encouraged in a breezy voice that she'd had to find to cover the horror beginning to gather and clog in her throat.

'Actually, I won't. I do believe I've indulged too much this evening. That rich gravy and then the custard. It's giving me indigestion, and I think one sip of coffee might send me to the bathroom.'

'Really?' Fleur said in a sympathetic tone. 'Oh, I'm sorry to hear that. You really shouldn't waste expensive coffee.'

Irma pushed the cup and saucer away from her. 'I know, but I just don't feel terribly good. A glass of water is a better idea. And I might go upstairs and rest.' She turned to Henry. 'You don't mind, dear, do you?'

'Not at all,' Henry replied. 'I'm off to the pub to catch last orders.'

Fleur watched them stand up from the table to head in different directions. She felt her father to be too sickly to be going anywhere, but she sensed he wouldn't stand for it if she tried to stop him. Irma did not look at Fleur again as she ascended the stairs, while her father kissed her goodnight and said he would see her later. Fleur barely registered the door closing or Nan coming in to clear the dishes, because her mind was trying to wrap itself around the notion that Irma was indeed poisoning her father. Fleur was now convinced that Irma had been lacing her father's coffee with the rat killer, to poison him carefully, invisibly and with a ghastly patience so no one would ever imagine it was anything more than his deteriorating liver from alcohol. The witch!

It was all very well to suspect, Fleur berated herself privately, and even to become convinced, but how would she prove it? Irma could easily deny it and laugh at her, cite their brittle relationship as a reason for troublemaking, and suggest Fleur was looking for any excuse to cast aspersions on her character.

Nan interrupted her musings. 'All done in here, I see.'

'Thanks, Nan. Can I help?'

'No, no, it's quicker if I just go through my routines. Oh, by the way, I've found the source of that dreadful smell,' she said, stacking the dishes from the table onto a tray.

Fleur couldn't stand idle; she gathered up the tablecloth to shake it free of crumbs outdoors. 'You have? Thank goodness. What was it?' she asked, following Nan into the kitchen and heading for the back door. She quickly opened it and shook the tablecloth.

Nan had put down the tray she was carrying and arrived to help fold up the cloth. 'You'll never guess what it was.'

'I can't,' Fleur replied. 'It was disgusting. I was becoming quite anxious about it, worried that any visitors to the funeral parlour might notice.'

'Well, they would of,' Nan said and Fleur resisted correcting her.

'So? Tell me.'

Nan took the folded cloth and grinned. 'Some old oysters.'

'What?' Fleur managed to sound amused, though she had a creeping sense of dread.

The cook shook her head, looking smug. 'Can you imagine? That terrible pong was from oysters gone off.'

'Where?' Fleur asked, filled with disbelief.

'Around the back behind the potting shed.'

The potting shed was Mae's little folly. Henry never went out there. Gardening was about as far from his interest as knitting might be. Fleur's mother, by contrast, loved to poke around in the small garden, but she especially loved her tiny 'haven', as she called the shed. Fleur remembered it being built to her modest specifications by a couple of lads Henry employed for the job, using hessian sacks from the port warehouses that Mae had cut up and sewn together to be stretched over a thin frame. It wasn't fully waterproof but it didn't need to be; it was mostly used for shade so that Mae could grow more fragile plants and herbs.

Fleur remembered coming into the space as a child and being fascinated by how the sharp summer light took on a softer, bronzed hue beneath the sacking. It was always cooler in there and she recalled how she'd rub her fingers against the garden mint and inhale, loving its clean freshness, and how she'd reap the rubbery spinach and marvel at the tiny strawberries her mother grew. Mae would allow Fleur to eat a few straight from the plants and feel the summer's warmth and ripeness splash in her mouth. Fleur remembered how her mother would encourage her to press freshly dug soil into terracotta pots she lined up on the lower level of the long bench, embed seeds and then water them from a miniature watering can that her mother had had made for the very purpose of encouraging Fleur to garden. Fleur had enjoyed potting with her mother but she didn't catch the bug to spend time growing plants.

'I'm better with the dead,' she'd once said with genuine gravity to Mae, who had chuckled.

'I think you're brilliant with them, my darling. And they are fortunate you are there for them.'

Fleur could still touch those golden moments for a few special seconds before Nan recalled her to the present, shaking her arm. 'Sorry,' Fleur said. 'I'm struggling to understand.'

Nan shrugged. 'Search me, Fleur. I just found them by chance. Perhaps they were thrown over the fence or something. Plus, kids jump over this fence all the time, you know that . . . probably a bit of a lark for them.'

Fleur nodded. It was true. Many of the local children dared each other to sneak a look inside the mortuary window to try to see a corpse.

Nan grimaced. 'Anyway, I flung them out.'

'Right, well, I suspect that will forever remain a mystery, but I'm just glad it's gone,' Fleur said, turning. 'Can I leave you to it, Nan? I have something rather urgent to attend to.'

'Of course. I'll see you tomorrow.'

'Thank you for a lovely meal and all your efforts.'

'I'm sorry your special guest didn't come.'

'I am too. But that's my urgent matter . . . I'm going to find out why Tom Catchlove didn't keep our dinner invitation.'

Fleur arrived at the Alberton Hotel feeling self-conscious about pushing through the hotel doors. The smell of spilled beer, stale ale, and even the cloying aroma of old sweat, seemed to come up and meet her like a gleeful host, wondering what had brought a well-dressed woman into this place.

Someone articulated that very notion. 'Now, what's a young lady like you doing 'ere?' a bloke asked as he rolled a barrel around. She couldn't tell if it was full or not and really wasn't that keen to know.

'Er, are you open?'

He cocked his head towards the front bar, where men were leaning up against the counter. No one seemed to be talking; all were sipping schooners of fizzing golden ale, and a woman kept herself busy wiping down the bar, while another dried and polished glasses. 'Always open, at least until the six o'clock swill time for last orders. Stupid idea if you ask me.' She hadn't, but he kept talking anyway. 'I'll be the first to sign the petition for longer opening times for pubs. It'll come, mark my words. No one will put up with all you crazy women and your pinch-faced temperance.'

She found a smile. 'Do I look pinch-faced?'

He grinned; an incisor was missing. 'No, you look like a reasonable sort, if a little posh for our pub.'

'Not posh, and not one of the Temperance Society either. I'm Fleur Appleby – you probably know my father.'

'Henry? Blimey, how did that fella with a long face like a horse manage to have a beauty like you?'

She could tell he didn't make the comment in a mean-spirited way and gave a little shrug.

He chuckled. 'I like Henry. He's a good man.'

'He is. Anyway, I'm actually looking for someone. One of your guests.'

'Oh, yes?' His tone turned conspiratorial. 'You're not an angry wife or jilted fiancée, are you?' He gave a wink.

'Neither,' she said, laughing off the remark. 'It's a friend of mine. Tom Catchlove.'

'Country lad,' he said, nodding.

'That's right, he's—'

'He's not here. Didn't come back yesterday. But I'm glad you're here, because you can fetch his stuff. And perhaps you can settle his bill?' This was said wryly.

Fleur frowned. 'Didn't come back? From where?'

'I don't know – work, the pub . . . who knows? Lad didn't fetch his key last night. And the cleaner tells me his bed hasn't been slept in, but all his stuff's still in the room.'

'I'll gladly settle his account, but is there nothing else you can tell me?'

The man started rolling the barrel again. 'Sorry, love. We don't pry. I know he was working at the woolstores but that's about all. He was a polite chap . . . hope he hasn't met with any accident.'

A chill passed through Fleur's body as though she'd suddenly stepped into a cool room. 'Tell me how much is owed, please. And I'll pay for another night, to keep his things safely in his room. Is that all right?'

The man shrugged. 'It's your money, Miss Appleby.'

Tom had come to his senses late on Monday night, his head throbbing but his memory clear. His tongue felt thick and stuck to the roof of his mouth, and pain now arrived in full force, singing like an opera diva in her finale.

The initial blow had caught him square in the ribs and he'd felt the first of his bones break. As he'd doubled up in pain, the fists began to pummel and the thought consumed him that he should have trusted his instincts. His head had been so full of thoughts of Fleur that he'd ignored the movement in the shadows. He'd worked hard and fast that day. Time had got away from him and he'd decided to get organised for the next day so that wouldn't happen again. He'd even swept the floor.

He didn't mind the physical work; it kept his body limber and kept him busy, like days in the shearing shed. But it meant his mind was free to roam and roam it did, daydreaming about life with Fleur and whether she was thinking along the same lines. He reckoned they'd make a great couple. Would she agree? She was a force unto herself and certainly didn't need a man, but her kisses! She'd meant them, he was sure. And he'd begun having ideas about how to help her realise her dream, while realising his own. He couldn't wait to see her again at dinner the following night, and to meet her father.

Charlie had suggested a beer before closing time; Tom hadn't really wanted an ale this evening because he'd planned to visit his mother's grave, but in the spirit of being sociable he agreed to one. And that's all they'd had.

After leaving Charlie outside the pub, Tom had begun striding up the road towards the hotel, intending to wash up first, but it was getting late, so he walked onwards towards the Cheltenham Cemetery. Charlie had given him directions. Distantly, he thought he heard voices and checked behind him, but apart from a couple of workers who looked to be making for the nearest pub and the usual thin traffic for a Monday evening, he couldn't see anyone or anything out of place.

Weariness came over him, but it washed over him on a happy wave of good feelings he hadn't felt in a long time, not since childhood. That was arresting. Had he been unhappy all these years? Probably not unhappy, he decided, but perhaps he had been moving through his days in a neutral gear – neither loving life nor hating it, but coasting through it, trying not to create any upheaval for himself. It suddenly felt as though he'd been avoiding life. This new mindset prompted the most pleasant of sensations, which he suspected came out of the delicious prospect of seeing – and kissing – Fleur again . . .

It was no small thing to carry a torch for someone over two decades, believing you'd never see them again. He remembered that first kiss from a precocious eight-year-old that had startled him, and laughed quietly to himself at her claim that he'd wiped his lips on his sleeve. To have met her again, and discover the fondness that had existed all those years ago was shared . . . He had become so lost in his thoughts that he paid insufficient heed to the animal instincts telling him to beware.

His intuition knew he was being followed by hunters who saw him as prey. Those hunters were moving in a pack, and they dragged him into a small laneway once he'd left Port Road and cut into High Street, which skirted the cemetery. Two of his attackers hauled him to his feet and he saw Jimmy Coglin's face stretched into an ugly snarl.

'You bastard. Stole my girl.'

You don't deserve to have Fleur on your arm ever, Tom thought, *and you'll have to kill me to stop me stepping in your way.*

Tom laughed despite knowing it was unwise. He won another fist in the ribs for that and felt something give. He began coughing and dragging in air. Although he was outnumbered and outmuscled, he would have loathed himself if he didn't speak up. 'Do you really think I stole her, Jimmy?' He nearly vomited but realised he had little or nothing to bring up. He gagged and coughed again, kept talking. 'Or was Fleur never actually your girl?' he panted. 'Perhaps she just walked away from the ugly bugger who she'd been forced to step out with by her bullying stepmother at home?'

Oh, he'd pay for that, he knew, but he enjoyed the moment as Jimmy's eyes widened in the dim light from distant streetlights and the moon as it emerged from a cloud.

Jimmy didn't like being mocked in front of the two apes alongside him, still holding Tom on each side. As they laughed, he rained down more blows and the blokes had to let go. It allowed Tom to curl into a foetal position and protect himself as his attacker laid into him with his boots.

'Enough, Jimmy, all right?' one said.

'I haven't got started, Brian,' Jimmy said, sounding breathless. 'Pick him up.'

'Nah. Pick him up yourself, Jimbo,' his mate said. 'He's taken enough, don't you think, Donno?'

Tom had taken the precaution of becoming still as he lay face down. Maybe they'd believe he was unconscious and leave.

The one called Don joined in. 'Yeah, you've made your point, Jimmy. He looks dead.'

'He's muscling in on my patch, lads. I'm going to marry her.'

'Yeah, well,' Brian, the less amused and more reasonable bloke, said. 'She didn't look all that interested at the dance, mate.'

Don laughed. He sounded like a donkey braying. 'Good luck with that, Jimmy. We told you she's too high and mighty for you.'

'My dad and I are going into business with her mother once the wedding's done,' he snarled. 'I can't have this country bumpkin getting in my way.'

'Well, he's not in your way. He doesn't even look alive.'

'Have you killed him, Jimmy?' Don asked, giving a fresh bray of laughter, although it now had a nervous quality to it.

'No, but I'd like to. He's breathing, look.'

Tom was aware of them pausing to scrutinise him. He kept his eyes shut, mouth slightly agape, pleased he was dribbling and hoping it was blood.

Brian tutted. 'He looks very bloody.'

'Good,' Coglin sneered.

'Let's go, Jimmy,' Brian urged. 'I'm not getting caught up in this.'

'Yeah,' the donkey said. 'You can buy us a beer.'

Tom anticipated it but hoped it wouldn't come. He'd hoped in vain; Jimmy's heavy-booted foot caught his chin and snapped his head back. He might have registered the blow as it connected with his jaw, but nothing else.

Tom now tried to move, and gave a soft moan as the pain shot through him again . . . and his world went quiet and dark.

18

Fleur spent a restless night, getting up before sunrise, not waiting for breakfast but leaving a message for her father that she would see him later.

No pressing tasks and no jobs on today to my knowledge. I'll be back soon. Off to fetch the oysters for your meal, among other errands. Fleur x

She wasn't trying to be mysterious but she didn't know how to explain what she was up to. On paper it would sound as though she was a jilted date stalking the man who let her down. If her father had been up, she would have explained face-to-face that she was genuinely concerned about Tom, and that she knew in her heart he would never have let her family down without good reason. She needed to know that reason, because she had a bad feeling about it.

At the woolstores she received the same frustrating and vague remarks as at the pub.

A man called Charlie Hunter introduced himself, looking almost appalled to see a well-attired woman arrive into the vast, busy space. 'Madam, when a woman arrives at the shearing shed, do you know what we say?'

He had ten years on her, with a pleasant face and a charming way about him.

'I don't,' she replied, going along with him.

'Someone will murmur the phrase "ducks on the pond".'

'Is that so?' She grinned. 'Am I a duck?'

'It's meant to be polite,' he said, grinning back. 'Everyone in the shed is immediately warned to be on their best behaviour. To be honest, it's very unusual for a woman to come here.'

'Am I really that frightening?'

He laughed. 'Quite the opposite. You're very lovely, and I would hate for you to be offended by the language or behaviour that working men sometimes . . . well, you understand.'

'I do. And I'm warned, thank you, but I shan't take much of anyone's time. Mr Hunter, I'm Fleur Appleby,' she said, holding out a hand, which he gently shook.

'Call me Charlie.'

She couldn't help but pause and take in a sweeping glance of the frenetic activity and noise. 'I've lived here all of my life and never seen inside the woolstores. All those bales!'

'Here, walk a little with me. Let me show you.' He inhaled. 'What do you smell?'

Fleur felt impatient but, knowing she needed his help, she again went along with his generous manner, knowing he was being polite. 'An earthy smell,' she said, frowning. 'Not unpleasant. I've never been to a sheep farm so I—'

'Not farm, Miss Appleby. They're called sheep stations. Comes from the military term, I reckon, but that's a guess. And earthy is right . . . you're smelling the lanolin, which is the grease from the wool.'

'Ah,' she sighed, understanding. 'It's enormous,' she remarked. 'So impressive.'

'All the wool from South Australia passes through here to its next destination. Most of this will be loaded onto ships, bound for Europe.'

'How exciting. And very busy, so I mustn't take up your time,' Fleur demurred, hoping she was being just unsubtle enough.

'How can I help?'

'I'm looking for someone – Tom Catchlove. Would you know him, by any chance?'

'Tom, yes, I know him. He didn't turn up for work this morning, or yesterday.' Fleur's inner chill turned icy as he looked back at her, puzzled. 'I don't know him all that well, but you take a measure of a man and I doubt it's his way to let people down . . . not without reason.'

She nodded. 'I agree. Tom's a friend of mine,' she said. 'We had . . . well, we had a dinner date yesterday.'

'He didn't waste any time then?' At her surprise, he added, 'You were at the dance.'

She recalled him now on the dancefloor, winking at Tom. 'Oh, that's why you seem familiar. You went together?'

He nodded. 'He took some persuading to attend, but once there, he couldn't take his eyes off you. And why would he? You were easily the prettiest girl in the room, and who could resist Tom's country charm?' He chuckled, grinning again.

She wanted to say *clearly not me*, but she kept her smile wide in return. 'He was expected last night at my family home, but Tom didn't turn up.'

Charlie's smile faded and a frown deepened. 'Ah, right. We worked together Monday . . . He seemed to have quite a skip in his step, to be honest, although he wouldn't explain why.' He winked. 'I could tell he was happy. Must have been you, Miss Appleby.'

She felt herself blush. 'Call me Fleur, please.'

He shrugged. 'He seemed perfectly normal. As I say, chirpy. He didn't say anything about his date with you, but Tom's not one for shooting his mouth off, I'm sure you've discovered. He did mention that he needed to find more permanent lodging but it really wasn't a problem yet for him. He'd had a good day's work, as far I knew, and I even persuaded him to have a beer together.'

'You did? What time was this?'

Charlie shrugged. 'We parted company before the six o' clock swill time, I remember that. We just had a small one . . . only time for a few swallows after a big day here.'

'And?'

'And nothing. He headed up Port Road. I went back towards Semaphore.' Charlie looked beyond her, his gaze narrowing in thought. 'Actually . . .'

'Yes?'

'We recognised a couple of blokes in the pub from the dance. And I'm only just realising it now that I see you standing here, but I think they were the fellows from your party.'

'Jimmy Coglin?' she said, startled.

'I wouldn't know the names. Tom recognised one of them, but nothing was said; they weren't paying us any attention and we weren't paying them any. He just casually mentioned they were in the pub as we left.'

'How many were there?'

'I really don't know, Fleur. Perhaps three.' Charlie opened his palms. 'What are you thinking?'

'I'm thinking that Jimmy Coglin is a jealous, dodgy, vicious—'

'Ooh, whoa, steady now.'

But Fleur's ire was up, as she imagined a scenario that could have led to Tom's disappearance that involved a trio of cowards, one of them with a grudge to settle. Fleur wanted to go straight to the Coglins but she calmly thanked Charlie for the information, then walked back to the Prince of Wales pub to purchase one dozen fresh Coffin Bay oysters for her father's dinner.

She returned home briefly, giving them to Nan. 'You'd better let Irma know I've fetched them,' Fleur said, but didn't tell Nan where she was going when the woman asked. 'Back out, another errand,' was all she was prepared to share.

Fleur took a tram and changed to a trolley bus at Black Diamond Corner to make her way up to Torrensville, counting her blessings that the Applebys had no dead to pick up or prepare today or tomorrow. That could change, of course, but for now she felt fortunate to have the time to make her way to the furniture workshop known as Coglins.

Outside, Bert Coglin was inspecting a series of products set out on small plinths. 'Miss Appleby. This is a surprise,' he said, taking a long suck on his cigarette.

Fleur gave him a polite smile. 'I'm here to see Jimmy, Mr Coglin.'

'Hope you're going to be a bit kinder to the lad. I was led to believe you would be marrying my son. He's not very good with the girls, but I'll work him hard and he'll do us proud. What a fine partnership that would be – the Coglins and Appleby's . . .'

'You were led wrongly, I'm afraid. Irma should never have given any such assurance. She is not my mother, and she is not my keeper.'

'You're a very headstrong young woman, aren't you?'

Fleur nodded. 'Yet another reason to cross me off Jimmy's list, Mr Coglin. We really aren't suited.'

'And yet he's quite struck by you.'

'I didn't have that impression the other night. He was rather unpleasant, actually. Mr Coglin, may I be honest with you, please?'

'Go ahead,' he offered, taking another drag and blinking as a flake of tobacco ember flew from his homemade cigarette.

'Rather dangerous to be smoking around all this timber and shavings,' she remarked.

He frowned. 'What did you have to say, Miss Appleby? I don't have all day.'

'No, and I'm glad we're at this point of truth. I have no intention of marrying your son. I really don't suit Jimmy. He did a nice thing in taking me out, but we were unhappy together,' she said, trying to put a spin on it so Coglin didn't feel that she was here to criticise his son.

'We like the idea of our families being joined.'

'That may be so for you and for Irma, but neither my father nor I believe Jimmy and I would make a good partnership in any sense of the word. May I see him, please?'

'Why? You've obviously got nothing nice to say to him.'

He was right, but Fleur couldn't let him know that. 'I want to be fair and I think it's only right that I say this to his face.'

'I thought you already had.'

'Mr Coglin, is there a reason I can't see Jimmy? Because I can hear his voice even over the lathe, and I can pick out his shape in the shadows back there.'

Coglin's expression twisted. She suspected exactly why the father was protecting his son. 'Do you know the difference between a casket and coffin, Miss Appleby?'

She was caught slightly off guard by his odd question. 'Erm, yes, I do.' It was temping to explain that the word coffin came from the French *couffin* – or cradle – and, before that, *cofin* – basket – but that would be deliberately provocative. 'The casket is usually hinged, and preferable for bodies that are to be viewed.'

'Very good,' he said, clearly trying not to bristle. 'And by contrast, coffins are not usually required to be opened, so they need no additional furniture, like the brass fittings.'

'They also tend to be curved or slanted from the shoulders rather than straight,' she said, helplessly wanting the last word. She frowned. 'Why do you ask?'

'Because, Miss Appleby, you're going to have to know your coffins and caskets, your biers and funerary boxes, for when you have to find your new supplier.'

She blinked with understanding. 'I see. A threat?'

'Not at all. Just business, Miss Appleby. Don't take it personally.'

'I shan't. Be assured, Mr Coglin, I am very well educated in all facets of undertaking, especially the carpentry.'

He smirked. 'We had a good thing going between the Coglins and Appleby's, but now you'll need to take your chances. I gather the next closest workshop is on the other side of Adelaide. You'll be waiting long for your orders and competing with all those pushy city firms for your carpentry.'

Fleur nodded. 'If that's the way it has to be,' she said, her words firm. She was glad her voice held up, but she was sinking inside. What would she say to her father?

'Right. Now, you can speak to my son. Jimmy!' he yelled. 'Get out here.' He stared coolly at Fleur while they waited for Jimmy to appear.

He sauntered up, hands deep in his pockets. 'Yeah? You called,' he said to his father.

'Miss Appleby's here; she has something to say to you.'

'Is that right? I didn't think we had anything more to say,' he remarked.

'It's true,' Fleur said, 'our words were more than harsh enough the other evening. But as business colleagues, I thought I should make some steps towards a conciliatory conversation.' That was the wrong word, she realised, as she saw his confusion. She hurried on. 'You deserve an apology,' she said, watching his eyes widen with surprise. 'There are so many reasons we are not suited to marriage, and I just wanted to say I regret that our exchange was so harsh.'

He gave a chuckle. 'You're strange, Fleur.'

Fleur shrugged. 'I've been called worse. Anyway, Jimmy, your father has just outlined to me the new arrangement, so I'll say goodbye and wish you well.' She took several steps forward and held out a hand.

He shifted awkwardly, not removing his hands from his pockets. She remained in place, hand outstretched. Now he was cornered.

She watched the Coglins exchange a glance.

'Well, get on with it, lad!' Jimmy's father rasped with disgust, flicking away the stub of his cigarette into the nearby bushes.

Come on, Jimmy, Fleur thought, smiling sweetly. *Shake my hand.*

Slowly, reluctantly, Jimmy removed his right hand from his pocket. He reached for hers, but she pulled it back. She could see all his knuckles were bruised.

'You coward! How many of you did it take, Jimmy?'

'What are you talking about?'

She nodded at his battered knuckles. 'I know you got them that way by beating Tom Catchlove in a cowardly gang.'

He shrugged, clearly realising there was no point in denying it. 'Had it coming.'

'Did he? Because he asked me to dance? I was the one who said yes. I was the one who asked him to take me home. I was the one who was yearning for anyone but you to dance with,' she hurled at him. 'Where is he?'

'How should I know?'

'Where was he when you set upon him?'

He gave another careless shrug. 'At the cemetery. He's obviously like you – prefers the dead. He's probably frigid like you as well.' At that, he raised his gaze to hers.

She blinked once at him and looked away as if dismissing him; he wasn't worth talking to any further. Instead she cut a scathing look towards his father.

'You can both go to hell. Don't ever come back to Appleby's looking for work.'

Fleur turned on her heel and, with her head high, walked away from the coffin-makers for good. She'd have some explaining to do to her father, but the feeling of taking control felt powerful . . . like a moment to remember.

19

Tom woke, confused to find himself on his back with a young woman in a starched uniform peering over him. It was as though he was reliving a previous scene in his life. His mother had told him there was a French expression that summed this up but for the life of him he couldn't bring it to mind.

'Hello, handsome.' The young woman grinned.

He groaned. 'Where . . .?'

'You're in the casualty hospital. I'm Jenny, but everyone calls me Jelly . . . always have since primary school.' She chuckled, smacking her wide hips. 'What's your name?'

He was sure they would have checked his pockets and wallet, so this was likely a test to be sure he hadn't cracked his head too badly. 'Tom Catchlove,' he ground out.

'It's nice to meet you, Tom. Good that your memory is intact. Looks like you've taken a thorough beating, or you were trapped in a room with a bull or something. Your face is a bit of a mess, but can't hide your good looks entirely,' Jenny said.

'What day is it? I mean, I know this happened on Monday evening, but—'

'It's Wednesday, Tom.' At his fallen expression she gave him an encouraging smile. 'Is there someone we can ring for you?'

'Please,' he said. 'Fleur Appleby from—'

'Oh, gosh, I know Fleur. We went to school together. How do you know her?' Jenny frowned with amused intrigue.

'Long story,' he croaked.

'Right. There's water next to you. Drink as much as you can, but be warned, everything's going to hurt. There's a policeman who wishes to talk to you. I'll just go and make that phone call for you.'

A senior constable was shown in by the friendly nurse.

'Tom Catchlove, is it?'

'Yes, sir.'

'You look like you've gone fifteen rounds with Young Palmer.'

'Who?'

'Who?' the policeman mimicked, astonished. 'Our champion prize fighter?'

'Ah,' Tom said, trying to smile. 'I've never been into boxing. But I know who you mean now. He played for Footscray too, right?

'Yes, indeed. Quite the athlete. Anyway, son, you've taken quite a beating. Know who did it?'

'I might.'

'Care to share?'

Tom shook his head. 'I'd rather not.'

'Right . . . Like that, is it?'

Tom shrugged and winced at the pain it cost him to do so. 'I'm not a dobber.'

'Fair enough.' The policeman sighed. 'But let me say this. I've spoken to the doctor and nurses who've cared for you and I'm assured these wounds were inflicted by a steel-capped boot, most likely. Would I be right?'

'I honestly don't know. I was down on the ground and trying to curl up to protect myself.'

'Well, if one of those blows had been any worse, you might have been no longer able to move. Or you could be dead. Or a rib could have punctured a lung and you might have bled to death if you hadn't been found. My point is, we can't have this going on. Folk have a right to feel safe on the streets of our neighbourhood.'

'Who found me?' Tom asked. He was the glad the policeman could decipher his words because the broken skin of his lips made it awkward to talk.

'The caretaker at the cemetery. What were you doing alone at night there, anyway?'

'I was looking for my mother's grave. I've never seen it. I'm from up north in the Flinders.'

The man's face softened. 'And what did you do to this joker to warrant such a punishment?'

'I asked his date to have a dance with me.'

The policeman cracked a smile. 'You're game.'

Tom sighed. 'I don't regret it. She's worth every bruise.'

'I guess she must be. Righto, lad. I admire your resilience and I do get that you don't want to dob someone in. But you need to know we don't tolerate this kind of serious breach of behaviour. It wasn't just a bit of biffo, Tom. This was dangerous, and you need to think about the next person this fellow might attack. They might not be so lucky. I just want to give him a clear warning that if I hear of him again in this situation, I'll drag him off. He needs to be afraid of the next time he loses his cool.'

Tom nodded. 'I don't think he'll do it again. His mates weren't happy, so they won't help him, and I think he's a coward, really.'

'Needs a pack?'

Tom nodded.

'All right, well, if you change your mind, and you want to press charges, I'll listen. Think on it for a few days while you heal. I'm going to keep my file open on this for a little longer. Sound fair?'

'Thank you, sir.'

'All right, lad. You take care and, remember, you don't have to be a hero.'

———————

Irma reached for the phone and put on her posh voice. 'Appleby's residence, Irma Appleby here.'

'Oh, hello, Mrs Appleby. It's Jenny Doonan from the hospital.'

'Oh, my poor Henry,' she began, making a presumption.

'No, no. It's not your husband. I'm actually hoping to speak to Fleur, if she's around.'

'She's not,' Irma said dully, trying to dampen the sound of her disappointment. 'I have no idea where she is.'

'Right, well, I wonder if I could leave a message with you, please?'

'If you must. Are you a nurse?'

'A sister, actually.'

'And what do you want with my stepdaughter?'

'If you could let her know that Tom Catchlove is with us at present, and he asked us to contact her.'

'Catchlove,' Irma repeated, playing ignorant but intrigued as to what Fleur's new friend was doing in hospital.

'He's Fleur's new beau. Surely you know?'

'Oh, Tom,' Irma said, sounding overly friendly now. 'Sorry, dear. My mind's a mess at the moment, as poor Henry has been so unwell. Both Fleur and I are rather worried.'

'Well, I don't wish to add another problem for Fleur, but she might like to get down here.'

'And what's happened?'

'Mr Catchlove has taken a very bad beating.'

Irma's eyes narrowed. 'Oh dear, that's not good.'

'No, and he asked me to ring her. Would you please pass on the message?'

'I'll do that, thank you,' Irma said and, without any farewell, put the receiver down. She gave a soft snort; she had no intention whatsoever of helping that impostor reach Fleur.

Frowning, Irma picked up the phone receiver again and dialled a number she had memorised.

'It's me,' she said, bluntly, when her call was answered. 'Get your son, would you? And be quick about it. I think he's just ruined our plans.'

Bert Coglin didn't rush off as she'd hoped. 'Listen, Irma, she's already been here, if that's what you're planning to give him a dressing down over.'

'Who's been where?' she demanded.

'Your bloody high-and-mighty stepdaughter, that's who! Came here smelling something bad and told us our fortunes.'

'What exactly did she say?' Irma demanded, feeling the flesh at the back of her neck turn into goosebumps.

'She was after my son to give him a boll— a few words in anger. She knew it was him who sorted out that country bloke.'

'How could she know?' Irma was disgusted.

'Jimmy's not very smart, Irma, you know that. He didn't hide his guilt well, but his damaged knuckles probably told her all she needed to know.'

'I see.' So Fleur was already ahead of her. Irma felt enraged; she would have to make her move immediately. 'I told your son not to do anything dopey, didn't I? I told him to cool his heels and wait, let me handle it. But he had to show he was a big man, didn't he, Bert?'

'You can't expect a bloke to sit by and watch another move in on his turf.'

Irma half groaned, half growled in frustration. 'Men! Who needs them!' she exclaimed. 'Listen to me, Bert, he's put the fellow in hospital. Did you know that? Now that is not going to give Fleur a warm and cosy feeling about the man we want her to marry. And you're as dimwitted as your son if you don't think this will involve the police. If you'd followed the plan, I'd have worked out a way to make this Catchlove fellow look bad in her view. I just needed time to get him out of the picture. But what Jimmy's done is help her to dig her heels in against the marriage – he's given her just the ammunition she needs. She'll go running to her father and he's too fair for his own good. He'll definitely see it from her point of view and our plans will be shot.'

Coglin sighed on the other end of the line. 'What about the other way?'

Irma pursed her lips. The very mention of it outside of her own mind terrified her. Not because of what she was doing; that was not the issue. But someone else knowing what she was up to . . . She should never had told him about the notion of ridding themselves of Henry, but at the time of her plan she couldn't see another way forward and needed him as an ally.

'It has to be slow. If I go any faster it will be too suspicious.'

'Is there anything else you can try?'

'Yes.' She had to give him something; she wasn't ready to tell him that her new idea was far more cunning and already underway. 'I may need your help. I'll come by later. In the meantime, rein your son in. I don't want to see Jimmy's face for a week!'

'Already too late, Irma. She's told us both – and these were her words – to go to hell. Said we shouldn't be coming to Appleby's for any work ever again.'

'She what?'

'You heard me.'

'That uppity bitch. Right. Leave it with me. I'll see you soon. Your son'd better start framing his apology to Fleur and to her friend. We have to make this idea work if I can't make the other plan go forward.'

'Make it happen, Irma. We'll buy the business off you at the agreed price within days. Don't let him get any thoughts in his head about a new will.'

'No, no, I won't,' she said, shuddering at the thought, and heard the door go. She knew the sound of those footsteps. 'I have to go,' she said, and hung up on Coglin.

———

Fleur arrived into the hallway feeling addled, where Irma was standing near the phone, her hand still on the receiver. 'Who was that?'

Irma gave her a perplexed look that said *why would you ask?* 'An old friend, if you must know.'

'Do you know where Dad is?'

Irma shrugged. 'I haven't seen him since breakfast.'

'I got the oysters. Did Nan tell you?'

'Yes, they're in the cool box – I asked Nan to organise ice. We don't want them going off, do we?'

'These are as fresh as can be. They're not going off in a hurry.'

'Even so, Fleur. We don't want to take any chances with your father's failing health.'

Fleur could feel her mouth thinning at the mention. 'Have there been any messages?'

'Who for?'

'For me?'

'None,' Irma lied.

'And how about for Appleby's?'

'No calls this morning. No one's dying apparently,' she chortled and bustled away, hitting the telephone table with her wide hip in the narrow hallway.

Fleur knew she needed to ring the local hospital and the one in the city, just in case. Going by the state of Jimmy Coglin's knuckles,

Tom had taken a hammering from him alone, so who knew what the others alongside might have done. As she began dialling, she was surprised to see Irma with her hat and coat on.

'Going out?' Fleur asked sweetly, hoping Irma could hear the fake tone in her voice.

'Obviously, Fleur. I don't strut around the house in my hat, carrying a handbag,' Irma sneered.

The casualty hospital number she had dialled answered in that second and cut off any further conversation with Irma, who left. 'Er, yes,' Fleur said, suddenly distracted. 'This is Fleur Appleby.'

'Oh, hello, Fleur. It's Anne Davies. Lovely to hear your voice.'

'It's been a while,' she admitted.

'How's your father?'

'He's well, thank you, and your family?' Fleur said politely.

'Growing! I've become a grandmother since I last saw you.'

'Oh, that's wonderful. You're very young to be one.'

'I'll take that compliment. But our Jess is now twenty. I can't believe she's been married for three years already.'

'My goodness. So, Anne, I have an odd question.'

'Go on, then.'

'I'm looking for someone.'

'Who've you lost?'

'It's a friend. His name is Tom Catchlove. We were meant to—'

'Ah, our very handsome new patient. I think all the nurses want to attend to Mr Catchlove. Your old school pal Jelly got the job.'

'He's there?' Fleur was astonished.

'Yes. We left a message for you. Tom asked us to call you.'

She closed her eyes. 'You left a message at my home?'

'Yes, Irma apparently took it from Jelly not so long ago. I heard her speaking with your stepmother. I thought you were returning the message.'

'No. Er, look, I've just come in and must have missed her,' Fleur said, angry with herself for saving face on behalf of the family – no one needed to know about the internal war – but even more furious that Irma was now lying confidently to her face. 'I think she's forgotten to write it down. I'll declare her of unsound mind if she's not careful.' She made sure to laugh.

Anne joined in. 'Watch out, Irma! Well, Tom came in early yesterday morning, but he was out for a good long while.'

'I've been looking for him. He was invited for dinner Tuesday evening and didn't make it to our house. I gather he was attacked?'

'Yes. Says he doesn't know by whom, or perhaps he just isn't saying. But they did a good job on him. He's lucky he isn't in worse shape.'

Fleur's heart sank and yet she forced herself to feel grateful he was alive, getting the right care. 'Can he walk?'

'Yes. Your Tom'll be all right. He seems determined to discharge himself and walk out, but he's not going to be terribly comfy for a while. He makes no fuss – I wish all our patients were as easy going . . . and as handsome.' Anne chuckled.

'Would you please tell him not to leave until I arrive? I'm coming now.'

'You'll be fine. The police are with him now, taking a report, but without an attacker's name, no charges can be laid.'

20

The policeman had left by the time Fleur arrived at the hospital.

'I'll show you to your Tom,' Jelly said.

'Thanks, Jelly,' Fleur said, giving her a hug. 'I didn't have many friends at school, but you were always kind to me.'

'You scared the others off, Fleur, but not me.' Jelly grinned. 'Far too clever and independent for the rest of us.'

'Oh, go on with you. Thanks for looking after Tom.'

'There was a queue,' Jelly assured and then winked. 'Here's your favourite girl, Tom,' she called before leaving.

'Hello,' Fleur said, approaching, trying not to show how appalled she was to see Tom's handsome features looking bruised and battered, one side of his face swollen, his lips cut. One eye was entirely closed, the other only open to a slit. Some wounds around his face still oozed blood, while others had scabbed. He was a mess.

She sat at his bedside, taking his hand. 'Oh, Tom. Would you like to come home with me?'

Tom shook his head. 'You come home with me.'

Fleur's breath caught. 'To the Flinders Ranges? I wish I could.'

'The Alberton Hotel will do,' he offered.

A nurse returned to help Tom dress, while Fleur sought out Jelly to discuss the care he'd need. Soon, they were on their way, Fleur hailing a cab to take them to Tom's lodgings. Eyes widened when Fleur stepped back into the Alberton supporting Tom.

'Bloody hell, I see you found him then,' the publican said, giving a low whistle. 'Hell, mate, how does the other poor bastard look?' He glanced at Fleur. 'S'cuse my language, Miss Appleby.'

She gave a grinning shrug as Tom blew an amused snort at the question. 'He and his mates jumped me. I never got a punch in.'

Fleur moved the conversation on. 'I'll pay extra, but I want to sit by his side while he sleeps. The hospital says he needs someone keeping a watch for a little while longer, but he didn't want to stay there another night.'

'You don't have to pay any more, Miss Appleby. You can stay all night if you wish.'

Fleur was grateful to him for not cutting her a sly look or winking in any suggestive way; he meant it genuinely.

'Thanks for keeping an eye on the lad. Let us know if we can help with anything.'

'Thank you,' she said. 'Come on, Tom. We'll head up and I have no doubt those stairs are going to test you.'

The ascent was slow and he paused to hold the stair rail twice, breathing hard.

'It's your broken ribs. I know it's painful to breathe. Just take your time,' Fleur soothed him.

She finally got him into his modest room. It was sparsely furnished but big, with windows that looked out onto the Port Road.

'Let's get you undressed and into bed, Tom.'

She sensed him blushing and didn't look up as she began unbuckling his belt.

He clasped his hands over her busy fingers. 'You don't have to—'

'You do know I undress the dead and work on them,' she stated, skirting the truth.

'Except I'm alive, Fleur. So, if you're going to undress me, I hope you plan to marry me.'

Now she did look up at him. He was staring at her with neutral features, although there was a question in his beaten face . . . along with some vague amusement.

'Er . . .' She was caught entirely off guard.

'No jest,' he said, taking her hands from his belt and lifting them to kiss her fingers. 'If you proceed, you have to agree to marry me, Fleur.'

Her mouth formed a brief gape of surprise. 'I don't know what to say.'

'Say yes . . . or if you don't feel how I—'

'Yes!' she interrupted happily. 'Yes,' she repeated, more calmly. 'Tom, I think I've always loved you since I was little. I know that sounds a little ridiculous, but this is what my heart says. I think I've been searching for a version of you all my life and why I've always felt hollow in the presence of men who were keen to see me. You're like . . .' She shook her head.

'Like what?'

'Well, you're like my other half that I've been waiting for to join me.'

He grinned around his bruises and his pain. 'Hang on.'

She watched him limp to the small chest of drawers and remove something tucked beneath a few items in the top drawer.

He hobbled back and sat on the bed. 'It was my mother's,' he said, opening a tiny box, shaped as a heart, its velvet rubbed off. 'It belonged in her family, and I think it's the only item she brought from them. I don't know how old it is or its value. I only know that she wore it every day, whether she was washing clothes or chopping wood. It once had a lovely engraving on the side – there, you can just see it?'

'Vine leaves?'

He nodded with a shy smile. 'And roses, I suppose, but most of that's gone, because her life was tough and she worked hard. I'd like you to have it. It's all I own of her, save a few photographs. I recall she told me these stones were old mine-cut diamonds of the finest quality.' He waited until she offered her hand, and then he slipped the slightly flattened circle of gold onto her ring finger.

Fleur touched the largest of the five diamonds that sat in a gypsy star setting deep within the gently glowing gold. She'd never been one for flashy jewellery, and she'd not worn rings previously because the claws and the raised stones created problems for her work. But this wonderful old Victorian setting and the bright warmth of the polished stones spoke to her. She too would want to wear this every day, no matter what she was doing. 'I do love its simple elegance,' she said, smiling at him.

'It loves you. It looks even better on your hand than hers. Really suits you.'

She leaned in to kiss him softly, not lingering, her lips grazing against his bruised ones. 'You know, Tom, you speak about your mother with so much tenderness, but you never mention much about your father.'

And the remark, like a key, opened some sort of locked door into their already emotionally heightened mood and Tom began to talk. By the end of it, both of them still perched on his bed, holding hands, she knew his story – all of it as best he could explain.

Tom stopped as abruptly as he'd begun and shrugged.

'Have you ever spoken so long or so much in one go?' Fleur marvelled, squeezing his hands.

He shook his head. 'Must be the drugs,' he quipped.

'May I ask something? You can tell me to mind my own beeswax – if anyone can, you can find a polite way to do that,' she offered, sounding uncertain.

'Go ahead. Nothing you say could ever hurt me. I'll tell you anything, I'll listen to you anytime.'

Fleur grinned. 'Let's see how you feel after ten years of marriage, Tom Catchlove,' she warned. 'What I want to ask is this: how would you describe your father?'

He wasn't expecting that, and she saw the slight surprise flash in his eyes. 'Well, er . . . hardworking. Loud. Funny.' He shook his head in a way that suggested he didn't really understand what she was asking of him.

'Your mother loved him, that's obvious. Did you love him?'

'Of course.' He didn't hesitate, now looking slightly shocked that she'd ask.

'You see, Tom, I think I'm in the rarefied position of being able to say what I'm about to with some authority.'

'All right.' He frowned.

'I am not Irma's child, as you know. She has never loved me. She has had to tolerate me as a means to an end – the end being marrying my father and, more cynically, inheriting his business, his property, his wealth.' She held up a finger as she sensed he was going to protest. 'Now, I was also not biologically Mae's child, but I never felt that . . . not once, not even when she scolded me and that was rare. Within our threesome, I knew only love and safety. So I have experienced both sides of that orphan equation. And if I've listened to you properly, and perhaps read beneath what you haven't said, you essentially belonged to a poor but happy, healthy home that had love, laughter and all sorts of enrichment through your mother's experiences and education, and it gave you the confidence you needed. You may be reticent, Tom, but you're not shy or lacking in self-assurance or self-reliance. Tell me. Did your father ever undermine you?'

'No, that's not—'

'Did he hit you?'

'I got the belt a couple of times when I deserved it.'

'Did he praise you?'

Tom thought about this. 'He was proud of how I looked after Mum in his absence.'

'And when you were together, you felt happiness?'

He nodded. 'I always looked forward to him coming home, and I felt secure in their love for each other. Dad wasn't affectionate like Mum, though.'

'Tom, as adoring as he is, my father is not one to lavish me with hugs and kisses. I used to take his smiles and encouragement as his pride and affection for me. Your father comes from an even tougher background. He couldn't look soppy, surely, in front of the other men?'

'The blokes are certainly rough and tough out there, especially in his line of work.'

'Well, there you are. He could be openly affectionate with your mother because that's how a man should be with a woman – tender. But as a father, he probably thought his role was to turn you into a man. I'm sure you'll say something like that to our son.'

'Our son.' He smiled softly. 'I like the sound of that.'

'Do you hear me, Tom Catchlove? Your father was a man used to the company of other men, out in the middle of nowhere, sleeping rough, drinking hard, eating what they could scrounge together. When he was with the woman he adored, he could show his gentle, fun side. But he was away so much of your life. He left raising his boy to her. I think you're hurting, Tom, and you're letting his role as a father, provider, drover and hands-off parent trick you into believing he didn't love you. You may not be his son, but I don't hear anything in what you've told me that says that. He did the best he could, and when your mother died, the light went out of his life. Can you see that?'

'Why leave me so alone? I was a child.'

'Grief is a curious drug, Tom. I've seen people acting strangely at funerals, and I've learned it's not deliberate. Your father probably never recovered from losing the love of his life, and you can imagine all the guilt he felt, the blame he allowed himself to bear for her death. Let's not forget he lost his daughter too – can you imagine his regret? And then you were there, a constant reminder of the woman he'd lost and the man she had once loved with all of her heart.' It was Fleur's turn to shake her head. 'I think I can understand him better than perhaps you do. Please don't allow your pain to override all those good memories of life with your parents. Don't go off on a wild goose chase to find the father who doesn't know you, doesn't love you, probably never knew of your existence. Where do you begin, thirty years down the track, to build that relationship with a stranger, when you have such colourful, vivid memories of life at Paradise? That was your life. Keep it bright. Forgive your father his shortcomings, for that's all they are, I'm sure of it.'

He stared at her, then dropped his gaze. 'You're wise beyond your years, Fleur. You always were.'

'I'm very good at dishing out advice, Tom. I wish I could take my own medicine, though.'

'What do you mean?'

'Well, here I am, blithely telling you to let go of your demons, but I can't let go of what Irma's done and is still doing.'

'It's different.'

'Is it?'

'Yes, because if you're right, then my father was simply careless, whereas what Irma's up to is wilfully committing a crime. If that's so, then it needs to be revealed.'

Fleur gazed at him for several heartbeats before finally giving a firm nod that accompanied a relaxing of her shoulders. 'Thank you,' she said, then sighed, leaning into him.

'For what?'

'For being Tom Catchlove.'

'Your fiancé,' he reminded her.

Fleur chuckled and looked at the ring once more. 'Hard to believe, and wonderful at the same time.' She kissed him again. 'Clearly now I have permission to undress you.'

He laughed. 'I tricked you into saying yes to marrying me, because I'm helpless to stop you, if I'm being honest.'

'Happy to be tricked. Lie back,' she said in a mock-stern tone filled with levity.

With great care, she began to remove the clothes that the nurses had helped him into. She paused at each wince and let him breathe through the pain. With his shirt off, she could see the ravages of Jimmy Coglin's steel-capped boots. The bruising was like a painting made by a drunken artist who'd lost his mind to the brush, with splodges of colour in some parts and trails of pigment in others. The word 'purpura' echoed in her mind from her training in physiology; she often looked at bruising in the elderly known as senile purpura, when the skin had become papery, more prone to injury and small tears. Some of Tom's bruises looked deeply angry, while others were still finding their wrath. There were more that looked like they were sympathising and trying to share the burden, showing pin-pricks of purple and red. Those last were known as petechiae.

She was showing off to herself, she thought, or perhaps she was anchoring her mind against the nervousness she felt at being this close and intimate with a man . . . a man who was alive and capable of returning her stares and her actions. The nurses had shown her where the ribs were broken or cracked and drew her attention to the more serious hematoma on one side, which they'd treated with ice and wrapped in a crepe bandage for compression. She reached gently for those places now as though her hands might heal him as she laid her cool fingers upon them.

'Jimmy did a good job,' Tom said, staring at the ceiling and having a brief rest now that his jacket and shirt were off.

Jimmy had. No doubt. But if Fleur was truthful, she would admit that she had stopped looking at the patchwork of pain on Tom's abdomen and was instead gazing helplessly beyond at the body of a man who was clearly used to physical work. She could point and name each muscle, so clearly defined from his regular labours. His skin, bronzed through summer, still looked tanned and his chest was broad, flat and mostly hairless. The arches and curves of his skeleton appeared sculpted by someone wishing to show a perfect form; from the sweep of his clavicle to the dip of his sternum, Tom's strong frame was carved as if from marble by the tools of a master. The slightly slanted ilium bones that formed the ridge of his hips were peeping above the tops of his trousers, which had fallen down slightly since she'd loosened his belt, and the taut skin that covered his hips dipped away from their high point into his belly.

She suddenly realised that Tom had spoken while she'd been gawping at him. She snapped out of her admiration of his physicality to breathe out slowly and hear in her mind what he'd said. 'I saw him,' she replied, glad she sounded less choked up than she felt in this moment. 'He's looking pretty sheepish, and I have no doubt his friends aren't too proud of his actions. Ganging up and kicking a man on the ground . . . over a girl who doesn't even like him, simply because he asked her to dance. It's pathetic. You'll heal, Tom, but as you noted, Jimmy has to live with his cowardice and his mates watching.'

'I think we both know it's not that simple, Fleur. To be fair, when I walked across that dancefloor, it was always my intention to steal you away from him. Frankly, I was feeling so brazen in that moment – as much as I was appalled by how he was publicly man-handling you – that I wanted to reinforce my theft by kissing you in front of everyone.' He gave a sigh. 'Men know. Jimmy knew what I was up to, what I was thinking, what I wanted to do.'

She looked down at his belt buckle. 'Well, in the spirit of fairness then, I think you should know that I wanted you to do just that,' she admitted. 'When I heard your voice and your invitation, I couldn't quite believe my luck. You were like a chivalrous knight of legend.' She chuckled at the fanciful notion.

'Good, because here we are. Exactly where we both want to be.'

'Not quite,' she said and smiled at his frown. 'I just need a couple more minutes,' she said, standing to unlace his shoes and drop them to the floor. She slipped off his socks and tucked them into the shoes. Without pausing or giving either of them a chance to hesitate, she set about undoing the button on his trousers and, as she had done many times in her work, she slid them off effortlessly, perhaps surprising him how easily she accomplished the task.

Neither of them had shifted their gaze from the other. Fleur rejoined him at the edge of the bed, as Tom caught her intention and winced to move slightly onto one of his narrow hips to make room. They were both keenly aware of the arousal that was filling the space between them like an entity, drawing them together. She daren't look towards Tom's shorts, knowing already what she'd encounter because his dilating pupils and the look in his expression told her there was suddenly something urgent and driven taking over his thoughts.

His voice was croaky, even if hers hadn't betrayed her. 'Fleur, I think—'

'Shhh,' she murmured and, without giving herself pause, she undressed, shocked by her need to feel his skin against her own and by her rising passion to heal Tom in the way women had been healing men since the beginning of humanity.

'Are you sure?'

She nodded. 'Not a single doubt,' she replied, undoing her satin bra, letting it drop before her – rather wantonly, she had the mindfulness to note – before she slipped in beside him carefully. 'Are you able to?'

He glanced down to where his arousal defied her query. 'I'll manage,' he said, his bruised and battered face still managing a crooked smile. 'Are we safe?'

'This time of the month, yes. But honestly, do I care?' She held up her hand to admire the ring again.

Tom pulled her to him.

They moved slowly, tenderly, Fleur trying not to hurt him and Tom sensing he mustn't hurt her. He didn't ask if he was her first and she didn't offer the information. The unhurried exploration of each other's bodies meant Fleur was almost ready to plead with Tom to take the next step. Finally, gradually and with such gentleness that surely hurt him to achieve, Fleur felt Tom fully. She'd expected pain but found only minor resistance, and she was also so desperate by then that her slightly ragged breathing matched his. And a new rhythm began between them. He never took his gaze from hers until the final heartbeat when he surrendered to her body. She adored the tremor that ran through both of them, and wished she could hang onto that sensation a few moments longer because it felt in that breathless space as though nothing else mattered.

And then relief seemed to sweep through him and Tom was sighing with the pain that followed the pleasure. She encouraged him to turn, so she could cup her body around his and feel her skin against Tom's. She felt his body from shoulder to toes shudder once and then relax as though she'd administered a drug – perhaps she had; love and lust were a powerful union. He was clasping one of her hands, the one that wore his ring, against his firm, warm belly. Her other hand got lost in his thick, golden hair, which she stroked until Tom's breathing turned deep and rhythmic.

It was only now that Fleur allowed herself private time for amazement. She was in a man's bed. How reckless, but how delicious too! In the bed of the man she loved, though, and would always love until someone like her would need to care for her lifeless body. *I want us to be cremated, and for our ashes to be shaken up together in a single urn and then scattered somewhere vast and spectacular*, she thought, to echo how her love for Tom felt.

She snuggled closer, inhaling the scent of his skin. At first it was antiseptic and all the places the hospital team had attended to on his battered body and face. But the back of his shoulder that she kissed gently now tasted and smelled different; this was the true smell of Tom. It was like a softly spiced wood . . . dry, of the earth, and wonderfully reassuring.

21

Tom seemed to be sleeping the sleep of the dead, but his breathing was even and deep – healing. Her wonder had lasted for hours. Pleasurable thoughts of life with Tom swirled about her as the night drew itself out of its darkest hours and into the first lightening of morning, and still he slept until she heard people moving around, then the sound of crockery and cutlery as the kitchen downstairs began to busy. And still Tom slept. His body needed it and she smiled, remembering how that body had felt some hours before. As if he could hear her thoughts of their lovemaking, he finally stirred.

'How are you feeling?' she whispered, getting out of the bed to make room for him. She quickly dressed.

'Are you leaving?' he asked, sounding wounded. 'I'm sorry that I ignored you since . . . well, you know.'

She laughed. 'You didn't, Tom. You did more for my emotions while silent and sleeping than anyone has since my mother passed away. I do have to leave, though. I shall pretend I simply sat and watched you all night. Tell me, how are you feeling?'

'Better. I haven't slept that well in years.' He smiled. 'Pain's coming back now, though.'

'Right. I'm going to organise for some soup, bread and cheese to be brought up and also some rich ale. My father drinks a little too much of it, but I happen to know that beer has healing qualities, plus it gets lots of liquid into you. I'll organise a chamber pot if—'

'No, don't do that, Fleur. I'm no invalid. I'll get to the bathroom all right.'

'Sure?'

'Yes. In the bush we get moving as soon as we can after any injury.'

'Well, I need to go home and check if there have been any deaths.' At his surprised look, she explained. 'I mean, any called in by grieving clients who need our services.'

'Ah. Right.'

'I'll come back later.'

'No, Fleur. You just go do what you have to. I'm going to be fine. I don't need mothering, I promise. I'll probably need a couple of days.'

She nodded. 'All right. I'll leave any messages with the publican and you can have him ring me if you need anything at all. Don't be bashful about asking for help,' she said, holding up her left hand. 'We belong to each other now.'

He grinned. 'Kiss me and go, or I'll find a way to make you stay.'

She checked her clothes were all straight and buttoned correctly, using the small mirror on the chest of drawers, then bent down and kissed him gently. 'Those wounds on your lips need to heal or they'll never get well.'

'Keep kissing them better,' he suggested, winning a smile.

She blew him a kiss instead. 'Tom . . . beyond loving you, I want you to know how much I completely adore you.'

'Now and forever,' he said.

Fleur left the room with a heart fuller than she could ever have dreamed. She was almost dizzy with happiness and gave the publican a broad, bright smile.

'You look well for sitting in a chair all night, Miss Appleby.'

She enjoyed a guilt-ridden private smile as she lifted her bag. 'I had a good book to keep me company while our patient slept,' she fibbed, permitting herself the white lie for the greater good. 'He's only just woken and seems brighter, but I think a good sleep has tricked him into feeling stronger than he actually is.'

'I'll keep an eye on him.'

'You will? You're very kind. Here, I'm leaving some money for food – it would be wonderful if you could send up some soup, bread, cheese, that sort of thing, and perhaps a bottle of healing ale tonight?' She even winked, surprising herself; how lovely the world felt right now. 'And here's our number at Appleby's. Will you ring me if he worsens or needs anything?'

'No worries,' the man said. 'It's Thursday – pay day – so you can imagine how busy it will be later on. My wife will organise some food. I'll send one of the kids up to check on him. Does he need a doctor?'

'No, no, nothing like that. Just rest now while his body does what it knows it has to do. That's what the nurses at the hospital told me, anyway. I'll be back soon enough.'

'Righto, Miss Appleby.'

She smiled and felt an almost childish desire to skip out of the pub and all the way down the Port Road home. She didn't, but she was humming the tune that she and Tom had danced to at the Palais. That melody would hold special meaning for her from now on. The distracted, vaguely smug smile held until she caught sight of the familiar black saloon car of the local doctor outside Appleby's. Her expression dropped suddenly, she stopped moving and there was a sensation of her organs, skeleton, flesh, mind – all of her – instantly deflating, as though it no longer had the equipment that held it straight and alert.

She'd encountered that car so many times in her professional dealings. The doctor was a lovely man, desperately overworked, paid nominally and sometimes too quick to ascribe a death based on everything he knew about his patients, rather than probing more rigorously. He was responsible for so many, not just day-to-day health needs in the community, but the more serious patients in the hospital, too. It was too much for one man, she understood, and his presence at a home might be a simple house call but was, more often, connected with dying.

An irrational and cruel thought ghosted that she hoped it was Irma, toppled down the stairs, fallen in the garden, or suffering an unexpected episode that had stopped her breathing. Fleur immediately chastised herself for allowing such heartlessness into her mind. She had not been raised that way and Mae would be ashamed, but Fleur, despite her guilt, knew this was the inherent defence system that everyone possessed. It was triggered to protect her from what her mind already knew and didn't want to face – the death of her father. And she knew as she began to run that he was already gone.

She burst into the house. Looking around, she could see only Nan peering out from the kitchen with watery eyes. Fleur didn't want to ask; she couldn't hear it from their cook. Instead she ran upstairs to find Irma, thanking the doctor.

'I am indeed deeply sorry for your loss,' he said as Fleur arrived onto the landing with a wild-eyed stare. 'Henry Appleby was of those one-in-a-million men,' he added, covering Irma's fat hands with his large, bony ones.

'No!' Fleur uttered and covered her mouth with both hands to stop a shriek.

'Oh, Fleur. My angel. My darling. I'm so sorry.' Irma rushed to her side, a study in indulgent sympathy.

Fleur felt those sausage fingers clutch at the top of her arm, as the doctor eyed her uncomfortably, dipping his gaze in respect. 'Good morning, Fleur. I'm so sorry.'

'Dad's dead?' She still said it, hoping she could somehow will it not to be true. Her lips felt numb. She couldn't bear for Irma to touch her, and she shook off her hold.

The doctor cleared his throat. 'Yes, Fleur. I'm very sorry to tell you that your father has succumbed to what was probably a raft of underlying complaints connected to cirrhosis of the liver.'

'No, no, that's not right.'

'Oh, Fleur.' Irma reached tenderly towards her.

She batted away Irma's arms, encased like bulging meat in the tight sleeve of her dress. 'Don't touch me!' she snarled.

'Oh, my dear, I know you're—'

Fleur ignored her, pushing past them both to confront her father, lying in his bed, the sheet pulled up neatly to his shoulders. He looked grey. Absently, she estimated he had died around three hours earlier. A helpless glance at her watch told her it was nearing nine. So before six, perhaps, as the birds had become noisy in their chorus, her father had sighed his last breath.

'He went quietly, Fleur darling, your name on his lips to the last,' Irma said in a soppy voice dripping with fake sympathy. 'Oh, my darling, darling, husband,' she wept, leaning against the door jamb. 'What am I going to do?'

Get rich? Fleur thought, relieved she hadn't uttered it. She hated this mindset of hers. Her father was lifeless and all she could feel was hate, instead of the love that she knew was desperately trying to ease past her despair to flood her, an almost drug-like defence for the bereaved. She knew how it went. People in true grief could feel utterly numb for days, unable to feel much at all because the angst ran so deep, so wide in their minds. If they moved, it was almost like they were one of the robots she'd seen in the shops. Functioning – sometimes rather well, with an almost daunting brightness – staying busy until the funeral and then the 'crash' would arrive into melancholy when all the architecture of the funeral arrangements and flurry of family and friends began to disappear. Others fell into a group that she believed she might belong to. They didn't really hit that false spiritedness; instead, they didn't really see anything, not engaging, their actions forced from memory rather than conscious movements. She was in an early stage of shocked denial and although she recognised it for what it was, she could do nothing to change it.

The doctor arrived at her side and risked touching her shoulder. 'To be precise, it's my opinion that Henry actually died of poisoning.'

'But—' Fleur began in a whisper.

'It was last night's oysters. Irma thinks they might have been off.' He looked over at Fleur's stepmother, who nodded in agreement and stepped into the room towards them.

'Impossible. I purchased those myself from the Prince of Wales. They smelled of the sea. Besides, Irma seems fine,' she said, keeping her tone neutral.

'Yes, obviously one that Henry ate wasn't fresh enough. That's all it can take, actually.' He continued, almost conversationally now. 'The Prince of Wales oysters are usually incredibly fresh. I eat them myself once a week. And, before you say it, I know that they keep them alive out the back, delivered fresh from Coffin Bay. I don't understand it either, but these random events never offer explanation.'

'Dr Parson, I chose those oysters myself. I would not have selected one that wasn't perfect. I carried them straight back to the house, not lingering anywhere in between the purchase and returning to the parlour, where Nan put them directly on ice. The ice was ordered in especially for them by Irma.'

'I see.' The doctor frowned. 'I can't guess at how this occurred, Fleur. Just a terrible turn of events that pushed an already fragile liver and kidneys over that precipice, if I might describe it that way.' He gave a tight smile and then let it go as soon as it arrived at his mouth.

Fleur ignored him, babbling now. 'They were unshucked, alive and as fresh as can be. I chose them.' She knew she was repeating herself, perhaps hoping that if she explained the facts well enough, it might change the outcome.

The doctor nodded and Irma's face softened further in contrived sympathy with each point Fleur made.

Fleur was shaking her head in disbelief. 'Each was large, with a distinctive cup and ridged shell. I know oysters, Dr Parsons. These were good.' The rotten oysters in the back garden were beginning to make sense.

Irma spoke behind her. 'I'm sorry to have called you out so early, Doctor,' she said, as if Fleur hadn't spoken.

'No, no. You did the right thing.'

'What happens now?' Irma asked, a tremor in her voice.

Fleur couldn't help wondering if it was feigned. She heard the doctor sigh; he too was ignoring the facts. 'Normally we'd organise for the, er, the body to be collected by the undertaker, but we're already here . . . that is, unless you wish some other firm to . . .?'

'No one but me is touching my father,' Fleur said, with menace in her tone.

Irma frowned. 'Is that wise, darling?'

'What's wise, Irma, is that you stop pretending. Stop calling me darling or dear, or angel or love. Just stop. And while you're at it, please stop pretending to care. Because we both know something's not right here.'

Irma's shock was so convincing that Fleur wanted to give her a round of applause, but the situation was so overwhelmingly dark that she couldn't muster the strength to be bothered with Irma any longer.

She didn't wait for her stepmother to act out her recovery from Fleur's cutting accusation any further. 'Thank you,' Fleur said to the doctor. 'I can take it from here.'

'Well, there is the business of a death certificate, which I can write up—'

'Please don't do that.'

'Pardon me?' the doctor said, frowning. 'I have to—'

'Not if the cause of death is in dispute,' Fleur said, her voice hard enough to throw stones at.

'Fleur . . .' he began

'Listen to me,' she said, forcing him to meet her gaze and not be tempted to flick it towards Irma. 'You've known me a lot of my life.'

He nodded.

'And you've known my father very well. I suspect you would credit us both with being of even temperament, not prone to histrionics or . . .'

He put a hand on her wrist. 'Fleur, you're in shock.'

She blew out a slow breath. 'That's true. I am. But my shock is not just that my father has passed away. It's the manner of his death.'

The man frowned. 'What do you mean?'

'Admit you know me to be sensible and calm.'

'Of course. What's this about, Fleur?'

Her stepmother cut in. 'Doctor, I really think that Fleur has—'

'Oh, shut up, Irma!' Both of them winced but Fleur ignored their alarm. 'I wish for a post-mortem to be performed on my father.' She was impressed at how calm and reasonable she sounded.

The doctor's alarm intensified. 'Good grief. What in heaven's name for, Fleur? That will only prolong the shock. You and Irma need to get on with your grieving and plans for Henry's burial, not—'

'I know you will have pronounced him dead from the complications of his alcohol consumption – no doubt cirrhosis – but you said yourself you think it was the oysters. I believe my father has been deliberately poisoned.'

'Deliberately?' he repeated, aghast.

'Yes, by fetid oysters, and I suspect arsenic has also played a keen role.'

His mouth formed an 'o' but no sound came out, his features slackening with horror. He blinked and finally found his voice. 'Arsenic? You cannot be serious.'

'I am always serious, apparently,' she said, her tone as dark and forbidding as a newly dug grave.

'Arsenic,' he repeated, incredulous.

Irma stepped back into the fray. 'Doctor, I think Fleur needs a sedative. She's rambling because she adored her father and, like me, she can't believe he's gone.' She gave another sob.

'Go away, Irma,' Fleur said, sounding almost weary now. 'Run if you want; you'll be hunted down. The police are going to be called and I swear I shall see you in handcuffs.'

The doctor took a step back, looking as if he'd taken a blow. 'I . . . I don't understand.'

'No, I know you don't. But I suspect Irma does.'

Fleur had to hand it to her: the woman had an amazing ability to give a performance. Irma's stance didn't change. She even managed to look injured by the accusation but, just a heartbeat before the doctor turned his head slowly to gaze at Irma with fresh shock, Fleur saw it. Irma's gaze narrowed slightly like a trapped animal looking for an exit and in the same moment Fleur saw the spark of rage and loathing flash in Irma's eyes before she closed them, apparently in mortification at Fleur's allegation. Fleur suspected her stepmother's mind was now racing into damage control . . . and especially how to refute the claim convincingly.

'How could you say such lies, Fleur?' she demanded, her voice wavering again, and her body now trembling too. 'Oh, Doctor, I think I'm going to need a powder or something to calm my nerves. I can't take this. You'd better plan another coffin, Fleur, if you're going to carry on like this – my heart won't stand it.'

Fleur turned to the doctor. 'She'll be fine,' Fleur said, bustling the poor man towards the door. She all but herded him down the landing and ultimately down the stairs, where she stood in front of the telephone. 'Would you please call the police, Dr Parsons?'

'Fleur, this is a most dreadful situation. Are you really sure you wish to pursue this course? Your father was not a well—'

'Let's not mince our words. My father was probably an alcoholic, and I have no doubt his liver would have given up at some stage. But not yet. He was not near death. So hold that death certificate. I forbid you to write it out, no matter what Irma demands of you.'

'But what if—?'

'Just give me the opportunity to substantiate my claim. Let the coroner make a decision.' Fleur suspected she'd just lost an ally, going by the pursed look of his lips. He wasn't happy, but he also wasn't going to obstruct justice; that much she could read. 'You've known me since I was a child. You know I don't lie and—'

'I know you to be very sure of yourself, Fleur,' he said carefully, but she saw a hint of annoyance ghost across his features.

'As I am very sure of myself now in my accusation,' she agreed, hoping that might satisfy him.

The doctor shook his head and began tutting. 'Fleur . . . this is an incredibly grave accusation. You're talking murder, by the woman who has looked after you since you were a child.'

'By the woman who has done no such thing. My father has looked after me. Irma simply tolerated me. Now she doesn't have to.

I'm a truth seeker; I'm not trying to set Irma up or besmirch her reputation out of mischief.'

'Hardly mischief, Fleur,' he admonished her. 'This could mean her life. Think on it.'

'Yes, it could. And I don't have to think on it any further than all the years I've suspected my stepmother of being insincere. I loved him. She didn't. We are talking about my father – your friend. You owe it to him to find the truth.'

He shook his head in a way that suggested he felt helpless. 'Right,' he said, showing his palms. 'I'll call the police now, and wait outside to speak to them. I'm very sorry for you both. There's only loss here.'

Fleur nodded, wrapping her arms around herself as if deeply chilled. 'I will deliver him myself to the city morgue for the coroner.' She pointed upstairs to the room where he lay, unable to hold in her rage any longer. 'Mark my words, my father was murdered. And now I must go to him. Good morning, Doctor.'

She turned and left him standing in the hall, still in shock.

22

It felt like she was participating in a gunfight in one of those Western films that her father had taken her to see at the cinema when she was young. She and Irma regarded each other, equally grim-faced, across the bed where her dead father lay. All that was missing were the pistols and stetsons.

'It's your own fault you weren't here, Fleur. You were out all night.'

'So what? I'm a grown-up.'

'People will talk. Act like a slut, you will be labelled that way.'

'Nothing slutty about where I was, Irma. It was wonderful,' she said, wishing she hadn't.

'So you reward your friend, even though he insulted you, by letting him have your body. My, my . . . how proud your father wouldn't be,' Irma said, making a tsking sound.

'Tom was beaten. That's why he didn't come.'

'But he could still take you into his bed.'

'Don't make it sound tawdry, Irma. I went willingly because I love him and he loves me. Do you know anything about love, Irma?'

Her stepmother laughed with a cruel sneer. 'You poor dolt. You likely won't see him again now he's got what he wants.'

'Well, I'll enjoy proving you wrong. Anyway, I thought you'd be packed, already on your way.' Fleur said, still helplessly impressed by Irma's ability to hold face, to go on attack and engage in full battle, even though she must know she was losing.

'What would be the point? It would make me look guilty.'

'You are guilty!'

'Listen to yourself, Fleur. You're going mad. I'm now convinced of it,' her stepmother baited. 'And I shall tell anyone who comes to hear your unfounded accusation just that. I swear I'm going to make you pay for this.'

'The only place you're going is to gaol. I'll bet my last dollar on it.'

Irma laughed cruelly. 'You don't have any money to be placing bets with. You do realise it's all mine, don't you?'

Fleur frowned. 'Why's that?'

'Your father has made a new will. In it he leaves everything to me.'

Suddenly Fleur could feel the pound of her heartbeat in her throat. She had not been given this information but she refused to betray her shock. And already she was letting it dissipate because her rationality was taking over quickly and making her accept that it didn't matter. All that mattered, now that her father was gone, was being with Tom. Even so, her anger outweighed her sensibility and it was demanding that Irma pay for her sins. 'I'm presuming you convinced him that you'd see to my best interests, did you?'

Irma smiled. 'Of course. You see, Fleur, I always knew how to get around Henry. A man is easy. You just have to have the right . . . shall we say . . . enticements on offer.'

'Ugh.' Fleur closed her eyes, helpless to control her revulsion at the thought of Henry rolling around with Irma but even as she did, she knew Irma wasn't lying. She would have used all her conniving charm and indeed her body to coerce her kind and trusting father to do whatever she wanted.

'My mother—'

'May she rot in hell! Both of your mothers, actually,' Irma said. 'The first for giving birth to you and not smothering you when she had the chance. The second for even bothering with you.'

Fleur wouldn't fall for Irma's word blows, designed to wound, to draw her into the trap of making a mistake. Irma clearly hoped Fleur would reveal her proof, maybe that she would lose control and try to physically harm her. But Fleur was wise to this woman after years of being conditioned. 'You know, you may have others hoodwinked but you really can't hide your cold-blooded nature from me. I see you. I see you for all that you are. Search though I have, I've found nothing redeeming about you. There isn't an ounce of empathy for others within you. I know you killed my father, and you will pay the price for your heinous work.' Fleur didn't let her gaze leave Irma's as she finished speaking.

'I'd like to see you prove it, Miss High and Mighty.'

'Don't underestimate me, Irma. You've been doing that for too long.'

Irma laughed and Fleur, despite her icy anger, couldn't help but feel slightly unbalanced by her stepmother's composure. She seemed fearless in her crime.

'It's curious, Fleur, because we could have been a good mother-and-daughter team.'

'I don't think so,' Fleur replied. 'We weren't even friends. I saw straight through you from the moment you started living in my house.'

Irma shrugged as if to say, *so be it*. 'All mine now,' she said. 'And I'll make sure you don't get a cent – I'm happy to see you cast out into the street with nothing.'

Fleur forced herself to swallow the keen fury that Irma believed money was at the heart of their feud. She leaned into that error now. 'Your mistake has always been measuring me against yourself. You see, Irma, I won't give a moment's thought to any of this,' she said, waving her arms in an arc. 'Money does not drive me, but it's all you think about. It's your weakness . . . and now it's become your downfall. You had it all – he would have given you anything you wanted. Why did you have to kill him?'

'You're so cocksure, aren't you? Well, others may not be convinced. The proof needs to be found,' she said in an airy tone. 'I'm not at all frightened by your threats, you stupid girl. Marry your poor shepherd, live in poverty . . . because that's where you'll be. Meanwhile,' she said, pausing to look around, 'I shall enjoy having all of this to myself. I'll sell the business, of course, and then spend some of the proceeds on redecorating and cleaning away the stink of Mae Appleby that I can still smell in every room.' She laughed again. 'Am I making your blood boil, Fleur? I do hope so. And look at that poor sod lying there. Gave his all for what? A dead wife, an ungrateful child and—'

'And a scheming shrew who will get her comeuppance,' Fleur snarled. 'Get away from me, Irma. Get away from my father too. Neither of us want you near us.'

'You can have a little while to say goodbye to your father, Fleur, but then I'd like you to leave. Please don't take anything that doesn't belong to you.'

'I'll be taking him,' Fleur promised.

'Go ahead. Good riddance to old rubbish. Henry became a burden long ago.' Irma turned to leave, looking over her shoulder. 'Oh, and if you're looking for his fob watch, don't bother. I've taken it,' Irma continued. 'Everything is mine, remember.' She picked up her large bag. 'I shall be out for a couple of hours.'

'When you come home, the police will be waiting,' Fleur threatened.

'And I've nothing to hide, while you've got everything to prove . . . beyond all reasonable doubt.' Irma chuckled at Fleur unkindly before slamming the door behind her. The clap echoed through the house and took with it Fleur's rage, whisking it away to leave her feeling empty. She doubled over as though in pain, and the action seemed to permit a great hole to open within and grief to suddenly flood it. It was like oil, thick and slick, that had been lit by the burn of her anger before it left. The viscous grief, flaming as it did, gave off no light, only heat, which moved slowly through her body, searing her heart, her cheeks and flaming at her neck, forcing her to tear off her coat and suck in gasps of air as though she were drowning. Suddenly it hurt to breathe, and her gasping only gave more oxygen to the invisible flames. Finally tears arrived and they were shed for several, long and gulping minutes over her father. Not her touch nor her weeping kisses could warm the lifeless body. He was gone.

She rose at last to open the window and usher his spirit to a happier place, and as she did so she saw two policemen arrive. She returned to her father and laid a watery kiss on his forehead. Her sense of loss was so great in this moment that she didn't want to confront it. It was as though she'd found a way to withdraw from the edges of herself so that nothing touched, not even her skin – and not grief any more. She would open herself up to all the pain soon, but Fleur urged herself to hold tight inside and to tense her body to stay strong, from the muscles in her face that would not betray her sorrow, to the muscles in her legs that would hold her upright and display no sign of weakness. Irma needed to see her strength, that she wouldn't be cowed by vicious words or threats, or her deliberate baiting.

'Trust me now, Dad,' Fleur whispered and left the room to greet the police as his spirit flew from her.

Irma took a pot of tea in a local café while she pondered her next move. Her plan was now in motion and how Fleur had reacted was no surprise. She had anticipated that Fleur would reject the doctor's summary and demand that the police be called. She was not frightened of the coroner being involved, but there were two elements that she didn't have control over.

The first was the Coglins. Hopefully Bert's greed would keep his mouth tightly shut and her threats would keep his loose cannon of a son under lock and key for a while. But the second, and more concerning, was Tom Catchlove. He had the power to exert influence over Fleur. She could already see that her stepdaughter had lost her head to this country lad. It was a hurdle but not insurmountable. She had wanted Jimmy for a son-in-law because it would have made it easier to control everything, to keep running the business and earning, but if it wasn't to be then she could sell up and move on, living off the proceeds.

An idea had been forming while she had watched Fleur rage at her. Her stepdaughter had appeared almost unbalanced in her grief, but that wasn't all there was to the powerful emotional outburst. Irma had always held the opinion that no one should underestimate her smart mind. She may not be educated to someone like Fleur's standard but she was naturally bright and gifted with an agile brain that possessed cunning. She felt cleverer than most of the people walking around.

What she had seen in Fleur was love . . . but not for Henry; that was an old love, a given one, part of the fabric of her life. No, it was this Tom Catchlove. Even his surname spoke of it. He'd caught Fleur's attention in a way no other man ever had and she had fallen for him . . . love was blazing in Fleur's body, and lust too, apparently. Irma smirked.

Irma's cunning crocodile mind, with its patient way of turning over a situation, considered this new love. To Fleur it no doubt felt so fresh and novel. She was in the height of her excitement at finding someone to love and return that love; her body was probably still tingling from his touch. This was a woman who had spent years without romantic involvement and now suddenly it was here and it likely felt glorious. Irma wondered how she might use all of this excitement against Fleur. She was likely still feeling untarnished, since presumably no one else knew about their tryst.

Irma rummaged in her bag and withdrew one of the Appleby notelets that Henry had had printed. She liked them because they were plain: a parchment-coloured card, tent-folded. It had the thinnest of black margins and on its back in neat, unobtrusive script was the Appleby name and address. He had used them to send thankyou notes to people within the industry and to pen a quick card to a grieving family a month or so after their funeral with Appleby's. Henry had had bold penmanship and he wrote in shiny black ink from an old fountain pen his father had given him.

Irma knew Fleur was following in his footsteps, copying her father's ways, and that she too wrote in black ink on these notes. Letting her mind dive freely, Irma refreshed her cup from the pot of still hot tea and withdrew a pen she kept filled with black Quink in case she ever wished to send a note from Appleby's and have it look official. She'd used this ruse from time to time to get orders hurried through or to have goods she wanted for her own end put through to Henry's business account.

She took a slow breath, frowned and began writing.

My darling Tom,

   My body is still remembering everything about our night . . . your touch, your kisses, your whispers of love. But night has become day, sweet Tom, and reality has found me.
   I have to tell you that I've returned home to discover, much to my anguish, that my father passed away during the

*night. I feel inconsolable that while we were making love, he
was taking his last breath on this earth and I was not there to
hold his hand, to comfort him or to farewell him. I came home
this morning to his cold body, and the doctor and Irma making
arrangements without me.*

*I'm not angry at you. I am not blaming you. But of course
it's natural that when I think of you now, I think of my father's
death. And that's no grounds for a happy future. I am bitter
at myself for being the worst sort of daughter. I knew he was
ailing, I knew how weak he was, and yet I put my own needs
above those of the only man I've loved.*

*I care for you, Tom, and I wish it could be different but
before this goes too much further, I think I must be honest
that despite what we shared yesterday, we can never be a
couple.*

*You see, there's something I must tell you – should have
told you before this but I couldn't. I was carried away by our
shared pleasure in each other. Darling Tom, you need to know
that I am already pregnant with another man's child.*

Irma didn't know she was going to write that and allowed herself
a shiver of delight at how cunning she could be. She sipped her
cooling tea, a small smile twitching and continued.

*Lying in your arms last night, I allowed myself to believe
that I could pretend the baby was yours. You could never know
and I had almost convinced myself that I could live with that, but
I cannot. You're a very decent man who deserves better, and so I
must walk away from us.*

*I am asking you now to respect my wishes. Walk away as
well. I want this baby, and while Jimmy Coglin is not the man
I wish to marry, I think deep down he will enjoy being a father*

and become a better man for it. I don't want this child of mine to grow up with a different father than his own as I did.

Irma wanted to laugh out loud now at her sneakiness. Time to finish the heartfelt note. She blew on the ink and took a second card.

> *We'll remember each other from afar, Tom, but we shall never be together. Go home. Go back north where you belong, I beg you. Please do not come for me. Respect that I am grieving too, and our family needs some time. Please do not write to me or telephone me. Don't hope I will ever come looking for you. I will not. Yesterday was wonderful and I will never forget being with you. But I have made the right decision to marry Jimmy and not allow my child to be labelled an orphan or rejected by their mother or father. They will be loved.*
> *Yours, Fleur x*

Irma read it back, then placed the cards in an envelope. It was a masterpiece. She struggled out of the cramped seat, paid for her tea and allowed herself a taxi up to the Alberton Hotel, where she stood on the pavement a while and waited for the right person.

A young lad came along on a bike. 'Hey, son. Want to make a couple of pennies?' she asked him.

'Yeah?'

'Take this into that pub and deliver it.'

'That's all?'

'One penny now and another when you've done it. I'll be watching.'

'Why don't you do it?'

'Because I'm grieving. Can't you see I'm dressed in black? Someone has died and I need to let people know. Now will you do it?'

'Where's my penny?'

She gave him the copper and her note. 'Off you go. I'll be around the corner.'

'Who do I give it to?'

'Anyone behind the pub counter, but make sure they know it has to be handed to this man.' She pointed to the envelope. 'His name is Tom Catchlove. Can you repeat that to me?' As he did, she nodded firmly. 'Good. I'll be waiting.'

———

Tom sat on the edge of his bed staring at the floorboards, watching a tiny spider wend its way towards him. What was it searching for? A mate? Food? A good place to set up a web? He pondered this, knowing it was simply a distraction from the words he'd just read. They were like a tornado of blades, each whirring up from the paper to draw blood as it struck home.

The letter sounded like Fleur and yet it was perhaps clumsier than he'd imagined she might be with a pen. However, he acknowledged that anyone shocked from the loss of a loved one rarely sounded normal.

The words felt like sandpaper against his mind as he played them through again to the final jagged cut of her letter, which, after the other small cuts, was too deep for him to stem the flow. Pregnant. Jimmy Coglin's child. Fleur had slept with Jimmy and then ruthlessly slept with him as a way of forgiving herself and indeed giving herself a different future.

It was as though he was watching a film of their night together, remembering the caresses, the smoothness beneath his calloused fingers of her pale skin that never saw the sun. The silken and erotic touch of her hair on his tanned chest like a feather as she moved above him. He wanted to watch her face contorting beautifully in the pleasure he was bringing to her, believing it was an indulgence she hadn't felt in a long time, or perhaps ever. But it seemed she had.

Or had Jimmy raped her? No, the repercussions of any violence against her would have been swift.

Slowly he paced, got his body moving; he could no longer be still and helpless. She was letting him down kindly, feeling the weight of responsibility from her actions and now her father's death. She had all but pleaded with him to leave her life. If he loved her, then he would do as she wanted.

He tried to find reason to go against that creed but no worthy rationale came up to challenge the fact. While she wanted him in her life, life was not going to let her have him. He did not want to raise Jimmy Coglin's baby. He'd end up like his father . . . raising another man's child because he loved the mother. There was too much potential to resent its presence and blame the child for intrusion, rather than Fleur.

Suddenly everything felt hopeless and pointless. Coming to Adelaide had been a mistake. He had run away from Farina, hoping to escape the emotional upheavals but all he'd done was add more to the rollercoaster.

And so, yes, he would go. He couldn't imagine ever getting over losing Fleur, because she'd been that unreachable treasure for most of his life, and just when that treasure was glittering in his hands, someone else was snatching it away. But this was her choice and he needed to respect her wishes or he would be compromising his own view of life. He would leave, and he would learn how to keep Fleur locked away in a private place.

He couldn't help dwelling on her loss. Her father's death would crush her for a while, and Tom began to wonder whether the foul play that Fleur suspected had indeed taken place. He wished that he could do something to help before he left.

Curiously, it was his own father's voice that arrived now. 'Always a solution, son. No problem is impossible to solve, but it will usually mean a bit of haggling.'

Tom smiled, recalling his father's laughter. He'd slapped Tom on the back as he'd given this pearl of wisdom. 'Life is all about bargaining, lad. You give some, you lose some. Sometimes you have the edge, other times someone else does. Look for the edge.'

The edge. Where was the edge in this scenario? Tom rolled it over in his mind. He had believed Fleur when she said that Irma had had a plan for Henry. It may not have involved killing him, but Tom suspected Irma wouldn't be mourning him hard. She would have been left a wealthy woman, going by what Fleur had said, and her plans to marry off Fleur to someone who could control her in the business was inspired. Dark, but inspired. He recalled Fleur telling him how Irma had spat on the photo of Mae Appleby so openly and with such glee, and that Irma had deliberately not passed on the message that he had been found in hospital. If he believed Fleur, then Irma was working against her in every way possible, and that included letting the Coglins know where Tom was staying. She may not have ordered the beating – he couldn't see how that served her interests, unless she thought it might scare him away from Fleur. Even so, she probably would not have discouraged Jimmy's anger. Did she know about Fleur's pregnancy? Maybe that was why she wanted any new men out of the way . . . It likely suited Irma's plans for Fleur to be helplessly bound to Jimmy through a baby. Maybe Jimmy was the answer.

The more Tom wrestled with this notion, the more it made sense that he needed to try to make a difference to Fleur's dilemma. An idea took form, and it seemed to be the edge that his father had referred to.

Well, he would use that edge now; it would be a farewell from him to Fleur. Tom swallowed two of the tablets he'd been given and pulled on his jacket. He knew what he had to do.

23

Fleur opened the door to the policemen. 'Miss Appleby?' There were two of them. Both removed their hats.

She nodded. 'Yes. Thank you for coming.'

'I'm Detective Inspector Peter Green from the CIB, and this is DC Bowers.' His partner nodded behind him. They wore dark suits with neatly knotted ties, both holding out their warrants for her to view. 'I was told there has been a suspicious death?' Green said, glancing up the stairs.

'Yes. My father.'

'Henry? Blimey. I'm so sorry.'

'You knew him?'

'Doesn't everyone know everyone around here?'

'Well, I don't know you.' Fleur frowned, wondering too late if that sounded rude.

He smiled. 'No. We did meet when you were an infant, not that you'd recall. I did my training in Victoria but I was born here. I left for a while but I just couldn't shift my allegiance from the Port Adelaide maggies,' he said, as if trying to lighten the mood. 'No Victorian team for me,' he added.

'Oh,' she said, not inclined to smile.

'Forgive me. The truth is, I returned to marry my sweetheart and make a life back here around the port. I've known your father since I was a lad and I'm very sorry to hear of his passing. Henry was a good man.'

'He was. Come in,' she said, holding the door wider.

His colleague nodded. 'Very sorry for your loss, Miss Appleby.'

'Thank you.' She showed them into the small sitting room. 'Can I offer you something?'

'No, no. Not at all. Um, is Mrs Appleby here?'

'No, she's—'

'I'm here,' Irma said, as though she'd been waiting in the hall to make an entrance. She was pulling off her hat and coat and bustled in. 'I've got nothing to hide.'

'Really?' Fleur said. 'You're all hide, Irma.'

DI Green cleared his throat. 'Miss Appleby, we need to keep this civil right now.'

'Yes, of course.' Fleur was wringing her hands and caught Irma's sneer.

'Right, er, may we sit down?'

'Gentlemen, please,' Irma said, taking charge. 'Can I offer you some tea?'

'I'd advise you not to drink the coffee,' Fleur said, unable to help herself.

'Why's that, Miss Appleby?'

'Because she may poison you as she has my father.'

Irma gave both men a look of indulgent disappointment as though she had fully expected this sort of attack.

'We won't have anything, thank you,' Green confirmed. He smiled gently at both women. 'I've only just recently finished one.'

'Then I'll just let Nan go. She stayed with me all night as Fleur was not here.'

'Just hold off a few more minutes, please,' Green suggested. 'Why don't you tell us what you believe has occurred, Miss Appleby?'

'I believe my stepmother, Irma Appleby, deliberately weakened my father's health with poison over a period of time and then, to hasten him to his death, she gave him spoiled oysters last night.' She blinked, amazing herself at how succinctly she had summarised her accusation.

Irma was shaking her head with incredulity as Fleur finished talking. 'That is so far-fetched, Inspector Green. Henry and I were a close couple and we were happy. I can't believe these accusations of yours, Fleur.'

'Can you substantiate what you're saying, Miss Appleby?'

'I can't show you anything because the rotten oysters we found in the garden were thrown away by our cook,' Fleur replied. 'But I believe Irma used them to contaminate the ones I bought for my father's dinner last night.'

'Mrs Appleby?'

'I think Fleur should write a novel, Inspector Green. Her imagination to tell a story is amazing. If there were rotten oysters around, I suspect it was some lazy local . . . perhaps those teenage boys you told us about, Fleur, who were always trying to sneak a peek into the mortuary?'

Green shrugged, his expression suggesting to Fleur that Irma's explanation certainly sounded reasonable – and it did.

Irma pressed her point. 'I don't know why you're doing this, Fleur, unless it's about your father's will. You see, Inspector, I think Fleur has always resented me being in Henry's life. She's rather obsessed with his property, his business, his bank account . . . always has been. Now that he's passed on – bless his dear soul – I think she wants all of it. She wants to cut me out.'

Fleur flinched as though she'd been slapped. 'How dare you.'

'No, how dare you accuse me of hurting the only man I've ever loved. I'm a widow. I can barely believe it. I lost him just hours ago, and you callously load on these dreadful claims. I think my heart is going to stop from the shock of Henry's death even without this ludicrous claim of poisoning. How can you make me go through this?' She eyed them all, looking wild and frantic.

It was a masterful performance, Fleur thought, and she hoped the police weren't falling for it.

'DC Bowers, perhaps you might escort Mrs Appleby back into the other room, fetch her a nip of something. Please calm yourself, Mrs Appleby. I would like to speak with Miss Appleby alone for a few moments.' Green took out a notebook and pen.

As Irma was escorted to the dining room, Inspector Green lifted his keen, blue-eyed gaze to Fleur's. 'We spoke to Dr Parsons on our arrival. I hope you don't mind that he gave me a brief account of your accusation.'

Fleur gave a shrug. 'Not at all. I'm sure Dr Parsons explained that he believes my father has died of liver failure complicated by food poisoning.'

It was the inspector's turn to nod. 'And, in your opinion, why is this not the case?'

Fleur paused to collect herself. She wanted to answer his question rationally and with a neutral tone. She knit her fingers to prevent waving her arms around with emotion; she needed to be cool and collected for this conversation. She explained about the oysters, and then took another deep breath. 'If you ask our cook, she will corroborate what I've told you.'

'Why didn't you say something to your stepmother?'

'I'd been complaining of a smell for a few days, and then our cook found the source of it – the oysters.' He nodded. 'It didn't occur to me the real reason for their presence, not until I'd heard about my father's food poisoning.'

'But you already had suspicions?'

She nodded. 'About Irma? Yes. She had been acting in a manner I believe was indeed suspicious. Inspector Green, on Tuesday night my father was fine. We shared a meal together and he seemed to be in very good spirits – more cheerful than I've seen him in a while.'

'Why might that be?'

Fleur blushed, unexpectedly shy. 'Because I'd just told him I'd met someone I like very much.'

'I see.'

'It didn't please Irma, because she had plans for me to become engaged to someone else. Anyway, that's irrelevant. I simply didn't know his life was in such immediate jeopardy,' Fleur answered, feeling her insides coil with tension. 'I didn't trust Irma, but I needed to confirm my suspicions that she wished to hasten my father's death.'

'And again, in your opinion, what was the original plan, the one that was moving more slowly?'

She took a steadying breath. 'I believe Irma was using rat killer to slowly poison my father with arsenic. She had been patient. I believe she had been adding it regularly to his coffee, morning and night, for some time.'

'You know this how?'

She told him about her father's complaints, the order for more rat poison when there were no rats present, and how she tested her theory by switching the coffees. 'It terrified Irma. She looked traumatised the evening I did that and immediately begged off, claiming she wasn't feeling well and would go for a rest. My father, however, was thrilled that the coffee tasted so good; he was convinced we were using new beans. We weren't. His coffee simply lacked the arsenic.'

'This was that same evening?'

'Yes, Tuesday.' Fleur watched him note the date.

'Why didn't you come to the police with this notion?'

'I suppose I hadn't fully formulated my thoughts; I tested my theory barely a couple of days ago. As far as I'm concerned, that test confirmed – for me, anyway – that she was adding something to my father's coffee that she wasn't adding to hers. But I knew it sounded unconvincing without some proof.'

'So you were waiting for proof?'

'Yes – to catch her in the act, maybe, or to find a witness. I don't know, to be honest.' Fleur shook her head in a gesture of helplessness. 'It was a notion, as you say. I was personally satisfied on Tuesday evening that I had her pinned, but imagine me giving you that tale, Inspector. By the time you had paid us a visit, the coffee would be thrown away, all trace of arsenic would be removed, as it surely already is, and Irma would quickly paint me – as she's trying to right now – as the petulant daughter making wild accusations.' She gave a sigh. 'No, I knew I needed more, but I couldn't have guessed about her plan to speed up his death with the fetid oysters. And she was cunning enough to allow me to fetch the oysters myself – fresh Coffin Bay oysters from the pub that has been supplying them for all my life.'

'Dr Parsons said you were not here when your father passed away.'

'No.' Fleur's voice was small and filled with regret, as she recalled where she had been and how happy she had felt while her father was sighing his last breath. 'I was taking care of someone who had been set upon by a band of thugs.' She explained going to the hospital and then seeing Tom back to his accommodation. 'The hospital wasn't happy about him discharging himself, and I was told by the nurses that he would need watching because he'd taken a knock to his head.'

'Is this your new beau?'

Again, Fleur blushed, hating that her emotions were on such vivid display. 'Er, yes.'

'I think I heard about this back at the station. Country lad?'

Fleur nodded.

'Right. Just back to the rat poison, Miss Appleby. In your line of work, is there a way of noting arsenic being present?'

Fleur gave a tight, brief smile, grateful that she could lean on her knowledge. 'I could describe skin pallor, for instance, but categorically?' She shook her head. 'Not without searching for its presence within the internal organs. I am confident it will show up in the post-mortem if we could be granted one.'

The inspector nodded; he appeared to be paying thoughtful attention to her remarks.

'I will say, though, if you're interested in the less categorical and don't mind me giving an opinion, then I noted a curious aroma on my father's breath in the last couple of months. I would describe it as stale in a mousey sort of way. I know that sounds strange, but to describe a smell or a taste, you need a metaphor in the same way that a connoisseur would describe wine or tobacco. My father's breath was not stale from age or an unclean mouth. He was fastidious with his hygiene, which is what made it all the more mysterious. No, his breath was recently tarnished by something coming from within. We were all eating the same food each morning and evening. I have read somewhere – one of my reference books, probably – that arsenic, if consumed, can give off an aroma not unlike sniffing at a mousehole. That's how the text put it.' She shrugged. 'I'm sorry, it's vivid, but perhaps not helpful.'

'For someone who doesn't sniff at mouseholes, you mean?'

She found a ragged smile. 'Yes, exactly, but it does paint a picture. It's sad; he seemed so delighted to be tasting good coffee again the night I switched the cups. He didn't know that the coffee wasn't the culprit.'

'And you have proof?'

'I have the test I've mentioned. I have the housekeeper, who will confirm that she was ordered to purchase more rat killer when we needed none, and that the previous tin had been finished quickly with no rats being killed or even sighted to warrant using the poison.'

'This is the same person who found the decayed oysters, which were thrown out? I assume the rubbish has already been collected.'

'Yes.'

'Of course, that find would be deemed circumstantial, Miss Appleby. There is no proof that Mrs Appleby was responsible for those. In fact, she could argue that you were the one who picked up the oysters and could have been responsible for the bad ones.'

Fleur looked back at him, aghast.

'I'm guiding you as to how a defence counsel might argue, Miss Appleby. Evidence has to provide concrete proof – no reasonable doubt. It cannot be your word against another.' He held up a hand. 'You could argue differently, but you cannot prove Mrs Appleby was moving around those oysters.'

Fleur shook her head in despair.

The inspector tapped the pen on his notebook in thought. 'Finally, Miss Appleby, can I ask why you think your stepmother would do this?'

Fleur didn't hesitate. 'I don't believe Irma ever loved my father, but she loved his status and his money. I think she always hoped he would die early and was almost comfy with the fact that he was an alcoholic, making the right noises but not really discouraging him from his drinking. It's my opinion that the rat poison helped his liver to decline faster. I was also in the way of her having everything she wanted – the house, income from the business, to live life exactly how she pleased and independently. At first her plan was to marry me off into a family that she knew would complement the business. It would keep the income steady and she felt she could control me via a husband who was in a business partnership with her. But when I refused, she shifted her plan, first to get my father to change his will, and then to speed up his death. Once Dad was out of the way, she would be declared his beneficiary and I could be asked to leave my home and my business, which she intended to sell to a coffin-maker who is keen to enter the undertaking business.'

'So it's money. That's what you allege her crime is about?' He didn't give much away in his tone but Fleur thought he sounded as though her explanation was plausible.

'Not just money – independent wealth. My father was a wealthy man who lived rather simply. He had no expansive tastes or desires. Irma is the opposite. She fancies herself quite the lady of the manor, and she wanted to live more . . . gregariously, shall we say. I suspect her plan was to move to the other side of the city – perhaps even to a new state, I don't know. I just imagine she would have wanted to put distance between herself and her crime.'

'You seem very sure, Miss Appleby.'

'I *am* very sure, Inspector Green. My stepmother is a murderess and I'm confident further investigation will prove my suspicions.'

He closed the notebook he'd been scribbling into, looking as though he was readying to leave.

'So what happens now?' she asked before he could stand. 'I have no doubt my stepmother is deemed the next of kin and will likely not insist upon a post-mortem.' She gave a mirthless twitch of a smile. 'Nor would I, if I had used poison to kill my husband. She says she's innocent, but will you let the coroner take a look, Inspector? If my father's liver failed from complications of alcohol – as the doctor would likely suggest – then there would have been more signs leading up to last night. I know a bit about physiology, Inspector, and a liver does not stop working as abruptly as a heart might. Please . . . we must respect my father enough to go through with a post-mortem to discover the true cause of death. That's all I'm asking. If I'm wrong, I will publicly apologise to Irma. I will leave this house and its contents, and my position at Appleby's – even this city, if that's what she wants. But I am prepared to bet my life's work on the fact that my father did not simply die . . . he was killed.'

'Miss Appleby, it doesn't matter what I think. I present the facts, and the coroner alone will decide whether or not a post mortem is necessary.'

Next, Nan was called in, arriving trembling and pale to be questioned, and Fleur was asked to leave the room so that the inspector could speak to Nan in private. And then it was Irma's turn, escorted in with the detective constable, but they still kept Fleur and Nan separated.

The phone rang. 'May I?' Fleur asked Bowers.

'Yes, of course.'

It was the Alberton Hotel. 'Is Tom all right?' Fleur asked, suddenly anxious that the publican was calling her and not the other way around.

'Sorry, love. I don't mean to scare you. When I last saw him, the lad was pretty much the same as you left him, perhaps moving a little easier. My wife says he should still be in hospital but I think he's doing well.'

Hearing about Tom should have cheered her but it did the opposite, as if hearing the publican's voice had pricked the tight skin around her emotions that she'd been managing to hold in check, like a balloon inflated to its fullest.

'How can I help? Does he need something?'

'Er, well now, that's why I'm calling. He's gone, love. He said to let you know if you called, but my wife insisted I telephone you.'

'Gone? What do you mean?'

'He packed whatever he had and left a few hours ago. He's left an envelope for you.'

'No, Tom can't have gone. We're . . .' Fleur didn't know what to say. *We're lovers, we're in love, we're engaged?* She chose to say no more.

'He has, I'm afraid.'

'Did he say to where?'

'He didn't. Shall I have the letter sent over?'

'Thank you. I'd pick it up, but my father died today.'

'Oh, Miss Appleby, I'm very sad to hear that. My apologies for interrupting you.'

She murmured that it was not a problem and, in a blur, put the receiver down, unsure if she'd muttered a polite farewell but uncharacteristically not caring in the moment.

Tom was gone? How wrong that sounded. It was suddenly too much to bear. Fleur leant against the wall and felt herself deflating as though the balloon she'd imagined had been untied, slowly letting out the air, and tears welled.

'Tom . . .' was all she could say in a small, wavering voice.

'Miss Appleby?' It was Bowers, helping her back to her feet from where she'd slid down to the ground. She had never been a dramatic person and could barely believe it was her now being hauled back upright. He looked concerned. 'Are you unwell?'

'I'm . . . I'm fine, thank you. Erm . . . just a bit of bad news.'

'More bad news?'

'Yes . . . no . . . I mean, it's not happy news but it doesn't matter right now,' Fleur lied. 'Only my father's passing matters.' She dug in her pocket for a handkerchief to wipe away her tears before returning to the sitting room, where Irma and Nan waited with Inspector Green. Bowers followed her in.

Green spoke first. 'Miss Appleby? Is there anything else you'd like to add?'

'Only to reiterate that I want a post-mortem carried out on my father.'

'Mrs Appleby?'

'Go ahead, I have nothing to fear. Henry died of alcoholism, and I think the accidental seafood poisoning just made an already weakened body and shot liver worse.'

Green continued. 'And the alleged contaminated coffee you spoke of, Miss Appleby? Is that available?'

It was Nan who shook her head. 'The coffee was thrown away.'

'Why?' Inspector Green asked.

'Er . . .' Her eyes flicked between her employer and Fleur.

'Speak honestly,' Green urged.

'Mrs Appleby told me it had turned.'

'Turned? Coffee?' Fleur exclaimed before giving a tight, mirthless gasp.

Irma straightened to her full height. 'Henry kept complaining about it, so I indulged him – why wouldn't I? I loved him. I thought we'd toss out the old coffee and buy fresh beans,' she said, somehow managing to sound affronted.

'Right,' Green said, bringing the conversation to an end before Fleur could erupt. 'Mrs Appleby, I would advise you not to leave home, as I'm sure we will wish to speak with you again – perhaps interview you formally at the station.'

'So I'm not under arrest for these ridiculous claims?' Irma cut a smug glance at Fleur.

'No, Mrs Appleby.' At her sigh of relief, he gave a look of caution. 'But heed my suggestion, please, to remain at home. Now, Miss Appleby, perhaps you'll accompany us to the car?'

'About my father. I can handle—'

'I'm afraid you won't be permitted to move your father's body, which is now officially in police custody.'

'I don't plan on tampering with it, Inspector Green.'

'Nevertheless. This is police protocol.' He gestured for her to lead the way. 'Good day, Mrs Appleby. Again, we're sorry for your bereavement.'

'Thank you, Inspector Green, Detective Bowers.'

They nodded and followed Fleur, who silently picked up their hats in the hallway and handed them to the men.

At the kerb, she rounded on Green. 'No arrest? She'll run.'

'It will only damn her if she does. You said you were utterly sure of the results that the post-mortem will show.'

'I am.'

He shrugged. 'While there is only circumstantial evidence at this stage, I thought you should know that I will be formally asking for the coroner's involvement. There's too much doubt, so we might as well follow through rigorously.'

Fleur felt relief flood her. 'Thank you.'

'I'm taking no sides, Miss Appleby, but Henry was a good man and I take your point that we must respect him. If he has met his end through a criminal deed, then I will not sleep straight at night if I have that on my conscience. Good day, Miss Appleby. I'll keep you informed.'

24

Fleur had gone for a long walk to calm down after the police left, and when she returned to the Appleby house, all the curtains had been drawn and a stern-faced Irma faced her.

'I want you out of this house and I want your key.'

Fleur removed her door key from the keyring in her pocket. 'I have no desire to share this house with you.'

'Good. You're no longer welcome in any part of it, or to anything in it, save the clothes you call yours.'

'I'll pack now,' Fleur said, making for the stairs.

'And go where?'

'That's my business.'

'To your country boy, no doubt,' Irma scoffed. 'Hope you enjoy living above a pub.'

'To my fiancé.' Fleur held up her hand and the ring obliged by glinting rather splendidly in the hallway's lighting.

Irma didn't look impressed. She simply laughed in her best cruel manner. 'Hope you enjoy being poor.'

Fleur did not overreact as perhaps Irma had hoped. It wasn't that the fight had gone out of her, but she'd come to the conclusion while she walked that she had contributed to her father's drinking problem, through all the tension with Irma. The revelation had reached her soul, she was sure. And now that soul wanted to be rid of the hate, rid of the pain, rid of everything connecting her to Irma. It wouldn't be easy, because the potential inquest was still looming, and there was the business, of course. No matter which way she tried to sell it to herself, Fleur knew she was still inextricably linked to her enemy.

The business would be a good distraction now. 'Any funeral calls?' Fleur asked, pausing at the bottom of the stairs.

'No calls. Just a visitor. Mr Wren.'

Fleur frowned, the name escaping her momentarily. 'And?'

'Their baby's dead,' Irma said, flat and heartless.

Fleur felt as though she'd taken a blow. How did Irma do that? How could she be so callous, to say that aloud and not show any care?

'I told him it wasn't convenient—'

'You what?'

'You heard. I let him know my husband had died and we were unable to help.'

'How long ago was this?'

'Barely five minutes before you walked in.'

'Did you get the address?'

'Yes, he'd written it down, but I've thrown it in the wastepaper basket.'

'This is why my father needed a secretary, not a new wife! We have a rule, Irma. Dad and I never turn away a grieving family.' And then it hit her. *Wren!* 'Wait, was his name James Wren?'

'So what if it was?'

Fleur closed her eyes momentarily in sorrow. The inevitable must have occurred; that poor child, and that poor family.

Irma went on speaking, ignoring her. 'And fret not. I will be taking calls and making sure you know about them. We don't want the business failing, do we? Or we'll both lose out.'

'After today, I'll be giving you my key to the mortuary.'

'What do I want that for?' Irma asked, looking disgusted. 'I've got no reason to poke around in there.'

'You'll need it if you take a call for undertaking.'

'And how do I reach you?'

'Irma, if you think I'm going to protect the business for you, then you have me wrong. After I handle the Wrens' needs, I shall step away. Apparently it's all yours now, anyway. You can find a new mortician from tomorrow, and good luck.'

'You can't do that!'

'I just did.'

'Watch your father's business go to hell?'

'No, I'll watch *your* business do that. I can always build another, because, Irma, you can't take away my skills or my reputation. In time, no one is going to come to you for a funeral . . . You might be able to convince a few with your clever acting for a while – relying on the name Appleby – but it won't last. In this I'm confident. You're a trickster and a con, and you'll be found out.'

Irma barely blinked. 'I'll just sell it, then.'

'Do what you like. All you have is the name. And that will only go so far once you've sold it on to the dodgy people you plan to.'

Fleur turned away to find the Wrens' address in North Adelaide and quickly changed into her special undertaking gown. She was out of the house in moments to find one of the lads washing the car. 'Quick, we have a call-out, Robbie,' she said. 'North Adelaide.'

As miserable as she felt for the Wrens, she was inwardly relieved to have important work to attend to. It would occupy her for the rest of the day at least and set the pain of Tom's departure aside, giving her a bit more time to confront that pain, which felt unbearable on top of the pain of losing her father.

She wound down the window and inhaled the fresh sea air, tasting the salt on the breeze. She needed it to cleanse her mind of visions of her father on a slab in the Royal Adelaide Hospital's mortuary, with a pathologist preparing to cut him open from clavicle to navel. She knew how the coroner's studies went, with nothing left to chance. All major organs were removed, weighed, scrutinised – even the tongue. She thought of all the fond words her father had spoken to Mae and herself and she began to cry again at the thought of her father being muted. She leaned back; she needed the wind to dry her cheeks before they arrived.

'According to the map, it's down here, Fleur. We got lost once, your father and I, and I know we drove down this street several times.' Robbie grinned and then his face fell as he saw hers. 'I'm sorry . . . I'm so sorry.'

'It's all right. Really. I want to hear the memories. Don't stop.' She felt sorry for his fallen expression. 'I know he normally didn't have city funerals to undertake, so I can understand you getting lost.'

Robbie frowned as he searched along the street. 'Number forty-three?'

Fleur nodded.

'Here we are. Want me to park and wait?'

'Thank you.'

'I'll be right over there.' He pointed.

Fleur left the car and opened the gate of an imposing pair of villas, adjoined and built in the trademark bluestone of this neighbourhood of Adelaide. Decorative iron lace added beauty to the first storey, and it was repeated at the fence and gate between the stone pillars. Daffodils lined the path lending a helplessly cheery air as she walked up to the door but Fleur noticed the curtains were drawn and the familiar silence of grief surrounded the house that now embraced the bereaved.

She swallowed. This was going to take all her composure, but she was known for it and now needed to prove it wasn't an empty claim. The door knocker was wrapped in black fabric, so she tapped gently at the door with her knuckles and was kept waiting a long time. She tried again, and once more there was a protracted pause before Jamie answered. The sleeve on his arm was rolled up and his braces dangled at his hips.

'Fleur,' he breathed. 'I wasn't sure—'

'I know, Jamie. I'm so sorry you encountered Irma. She's my stepmother and most unhelpful.'

'I was told that . . .' He didn't finish, looking uncertain of how to say it.

'I know what you were told and it's true I am newly bereaved, but I think your family's need is greater than mine right now.'

His brittle poise collapsed and he slumped at the door. 'I didn't know who to contact. Claire said there was only one person to call.' His voice shook. He too was in shock.

Fleur found a gentle smile. 'I like to think so. I'd consider it an honour to help your family.'

'Come in, please.'

Fleur let Jamie guide her into the family's sitting room, where Claire sat with her hair in disarray and red splotches on her cheeks. She lifted her eyes; even weeping hadn't dimmed their colour of a cloudless autumn morning. 'Alfie fell asleep,' she whispered, nodding to herself. 'He's just sleeping.' She hummed a little under her breath, a lullaby.

Fleur looked at Jamie, whose face told her everything she needed to know about this situation. 'Jamie, shall we have a cup of tea?' He looked like he needed something to do.

'Yes. Good idea.' He couldn't get away fast enough.

'Claire?'

The bereaved mother looked up again, slightly dreamy.

'Do you remember me?'

Claire nodded. 'Yes, of course. Thank you for coming,' she said and returned her gaze to her dead child.

'Where are the children?'

'They've gone to school. Only William knows.'

Fleur swallowed the rise of painful emotion at this news. She could try but knew she wouldn't get close to how Claire must be feeling.

Jamie returned. 'Kettle's on,' he said, pointing his thumb over his shoulder.'

'Has the doctor been called, Jamie?'

'He came early this morning and pronounced . . .' Fleur nodded firmly so he wouldn't have to say it. 'He, er, he told us to make our arrangements and I was able to drive down to the port to find you.'

'All right. Oh, I hear the kettle,' Fleur said and followed Jamie as he disappeared to switch off the flame, down a small hallway into a tiny kitchen. 'Jamie,' she continued as the whistle died and vapours settled. 'How long ago did Alfie pass?'

He trembled as he lifted the spout cover away, his arm shaking as he poured the water over the leaves in the pot. 'He didn't wake us up as he usually does around five. Always up with the birds, our Alfie,' he said, tears beginning to roll down his cheeks. 'Sorry.'

'Please don't be. This is the saddest of all situations. You're allowed to show it.'

'I want to be strong for Claire.'

'You will be. You'll be strong for each other. Claire's incredibly stoic.'

'What do we do next?'

'Well, if you can encourage her to drink a sweet cup of tea, I'll do the rest. You can trust me – I won't rush her. But I will have to take Alfie from you both, because I can tell it's been a few hours now and, well, I won't go into the details. It's important I take care of him for you.'

'Can you make all the arrangements?'

'Yes, of course. There's a small chapel attached to our funeral home that you are welcome to use, unless you'd rather—'

'No, that sounds good. My family are all too far away to antic-ipate they'd come. They're also . . .'

Fleur waited.

Jamie shrugged. 'As you know, I grew up in the north on a far-flung farm. Country people are just more . . .' He searched for the right word.

'Accepting?' Fleur offered, hoping she'd found it for him.

'Yes. Death happens. It tends to be more obvious when you live in an unforgiving landscape as I did, and I gather your Tom was raised in, too.'

She nodded, looked down, hating the mention of Tom. 'Yes, he mentioned how challenging it is.'

'My folk are not hard-hearted, but I reckon they would resign to the loss faster. They'd remind me that we have three bonny kids, all rosy-cheeked and healthy, and we've lost a baby who hasn't yet developed into a little boy who knows us or knows about life.'

Fleur swallowed. This was exactly where she sensed so many people – mainly men – went wrong. But she held her tongue and was glad of it when he continued.

'I don't subscribe to that, Fleur. I have to say I was as much in love with Alfie as I am with Will or Matti or my beautiful Susan. To suggest I'd miss him less is to reduce him somehow.'

All she could do was nod.

'But I understand their attitude, where it's come from and that it's not meant to be cruel. It's about finding resilience and accepting the reality of life . . . that it isn't always kind.'

Fleur gave a soft smile. 'Claire would know all this too. I suspect her time as a nurse in difficult places has prepared her more than any of us.'

'I would have thought so too, and she was certainly readying herself, but now that the moment has arrived, she's reacting like any mother feeling bereft.' Jamie shook his head. 'When should the funeral happen?'

'How about tomorrow? I know it's fast, but I've found in these instances, it's better to hold the funeral as soon as possible.' Fleur didn't want to start explaining about how quickly their little boy's body was cooling and changing. She needed to get Alfie back to the mortuary quickly. 'Don't worry. I'll make all the arrangements and I'll telephone you with the details.'

He straightened his hair and then did it again in a motion of fidgeting. 'Er, Fleur, we . . . we don't have a lot of cash just at the moment. We ploughed everything into this house for the children. But I do have an odd job and Claire starts her work shortly.'

'You won't need anything other than the cemetery's burial costs, which will be minimal. About three pounds. I will be waiving all costs for my involvement.'

'What?' He looked stunned. 'Why?'

'It's your baby, Jamie. I can't possibly do anything but donate my time, my care and everything else that an undertaker provides.'

'But the coffin . . . I was warned it could be expen—'

'As I said, don't think on any of that again. Let me do this for your family, as a friend.'

'I don't know what to say,' he said, embarrassed.

'Let's comfort Claire, and let me take care of Alfie from here.'

'I'm incredibly grateful and surprised. I'll pour the tea.'

Back in the sitting room, Fleur regarded Claire, again humming quietly to Alfie, who was wrapped in his baby blanket, with a gentle gaze and the realisation that as grief-stricken as she felt over losing her father, nothing could come close to losing a child. It was helping her find perspective on her own bereavement.

'Here we are, darling,' Jamie offered gently. 'Fleur here thinks you need a sweet cup of tea in you.'

Claire smiled affectionately at her husband. 'Thanks, Jamie, but I can't,' she said. 'Not holding Alfie.'

'Oh, here, let me,' Fleur said. 'May I hold Alfie for you?'

Claire looked unsure but Jamie nodded, urging her to accept the offer. She handed the still bundle into Fleur's arms.

'Ah, there now, I've got him,' Fleur said softly. 'Hello again, darling Alfie,' she murmured. 'Aren't you handsome?'

She wasn't lying. Alfie looked as though he were simply sleeping, a perfect-looking baby captured on canvas by a painter. Fleur looked up at Claire, who was smiling as she wept. The tears were good; she'd seen this before with mothers in shock. Once the tears arrived, it meant they were beginning to let themselves accept, or at least understand, that their child had died.

'He really was such a good baby,' Claire said, the tears flowing freely now. 'You met him on a bad day.'

And there it was. Another hurdle behind them. Once a mother began to speak in past tense about their baby, another enormous step had been taken towards letting go. Fleur knew now that she would be able to leave with Alfie soon.

25

No one but Tom could know just how much effort it took to arrive at Coglin's Carpentry, but he also knew he was not leaving there empty-handed.

Jimmy Coglin was sanding down a coffin in the yard when Tom limped through the gate. Jimmy glanced over, realised who it was and straightened, flinging down his sandpaper that was curled around a block of timber. 'What the hell are you doing here, Catchlove?'

'I've come to make you an offer.'

Jimmy's gaze narrowed and his eyes hooded with lack of under-standing. His lips stuck out when he made this gesture, adding to Tom's notion that he was dealing with a man of very low wit. 'What sort of offer?'

An older man approached before Tom could respond. 'Who's this, then? Bloody hell, mate, hope the other guy looks worse.'

Tom blinked but only his undamaged eye obliged. 'No, he doesn't. He brought his mates to hold me down.'

'Bloody coward,' the older bloke remarked and Tom simply nodded, letting his good eye find Jimmy's newly embarrassed gaze.

'I'm Tom Catchlove,' he said, offering his uninjured arm to the older man.

The fellow frowned as though it should be familiar. 'Bert Coglin.'

'You own this business?'

'I do, son. But if you're looking for work, you're no good to me all beat up.'

'He's not looking for work, Dad,' Jimmy growled, cutting a fierce grimace at his father.

'What are you here for then?'

'I just told your son I'd like to make him an offer. It will keep him out of the clutch of the police.'

'You what?' Bert took a step forward. 'What's this?'

'Leave it, Dad,' Jimmy said.

'I won't leave it, though,' Tom said. 'If you don't want me pressing charges, Jimmy, you have to come clean.'

'I'm not admitting to beating you up,' Jimmy snarled.

'You did this?' His father gawped. 'You stupid idiot. And I suppose you took your two numbskull sidekicks with you?'

'He did, Mr Coglin. There was nothing fair about it. They followed me and jumped me. They held me down so Jimmy could make a good fist of it, because I don't think he'd take me on alone. If he had, I doubt I'd be in this state.'

Bert Coglin pushed Jimmy aside, glaring sideways at him. 'Don't say another word,' he threatened. 'You, Catchlove – why are you here and not at the police?'

'Because I'm not a dobber. I'll take my punishment but, you see, your family has set out to hurt someone I care about and I've taken real offence at that.'

'Who's that then?'

Tom managed a wry smile even though it sent a trill of pain through him as a wound on his lip broke and began to bleed. He dabbed at it unselfconsciously. 'Fleur Appleby.'

Bert raised his eyebrows. 'Well, you country lads work fast, don't you?'

Tom shrugged. 'That's not relevant. What is relevant is how you and your cowardly son are going to fix things for Fleur. It's the least he can do under the circumstances.' Tom wanted to confront Jimmy over the baby, but this wasn't the moment. And he knew deep down that he was the intruder, the unwanted one.

Jimmy stepped forward, his bruised knuckles balled tight.

'Settle down, Jimmy. You achieved nothing with your fists. Let's use your head now, eh?' Bert turned his narrow-eyed expression onto Tom again. 'And what do you suggest?'

'Henry Appleby has died.' Tom watched the information land; it clearly came as no surprise. Regardless, they both tried to force sorrow onto their faces.

'Oh, really? That's no good. But he wasn't well, was he?'

'Mr Coglin, let's cut the false sympathy. This has come as no shock to you.'

'No, well . . .' the father began. 'According to Mrs Appleby, he's been ailing and I suppose—'

'Fleur knows that Irma helped him towards his last breath.'

Bert took a slow moment to blink and perhaps have the time to think about what to say to this remark. But it was Jimmy who looked down guiltily. So it was true. There *had* been foul play. They didn't have to say anything to incriminate themselves – it was there to see, plainly written on their faces and in their suddenly awkward body language.

'I don't know anything about that,' Bert said, not at all convincingly.

'Maybe, maybe not. What about you, Jimmy? You look suddenly uncomfortable.'

Bert whipped his head around but Jimmy couldn't help himself.

'I'm not involved in that. I told Dad not to—'

'Shut your mouth, boy!' Bert snapped.

Tom returned his gaze to the father. 'Or what, Bert? You'll use your fists on him? No point. You either come clean, or I go to the police.'

Bert sneered. 'I've got nothing to say about Irma.'

'I'm not talking about Irma. I'm talking about me pressing charges against Jimmy and his mates. They're not going to be happy to be roped into it, but I can remember each of them.' He reeled off first names that he remembered from the night he was jumped on and dragged off, along with convincing descriptions. 'I remember them from the dance and so does Fleur. The police officer in charge has encouraged me to press charges. He wants to stamp out this sort of hooligan behaviour, apparently. So, Bert, how do you feel about your boy in prison? I'll push all the way . . . Are you up for it, Jimmy?'

Jimmy let rip with a string of colourful language and curses. Other workers began sauntering out for smoko and to see what all the fuss was about.

Tom simply shrugged. 'It's up to the two of you. I'm leaving, returning north, so, Jimmy, you get what you wanted, but I can't imagine Fleur would appreciate a husband in gaol. Wouldn't be good for business, either. So what's it to be?'

'What do you want from us?' Bert demanded.

'The truth, that's all. Was Irma helping Henry Appleby to an early death?' Tom watched Bert draw in a long breath, taking that time to contemplate his answer and its repercussions. 'She can't hurt you if you tell the truth. But I will do my utmost to ruin your business if you don't.'

Bert shook his head. 'I never wanted any part of this. All I wanted was to get into undertaking. I could have opened my own funeral house.'

'Why didn't you?'

'Irma's very persuasive, and she offered a shortcut,' he said, sounding disgusted. 'And now look where that's got us.'

'What did she ask you to do?'

'Just an errand.' It was Jimmy who answered, winning a glare from his father. 'What?' he demanded defensively. 'I'm not taking the rap for bloody Irma.'

He returned his gaze to Bert, who sighed. 'She asked us to fetch some oysters, that's all.'

Tom was never one to be slow off the mark. He nodded, understanding in a heartbeat. 'And then she let them go off before serving them to Henry?'

Bert shook his head. 'She only used the juice of the bad oysters and put it on a couple of the good ones, I gather. Look, the fellow was as good as dead,' he appealed to Tom.

'Not according to his daughter. Do you know about the arsenic as well?'

Both Coglins nodded, looking worried now. 'But we had nothing to do with that.'

'Right. You're both coming with me to the local cop shop. Tell them what you did, what you know. Or I'll tell them what Jimmy did to me. One look at his knuckles is all it will take.' Tom nodded towards Jimmy, who shoved his hands into his pockets.

'We're damned either way!' Bert argued.

Tom nodded. 'But you can be honest. Contrite.' He could see them both frowning. 'If you can show your regret at the part you played, I'm sure you won't see the inside of the gaol. You were manipulated by a woman with a dark plan and she promised you her business. *You* didn't kill him. You were forced to run an errand, believing the reward was part of the business.'

'That's the truth of it!' Bert said.

'Then tell the truth.'

'Wait.' Jimmy frowned. 'What do you mean, you're leaving?'

Hell, he was slow. 'Don't think on it, Jimmy. You've got a full plate to contend with soon. Fleur is yours. I'm stepping aside.'

'I don't understand.'

And only then did it occur to Tom that Fleur hadn't yet told Jimmy about the baby. She must have been weighing up her situation when Tom had obliviously walked back into her life. Was she really that conniving? He would never have thought that of her, but there was no denying how smart she was. It hardened his resolve.

'Oh, I'm sure you'll work it out, Jimmy,' Tom said, and smiled, making the scab on his lip crack again. Somehow the blood that subsequently oozed felt appropriate.

Back at the house, Fleur could hear Irma upstairs. The wireless was on. How appalling that she could listen to music and the news of the day, knowing her husband had only died hours ago. Fleur swallowed the bile and didn't linger, moving straight through to the mortuary where she laid out tiny Alfie. He was beginning to look seriously dehydrated. She would attend to that now and ensure that, should the Wrens wish to bid a final farewell before their child was laid to rest, their son might look as plump and pink as he had looked in life.

Somehow she'd managed to get through that visit with only that single mention of Tom, which she had deflected well enough. Claire had been too preoccupied to ask after him, which was a mercy. Fleur would have to tell her friend soon, but it could wait. By then she hoped to be in far more control of her pain over losing him.

It still made no sense. After returning from collecting Alfie, she had taken delivery of the envelope from the Alberton Hotel. On the front it simply read *For Fleur Appleby* in small, neat lettering. Inside was cash and a note in the same handwriting that said: *Thanks anyway, Fleur, but no need to pay my bills. Yours always, Tom.*

Now she was more confused than ever. Those first ten brief words seemed to possess Tom's reticence, and the final three encapsulated the love she had felt in his arms, beneath his lips and in his bed. This was Tom, for sure, and yet it was surely an impostor. The Tom she had left that morning was not this Tom who had written the note and returned her money. Somehow that was incredibly hurtful. It was as though he was fully washing his hands of her; now they owed each other nothing. But why?

What occurred between this morning, when she had kissed him goodbye, and when he wrote that note? She could count the time in a few hours. Something had happened – something big – to change his mind from a man in love and wanting to marry, to a man walking away from her.

What had she done?

Tears welled as she pushed and pulled at the conundrum, and she let them fall. No one was watching – no one alive, anyway. Alfie was here and he was relying on her; he took priority over Tom.

She washed her hands with great care, pulled on her special apron and within moments had lost herself to her work, all her focus on attending to Alfie. The tasks were quick on such a tiny body but Fleur could not help lingering. It wasn't enjoyable so much as satisfying, and it created a warm feeling within her as she took extra special care with his fragile skin and delicate hair. And through it all, as she prepared Alfie for his final journey, she felt all the rottenness and canker of Irma's involvement in her life leaching away. It was as if Alfie's beauty replaced it; each dainty and precise action on the tiny body refilled Fleur's heart with affection.

She found it uncanny how death seemed to be bringing her back to full vigour; Alfie was reminding her about all that was precious in life. Irma was not important, and her sinister actions – true or false – were now in the past. That could not be changed. But Alfie was important. His brief life had meant joy, and Fleur wished she could brood on all that was brilliant in her life and leave the past behind. That meant no longer dwelling on her father's mode of death, which would be hard to let go of, but now, all of a sudden, Tom was her past too.

He'd represented her future for a brief, glittering period: love, marriage, a child or children of their own . . . *Find one thing*, she pleaded with herself, and she focused on her plan for a new business. A new enterprise, a new era for her, which she could run exactly as she wished.

And in caring for Alfie, washing his tiny body, combing his wispy golden baby hair, massaging the little hands and feet away from their stiffness, simply reinforced to Fleur that this was what she was born to do. More than that, she knew she was the best in her craft.

She didn't need this house any more. She didn't need the Appleby's reputation, or to be remembered for overcoming Irma's voraciousness. And as much as she loved Tom, she didn't need him for her business. She wanted to let that thought take root but a small voice followed up: *But you need him for everything else. He* is *you. You have become one.*

What she needed to do, she understood now, as she carefully buttoned on Alfie's white christening gown, decorated with tiny blue embroidered bunnies, was to let go. Let go of it all . . . all the pain of being an orphan, of losing the mother who had adored her, of losing the father who she knew had loved her unequivocally. And of losing Tom, the only man she had ever felt any romantic attraction to. They were all gone now.

She would have to start her life afresh . . . alone. She looked at Alfie, peaceful, pink and cherubic again after Fleur's careful ministrations and looking like the angel that she believed he'd become in her life. 'There you go, Alfie,' she whispered and placed a gentle kiss on the baby's cool forehead. 'Rest peacefully now,' she murmured as she lifted the tiny body into a satin-lined coffin wrapped in the softest of woollen baby blankets.

All of this, including the burial licence of three pounds and fifteen, she would gift to the family. And in that moment, Fleur decided that every infant under twelve months who came into her care would be given the same treatment, at her expense. It would be her new company's way of showing understanding to grieving parents, and they would use her business and recommend it, she was sure.

Alfie was ready now, and so was Fleur to set out on their new and separate journeys.

26

After making all the final arrangements for Alfie's burial and asking for a full account to be sent in the name of Appleby's, Fleur wrote a letter to the Wrens explaining everything. She summoned Robbie again and asked him to deliver the note. It was better than another phone call.

'You'll take the coffin to Cheltenham Cemetery for eleven tomorrow morning?'

He nodded. 'You're not coming?'

'Probably not, Robbie. I spoke to the parents earlier. Only they will be there – they want to keep it private.'

'Right. And all the paperwork is sorted?'

'Yes, I've taken care of it.'

'See you soon, Fleur.'

She smiled, not wishing to give him the truth yet. 'I don't really know what's going to happen beyond today, if I'm honest. Irma is now the owner of Appleby's.'

His mouth opened in surprise.

'But it will sort itself, I'm sure,' Fleur continued. 'In the meantime, your job is safe and should anything change, I want you to call me at this number.' She gave him a second note with the hotel's telephone details. 'You're not to worry. Tell Albert the same, will you?'

'Right.' He looked unsure. 'I don't want to work for Irma, Fleur.'

'I understand, but don't do anything rash for now. Let's talk when we know the outcome of the coroner's report. Will you stay patient for me, Robbie? I won't let you down.'

He nodded. 'I trust you, Fleur.'

'Thanks. See you soon.'

After he'd left, Fleur saw that it was nearing four and she phoned the pub. The wife answered this time.

'Tom left us this morning,' the publican's wife offered. 'I'll be honest, I didn't think he looked in any condition to be going anywhere but straight back to bed.'

'And he didn't say where he was going?' Fleur tried again.

'He didn't say, love, and I didn't ask. Not my place.'

Fleur's hopes sank. 'No, no, of course.'

'You got his letter?'

'Yes . . . if you could call it that. He was returning the money I left with your husband.'

'Like that, is it? You two have a tiff?'

'No! That's the thing,' she said, glad to be talking to another woman in this way. 'I don't know what's happened.'

'What do you mean?'

'Tom and I . . . Well, I thought we were going to be together for keeps.' Fleur didn't want to discuss the engagement so she kept it vague. 'We talked about marriage and family – you know how people in love do.'

'He didn't strike me as a Lothario, love.'

'Not at all. Truly. I consider myself a good judge of character, and whatever Tom might be, he's not that.'

'Quite a shy lad, really.'

He wasn't shy, Fleur thought, but she didn't want to explain it was Tom's way to be restrained, to listen more than he spoke. 'I just can't understand it. There's no explanation, so I don't know what happened for him to just leave, especially in such a wounded condition.'

'Well, whatever you wrote in that note, love, it obviously tipped him over the edge.'

Fleur felt a flash of alarm. 'Note?'

'The one we sent upstairs to him this morning. None of my business, of course, but we thought it was strange that you'd send a lad into the pub with a letter. But then I thought perhaps it's romantic. I used to do that sort of thing when I was young too.'

'But I didn't send anything.' Fleur frowned. 'You said a lad brought it in?'

'Yes, just a kid. I was the person closest. He gave me the letter and said it was for the person on the front. We sent it up to Mr Catchlove immediately.'

'And then he left?'

'About twenty minutes later. Thanked us, paid his bill and walked out.'

'It wasn't from me.'

'Really? I did ask and he said a woman gave it to him. Had Appleby's on the back.'

'Why would I ask someone to deliver a note when I had just been with Tom and was planning to return later today?' It was a rhetorical question, but the woman answered all the same with an edge of indignance in her voice.

'Search me, love. It's not our business.'

'No. I'm sorry. Please forgive my tone – I'm upset. My father has passed on, as you know, and this has been an awful few hours.'

'Nothing to forgive. I'm sorry it didn't work out with your young man. We thought he was nice fella.'

'I think I'm going to need a room later today. Are you able to accommodate me, please?'

'No worries, love. Easily fixed.'

Fleur was glad she didn't enquire further. 'I'll be up in a couple of hours. Perhaps I can have Tom's old room.'

'Fine. See you then.'

After bathing, re-dressing and packing a small suitcase, Fleur took a final look around her bedroom. She flicked off the light and closed the door slowly and deliberately, as though shutting off an era. She wanted to step into her father's room, to smell his presence, but she could hear Irma moving around in there and she didn't want to give her the satisfaction of seeing Fleur in such a private emotional moment. Perhaps when she returned to pick up the rest of her things, she might snare the chance to be alone upstairs.

'I'm leaving now, Irma.'

Fleur heard footsteps and the door was opened. 'Oh, good.' Irma sounded genuinely delighted.

'I'll leave the keys to the mortuary on the telephone table.'

'And that final body?'

'The funeral is tomorrow,' Fleur replied. 'I've got the coffin in the cool room. You don't have to worry about any of it. Robbie will collect it once we know the time. I'll need to make some final arrangements for the family, but I can do that from elsewhere.'

'Fine. Make sure you leave the keys to the chapel. I shall be changing all the locks,' Irma warned.

'No need, I have no keys.'

'Even so. Well, good luck, Fleur.'

'I'm honest enough to say that I don't wish you the same. I know what you've done, Irma, but I can't change the outcome.'

'Nor can you prove it. Now, hurry along – let's get all the Appleby stench out of this house. Oh, and you'd better grab that photograph of Mae, or I will certainly enjoy tossing it on the rubbish heap.'

'You're amazingly cruel,' Fleur said, her tone bordering on fascination. 'I'm sure you'd make a good study for someone who looks into personalities and disorders of the human mind.'

'It's not about being cruel, Fleur, it's about being pragmatic. What is happening suits me.'

'At any cost, obviously.'

'You've always had your head in the clouds. The real world is cruel, as you say. So you need to protect yourself and what's yours. You haven't done a very good job of that.'

Before Fleur could respond, there was a firm rap at the door. She was halfway down the stairs anyway so decided to answer it, hoping against hope that it might be Tom. A change of heart, a final conversation, a chance to find out what he was thinking . . . Whoever it was, it had to be important for someone to ignore the cloth wrapped around the doorknocker and the closed curtains. She opened the front door to see Detective Inspector Green, on his own this time.

'Oh, hello again. We weren't expec—'

He removed his hat. 'Good afternoon, Miss Appleby, Mrs Appleby,' he said, looking past Fleur's shoulder to where Irma stood not far behind. 'I have some news and wanted to give it to you myself and in person.'

'Come in,' Fleur said, feeling a pit open in her stomach. This didn't sound like the sort of news she wanted to hear.

'Thank you.' He stepped inside and followed them into the sitting room.

No one sat. Neither woman spoke. Fleur regarded the inspector with trepidation.

Finally he broke the silence. 'Er, well, I'll get straight to it. We've heard from the coroner.' He waited a beat but again was met with silence. 'Miss Appleby, I'm afraid to say there will be no coronial enquiry into your father's death, which means no post-mortem.'

'What?' Fleur stepped back as despair flooded her. 'How can this be?'

'Please sit,' he urged.

'I don't want to sit,' she snapped, glancing at Irma, who looked like she'd just won first prize in something important, licking her lips with glee as her fat fingers formed chubby fists of triumph at her side.

'Miss Appleby . . . Fleur, may I explain?'

'Is there any point?'

'I think you need to hear the rationale. You know I felt there was reason enough to at least pursue a post-mortem.'

Fleur just shook her head in dejection as he continued.

'You see, the coroner did give it due consideration, but it was explained to me that given everyone, including the doctor and you, agrees that Henry Appleby's liver was compromised through alcohol poisoning and would likely show cirrhosis, the other elements you were searching for were toxicity from shellfish poisoning and arsenic from rat poison.'

He paused and again no one said a word.

'We know Henry ate a dozen oysters. Your claim of deliberate poisoning was not backed up by any proof, and the cook's awareness of old oyster shells in the backyard is, at best, circumstantial, as I warned. The coroner assured me that even if seafood poisoning could be established, there's no evidence that can categorically point a finger at Mrs Appleby as the culprit.'

Irma gave a grunt of satisfaction and Fleur's shoulders drooped further.

'But the arsenic,' Fleur began anxiously. 'No one consumes that willingly. If it's in his body, he's been poisoned, and we have proof and a witness to say Irma was getting through an inordinate amount of rat killer.'

'Again, that's all circumstantial – you have no actual proof of her feeding it to your father.'

'Other than my test. She refused to drink it!'

'It's your word against hers. There were no witnesses.'

'And I would hotly deny any wrongdoing with rat poison, Inspector. It's a ludicrous suggestion,' Irma said, disappearing with a haughty expression into her chins. She stood straighter, with pinched lips that spoke of self-righteousness.

Fleur had to look away, beyond despondent.

'But it's more complicated than that. The pathologist at the hospital explained to me that arsenic is present in so many everyday items, from medicine to rat killer, but especially prevalent in—'

'Mortuary products,' Fleur spoke over him.

'I was told it's in plenty of fluids that you use every day in the mortuary: disinfectants, deodorising compounds, cosmetics and so on,' Green said.

Fleur nodded in gloom. 'He's right.'

Green sighed. 'So, just to be clear on what I've been advised, even if traces of arsenic had been found in Henry's body, it would not have proved what you wanted it to prove. Mrs Appleby's defence counsel would still quite rightly argue that Henry was around arsenic every day.'

'Not in the amount she was giving him,' Fleur bristled, but she knew there was no point arguing. 'I can tell I'm not going to be able to take this any further, Inspector.'

He shook his head. 'Not without some sort of corroborating factor.'

'Like what?'

'A witness or witnesses who would testify to what you allege about Mrs Appleby. They would have to be prepared to stand in the dock and affirm what they know under oath, and to be interrogated by her defence.'

Fleur sighed again. 'Well, I don't have anyone who can.'

He gave a small shrug. 'You have to let this go, Miss Appleby. The law sees that there is too much doubt in this instance to incriminate Mrs Appleby.'

'This means I'm free of all uncertainty over Henry's death?' Irma asked.

'It does,' Green said. 'You are free to arrange the funeral of your husband and the case is closed. I've organised for Mr Appleby to be transferred back here. Is that what you want?'

'Yes,' Fleur said firmly, before Irma could speak. 'I will prepare my father.'

'Well, thank you, Inspector Green,' Irma said, sounding buoyant. 'I'm delighted to cast off this shadow. Now I can get on with grieving for my beloved husband and working out how to live as a widow.'

'Yes, and I—'

The inspector got no further as another firm rap at the door startled them. This was suddenly like a poor pantomime, Fleur thought, and Irma was playing the role of the wrongly accused with spectacular credibility.

'I wonder who that might be,' Irma said.

All you lack is an audience out there in the stalls, Fleur thought.

'My word, people are insensitive,' Irma continued. 'Surely they know we're bereaved. Fleur, perhaps you could escort the inspector out and send away any other callers. I am going to my room to pray for Henry.'

Fleur had to use all her willpower not to walk over and slap Irma for her horribly hammy acting.

'Good day and thank you, Mrs Appleby. Shall we . . .?' Green said, but Fleur had not moved. She was staring at the swirling pattern on the carpet, knowing that once the policeman left, that was it for her father; he would be put in his grave without justice.

Green made to leave.

'Oh, look at the poor wretch,' Irma said. 'I can appreciate how upsetting it must be to realise her unfounded claim has been thrown out by the coroner.'

'That's not quite how—' Green started.

'Seems I shall have to see you out, Inspector,' Irma cut in, marching off and expecting him to follow.

Fleur heard Irma opening the door and a sudden shocked silence before she heard another man's voice in apology.

'Bowers?'

'Sir.' There was a moment's pause when she presumed the subordinate had removed his hat and nodded at Irma. 'Mrs Appleby.'

'What's going on?' Green urged.

'Can I come inside, please?'

Fleur moved to the doorway to see Inspector Green stepping back into the hall, giving Irma had no choice but to close the door, now trapped by the two policemen in her own home.

'Hello again, Miss Appleby,' Bowers said, catching sight of Fleur hovering. 'Er, curious turn of events. Down at the station, we've got witnesses who attest that Mrs Appleby was planning the death of Henry Appleby, first through the use of rat poison and then more recently using rancid oysters.'

Fleur couldn't believe what she was hearing and stepped up to form a trio of listeners, feeling light-headed with relief. Irma's jaw had dropped open in shock.

'Tell me,' Green instructed.

'It's a father and son. Coffin-makers who have had dealings with the Applebys over the years, but more recently with Mrs Appleby.'

'Bert and Jimmy?' Fleur murmured in astonishment.

'That's right, Miss. Your young man encouraged them to speak up.'

'Tom? But—'

Green sounded testy. 'Let me get this straight, Bowers. The Coglins have admitted to knowing about Irma Appleby's intentions?'

Bowers nodded. 'Yes. Mrs Appleby told Bert of her intention to hurry along Henry Appleby's death. She told him she was using rat killer in his coffee but it was taking too long.'

'Wait, why would she share that?' Green asked, as though Irma was not standing ashen-face just behind him.

'Her intention, according to Bert Coglin, was that she was going to sell Appleby's to him for a good price. They wanted to get into undertaking and funeral direction.' Bowers pulled out his notebook. 'According to the son, she'd suggested he marry Miss Appleby and I quote: "So you can control your wife, who is important to the business."'

Irma gasped. 'This is all rubbish.'

Fleur wanted to leap in and respond but Inspector Green shot her a warning look. He turned back to Bowers, frowning. 'This was recorded during a formal interview?'

Bowers nodded. 'Yes, sir. All done properly and by the book.'

'What else?'

'Bert Coglin was asked by Mrs Appleby to buy some oysters. Apparently just a few were required. She told him she was going to let them go off for a few days and then use their juice to taint the fresh oysters that she'd have the daughter – er, Miss Appleby, fetch. Coglin said she told him that it needed to be done this way so no one could attribute the purchase of oysters to her, fresh or otherwise. He went to pains to explain that he did nothing wrong. All he did was buy fresh oysters with her money and at her bidding. I quote again: "I knew her plan but she did all the bad stuff, not us. We're not going to gaol on her behalf."'

'So the Coglins have come forward with this incriminating information. Why now?'

Bowers blew out his cheeks. 'It's hard to say. They both came in, sir. Perhaps a guilty conscience that they knew something about the matter? Word's getting around about Mr Appleby's passing. And, er, I gather Tom Catchlove strongly suggested they come forward.'

A look of understanding passed between the two men before Inspector Green slid Fleur a sly glance. She frowned, unsure of what that look meant, but she presumed she was meant to stay quiet.

'They've signed their statements?' Green asked.

Bowers nodded.

Inspector Green turned to the quaking Irma. 'Irma Appleby, I'm arresting you for the murder of Henry James Appleby.' He began to quote her rights as Irma began to shriek abuse at Fleur and the two policemen.

Fleur looked on, open-mouthed in surprise but trembling with vindication.

27

Fleur had been told to wait. The room was sparse, with only essential furniture of a small table and two chairs. The window was small, high and dirty enough to not let much light in. An electric bulb hanging from the centre of the ceiling cast the room in yellow light, and the murky walls of drab grey did nothing to enhance her impression of this place.

She could feel the hard edges of the chair upon which she sat, and it seemed to speak of the whole building: spare, cold, unforgiving. She took the opportunity to escape into her thoughts, how she'd recently prepared her father for his burial. She'd kept the service private; it was held in the Appleby chapel, whose last grieving family had been the Wrens.

She recalled settling her father's black tie for one final tightening beneath his collar. The last time she would touch the first man she'd ever loved. He looked splendid; that ashen pallor had been warmed up with her tender and skilful ministrations. It was hard to close the coffin and she had wept as the young helpers had checked it was fast.

'We'll take it from here, Miss,' Robbie had said in his kind way. 'You've done him proud.'

Had she? Couldn't she have done more . . . maybe saved him?

Not from himself, a small inner voice assured. And that voice was right. Her father had never stopped grieving over the loss of Mae, and he had begun his decline from the moment of her passing. Resigned and sad, he had let life happen around him, never fully engaging again and perhaps his one final thought – Fleur hoped a happy one – was that his daughter had finally found someone she liked so much she wanted to introduce them.

She had not been ready for the gathered crowd on the day of the funeral. They had lined the length of Port Road, waiting for her father's hearse. As it rolled sombrely past, the women dipped their gazes and the men removed their hats to cast a silent nod to a man who had served their community faithfully and with a generosity she hoped now shone through her.

It was why she was here now. Her father would expect it of her.

———

Fleur found herself facing the only person she had ever hated. Hate was not a word that Mae Appleby had tolerated and she'd taught her daughter never to use it, but Fleur couldn't help herself; she sat across from the pale-faced woman who had not lost her sneer.

'Come to gloat?' Irma asked, sitting back in the rickety chair. She was being held in custody until the trial, but somehow didn't seem affected by the grim surroundings.

Fleur bristled. 'No, I brought you some clothes.'

'I won't need many, Fleur. They have to prove it all, and they won't be able to.'

Fleur nodded, schooling her features to neutral. She was determined not to be baited.

'I suppose you'll be running off to your father's solicitor now.'

'Hadn't crossed my mind, Irma.' Fleur sighed. 'I told you, I'm not motivated by money in the way that you are.'

'Then leave it all alone. It's mine.'

'You didn't earn a cent of it.'

'But I shall spend every cent when I get out of here.'

'I doubt you'll be getting out,' Fleur warned, helpless to stop herself. 'A murder charge is as serious as it gets.'

'That's on you. You put me here.'

Fleur had to ball her fists beneath the table to find her control. 'Irma, it will go better for you if you simply confess. The prosecutor might be willing to go for manslaughter rather than murder.'

'I thought you'd want to see me hang, Fleur,' Irma replied, surprisingly casual in how vicious she was.

She might as well have stuck a blade into Fleur's belly; it felt like a brutal attack. 'No,' she stammered. 'That's not what I want.'

Irma shrugged again. 'Then why do this to me?'

'My father's death was deliberate—'

'You're like a stuck needle on a seventy-eight! The man was near death anyway.'

'But you have no right to be his judge and executioner.'

'I don't believe I was.'

'We both know you poisoned him.'

Irma folded her arms on the table. 'Have you ever wondered if that's what Henry might have wanted?'

'No. I think I know him as well, if not much better, than you do. He would not do that to me.'

'Why is it always about you, Fleur?'

'Because I was all he had. You had long ceased holding interest for him.' Fleur looked shocked by the cruel words she'd just said. 'I didn't mean that.'

Irma actually laughed. 'Yes, you did. But he had lost interest in everything – including you.'

Fleur swallowed. 'He didn't have the opportunity to put his affairs in order.'

'He did. It's all mine, I told you that.'

'Irma, we're going around in circles. Would you prefer I don't come again?'

'Yes. I have no desire to look at your smug expression. What happened to that young man you were so keen on, by the way? Did he not stick around?'

'I don't know where he is.'

'So you drove him away too, did you?'

It hurt to even ponder it. Fleur shook her head.

'You should have stuck with Jimmy. Could have been married and in the family way by now, and no need to lie.'

Fleur frowned while she watched Irma's eyelids flutter as though she hadn't meant to say that much. 'What do you mean?'

Irma simply smiled, putting a finger to her lips. She was enjoying herself, but she had underestimated Fleur's ability to make connections with speed. Irma had let something slip,

Fleur wouldn't let it go. 'What did you do, Irma?'

Now her stepmother laughed openly, deciding there was little else to lose anyway. It was like entertainment for her on a boring day, Fleur decided, and if someone was watching, they could not be blamed for imagining Irma was not the one accused or facing a trial.

'Tell me,' Fleur said, trying to keep it firm: a demand, not a plea. Irma's self-assured smile triggered her mind to chase down what her stepmother could possibly feel so conceited over, and then the jigsaw piece fell into its rightful place – the one she'd been searching for, for days since Tom had disappeared. 'The letter!' Her voice sounded small and hoarse. 'You sent it?' she said in an incredulous tone, shaking her head as if warding off evil. 'Oh, Irma, what did you write?'

Her enemy chuckled. 'Whatever it was, it sent him scuttling, didn't it? I'll be damned, Fleur, if you get to live out your happy life at my expense. You could have left things alone, even walked away with your young man and gone to live anywhere you please. I would have left you alone. Instead you decided to ruin my life. So I decided to ruin yours.'

'What did you tell him?' Fleur hadn't realised she'd now stood and was yelling.

A policeman moved alongside hurriedly. Over Irma's laughter, he cautioned Fleur. 'You'll have to keep your voice down, Miss Appleby, and return to your seat.'

'Yes, yes, I'm sorry.'

He moved away and Fleur did as asked, directing a scorching, almost fevered gaze towards Irma.

'Look at you, Fleur, so much passion. At least we know someone can ignite your lust, because I've always thought of you as sexless. It's as if—'

'Irma, I know you're enjoying yourself, so why not keep up your entertainment and enjoy watching me learn about your latest sinister actions?'

'Nothing much to tell,' Irma replied conversationally. 'I simply warned him off.'

'With what? I don't think Tom is easily spooked.'

'Seems he was once he learned that you had reconsidered your situation and decided to do what your family wants by marrying Jimmy.'

'He would never have accepted that. We were planning—'

'Clearly he did once he learned you were pregnant—'

Fleur's mouth opened but no sound came out.

Irma filled the silence with a nasty sound of amusement before continuing '—and that he shouldn't come sniffing around between you and Jimmy now that you were going to have Jimmy's child to care for.'

There was nothing more to say. Fleur put her head into her hands and allowed the sound of Irma's laughter to deafen her thoughts.

28

While Fleur had been preparing her father's body for burial and awaiting news of a trial date, Tom was making his way to an address in Carrington Street. He knew that Irma Appleby had been arrested and that two witnesses had come forward with incriminating evidence that would most likely lead to a conviction. He didn't want to know more; did not wish to be involved. The police had told him he was not required for the investigation, but they wanted an address where they could reach him. He'd given the post office at Farina, not knowing what else to say; he had temporary lodgings in the city but would be leaving soon enough. And ever since that moment, Tom had realised, not sure whether it was with a sinking feeling or just comfortable resignation, that he really would be returning home. He knew how to live in the bush, and it seemed that city life, as exciting as it was, might not be for him . . . not alone, anyway.

He helplessly reached towards memories of his mother. He could see her sitting at his side on his favourite big branch of the coolabah, using its vantage to appreciate a spectacular sunset. She was smiling the smile he loved, which seemed to shine straight from her heart. Her eyes, he recalled, were the colour of faded

Vaseline glass. They could 'fire' when she was happy, as though the uranium in that glass was being illuminated.

She had given a sound of delighted awe at the sky. 'Tom, will you look at that!' she said, even though his attention was already riveted on the same spectacle. 'It looks like a peacock's tail. Remember that picture I showed you?'

He nodded as she glanced over at him.

'Well, the colours in the sky are shaped like the fan of the peacock.' She pointed. 'I can just see the last tip of the sun, like a fiery halo. And it's throwing those burnished golden-striped feathers towards us.'

'I wish I could touch them,' he'd replied.

'That's a mix of cirrus and cumulus, do you remember?'

He had nodded but had told a fib; he couldn't remember which type of cloud was which. She knew so much about lots of things. She was the clever one, and he often sensed that his father felt awkward around her knowledge. Tom had never thought them well suited, but as long as his father was in her presence, his mother was laughing. As young as he was, he sensed their love and that was enough, wasn't it?

'You're so like your father, Tom. Handsome and awfully taciturn.'

He hadn't known that word. And his eloquent mother liked to use words like this. He figured it must mean quiet, because that's what he was. He didn't feel a need to be noisy like his father; he preferred to observe, to speak when there was something to be said. Was that taciturn? Perhaps. His father wasn't quiet. He'd never considered his father handsome either and had never heard him described that way, but he had liked the compliment all the same.

But now Tom understood. She hadn't been referring to Vern, but Tom's biological father, who had obviously been handsome . . . and taciturn.

Tom returned to his recollection, which he found comforting. Moira had explained the differences between the clouds. 'The slightly puffy ones are cumulus and they're sitting below the sketchy cirrus.'

'They look like inkblots,' he remembered saying, hoping to keep her engaged.

It had worked. Moira Catchlove had laughed and being the one to prompt it lifted his spirits. 'They do; well noted, Tom.' He could even remember how she'd clutched her hand around his shoulder and hugged him close, as though only the two of them mattered. 'The colours are so beautiful they make my heart ache.'

That was his mother neatly summarised. She spoke like this often, especially just before she was about to cry. He couldn't have that.

'Shall we mark off another day, Mum?' he'd suggested, leaping nimbly down from the tree, hoping to distract her.

He'd watched her look back at him with damp eyes. 'Yes, Tom, let's do that. And hopefully we'll have news of Vern by tomorrow.'

Now that Tom had a certain amount of distance from life in the outback, he could look at it with some amazement. Surely it was the last place on the earth that anyone should want to live, and yet here he was. This was home. His enquiring mind had learned from his father and some of the other adults who moved through his life that, long before the Europeans and British had arrived, the original people of the region had used highly prized ochre for their art, as well as for painting their bodies, and sometimes even as protection from the ferocious sun. There had been Chinese folk in the region – Tom wished he had met some of them – but they had left by the time he'd reached adulthood. Now the town had Afghan people, like Gool Mahomet, who led long, snaking camel trains across the northern border. Tom's own folk were British, his father

Scottish and his mother's people originally from Hampshire, in the south of England. The climate did not suit either.

'We're at your stop, mate,' the bus conductor said, interrupting his thoughts.

'Oh, thanks very much,' Tom said, flicking him a grin.

'Looks like you've had a rough trot, mate.'

Tom nodded. 'A misunderstanding. I was the wrong fella,' he added, feeling those words resonate.

'Ouch,' someone else, also moving downstairs to alight, joined in.

'I'll be right soon enough,' Tom assured them, and lifted a hand to wave farewell to both. As he walked away, he tried to disguise his limp, which was nothing to do with his legs but the sharp and shooting reminder that came from his ribcage with each step.

He looked around to get his bearings. He was on Wakefield Street, and now crossed the wide road, turning to face a shopfront called Central Motors. This is what he had hoped to see, according to the directions he'd been given. *So, not lost yet*, he thought wryly. A line of cars were parked on an angle in front of the buildings but where he stood, the cars were parked parallel to the curb. He recalled word for word what the bus conductor had told him: 'If you're facing Central Motors, keep walking to the right and you'll come to a wide street called Pulteney. Turn right there, cross over Angas and the next main street you come to is Carrington. You'll need to work out the house number, but it's not such a long street that you can get into much trouble.' The conductor gestured with his hand as he continued. 'If you go too far, you'll do a sort of zigzag on East Terrace around the East Parklands. Just remember, Adelaide was built on a simple grid. You can always find your way back.'

Tom headed east and found Pulteney, which felt like a main road; it cut through the city north to south. Carrington Street was only a minute or so away by his reckoning, and despite the limp and the aches, he soon found himself standing in front of a familiar two-storey residence that appeared as grand now as it had two decades ago.

He felt vaguely sick to be back here, and memories began flooding in of the day he'd arrived to such a cheerless welcome. His single bright memory of the experience was Fleur, and he leaned on the knowledge that without that awful experience, they'd never have met, fallen in love, or have been planning their life together.

Be grateful for every good thing in your life, Tom, his mother had told him. Because it was said so often, it had tended to flow over him, but now he focused on it. Every good thing was Fleur. And while he couldn't be grateful for the sorrows of his life, he felt the push and pull of destiny that every sad event had led him further along this path to rediscovering Fleur.

He squared his shoulders, ignoring the pain it caused, and rapped on the door.

It took an age to be answered. A man with rolled-up shirt-sleeves opened the door. He looked distracted and had a burning cigarette between his fingers. 'Yes?' Before Tom could speak, he held up a hand. 'Ah, no travelling salesmen, please. I thought we'd told every one of you enough times, although I don't recognise you, so I'll give you the benefit of the doubt.'

'I'm not a salesman,' Tom said bluntly.

'Actually, you look like you're a boxer,' the man replied with the slightest of sneers. 'But whatever you are selling, we don't need it, thanks.'

He began to close the door and, uncharacteristically, Tom felt a rush of anger at being dismissed with such disdain. This was how they'd likely treated his mother. 'Wait up, mate. You're being rude. I've travelled a long way to come here.'

'I don't care where you hail from, you country bumpkin. Please leave or I'll have to call the police.'

Tom laughed. 'For what reason? Knocking on your fancy door?'

'Trespassing. Go on now, bugger off. Knock on another door.'

Tom's gaze narrowed and this time when the man started to close the door, he stuck his foot firmly in the way. 'Not so fast, Mr Darnell. You are Darnell, right?'

Tom saw the flash of surprise in the man's eyes and then his gaze clouded quickly into suspicion. 'What if I am?'

'I'm Tom Catchlove – but you and your family might understand quicker if I used the surname of Wintrow.'

Now the eyes widened, but before Darnell could speak, a pale-faced woman with thick, dark hair cut fashionably short sidled up behind him. 'Who is it, Father?'

'Er, it's no one, dear.'

'I remember you!' Tom said. 'You're the girl at the window.'

29

At Tom's words, the dark-haired woman took a step back from the door. 'Pardon me?'

'Emily, go back into the drawing room, please,' Darnell said. 'I'll deal with this.'

'Yes, that's right, I think you may be my cousin,' Tom continued, ignoring the snub and the person who gave it; his anger fuelled his confidence. 'My mother was Moira Wintrow.'

Emily gasped. 'Aunt Moira? I went to her funeral many years ago.'

'Well, I didn't. I wasn't allowed.'

'Look, what do you want?' Darnell asked, the tetchiness gone and swiftly replaced by open hostility.

'I wish to speak with Mrs Darnell, please.'

'Well, my wife doesn't wish to speak with you, Catchlove. She didn't want you in the house all those years ago and I doubt her perspective has changed.'

Tom shook his head with both disbelief and amusement. 'You really are the most awful people. I'd hoped it was just childish memories but no, you're every inch as ghastly as I recall.'

'Father! Please invite Tom in. If he is my cousin, let us at least hear what he has to say.' Emily turned to Tom. 'You're surely here for a reason.'

'I am. And it won't take long. I just need some information.'

'There you are, Father – nothing too hard about that. Come in, Tom. I'll fetch my mother. She's hardly busy, she's reading.'

Reluctantly, Darnell stepped aside. 'Well, my daughter seems to want to make you welcome, Catchlove, so you might as well come in briefly and not keep the doorway looking untidy.'

'As I said, Mr Darnell, you're pretty bloody awful folk – apart from your daughter – so I promise not stay longer than I have to.'

'Through there, Catchlove. Try not to touch anything.'

'Steal, you mean?'

'That too. You could be down on your luck and here to extort money from us, for all I know.'

'I could be, yes,' Tom said and he liked how that made Darnell blink. 'This is a very nice house you have here, Mr Darnell.'

'It belongs to my wife.'

'I thought so.'

'What's that supposed to mean?'

Tom didn't have to answer because Emily arrived back with her mother in tow. All the memories crashed back into Tom's mind now with vivid colour, texture and sound. Elizabeth Darnell might have been two decades older, but she hadn't lost her pursed-lip appearance and, as her gaze landed on him, her mouth twisted slightly as though she was tasting something bad.

'Tom Catchlove, indeed. I do remember you. You haven't changed much.'

It was clear they weren't going to invite him to have a seat, so he faced the trio where he stood; Emily slightly behind her parents.

He gave a wry smile. 'I don't know whether to take that as a compliment, Mrs Darnell.'

'No, it's not. You look identical to your father.'

'Do I?'

Elizabeth's stare locked with his and it felt like pistols at dawn. She was challenging him and he wanted to say aloud, *I'm up for it.* Instead he smiled.

'Are you talking about Vern Catchlove, or my real father?'

'Oh, so you know about the other one, do you?' She sniffed. 'Well, they were both wastrels.'

'What does that mean, Mrs Darnell? I can't imagine you knew either of them well enough to make such a presumption.'

'Your mother was going to make a good marriage in this city. She could have had any of the eligible bachelors she wanted, but she decided to throw it all away with—' She pulled herself up abruptly.

'With whom?'

Elizabeth shrugged and it looked theatrical. 'I have no idea. All I know is Moira was with child and used goods, as far as Adelaide society went. We all offered to help, didn't we, Giles?'

Her husband took the cue. 'Your mother was a dreamer, lad. That's the kindest I can say about her. It seemed tarnishing her name and threatening this family's reputation wasn't enough; she decided to flee to the back of beyond with a shepherd or drover or some such peasant.'

'Can you two hear yourselves?' Emily burst in. 'Heavens! I'm frankly disgusted but rarely surprised by your superiority. A guest comes into our home – family, no less – and you treat him like a leper.'

'This man is not our family, Emily dear. Just look at him – he's a mess. He's probably here to ask for money. Giles, write him a cheque and get him out of here, would you?'

Tom held onto his temper and found the calm he was known for, honed over years to be his place of retreat. 'No need, Giles,' he said, his tone so dry he wanted to cough. 'I don't need your cheque.

You know, Mrs Darnell, if only you were civil, I wouldn't have to take you to court for my mother's rightful share of this house.'

If Adelaide had frozen over in that heartbeat, Tom would have believed it because the temperature in the room – which only a moment ago had been hot and heated from their scowls and barbs – dropped dramatically. He heard Elizabeth inhale with a hiss at his words.

'You bloody bastard, walking in here,' Giles began.

'Back off, Giles,' Tom snapped. 'This is between me and my aunt. I've spoken with Tillet & Associates.' He gave a mirthless smile. 'I'm guessing you didn't think I'd know the family solicitors. My mother told me all about them, had impressed upon me to remember that name since I was old enough to listen. I've never forgotten it and decided to have a chat to them a few days back when I had nothing better to do.'

'Are you threatening me, young man?'

'I could be,' Tom said and saw Emily twitch a swift smile that disappeared as quickly as it arrived. He felt encouraged by her amusement. 'But I choose not to. I know my mother was left a sizeable amount in your father's will because, although your mother disapproved of her marriage, your father still insisted that she was to benefit. And I know half of this house is hers. I can prove I'm her son – and claim all that belongs to her.'

The Darnell couple couldn't hide the horror from their expressions, while their daughter could no longer fully hide her enjoyment of their discomfort.

'And will you?' Elizabeth demanded.

'If you cooperate, I shall not press my claim.'

'Cooperate?' she repeated with a frown.

But Giles leapt at the opportunity to avoid sharing any money. His tone took a conciliatory note. 'Now, listen here, we were perhaps a little hasty. We've had nothing to do with you over the years—'

'Because you chose not to, Giles,' Tom reminded. 'I didn't know I had a pretty cousin, for instance.' He threw a smile Emily's way. She was far from pretty in the way that Fleur was, but possessed a sort of wan beauty that really rested in her sharply intelligent eyes. Tom would lay money down that Emily would have been a suffragette if she'd been of age back then and would likely relish the chance to get away from her parents' overbearing manner. 'But you deliberately kept her away from me all those years ago.'

'More's the pity, Tom,' Emily said. 'Tell us how we can make amends,' she offered.

'I want to find the man who fathered me,' he said. It came out baldly but there was no easy way to make his request.

'Whatever for?' Mrs Darnell said, her tone critical.

'Now, now, Elizabeth. It's a simple enough request,' Giles cautioned. 'And that's all you want . . . er, Tom?'

'That's all I came for,' he confirmed. 'I want nothing else from you.'

'Would you be prepared to put that in writing, per—'

'Father!' Emily admonished. 'Don't be ridiculous. If Tom says that's all he wants, then please do not make him prove anything. Furthermore, don't humiliate me any further in front of him. Forgive us, Tom.'

'You're forgiven, Emily . . .' He left the rest unsaid.

'Right, well. Elizabeth, do you have . . . um . . .?'

'No, I don't. You know I don't. I can't even remember his name, Giles – can you?'

Giles shook his head forlornly. 'Bill? Or was it Hugh?'

Tom searched their faces for guile, pleading inwardly for them to remember. But he found no pretence; they genuinely couldn't recall.

'I met him,' Emily declared. 'And I have a very good memory.'

'What?' Her mother swung around.

'He came to the house to see Aunt Moira, as you well know. I was only about five or six at the time. Nasty Miss Jackson tried to send him packing on your instructions, Mother, or did you forget that?'

'I have forgotten that,' Elizabeth admitted, although Tom sensed she was lying. 'I spoke to him for about two minutes, Tom,' she reiterated defensively, as though she knew he saw through her.

'Where was my mother?' Tom asked.

'Locked up,' Emily said. 'My grandmother took all her clothes and locked her in her room for days. We weren't living in this house; we were still at College Town, but we were staying here while some building work was being done at our home in Harrow Road. I clearly remember all the screaming and crying . . . so many arguments through that bedroom door. Grandpa was very upset about it all and never agreed with how Aunt Moira was treated. My memory of it is vivid, Mother. I can't lose recollection of it, much as perhaps you'd like me to.'

'Really, Emily, do you feel clever stirring all this up?'

'I'm sorry, Tom,' Emily said, before addressing her parents. 'I'm simply giving Tom the truth. This is all water under the bridge. We can't change anything. But he has a right to know; he's trying to find the man who fathered him, for heaven's sake. I'd want to know if Father didn't actually—'

'Right, that's quite enough, Emily,' Elizabeth broke in. 'I swear it's that university giving you such independent thinking.'

Emily cut Tom another amused look. 'Wicked to think for myself, isn't it, Mother?'

'You'll never get a husband carrying on like that,' Elizabeth warned.

Now Emily laughed and she became prettier for it, Tom noted. 'If I decide to marry, Mother, I'll choose him when I'm ready.'

'Are you listening to this, Giles? She sounds like Moira all over again.'

'Just a lot older,' her father said and Tom suspected it was an old family argument that their daughter was still a spinster.

Emily wouldn't back down. 'I did always admire Aunt Moira's spiritedness. She lived life on her terms.'

'Like a beggar!' Elizabeth spat.

'No, she didn't,' Tom interrupted. 'My mother lived a hard life – there's no denying that – but I shared it with her, and I have to say it was a happy one. She loved the man who raised me and he loved her with every ounce of himself. He would have given her the world if he could.'

'Except he couldn't. He was poor,' Elizabeth scoffed.

'He was an overseer on a property and, to be honest, I think Vern would say he had everything he needed. All the space in the world, all the peace in the world and the most beautiful woman in his bed.'

Both Darnells gasped as he'd hoped they would and Emily chuckled quietly.

Tom continued. 'Being poor isn't a crime.'

'He stole her life,' Elizabeth bleated.

'I doubt it. I think her family stole it. She wasn't allowed to be with the man she wanted to marry – her first love – and so, as I understand it, when the opportunity rose again to be with someone she genuinely liked, she took it. She was pregnant, after all, and her chances to raise her child in a family environment would have been slim at best. I'm sure you offered her a way out of having me.'

Elizabeth didn't confirm his suspicion but had the grace to look back at him sheepishly. 'We only wanted what was best for her, what she deserved. Your mother was the most beautiful and gifted person. There wasn't anything she couldn't do if she turned her mind to it, whether it was music, or sport, or art. She was educated and she was fun. And she gave it all away for nothing.'

Tom gave a small laugh, refusing to feel insulted. 'She gave it up for me, Mrs Darnell. My mother never let a day go by without making sure I understood how loved I was. And I felt the same way about her, which is why it was so cruel to deny me that final farewell to her and my sister.'

Elizabeth looked down and her lips pinched. 'That was all a long time ago, Tom.'

He nodded. 'And I've been stewing on it for all that time. What you may not know is that my mother left me very well set up.' The Darnell family frowned as one. 'The solicitor told me that she'd established a trust for when I came of age. And my grand-father – the same one who felt badly about how his daughter was treated – regularly put money into that trust for me. I know now why my mother impressed upon me to never forget the name of the law firm. She didn't tell me why, but she knew my curiosity would get the better of me at some stage – as it did.'

Giles and Elizabeth shared shocked glances. 'My father never spoke a word of this,' she snapped.

Tom shrugged. 'I can only presume he didn't wish you to know – or indeed anyone except my mother. And she didn't touch it, according to the solicitor. It has quietly amassed over the years and earned interest . . . so you could say that I am now an independently wealthy man too.'

'I . . .' Giles looked stunned. 'How much money are we talking about?'

The laughter as it came felt good to Tom. 'Now you're an educated man, Giles, and you know that's a rude question – even this country bumpkin wouldn't ask such a thing. Just know I don't need or want your money, but I will demand my share if I don't get what I do want, which is simply the name of my father.'

'I think my mother needs the smelling salts,' Emily said to her father, nodding towards her mother, who was tottering to the wall to steady herself. They both helped Elizabeth into a nearby chair. 'Come with me, Tom.'

'Where are you going?' Giles demanded.

'I'm seeing Tom out,' Emily said, squeezing Tom's arm to prevent him from saying any more. 'You tend to Mother.'

She led Tom to the front door and opened it. 'I think you're marvellous and I'm so happy to be your cousin. Can you wait here a moment? I didn't think you needed to spend another second around their appalling rudeness.'

Tom grinned. 'I'll be by the gate.'

'Back in a tick,' she promised.

Emily emerged from the house a few minutes later holding out a small white calling card. 'Here, Tom. I can't say whether this is still current in terms of an address, but I doubt his name has changed,' she said.

He took it and read the name: *William John Stern.* He looked back at Emily, eyes shining. 'My father?'

'The man who wanted to marry Aunt Moira and presumably fathered you. But I think you said your real father was Vern Catchlove and that, I hope, won't change . . . Unless he wasn't good to you?'

'He's the only father I've known.'

She nodded, tapping the card. 'This man came looking for Moira. I happened to answer the door, even though I wasn't meant to.' She gave a sound of frustration. 'But I was always doing things I wasn't meant to, and he gave me this card to give to my aunt or someone who might get it to her. But your mother had been moved to another of the houses. Of course, they soon came up behind me and sent him packing before I could tell them about the card, and then I decided I wouldn't because they'd been so mean to Aunt

Moira and this nice gentleman of hers. Never gave him a chance and told him my mother never wanted to see him again.'

'Did they tell him she was going to have a baby?'

'No. I eavesdropped on the brief but wretched conversation – it was as rude and terse as you can imagine.'

'Do you remember much about him?'

'Well, from a child's perspective I recall him as tall and extremely good-looking, with lovely teeth and a bright smile that reached all the way to his eyes – one of those smiles that made the leap to me, and made me want to smile back. His hair was like yours, thick and blond but slicked down with hair oil and a very neat parting. He was dressed in a suit and his shoes were polished.' She gave a tight smile. 'I can't give you much insight into him because I barely had more than a minute or so in his presence and then I was shooed away. But he had a nice voice, not dissimilar to yours, and he was polite to my mother even though she was rude and dismissive towards him, as she always is.'

'And they never knew you had this?'

She shook her head. 'I've kept it for years in an old trinket box and frankly had forgotten about it until you came in today.'

'I remember you at the window when I was here as a child.'

Emily smiled. 'You and that little girl. I envied you.' At Tom's frown, she continued. 'You were both laughing at the things you were talking about, and I wanted to be like that – to be with you both, but I wasn't allowed to meet you.'

'Even though I was your cousin.'

'*Especially* because you were my cousin. They wanted absolutely nothing to do with poor Moira and her bastard child. But Grandpa insisted – and caused a huge stink until they agreed – that they bring your mother's body back to be buried in Adelaide. Grandma refused to have her in the family plot, but Grandpa bought her a special place at the Cheltenham Cemetery, where another of our wayward family members was buried – Uncle Albert. I don't know his misdemeanours but we're not even allowed to mention him.' She giggled.

'Thank you for this, Emily,' he said and stepped forward to kiss her cheek.

She touched her face, blushing. 'You're welcome, Tom. It was worth holding on to for all this time, because it brought you here. I don't know how much help it might be – it doesn't say what he does for a living – but hopefully that address is a start. I hope we'll see each other again. I'm sorry for the circumstances, and for my parents' appalling behaviour, but you went for their softest spot – well done. Money and status are everything to the Darnells. I wish I was a Wintrow, to be honest, because Grandpa was wealthy but generous and a real sweetie. You'd have liked him.'

'Well, I plan to get to know his granddaughter from here on.'

Emily hugged him. 'Oh, this is going to really make my parents' day. You know they'll be watching from the shadows.'

He grinned, then turned to leave.

'And Tom?'

He turned back.

'If you're happy in your present, maybe don't go digging back into the past.' Emily shrugged. 'Just a thought,' she said with a bright smile as she closed the iron gate between them. 'Take me out of this gaol soon.'

'I'll write.'

'You'd better.'

His grin was his promise and as he walked away he realised how novel the feeling of happiness was. Since leaving the Alberton Hotel and meeting his cousin, he'd known only a dark mood as he made plans to return north. Tom had telephoned the woolstores to explain he was going home, using the excuse that life in the big smoke did not suit him.

'I miss the big space and the peace,' he'd said to his boss. 'Can you let Charlie know I'll drop him a note and sorry I didn't get to say goodbye?'

'You all right, lad? Heard you took a hiding from a jealous fella.'

'Something like that. I've had worse,' he lied. Or was he lying? No. He could admit to himself he was far more broken from the wounds of Fleur's letter than anything Jimmy's fists or boots could do to him. He said none of this, of course. 'I'll be fine, Mr Chapman.'

'Sorry it didn't work out, Catchlove. I liked your style but I especially liked your speed. Easy to tell you've come from a shearing shed.'

'And where I probably belong,' Tom said in a rueful tone, not wanting to believe it. 'Bye, Mr Chapman.'

Tom put the phone down in the hallway of the hotel called the Seven Stars that he was staying in. He could hear the drone of men from the front bar, punctuated by bursts of laughter or roars of ridicule and the clash and clatter of glasses.

A man lurched out through the swing doors into the hallway and turned towards him, looking confused. He was intoxicated but not yet fully drunk, with the presence of mind to smooth his clothes and his hair. 'Mate,' he said in greeting.

Tom nodded in response. 'I think you want that direction,' he said, gesturing towards the doors that led out onto Angas Street.

'Lost my girl today,' the man groaned.

Tom felt his insides flip but he didn't let his expression betray the feeling of brotherhood. 'Sorry to hear that.'

'Her friend told me lies about her,' the man said, his gaze swimming slightly as he moved towards Tom.

'And you believed her?'

His companion held up a forefinger and waggled it before Tom. 'She's a cunning one, that one. Very . . .' He let out a small burp. 'Very convincing.'

Tom nodded. 'Girls can be cunning.'

'Yes!' the man hissed. 'She lied, told me Sarah – that's my love – fancied another. Always had. But that I was a good catch and Sarah thought I'd make a good husband, good father.'

Tom smiled gently. 'Didn't you ask Sarah?'

He shook his head. 'I accused her. We rowed. Too late now. She doesn't want anything more to do with me.'

'Try again. Don't give up.'

'Says she can't forgive me for believing lies before giving her the chance to deny them.'

'Why did her friend do such a thing?' Tom asked.

The man shrugged dramatically. 'I don't know.' He belched again. 'Jealously, mischief . . . or just not right in the head. All I know is I love Sarah.'

Tom grinned, and then put his arm around the bloke, leading him to the door. 'Go and tell her. And then prove it every day of your life. Women, from what I know, respond to honesty, especially if you share your feelings . . . what you feel in here,' Tom said, tapping the man's chest over his heart. 'Can you get home all right?'

The man gave a crooked smile and nodded like a child. 'I'll walk it off. And then I'll go and sing outside her home, shall I? Tell her how much I love her.'

Tom laughed now. 'Sleep it off first, mate. You don't want the neighbours pelting you with rotten fruit. Don't let her get away, though, over a misunderstanding.'

His new friend brayed a laugh. 'Bye, mate.'

Tom watched the man walk away, swaying slightly but not unsteady. Tom sighed, wishing his situation was just a misunderstanding, a lie that could be refuted and the damage repaired. But Fleur had made it clear he was not to contact her, and he had been raised to respect a person's wishes.

Time to go then, back to Witchelina. She really did not want him, but maybe they would and he could accept his life as a wool classer. He'd also need to accept that his future days would hold private yearning for something he'd always wanted and now would never have.

He glanced at his watch. Yes, enough time to gather up his few belongings and head back to the Adelaide Central Railway station, which had promised so much when he'd arrived, full of wonder and the lightness of leaving behind a heavy load. Except the burden of lost love felt somehow heavier than the grief. Finding Fleur, discovering a door opening into so much potential with her and knowing she shared the same affection, had been like entering a new world. And now that world was shunning him, pointing him back to the familiar world he had come from. Though it offered none of the sparkle and promise he'd glimpsed in Fleur's arms, it was a safer world. He knew how to live in it. And although his heart wouldn't heal, it was reassuring to him in a way that now it could never break again. He'd leave one half in Adelaide, on a moonlit jetty with the sound of the shoreline where waves surged and receded, mingling with the sound of a woman's laughter, while the other half would seek comfort in the outback's isolation and peace.

30

Irma's case had gone to trial because she had maintained her innocence. Two months after her father's death, Fleur had been called to the witness stand, where she had answered all the questions from the prosecuting barrister with care and precision as he masterfully guided her through her memories of Irma's behaviour and the question of Henry's death.

And when the defending barrister took to his feet with an expression of disdain that was meant to throw her off balance, Fleur hadn't reacted to his withering stare or the protracted silence as he made a theatrical tour of the space before her. She'd forced herself to regard Irma and was deeply surprised to find a sense of pity that someone would go to such lengths for money. It remained perplexing to Fleur because Irma had wanted for nothing as an Appleby, and Henry was far from an ogre as a husband.

It was only during the trial that Fleur had learned about Irma's family, as her backstory began to take shape for the judge and jury. She'd birthed twins in her teenage years: a boy and a girl, now nearing forty, the son disabled with a twisted leg. They were both in the courtroom daily and Fleur found it her greatest challenge to face them from the witness stand and speak out against their mother.

She had been warned by the prosecutor not to elaborate when responding or the defence would find ways to constantly interject or ridicule her. The prosecuting counsel, in his formidable wig and robes, had impressed his guidance upon her. 'Answer only what they ask. Be concise but explicit in your answers, and take your time to think before you respond. It's your right to be careful.'

The advice – and indeed warning – had burned in her mind as the man defending Irma began his interrogation, doing his utmost to corner Fleur into yes or no answers that worked against her testimony. She'd calculated soon enough that his intention was to make her claims against Irma feel circumstantial, unable to be proven without doubt. Even Fleur could sense that her claims were coming across as simply her word against her stepmother's.

But she had her ace card, which she now knew her beloved Tom had brought into play. The powerful admission by the father and son coffin-makers, which had added all the weight for the case against Irma, could not be doubted. Bert Coglin even produced a damning note written by Irma, instructing him to buy the oysters that she would leave to decay so she wouldn't be associated with their purchase. Fleur had looked down when this piece of irrefutable evidence had been produced, knowing it was the proverbial nail in the coffin for Irma.

She had proven to be as capable an actress in court, fighting for her life, as she had been in the Appleby home where she had outmanoeuvred Fleur. Nevertheless, even Irma couldn't wriggle out of the statements made by the Coglins under oath, which corroborated all of Fleur's claims. And the more the barristers delved into Irma's life, the more she seemed to damn herself as a person prepared to risk everything for self-interest . . . or at least the interest of the children she seemed to truly adore.

The treachery against Fleur and Tom was not presented, considered irrelevant to the main thread of the case. It wounded Fleur privately to think that the great love of her life and the betrayal that had taken him from her was considered immaterial; it felt like her whole life had been rent twice over by Irma.

Perhaps the biggest surprise of all was watching Irma weep when she had to take the stand and talk about her children. Fleur had spent too long in Irma's company not to have developed a keen sense for her stepmother's guile, but in this instance the sound of her sobs seemed genuine. Fleur hadn't known until that moment that Irma had the capacity to love, or that she possessed a single mote of authentic tenderness within.

This epiphany had begun as a small tangle of uncertainty in Fleur's gut that, over the course of the trial and in the days leading up to sentencing, grew bigger until it squirmed uncomfortably in her belly. Fleur knew what her conscience was demanding. She'd looked around the courtroom and despaired; from the accusations to the onlookers salivating over the details of greed, jealousy and murder, it was everything her father would squirm away from. She could feel its stain spreading over her as she tried to keep her expression even and her posture straight when it wanted to curve under the weight of the trial.

She wished she could share with Tom that Irma's guilt felt like lead weight. She felt like yelling at the judge, *This shouldn't be my burden and still it is!* All she wanted when the trial was over was to walk out into the sunshine and Tom's strong, safe arms and not have to feel any of the trial's guilt following her.

But he was gone and the heaviness of Irma's trial was pressing on her shoulders. On the day of the sentencing hearing, when the newspapers were clamouring to report on the decision – anticipating that it would be a death sentence – Fleur had asked to be heard. She sat quietly, looking down at her lap as the judge opened the session.

Various people spoke about the guilty verdict that had inevitably been announced at the end of the trial and then Irma's defence counsel had his chance to argue for a lenient sentence, taking into full account her background and lack of prior involvement in anything remotely close to murder. The prosecution had an identical opportunity and naturally pressed for Irma to face hanging, irrespective of her sad background, based purely on the gravity of her crime against an innocent, good man of South Australia, so well regarded in his community.

The demand chilled Fleur.

All the anger and despair that had built over the years of living alongside this horrible woman since childhood, culminating in the day of Irma's arrest, seemed to flee in that moment as the prosecution made its advice known. The barrister pressed on the fact that the jury had accepted Irma's premeditated actions in the murder of Henry, that she had set about causing his death using two forms of poison over the course of a protracted period.

Fleur's mind raced as Irma's children were allowed to speak. She couldn't bear to listen; instead she withdrew into her thoughts. *I can't bring Dad back*, she told herself repeatedly, the truth of it knocking about in her mind like a fly banging against a window pane. And a second urgent fly banging against the same pane: *Irma's death achieves nothing.*

As Irma's daughter finished giving an impassioned plea for her mother's life, the judge finally turned to Fleur.

'I believe Miss Appleby would like to address the court.'

Everyone shifted in their seats. It seemed obvious to all that Fleur was going to make an equally impassioned plea for the judge to use the full weight of his power against Irma for the murder of her father. She had planned to read her statement but instead she folded up the page upon which she'd scrawled her thoughts, slipping it into the pocket of her summer jacket.

Fleur drew in a deep, inaudible breath, reminding herself that nothing in her life would be as important as what she did in this moment. She swallowed, lifted her chin and regarded Irma's children before she finally let her gaze land on Irma, who, to her credit, met Fleur's eyes with scorching defiance.

'Thank you for this opportunity,' Fleur began. 'I wish to express my keen desire for this court to show mercy, and I wish to argue strongly for leniency to be shown to Irma Appleby.'

She paused for the inevitable gasp, which came as a collective noise. Pandemonium erupted as court reporters rushed to scribble down her exact words and everyone began talking at once. The judge quickly regained order of his court with a couple of deafening bangs of his gavel.

Fleur hadn't taken her eyes off Irma, who blinked in clear surprise. She continued. 'Having listened to all that has shaped my stepmother's life, I feel it would be a travesty to punish a woman whose childhood began in poverty, in fear, in hunger and in abuse. I was an orphan, but I became one of the luckiest to ever live. I have known only love, laughter and plenty in my life from Mae and Henry Appleby, who adopted me. They knew how to provide all that a child needs to thrive and if my mother had not died so young, the three of us would still be living in harmony and happiness.

'I've learned over the course of the trial that Irma was attacked as a thirteen-year-old. Still a child! Thirteen and pregnant – it's horrific for any of us to imagine. And the nuns who were supposed to care for her blamed her instead. They took away the children she carried in that all-too-young body, but she found them again years later and I have only respect and indeed admiration for her courage.' Fleur had looked away as she spoke to be sure the whole court was hanging on her statement, but now she looked back at Irma, who appeared shaken, tears watering in her eyes. It was a rare moment of genuine respect between Fleur and Irma. Fleur swallowed again, emboldened by Irma's reaction, then continued.

'I mean, can you all imagine yourselves as an abandoned child who feels ignored and unloved, and is then abused by a stranger – an adult with all the power? And then you are blamed for the horrific incident? But the pain didn't stop there. At thirteen, when most of us were playing in gardens or building sandcastles at the beach, she was carrying twins from the rapist, along with all the guilt and blame. These are defining years for a girl, and they shaped her view of the world in a way few of us can probably understand.'

Fleur took a breath. 'I would like to say to the court that if any of us had been treated in this manner, then most of us were either going to die or, if we were somehow to survive, develop a selfish attitude just to survive – as Irma chose to do. For all my loss and heartache at how my father passed away, I am convinced now that Irma had never known any love from anyone. I think my father was the first man to show any tenderness or respect towards her and of course she clung to that, but I suspect she never trusted it. She certainly didn't trust me – the indulged, precocious child growing up in her midst with all the opportunity in the world, when her own children had so little as they battled into adulthood, separated into various foster homes. I feel ashamed that I didn't know about my stepbrother and stepsister – I wish I had, because I would have welcomed them into our home.'

Irma broke into audible sobs at Fleur's admission, and beneath those sobs all in the court could hear her repeating 'I'm sorry, I'm so sorry.'

Fleur took another deep breath, moved by Irma's apology. 'My father was dying, I cannot deny that. Irma made it happen sooner than was necessary and, while she had no business playing executioner in her own interest, I think we can all see that she wanted to give her children some hope – a chance at a better life. I might make it my business to help in that regard with my brother and sister.'

Irma's sobs intensified.

'Judge, I make this plea for leniency because Irma never stood much of a chance. Her life was moulded in such a way that she would never trust, never accept affection, and she became entirely self-centred, losing sight of right and wrong. I cannot ask the court to forgive her sin, but I am asking it to help her to atone for it. If I can find mercy – the person who has lost the most to Irma, including . . .'

She didn't finish that sentence, preferring to keep Tom out of this dark place. Instead she cleared her throat. 'I am pleading with the people of South Australia to do the same. Show mercy. Irma will likely spend her remaining years behind bars, but perhaps if we can show her mercy, then she might just be able to change the trajectory of some of the younger offenders in prison alongside her. I suspect Irma will take on that role – it will give her purpose for the first time in her bleak life, and in my view it turns something that was once bad into something that can work for good. I think that's what punishment for crime is about. I don't see how my stepmother losing her life achieves anything for anyone who has suffered from her crime – certainly not my family.' Fleur paused to look around at those in attendance and the judge. 'I want no vengeance. I simply want peace of mind. If we all take a more gentle approach to the welfare of those around us, the world will be a better place, so I am pleading with the court to spare Irma Appleby's life.'

She finished, breathing hard.

The judge took a long, slow breath, staring at her over the rim of his glasses. 'Thank you for your honest and heartfelt thoughts, Miss Appleby. I shall give due consideration to them.'

Back in the courtroom one week later, Irma Appleby was sentenced to life in prison and a look was exchanged between the two Appleby women that anyone in the courtroom might have understood as a peace being made.

While Irma was taken down in handcuffs, whispering whatever she could to her weeping daughter and her son who wore a stoic expression, Fleur left the courtroom, scurrying down the steps into the soft sunshine of an Adelaide winter.

She breathed out in relief. She knew both her parents would be proud of her and that was enough. Something about the dry warmth as she took a deep breath spoke of the place where the man she loved had likely returned to a desert winter. While she had been pouring out her thoughts to the court, her heart had poured something else into her mind.

Find him. Make him understand it was a lie.

31

July 1935

It had been nine weeks since Fleur had spent a night in the arms of Tom, since he'd been told a terrible lie and he'd left her. They'd been in love and committed to one another just nine hours before he'd disappeared. Nine weeks since her father had died. Less than nine months before Tom believed she would be giving birth to Jimmy Coglin's baby. Nine days since Irma's sentencing hearing: life imprisonment.

It was a win. The judge could have demanded that Irma give her life for her wicked and murderous deeds, but the sentence had been commuted and a glance of thanks had been cut Fleur's way, not just from Irma Appleby, but from her two children, who Fleur had come to think of as family. She had not acted on her resolve to formalise that relationship – but she would. But first there was something far more important to be done.

She'd felt queasy this morning. Nerves perhaps, or the strain of the previous dramatic weeks. Her body was asking her to give it some time, but she didn't have time. She had to find Tom, had to have her chance to set things straight between them.

She'd taken the precaution of reserving a seat on the train because it meant a class of ticket that had only a few people in each carriage. Her head was pounding a little with all the anxiety and change; she needed to be kind to herself. Fleur could almost imagine her blood fizzing with the excitement of her decision to go in search of Tom. People likely thought of her as wilful and independent, but the truth was that Fleur had never travelled further than Adelaide's city from its port. The decision to hunt down Tom might appear determined, but it was not without the feeling of butterflies at leaving all she knew.

Fleur understood that her certitude in most aspects of her life originated from its familiarity, routine and even, yes, its humdrum. While each corpse was individual and she treated them thus, humans were packaged in the same flesh that clung to a reliable skeleton that was protecting the same order of organs. Bodies worked in the same way, and only age or ill health – or something more sinister – changed their functionality. She knew her work, and felt sure of her place within that structure.

But this was an adventure in which there was no certainty – not even of finding Tom. She presumed he'd returned to Farina as he'd told her he would, but she might discover that, on a whim and hurting from Irma's lies, he'd left the state. But Fleur wouldn't allow herself to consider that until it actually faced her. It might never come to it, so there was no point in getting herself into a lather.

Hers was a long train among eleven others in various stages of departure or arrival that morning. Only one platform was empty in the Adelaide Railway Station and that would soon be filled. The station concourse was a beehive of activity, humming with people moving in a constant flow in various directions as they began their busy day.

But that was all minutes ago. Now she was feeling a little more secure, ready in her seat near the window and anxious to be on her way. The train seemed to mimic her state of mind; the engine that would haul them north to Terowie was like a snorting bull, pawing the ground, straining and ready to charge.

There were eight seats in her compartment and only four others were filled, leaving the seats directly opposite and next to her empty. She wished they would remain vacant but finally a young man in uniform stepped on, looked at his ticket and smiled at her.

'May I?' he asked politely.

'Of course,' she replied, crossing her legs at the ankles and tucking them neatly beneath the seat.

He appeared younger than her, going by his soft, clean-shaven skin. She watched him put his kit bag overhead before settling opposite her. There were two other couples within the compartment, older than both of them and each reading either a book or newspaper.

Once seated the young man gave her a grin. 'How far are you going?'

'All the way to Farina,' she replied.

'Good grief, so am I,' he said, then frowned. 'I thought I knew most people from Farina. You aren't familiar.'

'Did you grow up there?'

He nodded. 'Born in Adelaide, but my father and uncle took over the general store at Farina when I was only a few years old. Our family moved there and I left not so long ago to join the RAAF.'

'Congratulations. Your family must be proud.'

He shrugged. 'I used to watch the odd aeroplane landing in the desert nearby – often crash landing,' he said with a chuckle. 'And I'd dream of what it must be like to fly in those huge skies over the Flinders Ranges.'

Fleur smiled. 'I know someone like you from Farina who used to daydream about what lay beyond the ranges.'

'What's his name?'

'Er, Tom Catchlove.' It felt nice to say his name, but it also frightened her to speak it, as though she were casting a spell over a happy outcome for her journey. She'd told no one where she was going or why. Appleby's, now hers with no protest from Irma, would be closed for at least a week . . . perhaps longer. It felt thrilling but at the same time reckless, and she knew she risked desperate disappointment at the end. But Tom was worth it.

Her companion's big smile warmed her thoughts and banished her fears momentarily.

'Tom? I know Tom. He was always nice to me. Used to encourage me in my dream to join the RAAF.'

She nodded, feeling her throat clog with emotion. 'That sounds like him,' she said.

He sat forward and reached out a hand. 'I'm John Napier Bell.'

Fleur shook it. 'Fleur Appleby. So you're going home,' she said, sounding pleased for him.

'Yes, but only briefly. I've recently finished training in Victoria and so we've all been given some time to visit our families.'

'And then you return to your base?'

'Yes. Although there's talk that some of us may go to England.'

She frowned. 'Why's that?'

He gave a light shrug, dashing in his uniform whose buttons he had loosened for sitting. 'There's talk of war with Germany.'

One of the other men looked up and Fleur thought he was giving them a sour look for talking.

'Oh, surely not,' she said, sounding incredulous. 'We're all only just getting back to normal after the last war.' But even as she said it, she recalled how her father would shake his head at the breakfast table, reading his paper, and remark that a new chancellor in Germany had big plans.

Bell nodded. He didn't look at all bothered at the notion of war, with all the youthful energy that his age had in vast reserve.

'Seems unthinkable, I agree. But this Hitler bloke, who is on the rise in Germany, shows a lot of hostility in his nature. He fought in the Great War and feels the soldiers were betrayed.'

'Oh, I don't want to think about this,' she said, feeling her belly clench.

'Sorry.' He grinned. 'But, if it comes to it, I want to be in the skies over Europe with whichever squadron I belong to.'

'Gosh, so brave,' she said with an uneasy but affectionate smile.

A shrill whistle in the distance demanded attention.

'Sounds like we're about to get going.' He changed the subject. 'Is this your first visit to Farina?'

'I'm afraid so. I have no idea what to expect.'

'Well, those lovely polished brogues will have to be put away. You've chosen the right time of year to visit, because it's not sweltering, but if it's been dry, the dust will clog that lovely pinprick pattern on your shoes, and if it's rained, then it's going to be muddy.'

'Oh,' she said, looking crestfallen. She'd wanted to look perfect for Tom. 'Lucky I have others, then.'

He nodded. 'Save those for church.'

The whistle sounded again and doors banged down the train.

'Here we go,' he said, grinning again from his long, square jaw. His thick hair, which clearly wanted to be unruly, was cut short at the sides and neatly parted on the left.

The bull was finally allowed to charge and, in a bellowing rage of steam and smoke, hauled its carriages out of Adelaide central station and headed through the suburbs until they left the final one, Kilburn, behind and hit the small, open farmland of Salisbury.

'We're headed for Gawler,' John helpfully offered, 'and then we'll start the small climb up the Roseworthy bank. You'll know when we reach that because you'll hear the train strain and complain.' He won a grin from her. 'And you'll know we've reached Hamley Bridge, because we make quite a clatter going over it.'

'What time is the next stop?'

'Nothing precise about this train, Fleur, I must warn you. But it's now, what . . .' He glanced at his wristwatch. 'Just reaching a quarter to nine, so we'll be at Terowie for noon or thereabouts.'

'What happens then?'

'We change trains and on to Peterborough,' he said, settling deeper into his chair. 'Until then, forgive me if I catch forty winks, will you? I've been travelling for a couple of days.'

'Please rest,' she said, smiling. She was happy to let the scenery pass slowly by and give her a chance to let her racing pulse find a quieter rhythm.

Please be there, Tom, she cast out into the wilds beyond Gawler, the last glimpse of humanity before Mother Nature had them fully in her clutch.

———————

They'd changed carriages at Terowie and continued their journey, Fleur's companion still nearby and just dozing now. John stirred as the train slowed into Peterborough. Fleur was astonished that his body just seemed to know where they were.

He blinked and yawned as he stood. He had no need to stretch or worry about stiff limbs; his were too young and strong. He didn't wait for her to ask but lifted down her small holdall and politely handed it to her.

'Thank you. Er, John, do you mind if I stick with you?' She hoped it didn't sound too forward or like an invitation.

'Not at all. I'm sure this all feels rather strange for you.'

As she stood on one of the two station platforms and regarded the sudden mass exodus, she frowned. 'Does everyone alight here?'

He nodded. 'Yes. It's from here that people take their connections to the far west to Perth, or to the far north to Alice Springs—'

'Or to Farina and beyond,' she finished, sounding awed. 'I love that. We're all together for a while and then we bundle off and go to all corners.'

'Train travel is brilliant, but wait until you fly, Fleur.'

She laughed. 'I can't imagine that will happen.'

'Oh, it will. One day you'll take a flight across our great nation and visit friends in Queensland or Darwin . . . or London,' he said with wide eyes and an excited expression.

'I'll trust that if you're the pilot, John.'

'How about a pot of tea while we wait? I'm starving.'

'Come on, the refreshments are on me. You've been most gallant.'

As they each drank a cup of tea, they shared some sandwiches and a wedge of cake. It was about half an hour while all the luggage was unloaded and then reloaded onto their train, which John pointed out.

'We're lucky, we get a good connection. That's a T-class engine and we now move to narrow gauge, so it's a smaller train. Life's about to get rattley,' he warned. 'I know that's not a word,' he added with a smile.

'Maybe not, but I understand exactly what I'm being warned about,' she said. 'You eat the rest,' she urged and he did like any twenty-year-old with a bottomless stomach would.

'It's quite flat from here to Orroroo, but then you'll hear our engine struggle through the higher country before we drop down into Hammond and onto Quorn.'

Normally Fleur might have tuned out to this sort of conversation, but the truth was that she rather enjoyed listening to John making polite chitchat. If she remained engaged, it prevented her from allowing her mind to drift to Tom and whether they still had a future.

———

The Ghan was the name of the train that would take them to Farina and John hadn't lied; the carriages were smaller and filled with hard, sit-up seats, although in First Class they were padded. Fleur and John were both lucky enough to be in that compartment.

'I never usually travel First Class,' John told her. 'But finishing my training and becoming a qualified pilot felt special, so I treated myself.'

Fleur grinned. 'Well, I've never taken such a long train journey and I purchased a first-class ticket because I had no idea what to expect. For instance, what's all that noise at the back?'

He laughed. 'They reserve the last carriage on these trains for the gangs of fettlers and railway workers. They've all done a week or probably more, hard at it on the tracks, so now they're heading home to their families. The train will stop at every tiny, far-flung railway station to let them off and the further we go, the drunker they become.' As he finished saying that, they heard a crash of glass. 'Another longneck shatters in the dust,' he explained. 'They're all pretty rough lads. You'll never get their names. They go by the nickname of Lefty or Jacko, Crow or Budgie.'

Fleur chuckled. 'Tom used to work in a shearing shed and explained it's much the same.'

'Yes, exactly. All characters. Some staying out of the way of mainstream life, others dodging the law, but all of them drink and smoke a lot.'

They heard more bottles shatter beside the slow-moving train as it continued its journey into the late afternoon.

They crossed some bridges and the train started to rattle loudly, the chairs squeaking, and Fleur began to feel her body bouncing in a way it hadn't previously. 'Where are we now?' she asked.

'Coming into Quorn and onwards to Hawker,' he said.

It meant nothing to her, though she called that Jamie Wren had mentioned the town of Quorn. She told John.

'Ah yes, all the new recruits from stations all over this region would have left for their training, and perhaps for Europe, from Quorn Station. It's where east meets west in railway terms,' he said with a grin. 'Great romantic train journeys that cross the vast continent, and all the young men of our state gathering at Quorn to defend their King.'

It did sound romantic and so brave. Fleur wondered if John would have to defend his King soon. She gazed across the saltbush plains where, in the far distance, she could see a blue outline of hills to the east.

After their stop at Quorn, the sun was dipping low and the temperature was falling. The train began to pick up speed as it strained to get over the hills to reach Hawker.

She pointed and John craned his neck around to see. 'That's the start of the Flinders Ranges,' he explained. 'Soon you'll see that blueish line become a purple range. They're incredibly beautiful at sunrise or sunset.'

Pulling into Hawker at around six thirty, Fleur was beginning to feel the hours of the journey tugging at her eyelids, and her body no longer sat pertly upright. Sagging into the evening, she hoped it wouldn't be a long stop but it was another half hour to take on water and the railway gang at the back had become increasingly rowdy and raucous.

'They'll start to thin soon. We'll be dropping them off regularly from here on,' John assured her. 'Do you want anything from the refreshment room? It's my turn.'

'Nothing, thank you.' She yawned.

'I might get another tea,' he said and while he was gone, Fleur wandered the platform in the other direction from where all the singing and explosive laughter emanated. She looked back over the train with its maroon paint, now covered in the thick rust-coloured dust of the landscape they wended their way through. It was twilight; there was still just enough light to enjoy the scenery but Fleur felt a true sense of the day ending by the time they stepped back on the train. The climb began north into the Flinders Ranges proper now, towards a place that John called Hookina.

All these curious names, like Parachilna and Beltana; she'd never heard of them. John pointed out places called Devil's Peak and Willow's Halt. Wilpena Pound, which John mentioned with a note of awe in his voice, was not something she could pick out, but she nodded as he gestured at a tall range that looked to be on fire from the way the setting sun lit stripes of craggy mountain tops, a burnished glow of orange reflecting its furnace.

It was beautiful enough to win a sigh from her. The response was pure and primitive, bathing her heart, it seemed, with an emotion she couldn't name other than a sense of reverence. The fiery ranges made her feel small and inconsequential, a mere mote in time for these giants who had guarded the land, looking down upon it for millennia. Curiously, the surge of sentiment made her want to be in Tom's arms even more, and she hadn't thought her passion could run any harder or deeper for him. This was Tom's country; the Flinders Ranges had held him in their wrinkled, encircling ruggedness for his whole life, and then they gave him to her.

As far as Tom knew, she'd rejected that gift. Irma's cruelty knew no bounds. *I have to make this right*, she repeated in her mind and cast a thought to the rough, stony mountains that she would make good on her promise. The train frequently slowed to a halt but barely paused longer than a minute, and Fleur guessed this was to drop off the now drunk and disorderly fettlers in all the small towns along the way as John had warned.

After a mighty rattle and shake winding up through the ranges past Beltana and onto Leigh Creek, she got the nod from John.

'It will be flat to Lyndhurst, and then Farina is next.'

'Will anyone be waiting for you, John?'

He laughed. 'Probably the whole family.'

And John had not lied. By the time the train sighed with a great bellow of steam into what was apparently the station at Farina, there were plenty of people standing alongside the equally small hut that served as the platform and ticket office.

'There's my lot,' John said, hanging out of the window. He yelled and waved, then dipped back into the carriage to grin at her. 'They're all here. Don't drift off – it's too dark. Let me introduce you.'

32

Fleur was taken aback by how many people had been awaiting the train.

'These can't all be for you,' she quipped as John helped her to alight.

'The townsfolk like to come and collect their mail,' he explained. 'Even at this time of night.'

It was past eleven – what a strange time to arrive – but she was secretly grateful. She'd never seen skies like those above her. It looked like black velvet sprinkled with millions of small diamonds. Again her mind roamed to Tom; she could finally understand his love of this landscape and his awkwardness in hers.

Both of John's parents were at the station to meet their son and Fleur stood back, watching his mother hug him, feeling her emotions tugging as she witnessed the affection between them. She was smartly dressed in a coat buttoned to her throat. John's father was slapping his arm with a proud smile, and Fleur thought John Bell looked extremely fine in his uniform for his homecoming.

Plenty of other locals were hailing John, welcoming him back. Fleur wondered if anyone had done the same for Tom when he'd returned. Finally, John beckoned to her. She couldn't avoid it; there was a round of introductions to his parents, Jack and Eva, also to his younger brother, Bruce, who was looking adoringly at his older sibling. Fleur guessed he was around twelve. She graciously moved through the greetings, including from others who'd clustered around the family to eagerly say hello to John, admiring his garb. Finally, John asked about Tom on her behalf.

'Tom Catchlove? Ah, now, I did see the lad,' Eva replied. 'He came by to fetch some stores.'

Fleur grinned, thrilled. So close now. 'Oh, good.'

'He was headed out, though,' Jack followed up.

'Headed out?' Fleur repeated, a trill of anxiety sounding within herself like a lone bird calling into the night.

'Yes,' John's father said, frowning as he tried to recall. 'I think he was joining a mob of fellas going north. I'm sure he was muttering to me about perhaps even travelling to Perth and into the great stations of the northwest.'

Fleur swallowed but she couldn't fully hide the distress in her expression.

'Oh, look now,' Eva exclaimed. 'We've upset you. You've come a long way and it's very late. Is Tom your sweetheart, love?'

All Fleur could do was nod, unsure of what to say. She dared not say fiancé, because she wasn't sure how Tom was feeling about her right now.

'Brucie, run down to old Alf at the Exchange – it will be closed but he'll be around, probably outside with some of the other blokes with no home to bother with. Find out if the Witchelina mob have hauled out,' Jack said. He looked at Fleur again, apologetically. 'If anyone knows, Alf will. Hurry now, lad.'

Bruce paused only briefly to cast his big brother a look, nodding conscientiously, and won a grin.

'See you back at the house, Brucie,' John urged. 'I might even have something for you.'

They watched Bruce skip off into the darkness, patches of the town lit by minimal ambient light from the pubs, of which she could count two in the distance.

'They keep a few lights on so the blokes can see what they're weaving their way towards if they're in their cups,' John explained. 'Very dark out here.'

'In the meantime, you come with us,' Eva said, with a serious expression that brooked no protest.

Fleur tried to protest, unsure of what her next move might be if left alone; she had no plan. 'Oh no I couldn't, I—'

'We insist,' Eva said firmly. 'Come to the house while you wait for news, at least, and help us celebrate having our boy home for a little while.'

The family's store, which Fleur had remarked to John that yes, she would like to walk through, felt like an emporium and took her by surprise. 'Is there anything you don't have here?' she asked him.

Jack thought about it. 'Elephant feed,' he said and laughed. 'We try and have all that our folk around here could possibly need.'

It was obvious that Eva was keen to take Fleur to their home. Soon seated around the parlour table, Fleur stood to help but Eva immediately flapped her away. 'No, no, we have a girl to help,' she said. 'Here she comes now. Frieda, tea for everyone and how I like it, mind.' She returned her gaze to Fleur. 'You go and join the others.'

Fleur noted the sleepy young woman who had obviously been woken abruptly or perhaps not permitted to go to sleep this evening until the young master returned. There were shades of Irma here, Fleur thought, learning as they made conversation that Eva was the organist for the Anglican Church and had a lot to do with Farina's girl guide troupe. She told Fleur how much she loved fine music and liked to travel into Adelaide to hear recitals.

'But I can never wait to get back to the desert,' she said. 'Adelaide's so green all the time.'

Fleur blinked. She hadn't expected such a remark, imagining the woman pining for the snobbish sitting rooms of the capital. 'Is your family local, Eva?'

The woman nodded, smiling. 'I have four sisters here, and my mother came here as the schoolteacher before the Great War. She was very elegant, and the locals nicknamed her "the lady". I think most found her formidable, but that was because Mum was very proper and she liked to have afternoon tea with a silver service and a starched tablecloth.' Eva looked around. 'Not like here, with my three boys growing up around me,' she said but with affection. 'People said that when my mother invited you to tea, it was like being invited by the Queen Mother.'

Fleur laughed but hid her amusement that mother and daughter didn't seem so far apart in their habits. The Napier Bells lived well, which she noted, and Eva continued.

'I've done all right with my Jack. I think I'm a privileged soul in Farina. I bathe daily in a fresh bucket of water.' At Fleur's soft frown, she qualified her remark. 'Water's very expensive, and firewood here is triple the price you'd pay in Adelaide.'

Bruce burst back into the room.

'Manners, young man,' his mother remarked.

'Sorry. Er, Miss Appleby, yes, the gang left yesterday.'

Fleur had never fully grasped the meaning of the phrase of a sinking heart but she did now. It felt like hers had dropped several inches, and she had the sensation of being at the tallest point of a playground swing's arc and then falling backwards in that inevitable downward sweep. But unlike the fun of a children's playground, she felt momentarily nauseated, almost dizzy with what she heard.

'Is Alf sure, Brucie?' John pressed his brother.

The lad nodded. 'He said he delivered the longnecks onto the wagon. Plenty of them, he told me. And Tom Catchlove was at the reins. Tom told Alf he'd see him in six months or so.'

The walls of the Bell's house seemed to collapse inward, mimicking Fleur's mind, which seemed to invert on itself. 'Gone,' she whispered. 'I've missed him?'

John looked around awkwardly at his family and then took a step to crouch by where Fleur was sat. 'Look, Fleur, um . . . I'm sure he'll make contact.'

'He doesn't know I'm coming, John. He doesn't think I want him. He doesn't know yet that I'm having his baby.'

Fleur heard Eva Bell gasp, noting the slight hitch of indignation.

'They were to be married,' John snapped at his mother, but his attention was back on Fleur. 'I'm so sorry. We can try and get word to them but not tonight, I doubt.'

'Well, there's nothing for it, Fleur,' Eva said. 'You shall have to stay here this evening. I can't have a young woman from the city walking off into the night in your condition. Did you have nowhere planned for your overnight?' She had suddenly become haughty.

'No,' Fleur bleated, feeling uncharacteristically helpless. In her mind Tom would have learned she was here and come running, kicking up the dust behind him as he leapt off the wagon, with the famous Bonny he'd told her about bravely pulling him all the way to Farina as she had all those years ago when his mother had been in labour. But that clearly wasn't going to happen.

She allowed herself to be ushered to a spare room that Eva Bell and Frieda hurriedly made up. She heard them telling her about the outhouse and other such mundane information but none of it sunk in because reality was forcing its way through all the detail and her sorrows were crowding in.

Bonny was surely dead and Tom was no longer here. So why was she? She had no immediate future that held wedding bells and lots of smiles. Her love had disappeared. Her mother dead, her father dead . . . an orphan again. She had not had the chance to explain the terrible lie. How could Irma have known? Fleur herself had barely realised what was happening in her body until she had encountered the doctor signing a death certificate as she arrived to help the bereaved family.

They'd both stepped into the hallway while the family said their final farewells.

'You're looking a little peaky to me, Fleur. Are you well?' Dr Parsons asked.

'Oh, I'm fine, thanks. It's just, you know, these last few months have been taxing.'

'No doubt, no doubt,' he said softly. 'Even so, Fleur, you look wan. You should come and see me.'

'I'm fine, truly.'

He persisted. 'No symptoms of anything?'

She sighed, realising he was not going to let it go. 'I seem to be very tired suddenly, lacking the energy I have always been able to count on.' She shook her head with a wan smile. 'Just unused to my body not obeying. It will pass. As I say, it's been a rough few months, and I suppose this is the result of a lot of suppressed worry and, well, grief.'

'Hmm. Do you take much sugar?'

She hadn't expected that. 'No, not really. My father never did and so I tended to copy him. I don't have a very sweet tooth – no real cravings, although, funnily enough' — she chuckled softly — 'just recently, all I want is ice-cream . . . and I seem to want the smell of coal.'

He snapped her a fresh glance. 'You crave them?'

She shrugged. 'Silly, I know. But if I do treat myself to an ice-cream, all I do is sicken.'

'When?'

'When?' Fleur repeated, confused.

'Yes. I'm guessing this isn't an isolated event simply after ice-cream.' He peered at her over his spectacles.

She blinked at the scrutiny. 'Well, the truth is, Dr Parsons, I feel nauseated most mornings these days. Usually when I wake, but the queasiness can hang around. I'm sure it's nothing.'

It was his turn to chuckle. 'Fleur, my dear. How are your monthlies?'

She stared at him. Then her mouth slackened in surprise.

'Haven't seen one in a while, I'm guessing?'

Now her mouth opened but she didn't know what to say because her throat was so dry and all the words felt jumbled in the shock of what he was intimating. No, not intimating – telling her.

She cleared her throat. 'Surely not?' she asked in a small voice.

'Well, as I'm presuming you know how it happens, I'm also presuming that ring on your finger was given to you by the young man in question. You'd better be suggesting to him that he come up with a wedding day, and fast.' He laughed. 'I met him. I liked him. He seemed moonstruck with you.'

'When?'

'At the police station. He came in with the Coglins, for some reason, rather banged up, and I asked him to let me check his wounds. I lanced a blood blister that was keeping his eye closed. Anyway, we talked and Henry came up in conversation, then you did and . . . well, he struck me as a reticent fellow but when it came to you, his eyes lit. I wish you much happiness, Fleur.'

'Dr Parsons, you won't—'

'Not a soul, my dear Fleur. If you hurry, no one will be any the wiser.'

But now she'd missed Tom. If he wasn't home for six months, their baby would be nearly due. Would he want them? Could she convince him this child was his, and not Jimmy's?

She began to cry, no hard sobs but a leaking of tears that wouldn't stop as they dampened the pillow. She had no idea when she finally fell asleep and delivered her from her sorrow.

Fleur was up early. She had no choice but to wear the special green dress she had bought especially to see Tom. He had once whispered to her that green was the colour that was missing in the outback.

'We have silver greens, and greyish greens, and even blueish greens,' he'd explained, twirling her hair through his fingers. 'But my mother used to talk about the grass on her travels through Europe being this sort of luminous green, full of rich chlorophyll.'

She loved that Tom used words like this, and she wanted to smile imagining what sort of expression would appear on Jimmy Coglin's face if she mentioned chlorophyll to him. It wasn't about being superior; it was about knowledge and a love of learning and acquiring new information.

'This green – she talked about it a lot and one day I want to see it. We'll go together.' He'd smiled into her eyes.

Fleur had searched and found a dress that was deep emerald, with a small floral print in a lighter shade and spots of black, like tiny flecks of ink beneath the flowers. The long sleeves were cuffed and at her neck, a length of the same fabric formed the collar and tied into a neat bow. She had known immediately that dress was for Tom but she had no choice but to wear it now because she'd managed to get yesterday's dress rather grimy with all of the changes of seats and the dust. She could wear it with her neat black brogues as John had advised. Tom would never see her in the green he dreamed of, and she breathed out her frustration and melancholy, determined to not force her mood on anyone else.

She arrived into the parlour before most in the family had stirred – even Frieda hadn't arrived – but it didn't take long for others to start emerging.

Eva swept in, wearing a silken day dress. It seemed rather fancy for Farina but Fleur admonished herself that she didn't know what was appropriate or not for the region.

'You look lovely, Mrs Bell.'

'Thank you, dear. You, however, don't look as though you've slept.'

Fleur gave a soft sigh. 'Not much, but I'm very grateful for your kindness and the bed. Thank you.'

'What do you plan to do?'

'I shall go home. Um, I gather there may be a returning train today?'

Eva nodded as John arrived and not too far behind him, his brother, Bruce.

'Fleur is taking the morning train back to Adelaide, John. Perhaps you could accompany her to the station before our visitors start arriving?' Eva urged. She looked back at Fleur. 'I'm hosting a welcome for John, although I suspect it shall probably be more of a farewell to my boy, who is travelling to England.'

Fleur nodded. 'So I hear. I'm sure the gathering will be splendid.'

'So, Fleur, the Ghan is not terribly reliable but, even so, if it leaves Marree even close to its scheduled timetable, then it will be at Farina station for nine. Frieda should be here shortly, and I'm sure she can give you breakfast and pack up a small picnic for your journey home. I must go and see to the table set up for our guests, and so I will bid you goodbye now.'

'Yes, of course. Thank you again. And if you're ever visiting Adelaide and can give me a little warning, I'd be delighted to take you for afternoon tea at the South Australian Hotel.'

'My, my, how grand. I'd be delighted.'

They embraced briefly and then Mrs Bell was gone to attend to her hostess duties.

'So you're going?' John asked, sounding sympathetic.

She nodded. 'Yes, no reason to linger.'

'I'm sorry, Fleur.'

'Don't be. No one's fault. Um, I'm sorry about breaking down and being pathetic yesterday. It's been—'

'Nothing to apologise for and, er, we're all rather upset for you in your . . . condition.'

Fleur smiled softly, imagining that Eva Bell likely couldn't wait for her, an unmarried pregnant woman, to be out of the house. But that was churlish given the family had looked after her. She really was grateful, but she was also miserable and it was hard to maintain her composure. 'Thank you for taking me back to the train. Where's your father? I should thank him too.'

'He'll be in the store. Customers would happily have Bell's open all day and night. My uncle will be there too.'

She looked at her wristwatch. Less than an hour before they left for the station. Her departure couldn't come quick enough.

———

They decided to walk to the station.

'I want to know I didn't leave without at least seeing the town that Tom was born into.'

'Not a lot to see,' John began, but Fleur gasped.

'Look at that!' She pointed as a long camel train in the distance moved slowly north. 'What are they carrying?'

'Water,' he explained. 'Those oblong containers either side

of their humps are called shippers. That's how we move the water around to various places nearby.'

'Amazing,' she breathed. She'd only previously seen camels at the zoo and that thought reminded her of being there with Tom. She banished the memory, forbidding herself from getting upset again in front of John. Plenty of time ahead for that.

'That's the bush hospital,' he said, pointing. 'It's an old hotel that's been converted.'

So that was where Moira Catchlove had given birth to Amy, and both had died. That poor family. Everywhere here was a reminder of Tom.

John continued, unaware of her musings. 'Because you're travelling in daylight, you'll see some sights this time. Maybe a long bullock train . . . you'll certainly see teams of donkeys pulling a load of wool towards the train. And camels, of course; they haul everything from food to ballot boxes and go as far as Cordillo Downs.' He sounded impressed.

Fleur gave a grin as she shrugged. 'I have no idea where that is.'

'Well, let's just say it's over three weeks journeying in one direction on a camel train.'

'And still in South Australia?' She sounded aghast. 'That's hard to imagine.'

'Yep, it's a huge cattle station.'

'And what's happening there?' she said, glad to have this interesting walk to take her mind off Tom.

'Oh, apparently they're dismantling the Catholic Church and moving it to Murray Town, or so I'm told.'

'Good grief.'

In the distance, the Ghan signalled its imminent arrival with a loud blast on its horn, and Fleur and John watched great clouds of steam billowing up from far away, dispersing against a cloudless, turquoise morning.

He laughed. 'What impeccable timing. It's so rarely on schedule, it must be you. And here's the station again,' he said, as they neared a hut.

'It's even smaller than it appeared last night.'

He grinned. 'You know we have horse races, dances, concerts, fairs, tennis, bowls . . . We have hotels, a library, even an underground forge. We have schools and churches. You name it. It all goes on.'

'I didn't mean to suggest—'

'I know,' he said, smiling. 'I'm just proud to be from here, that's all.'

'And they're all very proud of you, John. Thank you for being so kind to me yesterday Your whole family is lovely and so generous.'

'Mum's a bit of a handful at times, but she's very good for the town, always pushing hard to improve things around here as best she can.' At Fleur's nod, he continued. 'I know she gave you the impression that she—'

Fleur squeezed his arm. 'No need to explain. I'm not offended. I'm a modern woman with broad shoulders and I can handle the pursed lips of the previous generation. I didn't plan this, John; life's just gone a little crooked for me, that's all.' She gave him a hug, keeping it deliberately brief so she wouldn't cry.

The rattle of timber and the screech of iron combined with clouds of steam to announce the train's arrival. She could taste the metal of the engine and the tracks. People were hanging out of the windows and calling out to others at the station, passing on messages from family and friends. Bursts of laughter and whistles to catch attention were all part of the cacophony.

Men rushed up with bags of mail and other product to be loaded, while passengers alighted or stepped on board alongside Fleur. She found a seat and lowered the window to say a final farewell to her friend.

'What will you do?' John asked.

Fleur smiled more bravely than she felt, adding a breezy tone she certainly wasn't feeling. 'What I know . . . back to Adelaide and the business.' She put a hand on her belly. 'And what will be, will be.' She reached her other hand out to squeeze his. 'Happy flying. Good luck, John.'

'You too,' he responded, squeezing it back. 'I hope . . .' He trailed off, unable to find the right words.

She nodded. 'I know. Now, go . . . get back to Eva or she'll have something to say. High tea and all that!'

He laughed aloud. 'She's unstoppable.'

Fleur waved and John reluctantly turned away, slowly loping back in the direction they'd come from. Fleur deliberately avoided staring out wistfully at the desert, reminding her of what might have been. She pulled out a book and was determined to lose herself. She did not wish to speak to anyone, so she hoped the book and her focused attention, even if she didn't take in a single word, would dissuade anyone from striking up a conversation. She was grateful that today, at least, she was not feeling the familiar nausea.

A baby. If she was honest, it was privately exciting and something to look forward to, even without Tom. She would raise her child with love and all the tenderness that Mae and Henry had raised her with. She had the means to give her child anything that was needed in life and for that alone, Fleur knew she should be grateful.

Her baby would want for nothing, except its father.

And she would want for nothing except its father too.

Tears stung but she would not let them fall. She opened the book and blinked them away. Absently she heard whistles, doors banging and an increase in the sound of the engine revving to be on its way.

A man and presumably his son sat opposite her. She couldn't avoid the eye contact, so she smiled.

'Good morning,' the man said, lifting his hat and then removing it to his lap.

Fleur looked at the boy; he was probably twelve. 'Hello,' she said.

'Dad says the train struggles to get up the hill and out of Farina,' he said, by way of introduction. 'I'm Billy.'

Fleur grinned, then glanced at the father, who shrugged and said, 'It's true. You might have felt it on the way into Farina – it all but coasts down the hill after a struggle to get to the top just before it reaches town.'

'I came in late last night and I have to admit I didn't notice because I was so tired.'

'That's a quick visit.' He raised his brows, opening a question but she didn't answer it.

'Yes, very,' she said, dipping her gaze.

'Well, the point is, we don't always get up the first time,' he said. 'I think Billy's hoping that happens.'

'I am . . . Hey, Dad, can we go more to the front to look out?'

'Er, Miss . . . ?'

She obliged. 'Appleby.'

'Thank you. Miss Appleby, could I leave our things here, and we'll return? It's the lad's first train trip, so I should take him towards the engine.'

'Of course. Your stuff is safe. I'm here all the way to Adelaide, so I won't let anyone take your seats, I promise.'

'Oh, excellent, thank you. Come on, then, Billy. Let's see if we can get you a peek at the front.'

It was a mercy for Fleur that they'd departed. Maybe they'd be gone for an hour and she'd have that time alone with her thoughts.

The train began to roll, but it also seemed to be pushing hard. Now that she understood the reason, she too was intrigued to see if they could crest the hill on the first thunder towards it. It seemed everyone else in her carriage knew the track record too and an excited tension rippled through the air.

The train was gathering speed, travelling much faster out of the town's reaches than she thought was possible in such a short run. She sat forward and watched. They were moving up the hill now and it was as though everyone, including her, was holding a collective breath as the train searched for the summit . . . and failed.

Wheels squealed, iron complained and there was a shuddering pause as, gently at first and then gathering to a slow but steady speed, the train began to roll back down the hill into town accompanied by whistles, laughter and sarcastic but somehow affectionate cheering.

She joined in with the laughter; her first genuine amusement in months. It was good for her.

The Ghan tried again. This time everyone in her vicinity began a sort of soft and encouraging cheer.

'Come on!' one bloke yelled.

'You can do it!' another called out.

Everyone shared smiles and chuckles as the train gathered speed again. Billy must have been chuffed, Fleur thought, before imagining the frustration of the engine driver hearing all the catcalls – but he'd be used it.

They were hurtling towards the incline now. Out of the corner of her eye, she saw a streak of someone running alongside the train and that person waving, probably in farewell, the train hooting as if in response – *See you next time.*

'Yeah, we'll make it,' someone said.

But Fleur wasn't so sure. And her instincts were right; as if the train were clutching at the crest with its fingertips, the top of the hill slipped away and, once again, the train slid backwards into town.

Inside the carriage, the cheering intensified. Fleur imagined this must be a regular sport for the travellers; they might even lay bets on how many tries it would take. She was openly laughing now with everyone else in her compartment.

'Third time lucky,' she said to a neighbour.

'Maybe,' the woman said with a chuckle.

The men in at the engine were obviously feeding it furiously for this third attempt. The sound of it was different now – more like a hungry beast. As it sped forward at what felt like full pelt, there was a sudden clatter to Fleur's side. Her neighbour gave a small, alarmed shriek as the window nearest to Fleur was darkened by a shape; a man had leapt onto the moving carriages. *What on earth was going on?* Fleur thought, her hand instinctively going to her belly once more.

The train was reaching the base of the incline, travelling at the highest throttle it could under the circumstances, when the man bent his head to look inside the carriage.

Impossibly, Fleur saw Tom Catchlove grinning his crooked smile, and then his mouth widened to a full beam of white teeth, his laugh crinkling his eyes in that way that melted her, the rush of wind whipping at his hair.

'Tom . . . Tom!' she shrieked, half crying, half hysterical, with just enough presence of mind to know neither of those qualities usually belonged to her. 'Tom!' she screeched again, unable to believe it was him.

'If we get over the top this time, I'll have to go all the way to Quorn out here,' he called through the glass, grinning lopsidedly.

People were moving to open the door and haul him in, with Fleur anxiously standing by, terrified he'd fall off or fall under the wheels on the track. And then suddenly he was inside. The door slammed and three burly men watched on helplessly as both Tom and Fleur collapsed to their knees in each other's arms.

Her shoulders shook with the helpless tears that came . . . real sobs this time, as she felt the warmth and hard, muscled body of Tom holding her close, saying nothing, both of them listening to the raucous cheers as the train failed yet again to tip itself over the summit.

Through the cacophony, Fleur finally pulled back from Tom. 'I have so much to say.'

He grinned. 'You've said it all by being here. And you're wearing green . . . You look so beautiful.'

'No, there's more. But how come you're here? They said you'd gone!'

'I should have been gone, well out of Farina by now, but my horse pulled up lame. I brought her back and was intending to catch up tomorrow, but an old bloke called Alf whistled for my attention.'

'Alf from the Exchange Hotel?'

Tom laughed. 'Yes. Are you old friends, or what?'

She gave a watery laugh back. 'No, Brucie Bell found him last night.'

'My gosh, now you know the Bells? You haven't been here more than twelve hours.'

'Met them all, slept over,' she said, drying her tears.

He looked amused. 'Anyway, Alf said some woman from Adelaide was looking for me. It had to be you. And then someone at the station said they'd seen a "beautiful city lady in green" leaving on the train, having hugged a local lad.'

Fleur nodded. 'John Bell.'

'So I chased the train, hoping against hope it would fail to reach the top of the hill as it often does.'

She looked into his eyes, so full of sparkle and affection, and knew her visit, every last tear of fear and sorrow that she'd missed him, was worth it. Because here he was, staring at her in what looked like similar wonder.

'We've found each other once more,' he said, as though he were listening in on her thoughts.

'I'll never let you of my sight again. Never!'

'Good. I want you to marry me today.' He pointed out the window; the train had come to a stop once more just outside the station. 'Come on, let's get off the train and go to see the mayor or our local constable. One of them can marry us.'

'Tom, I haven't anything to wear to be a bride.'

'Doesn't matter what you wear, Fleur,' he murmured, 'it will be coming off soon after.' He lifted an eyebrow, grinning at her.

She toppled into his arms once again, kissing his neck and hugging him hard.

'Come on, you two lovebirds. We're all getting off,' one of the rescuers said. 'Hurry up, or we'll have to book you a room at one of the pubs.'

Tom leapt up and helped Fleur to her feet. 'Thanks for helping me on board.'

'Seems you had urgent business,' another man quipped.

They all shared an affectionate grin.

'We're off to get married,' Fleur said, sounding breathless and entirely caught up with the excitement of the morning.

'I should think so, with all that canoodling in public,' another said, but without malice.

A round of congratulations followed as more people arrived into the tiny corridor to get off the train.

'What are they going to do?' Tom asked as the train backed alongside the station platform.

'Try again in an hour. Engine driver's cursed so much he needs an ale to calm his throat.'

———————

Fleur and Tom were married that day as he'd threatened. Eva Bell, despite all her own event preparations, flew into action and found a suitable cream silk dress; Fleur, beyond grateful, didn't ask where from. Eva also insisted that the whole group of guests arriving for John's event first stopped at the local hall – really just a shed behind the Patterson House, where they used to hold dances and concerts, with a piano – so that they could all bear witness to the civil ceremony, which everyone cheerfully did.

Eva sent Brucie scuttling off for some wildflowers and he returned with a small bunch of wild daisies in pinks, mauves and a few white, which Eva laced through Fleur's hair.

'It will do,' she pronounced.

'I find myself thanking you again, Eva.'

'I'm very happy for you, and especially because of the child. Does he know?'

'Not yet. It will be my wedding gift to him.' Fleur grinned and put a finger to her lips.

The hurriedly pulled-together shotgun wedding – not that Tom knew – was over in a few minutes and suddenly they were being urged to share their first kiss as Mr and Mrs Catchlove.

Old tins had been tied to the cart that Tom had driven into town and, with some stores thrown into the back of it, they set off for Witchelina Station, half the town waving them off with catcalls and cheers.

Privately, Fleur thought that she couldn't have planned a more perfect wedding. Brief, painless, almost no socialising and back in Tom's arms in less than an hour since she'd clambered into a borrowed dress.

Fleur snuggled up to Tom, holding his arm tightly.

He grinned. 'You meant it, didn't you? You're not letting me go.' He kissed the top of her head.

'Tom, there are things to be spoken about.'

'I know. But can we talk about them later?'

She shook her head. 'No. I want you to know that I did not send that letter.'

He stayed quiet for a few breathless moments and then nodded. 'Irma?'

'Yes. I can show you how different my handwriting is.'

He shook his head with disgust. 'Why didn't I guess that?'

'Why would you?'

'Because you left me so in love . . . I should have trusted your love and how honest you are.'

'Perhaps you should have, but I'm well aware of how cunning Irma can be. I imagine she was extremely convincing.'

'It even sounded like you when I read it, Fleur.'

'So I don't blame you.'

He hugged her tighter. 'I'm glad you came after me. Blimey, Fleur, you could have missed me by a whisker.'

'I thought I had. I could kiss that lame horse of yours.'

'She's called Ginger.'

'Will she be all right?'

'Yes, with the right care, but I couldn't risk taking her further.'

Fleur nodded gratefully. 'Listen, Tom. While Irma told a raft of lies in that letter, she did manage to stumble upon the truth of one aspect.'

He glanced at her. 'Which is?'

'That I'm pregnant, Tom. But I'm having *your* baby.'

He hauled on the reins and the wagon juddered to a halt. He stared at her, up and down, his gaze helplessly returning to her belly. She realised she had once again placed a protective hand across it. 'Mine?'

She nodded, tears welling. 'I've never slept with anyone but you, Tom. You must have sensed that, surely?'

'I don't know why I allowed myself to believe you would let anyone like Jimmy Coglin get that close.'

'Ugh,' she said, giving a shudder. 'Perish that thought.'

'We're having a baby?' Tom asked again and she nodded, matching his loony grin. He stood, still holding the reins, and let rip with a howl that echoed across the landscape. 'I'm going to be a father!' he yelled.

Laughing at his joy, she hushed him. 'I think we need to keep it a secret for a while. Only John's family knows. Promise me.'

'I promise. So can we still . . . you know . . .?'

'Yes, you dolt! Our baby's only about an inch in size. It won't know what you're up to.'

And now their laughter sounded against the red desert.

33

They agreed to remain at Witchelina for a week. Conveniently, everyone was away, so the house was theirs but they left no traces other than a track between a back bedroom, the bathroom and the kitchen. The week had passed in a tumult of lovemaking, grazing on whatever stores they had carried with them, and watching the stars each night from the wide verandah of the first floor, sipping tea as they sat close on an old armchair that had been dragged out there.

Fleur listened, enraptured as Tom guided her through the Milky Way, pointing out celestial bodies she'd never heard of and others that were simply fun to listen to.

'That's Venus, pretty close to the teapot of Sagittarius,' he said as she squinted. 'And the waxing moon is near Saturn, do you see?'

She nodded, just enjoying the sound of his enthralled voice. 'I want you to teach our child all of this,' she said.

'Then you'll have to agree to make regular visits into the outback, because you can't see much of this from the city, Fleur. It's only in the desert you get to commune with the firmament.'

She smiled. 'Then each year we shall come and spend early spring here.'

He leaned down and she kissed him slow and tenderly.

'Now I have a couple of pieces of information to share,' he said.

'You do?' She sounded intrigued. 'Good information, I hope. I can't take any more bad news.'

'It's not bad, but it's only good depending on how you view it.'

'Do you mean *you*, as in generally, or do you mean me in particular?'

'Everything for me is about you in particular, Fleur. You and our child.'

She felt her heart give. How could she have ever lost this? The Flinders Ranges, those oldest of gods, had been very generous to her with their gift. After all her sorrows of this year, the happiness she felt in this moment couldn't be overstated or overwhelmed. 'All right. Tell me,' she said, shifting her position so she could look at him squarely.

'Do you remember the family that you and your father had to visit when you picked up my mother and my sister for burial?'

'They're hard to forget, Tom.'

He gave a soft snort of agreement. 'I met them again recently.'

'You did?'

'They're as repugnant as we both recall.'

'That's disappointing,' she said, unsure of where this was leading.

'By they, I mean Mr and Mrs Darnell. Knowing your memory, you'd remember my aunt, Elizabeth Darnell.'

'She accused me of being precocious when I was just displaying good manners.'

He nodded. 'Do you remember the girl at the window? We saw her when we were in the garden.'

'Yes, a pale creature.'

'Well, she's still pale but she's also great and she's my cousin, I've discovered. Her name is Emily and she's everything her parents are not. She's normal, for a start. And she takes no prisoners, Fleur. She reminded me of you, and I've promised I'll introduce you both.'

'If you like her, then I know I shall.'

'She's single-minded and desperate to get away from the clutch of her parents. I mean, she probably loves them but their attitude frustrates her. She's a modern woman and shows none of their hideous pretension.'

Fleur nodded. 'How did this come about?'

Tom explained.

'So now you have family . . . even if you only count that one lovely cousin.'

He nodded. 'Feels good. But the best bit about Emily was that she could tell me more about the man my mother loved, the man who fathered me.' Again Tom explained all he'd discovered. He pulled out the card and showed Fleur.

She was quietly shocked but was careful not to show it. 'It isn't much to go on.'

'No. I've been thinking it all through since she gave it to me and I've decided I don't wish to find out more about him. I had a mother and father – the only ones I knew about – and the man who came before is simply that. A man. A stranger. I'm wondering about the proverbial can of worms, Fleur. What if finding him sets off a new pile of problems and emotions I don't need? I just want to get on with life with you. I've imagined how me arriving into his life – if I can find him – would be disruptive. He may have his own family now . . . a wife, other children, perhaps even grandchildren. And all I would do is create new turmoil for all of those people. It might unsettle him as he remembers Mum and their love and being forbidden to be together.' Tom shook his head. 'I think it's not worth risking upset.'

She nodded, hugging him tighter. 'We were so fortunate to find each other again. I agree, perhaps you should let that be enough and not hold on to old hurts. The hurt was your mother's and she came to terms with it. And as you rightly say, he's a stranger, whereas Vern Catchlove was your father in every way.'

Tom pondered this some more, nodding finally. 'I'm glad you agree. Our child will never know his or her two grandfathers but as far as they're concerned, that's Henry Appleby and Vern Catchlove.' He seemed to hesitate.

'Sounds like you have more to say, Tom.'

'There is more.' He took a deep breath. 'I heard about an old house while I was at the woolstores, and was interested in seeing it.' When she gave him a look of enquiry, he added, 'I think my mother gave me an interest in history. The house holds many stories of past lives.'

Fleur knew to remain patient with Tom. 'I'm listening.'

'It's a rather grand old place on a hill, overlooking pasture for as far as my gaze could reach.'

'You've seen it?'

He nodded. 'I've been in it. They let me have the keys,' he admitted, sounding embarrassed. 'It's been left to go to ruin, I gather. It was built by a gentleman landowner in the previous century – one of the early settlers of South Australia. It's called Drumminor.'

'Where is this house? Is it out here in the middle of nowhere?'

He laughed and she gave him an apologetic shrug.

'Sorry.'

'I do like the middle of nowhere at times. No, this house is north of Adelaide, further out from Prospect, and I have a feeling that the region will become part of the Adelaide metropolis as it begins to sprawl.' He warmed to this topic, sitting forward eagerly. 'Fleur, it has to be the next region that will feel the effects of population increase. It's not too hilly and has a near enough straight line to the city. I think they'll build proper roads and they'll start carving up the land quite soon into suburbs, then begin building houses, schools, hospitals and shops.'

She turned to regard him with an interested frown. 'Tom, you sound convinced.'

'I am.'

'All right. You've thought this through, but why?'

'People have to live somewhere and the population is exploding. Not everyone can afford to live in North Adelaide or Unley or Norwood. The Port is already crowded. Prospect is booming and becoming densely populated, and I reckon they'll just keep going further north from there.'

'So?'

She watched him tense slightly. 'So, I bought it.'

Fleur resisted the natural response to say 'pardon' in her surprise and have him repeat what she'd heard perfectly well. But it didn't stop her needing to repeat it in her mind to comprehend his words. 'I don't understand.'

He gave her a sheepish shrug. 'Recently I discovered my mother left some money in trust for me for when I came of age.'

'Oh, Tom.' Fleur sighed. 'Why didn't your father tell you, given she died long ago?'

'If Dad knew about it, he chose not to mention it. At first, when I found out, I thought he mustn't have wanted me to have it – jealous, perhaps, or maybe he reasoned that we've never had money, so why have it now? I was doing fine as a wool classer. Dad had an opinion that money – a surplus of it, that is – only caused problems.'

'Irma being a very good example,' Fleur said, in a dry tone.

Tom nodded. 'He was someone who earned and spent all he had on living. He didn't think to save or aspire. But if he kept it a secret, then I forgive him. He wasn't trying to keep it for his own use – he simply didn't want to bring that problem of money into our simple lives. And maybe he never knew.'

'And you're comfortable about the money?'

Tom gave a slight lift of his shoulder to show he was not entirely convinced but said, 'I've reached a place of understanding, and perhaps resignation, regarding Dad. I think to him this money was likely another reminder of all that he wasn't and could never be. He didn't come from money like my mother, and he didn't have the potential to earn a lot. So I imagine that, while he adored Mum, he knew she deserved more and he'd never provided much for us . . .'

'Other than love and laughter,' Fleur said softly.

Tom nodded with an appreciative smile. 'For sure . . . and in droves – at least until Mum passed away. I think the money also just reminded him about Adelaide and the life she'd left behind for him. I know from conversations I overheard when I was young but didn't fully understand that Mum's family never enquired after us. They really did not care.' He sighed. 'But when I came to Adelaide, I remembered the solicitors Mum had talked about and I learned of this money. I had no idea what to do with it. And then I met you again and you told me your dream.'

'My dream?'

'That you want to open a new business that trains women to be the very best undertakers and morticians, and a specialist funeral home that caters to bereaved parents of newborns and young children.' He gave a gentle smile.

Fleur felt her emotions being stirred on so many levels; the fact that Tom had absorbed her hopes with such gravity felt like the sun was sending its rays directly into her heart to warm her. But, more importantly, they were speaking this aloud as though it was not just plausible but something to follow vigorously, like a new pathway opening for them.

Her father had never taken her suggestions very seriously; he had been tolerant of her ideas, appreciative that she was always thinking ahead for the future of the business, but she knew that deep down he was set in his ways. He had felt he'd already taken the business into a new era, and Fleur suspected he couldn't quite look forward as far as she could to a time when women might lead a new way in undertaking. Tom being her own age, a child of the twentieth century . . . well, it meant he was more open to a new age of women's rights and their aspirations. He'd been born to an independent thinker, not manipulated by wealth or society. If anything, Moira Catchlove had defied all the rules and, in doing so, had raised a son who admired women with agency.

'I do have a lot of ideas. Like cremation – it feels primitive, but it's catching on with the liberal-minded and the forward thinkers, who can see that cemeteries are going to become full. Once that happens, they'll have to start being positioned further and further away. And you know, Tom,' Fleur finally said, grateful for his silence while she gathered her thoughts, 'when I was young and still learning about undertaking and work in the mortuary, a newborn who died didn't get their own burial.' She swallowed. 'If they could, funeral homes would place a dead child into the coffin of a dead woman, rarely its mother. They thought the child should be in the arms of a female.'

She watched his expression turn slack with surprise. 'I had no idea.'

Fleur shook her head. 'Why would you? And you must understand that this was not cruel. If anything, I believe it was a tenderness being shown. No one wanted to put a tiny newborn into the earth alone, but no one wanted to go to the expense of a coffin and all of those trappings. Add to this that at the turn of the century, many children didn't live past the age of five, so mothers were losing every third or fourth infant. They couldn't possibly afford all the burial fees.

'My father and other reputable funeral homes never charged for undertaking services for an infant; they felt the sorrow of the loss and showed great empathy. But as a woman in undertaking, I have never thought that was good enough. To lose a person who has lived a life is hard enough, but to lose a child at any age is unimaginable. No one wants to outlive their children and so I've always felt that we need to do better for grieving parents . . . especially mothers. And that means everything from how we approach the removal of their child to how we convey them to the mortuary and how we prepare them for their final rest . . . and how we work with the mothers to let them know we understand their grief. I would ensure their lost babies have their own casket, their own private resting place, and not be buried with a stranger.'

Tom straightened. 'So do it!'

She let out a soft gasp of surprise and smiled at him. 'I want to . . .'

'Start afresh,' he urged. 'I will build you a funeral home like no other. I've done plenty of carpentry alongside wool classing, and I can learn how to make coffins for you. There's nothing hard about them as I can see, but I'll make each with care and that will echo yours.'

'Tom . . .' She sounded breathless, unable to say any more.

'I have loads of ideas, Fleur, but I didn't want to presume,' he admitted. 'I want to make you tiny white coffins for babies, and light wood coffins for children, and I figured I might run some sheep on the land . . . That way we can have our own wool spun and turned into beautiful miniature blankets that you can give to any bereaved parents to wrap their child in before they lay them to rest. We'll build a chapel at Drumminor, and if we pool our resources, we can build you the most modern mortuary with all the proper air extraction and latest equipment. And over there' — he gestured with his hand over an imaginary map, hardly daring to take a breath, it seemed — 'we could set up a series of gardens with rose arbours in summer and wisteria in spring for you, because if people are becoming more interested in cremation, they can scatter ashes there or bury them, or have a plaque to commemorate a loved one. That way they can visit the most pretty of scented gardens and remember those they love. We can even build a fountain and embed memorial plaques around it . . . It would be the only private cemetery and memorial gardens in all of South Australia – perhaps the country.'

Now he did stop talking, searching her face.

'I didn't know you had so many words to use in one day, Tom. And for once, I'm lost for words. I really don't know what to say,' Fleur smiled, knowing her eyes were shining with the excitement of all that Tom's words prompted.

He waited. 'Please, Fleur. Let me help you to make this dream a reality. Just say yes.'

She nodded, her mind already racing around his ideas; she loved him all the more for thinking so big on her behalf. 'Yes.'

He clapped in relief. 'And the house, Fleur. Will you move there with me and make a large family? It's beautiful, you will love it.'

She laughed. 'Who could say no? Yes, we'll turn it from a house into a home. But what about Alberton?'

Tom's eyes were shining with his own excitement and she understood. Now he had a purpose – a big project to mastermind.

'You don't have to close up shop,' he said. 'You can appoint people and train them to take over when you move up here. Perhaps the manager's job comes with the home down there? Or maybe you provide it for your staff to use when on shift, because you will always be open for the bereaved,' Tom continued, unable to stop the ideas from pouring out. 'You still want to offer undertaking services to the people who know you and count on you but, if you don't mind me saying, I think it will be the best decision you make to leave that house. I know it was once a happy home, but it became a miserable one. Leave all that sorrow behind, Fleur, and build your own home, fill it with love and laughter . . . and lots of children.'

She grinned; his excitement was infectious. 'Lord and Lady Catchlove of Drumminor, eh?'

———————

This was their last day at Witchelina. Tomorrow they would take the train back to Adelaide and start their new life. But first, Tom explained, he wanted Fleur to experience a moment from his childhood.

She'd allowed herself to be persuaded to journey with him in the dark to his old childhood cottage at Paradise and to climb a tree before the sun rose. Tom helped Fleur to sit beside him in the same coolabah tree that had stood the test of time through drought, winds, rain and even earthquakes. There was no water in the old creek, but the weather was mild and a soft breeze was tumbling over the range, wafting at her hair. She was wearing her green dress for him.

'Tom, is this safe?' she asked, swatting at tiny flies.

'Safe as houses. I used to climb up here when I was a lad and daydream. I used to sit on this very branch and now it's supporting both of us – it's as strong as ever.'

'And what did you daydream about?'

'About the world out there, how big it was and how much I wanted to see it. But now, as I sit here, I realise life was simple and good here.'

She sighed happily. 'I can see why.'

'Can you?'

She smiled. 'Listen.'

He did, waiting for her to explain.

'I can't hear much above the rustle of the leaves, that bird over there making a racket and the soft breeze.' She frowned. 'If I really concentrate, I can hear something clanging gently on metal.'

'That's at the railway track.' He grinned. 'Probably some ties come loose at the siding; nothing to worry about.'

'My point is, everything is so still and quiet that I can hear a single bird's song. I grew up around constant noise, I now realise. The port was always heaving with people and ships, trucks and animals, machinery that lifted things or pushed things or moved things. I've never really thought about it until now. Men were always shouting or whistling to get each other's attention and then there were the ships themselves; their foghorns announcing their arrival or farewelling Adelaide. The sound of the sea, the sound of the traffic, the sound of people going about their lives. I have never, ever known such tranquil surrounds as I do right at this moment. I can hear myself breathe.'

'You're right, but it was lonely growing up in this. You have to get lost in your own imagination.'

'But that's why you can think things through so clearly. You know how to disappear into your thoughts and weigh everything up swiftly.' She smiled. 'Plus, the scenery is breathtaking,' she said and it wasn't the desert before her that she was referring to. Her mind was still swollen with vivid images of the grand range of mountains that the train had cut through to bring her here. The Flinders, as Tom referred to them, had mesmerised her and John had sensed that she didn't wish to talk while they watched their majesty, even as dark shadows in the night.

Out here with this big sky, the horizon seemed to burn golden while the weight of darkness still hung heavy above. Then the sky behind the shadowy clouds began to lighten, like heaven was waking up, stretching and switching on the lights. And with each yawn and stretch of the souls she liked to believe lived there, areas of the sky flashed white, their luminosity breaking through the cloudy blanket. In the east she watched the horizon's cauldron begin to simmer with copper light that continued to change as it broadened its reach into a fresh golden promise of a new day. Mild warmth chased away the night clouds and cleared the sky for morning's sun to make its ascent. In awe, Fleur watched as daylight stippled the craggy summits of the ranges with a golden burnish that soon became long sweeps of colour, picking out the faces of the rocks against their still purple and brooding depths. The rocks turned red and then bronze until they finally gave way as the Ghan snaked from the clasp of the mountains' jagged peaks to emerge fully into the great outback of South Australia, where the rusted earth stretched for as far as she could see.

She threw out her arms and repeated her word. 'Breathtaking!'

Tom caught one of her arms. 'Be careful.'

'Oh, don't fret. My body knows how to carry a child like every pregnant woman who has gone before me.'

'Yes, but none of them were carrying *our* child,' Tom pointed out in an arch tone.

Fleur leaned into him. 'It is exciting, when I'm not feeling nauseated. I told Claire Wren I was having a baby.'

He gave her a look of surprise. 'Before me?'

She grinned sadly. 'I had to tell someone and you'd run out on me.' Before he could object, she kissed him. 'You know I don't mean that, but I was bursting and there's just something about her. She has a wisdom that I appreciate.'

'She's a nurse; she's seen a lot.'

'Yes, but it's more than that. I think Claire celebrates life. Losing Alfie must have been so hard and yet, in all that sorrow, she somehow found time for her other children, time for Jamie . . . time to feel pleasure in my news. A kind of balance, so I felt joyous, not hesitant in sharing it.

'I've learned that she was stationed in the Middle East during the war and then she volunteered to go to the frontline in France with artillery dropping all around her. She didn't care – she'd lost faith in life for a while because she'd believed Jamie dead. She told me she found her way back through the friendship of a former enemy, believe it or not – I can't wait to hear the whole story. Something to do with a Turkish scholar in Istanbul, who was very kind to her at a time when she felt so alone and without a compass. His compassion and companionship brought her back from a dark place, and then she found Jamie again. Theirs is a magnificently romantic tale, and I think Claire just knows to look for and hold on tight to all the good bits.'

Tom nudged her. 'I think our story is romantic too, given we first kissed when you were eight and then we were separated for two decades.'

She gave him a soft, playful shove in return. 'Ours is, you're right, especially in spite of people trying to keep us apart.'

'And now you're Mrs Catchlove.'

She nodded. 'Never been happier either. I decided as I woke up to this beautiful morning that I'm going to call the new business Appleby & Catchlove.'

'Catchy,' he admitted, his dry tone making her laugh.

'Seriously, though, it has a rhythmic elegance and it keeps the memory of my father strong, all the way back through the Appleby men who pioneered the funeral business. But it starts the new era.' She placed a hand on her belly. 'Maybe this little Catchlove in here might follow and take on a role in the company.'

'Fleur, I think it's perfect, and I'm proud to be part of it.'

She leaned in to kiss him and wondered if the boy she'd met so long ago had dreamed of kissing a girl in this tree. It made her smile. 'Tom, I doubt you'll ever appreciate how much confidence you give me, but you do it in a way that makes me feel strong without having to be brusque or quite as prickly as perhaps I used to be. What's more, I haven't had support or affection of this kind since my mother died.'

'Ditto,' Tom said and stopped her saying any more by kissing her again.

They heard a foghorn sound in the distance.

'Ah, there it is!' Tom said, leaping easily down from the branch and landing lightly on the creek bed in such familiar fashion that Fleur knew he'd jumped from this branch many dozens of times. 'Come on, let me help you down.'

'I'm pregnant, not an invalid.'

He ignored her remark and showed her where to put her feet to clamber back down.

'I wanted to jump.'

'That takes years of practice,' he said in a teasing tone, grabbing her hand and twirling her around the lower reaches of the tree and down to the red earth.

Fleur gave a soft gasp of awe and Tom followed her gaze to where the highest branches were hosting feathered visitors.

'Galahs,' he said.

'Do you know I've never seen one before?'

'You're kidding, right?'

She shook her head. 'They really are very bright pink, aren't they? Beautiful.' She sighed.

'Noisy, too,' he admitted. 'Well, if *they* impress you, let's hope you see a Mallee ringneck – now there's a parrot to stare at. He's turquoise and orange, yellow and green, he's got violet and chocolate . . . and across his beak is a red stripe with a lemon scarf around his neck.'

She looked back at him with a look of mistrust.

'I tell no lie, Fleur. Honest. They really are beautiful.'

'Well, find me one!' she demanded.

He laughed. 'At night we get geckos, and you'll find skinks scuttling around everywhere. There's even a legless lizard that will convince you it's a snake and send you hurtling in the other direction.'

She took his hand. 'Tom, I'm terrified of snakes.'

'Have you seen one?'

'Only at the zoo.'

'That was a python. Look, the snakes out here are some of the most venomous in the world, but they're pretty shy. We make a lot of noise just walking on the land and they can feel us coming and they take off.'

'Feel us?'

'Our footsteps vibrate across the earth.'

She laughed, clapping her hands. 'Brilliant! And you're not scared?'

'I'm respectful and wary of them. You learn to be cautious around wood piles or dark corners – or boots that have been left too long somewhere.' He grinned. 'I've heard all the stories but if we're careful, we don't have to fear them . . . they fear us more.'

'No, I'm sorry, but I don't believe you. It's not like you can accidentally tread on one and offer up an apology.'

He laughed aloud. 'Well, that's true. So out here you learn how to live around all the dangers and take the right precautions.'

She gave another shuddering groan. 'I think you have to grow up around it.'

'Like you in a mortuary, I guess. What you do would frighten a lot of people.'

Fleur stared at her husband before nodding. 'You're right. And for me it's second nature, so I struggle to put myself into their shoes and feel what they fear.'

'There you go. That's how bushies feel about snakes, spiders, scorpions and so on.'

'I think you're one of the most insightful people I've ever known, Tom.'

He looked around, smiling shyly at the compliment. 'When you're raised in a place like this – a place that guards the knowledge of the world – and pay attention to it, then I guess it helps shape your judgement.'

Fleur gave a smile, wide and full of loving warmth. 'I adore the romantic way you think.'

The foghorn sounded again, closer this time. 'Is that the train?' she demanded, frowning.

'Yes, the one from Adelaide. As a boy I'd wait for that sound, sitting in the coolabah, and the moment I heard it this close I'd begin to run . . . like this!' He took off, one hand clasped to his hat, the other grasping her hand. 'Come on!'

Fleur let out a shriek of amusement. 'Why?' she said and was so glad she'd worn the flattest of her shoes.

'Because it was ritual for me,' he said as they galloped along. 'I had to arrive as the train went past and feel all the breath it brought, hundreds of miles from the big city,' he yelled. 'I used to believe it brought voices and amusement, tears and secrets. Come on, Fleur, faster . . . Can you do it?'

'I told you – pregnant, not incapable!' She increased her stride to match his, although she knew he was letting her catch up and could probably go faster.

'Jump!' Tom called, and Fleur cackled with a laugh of the most carefree kind as they leapt in unison over a small cottonbush. Now she could see it, the steam train's engine emerging into her view, and its horn sounded loudly once more. Perhaps the driver could see them, but even if he couldn't, it sounded joyful, and their yells in response were full of welcome.

'Faster, Fleur! I want you to feel it as it passes.'

She couldn't believe she had the stamina to do so but somehow she found it within her, and they reached the tracks just as the huge metal beast powered past them.

Fleur watched Tom arch his back and close his eyes to the sky and she did the same, feeling the wallop of the air that the train pushed over them. Tom was wearing an almost dopey grin and she felt a rush of affection for this man, who had brought true love into her life, something she'd never thought would happen for her. And he'd brought new life into hers with the baby nestling and growing within.

And as the roar of the train continued towards the final yards of its track, Fleur felt her own sense of power bloom inside, and an awakening to a new knowledge.

Finally, she alone was in charge of her life.

She would never think of herself as an orphan again. She would never seek permission to do as she wished, because decisions were now hers to make. In less than a year, life had tipped dramatically. She was a wife, soon to be a mother. She was the owner of her own business, and with it she was going to change the face of the industry that had kept her frozen out of its inner sanctum. She already knew women were going to turn the funeral industry on its head, for the better, and Fleur intended to be at the helm, driving that change.

And here, with the man she loved more than anything in the world, clasping his hand as they ran across this timeless land, she made the decision to live their life to the fullest. Life could be short – she knew that better than most – but she would not allow time to be stolen from them, and she would not allow herself to ever be too busy to recapture this moment of childlike abandon and pleasure. She felt in this moment that no endeavour, no wealth, no status and no reputation could ever match the feeling of wellbeing that loving someone and being loved in return brought.

The train passed them and Tom turned, his cheeks flushed with happiness. And as if the gods themselves had orchestrated it, they both lifted their faces to the sun and yelled into the roar of steam their own cries of sheer joy to be alive, to be together, and to belong to someone; orphans no more.

Acknowledgements

This is the first Australia-based story I've crafted and so it brought with it plenty of nervous energy. A host of people, sensing my need, became involved in helping me to achieve authenticity for this story. Building an era is hard at the best of times but it was especially tricky through the lens of an industry that was once the sideline of butchers and not well documented.

Harrison Funerals came to my aid twice when I most needed it. The first was when my father passed away and our family was in that stage of early bewilderment; this is when a funeral director really needs to shine. Brenton Hill, a fourth-generation undertaker, stepped in and took care of my father – and our family – in a seamless and yet generous, professional way. I couldn't imagine the experience being made any easier; his team was nothing short of brilliant.

Still a bit lost in grief but knowing I had to craft a story for 2022, I found myself dwelling on Dad – that moment of him being taken away – and I kept wondering what happened next. Brenton invited me back to Harrison's to learn more and so began an enriching experience. He told me the colourful history of the family firm, which began with a busy milk round in Adelaide and morphed somehow into an undertaking business. I found the story of his mother's involvement especially intriguing and felt the first seed of a story growing in my mind. He walked me through a small museum he built down at Port Adelaide that highlights the company's history and memorabilia, which I found fascinating, and gave me a guided tour of the port region and its neighbourhoods, helping me to grasp the atmosphere of the 1930s. Finally, and with great care, he asked whether I would like to visit the mortuary and learn how our loved ones are cared for. How could I resist?

Once I met retired mortician Peter Edwards, who now trains young people in this very special art, I was trapped by my own fascination. I simply had to write a story based around a little girl growing up with an undertaker father, helplessly interested in a business so firmly owned by men that the very thought of a woman in a mortuary would have created waves of consternation and offence. I have a character inspired by Brenton's mother but wholly fictionalised, called Fleur Appleby, who pushes back against society's expectation that only men can be undertakers and morticians.

I cannot thank Brenton and Peter enough for their joy at teaching me, the regular visits, the books, and reading my work for accuracy. Can I add that Amelia Whitbread, daughter of Brenton, who I met through my sons' circle of friends more than twenty years ago, impressed me when she told me she was so nervous of public speaking that she used to practise in the mortuary, chatting to the dead as her audience. I never forgot that and so it seemed I was destined to meet her father and write this story, giving Fleur Appleby a similar habit.

Other people who must be thanked are Chris Reed, his wife, Maria, and family from Wandilla Station at Burra in South Australia. I first met Chris when I was lurking around Witchelina, which is the main property on the once massive sheep station in the

far mid north of South Australia. Vern McIntosh, son of the original
pioneer, Donald, lived with his family in a cottage at 'Paradise' on
the station. He was initially a cattle drover and then became the
station manager. My husband Ian's father and aunt were raised in
their early years at that cottage, about 50 kms from the outback
town of Farina, hugged by the Flinders Ranges. We were tracing
some McIntosh stories when I became entranced by the notion of
this mother – Ruby McIntosh – and her two small children living
in the middle of nowhere with no running water, no power, no
people around, husband gone for months on end, and the elements
doing their best to thwart their hard lives. The desert, the heat, the
cold, snakes, scorpions, the earthquakes, the dust, the sand storms,
drought, floods, loneliness, depression . . . Everything about their
lives was so hard I found it hard to believe anyone could survive.
As a result, another character, this time inspired by Ian's father but
wholly fictional, grew in my mind and became Tom Catchlove.
I initially thought Tom would be a shearer but after meeting Chris
Reed, who is a volunteer restoring the landscape around this
station and a retired wool classer, I knew that's what Tom needed
to be and Chris was a fabulous help in teaching me how to build
Tom's working life.

And there are others . . . Anne Dawes at Farina was such a
brilliant support in inviting us to her home and teaching us about
the town and its history. I'd like to thank Tom Wilson for sharing
his knowledge of Adelaide buses, trams and trains during the 1930s
and to Lindl Lawton from the South Australian Maritime Museum
for helping me understand the woolstores. Denise Schumann, his-
torian, and Michele Bayly Jones from the Coroner's Court of South
Australia, thank you. Rob Ball from the Farina Restoration Group
and his amazing knowledge of the train network to Farina was vital
in getting the final chapters correct . . . especially how it used to get
up and down the hill.

Bill 'Swampy' Marsh's book *Great Australian Shearing Stories* is a hoot and became a wonderful resource that helped to build the atmosphere of the blokes working in the shed, while Rob Olston's book, *Farina: from Gibbers to Ghost Town*, was a major point of reference for my history.

Amanda, Jeff and Chelsea from the Adelaide Zoo were an amazing help in recreating the history of the Zoo in the mid 1930s and I spent a splendid day poring through archives and photos and walking around to rebuild it from the era I needed. Many thanks.

The usual suspects, Pip Klimentou and Sonya Caddy, read my drafts and encouraged me, as I was especially nervous about writing my first all-Australian novel. I wanted it to feel different and steer away from cliché while paying respect to two industries . . . one so well known – wool – and the other hardly known at all – undertaking. It was a strange coupling but it works. Thanks to them both as always.

The publishing team – you know who you are – big thanks for helping me to feel confident with this particular project, and a special thank you to my publisher, Ali Watts, and my editor, Amanda Martin, for helping to finesse the story and guide its path to completion with generosity and laughter.

I've taken liberties that I must confess to. The big earthquake I mention was in 1910 but I've shifted it a few years later. The kiosk at the Adelaide Zoo was not opened until 11 March 1936, whereas I've got it open in 1935. Fleur sings the very famous 'Click Go The Shears' to Tom, but she probably wouldn't have known it as it wasn't popularised until some years later. If there are any other complications, they're mine alone because I had loads of solid advice from so many people, as you can see.

And finally to my family . . . always so indulgent of my hours at the keyboard, especially Ian, who puts fresh flowers on my desk each week, vacuums the office, changes the bedlinen, builds fires in winter, keeps me cool in summer and fully grounded the rest of the time, not lost completely to my imagination. Our trips into the desert were fun and all the countless support often goes unnoticed when I'm busy. Thanks, Ian. Will and Jack, here's another one for you to ignore because it doesn't have warriors or wars in it. Mum, keep powering; Dad's smiling at this one.

Fx

Book Club Notes

1. Fleur and Tom are both orphans but they come from very different families. In what ways did their difficult childhoods influence the adults they became?

2. Fleur believes that women can bring something very special to the funeral industry. What are those qualities, and do you agree they are important for end of life rituals?

3. When Tom spots Fleur on the dancefloor, more than twenty years after their first meeting, he wonders whether it was destiny or fate that brought them together again. What do you think?

4. 'Well, there you are. He could be openly affectionate with your mother because that's how a man should be with a woman – tender. But as a father, he probably thought his role was to turn you into a man. I'm sure you'll say something like that to our son.' Do you think this idea of fatherhood still exists in today's society? How are things different now to the early 20th century when Tom grew up?

5. 'Grief is a curious drug.' How do you think grief affects each of the main characters' actions: Fleur, Tom, Henry and Irma?

6. Fleur says: 'I love my work. People think it's bleak or frightening, but really it's the opposite. It's uplifting . . . an honour to take care of the beloved for *their* beloved.' Discuss the ways in which this is so.

7. *'Be grateful for every good thing in your life, Tom,* his mother had told him.' Tom and Fleur both resist becoming bitter despite their hardships. What role do you think gratitude plays in this?

8. Do you think Fleur did the right thing by Irma in court? What would you have done in her situation? Do you agree with Fleur's belief that Irma's death achieves nothing?

9. Irma's lies wreak havoc in Fleur's life. How might Fleur's future have played out if her train journey had ended differently?

10. Did you recognise Jamie and Claire Wren from another of Fiona's novels? Which other books by Fiona McIntosh have you read and enjoyed? Which is your favourite and why?